Imperial Jade Dragon Pendant

Bleue Rose

Imperial Jade Dragon Pendant

Bleue Rose

Front Book Cover Illustration by LaLanaArts
Back Cover Illustration by Lacegarden
Formatting by Istvan Szabo
ISBN 978-1-7338194-5-9
ISBN (e) 978-1-7338194-4-2
Text copyright 2023
Published by Bleue Rose
BleueRose.com
BleueRoseNovels IG
Printed by Ingram Spark

Dedication

To Ruth and Joseph, whose generous and tolerant world views shaped mine.

To Josh, whose generosity of spirit warms my insides daily.

To Julia, whose creative vision has no boundaries.

Honoring Mahatma Gandhi's Buddhist thoughts on Marriage:
Marriage for the satisfaction of the sexual appetite is no marriage. It is uyabhichara-concupiscence.

The wife is not the husband's bond slave, but his companion and his help-mate, as equal partner in all his joys and sorrows- as free as the husband to choose her own path.

The Teaching of Buddha:
A family is a place where minds come in contact with one another. If these minds love one another, the home will be as beautiful as a flower garden...

Table of Contents

Carefree Summers in Sag Harbor

"Grandma, will you tell me another story about when you lived in Hong Kong?"

"Haven't you heard them all by now, Lily Rose?"

"No. You always surprise me with something new."

"Hmmm…let me think." Marina eyed her granddaughter over her electric blue reading glasses, then finished rinsing the dinner dishes and loaded the dishwasher. "Here's the deal, Missy. If you shower and get ready for bed, I'll think of a story I might have missed."

"Ok, I know you'll find one. You always do.

"You may have me there. Now that you're almost eleven, maybe I'll tell you one of the adult ones." A smile formed at the edge of her lips.

"About Jin and Mei?" Lily Rose's eyes widened.

"Yes."

"Oh good. I already know they're madly in love, you know."

"Aren't you the perceptive one. And here I thought I only covered their PG adventures. Off you go then."

Marina smiled and turned to look out the window as Lily Rose scampered up the stairs. She didn't want her granddaughter to see her barely contained laughter. The fact that her daughter couldn't afford summer camp for Lily Rose worked out perfectly. She loved spending the summer months with her granddaughter and savored moments like this when they traded intimate secrets and treasured memories. Of course, she did filter the inappropriate material, most of the time, but Lily Rose was particularly perceptive and often read between the lines.

City kids!

Marina's cozy little cottage in Sag Harbor was heaven during the summer months. In the dead of winter, she tried to escape to somewhere warm, hitting different destinations every year, but the other three seasons were happily spent in Long Island. Her daughter and granddaughter were frequent visitors, especially in the warmer months.

Post-retirement, Marina occupied herself with book club meetings, playing bridge, yoga, tennis, pickle ball and kayaking with her friends and neighbors. When she arrived from New York City, Lily Rose joined the activities, seamlessly, thriving like a desert bloom.

After a vibrant career in the city, retiring to the east end had been a blessing. Marina never got tired of the magnificent scenery. Neither did her granddaughter it seemed. Tonight the sun was setting in brilliant pink and yellow striations over a glistening cobalt bay. She feasted her eyes and sighed. Life was good, especially when Lily Rose was home.

Marina heard the plumbing groan to a halt as the upstairs shower was turned off in the guest bathroom. Quickly, wiping down the butcher block table in her rustic country kitchen, she began to set up the dishes for the morning. Tomorrow, Lily Rose had to return to the city, to her working mother. School was back on the calendar. Summer flew by. It always did. She would miss their shared adventures and private talks. Lily Rose warmed her heart and kept her young.

"Grandma, I'm ready," came a small voice from the top of the stairs.

"Coming." Marina poured hot water into a lotus mug, adding her favorite herbal passion fruit teabag, and climbed the creaky stairs. Lily Rose was splayed on her plush, oversized pillow, her wavy, long blonde hair fanned around her, ocean blue eyes alert under long curly lashes. Marina dimmed the lights and settled into the pastel paisley armchair next to Lily Rose's white cloud bed. The home's pastel colored hues, paired with natural tones, screamed vacation beach house and both women loved it.

"Let me tell you about Jin and Mei's final days together," Marina began. "You've only heard about their adventures around Hong Kong, but you don't know what happened to their friendship. As you know, all good things come to an end.

One Monday morning, out of the blue, after a particularly beautiful weekend visiting Kaiping *City* with Jin, Mei's boss called her into his office. In short order, he informed her she would be relocated to the Shanghai office on mainland China. This unexpected announcement caught her by surprise and left her devastated. It meant leaving Jin, her best friend, behind. She couldn't breathe for a moment. Her mind raced through all the wonderful times they had shared like a series of flashbacks spliced into an action film. She had become so very fond of Jin, she couldn't imagine not seeing him regularly. They had shared so many extraordinary experiences in the four years she lived in

Hong Kong. Remember when they went to films from the Shaw Brothers Studio? Or their many Xiaomeisha and Stanley Beach excursions? Or the Star Ferry tours, the Peak Tram and rickshaw rides?"

"Or Lantau Island? I remember that one too." Lily Rose nodded emphatically. "I remember it all."

"Mei was also concerned about going back to Shanghai. Hong Kong was a much kinder city, especially to educated women with jobs. Mei worked as a journalist, like me."

"I know." Lily Rose's eyes focused on her grandmother with a serious expression.

"Now all those fun excursions I told you about would become distant memories, never to be repeated. Mei kept it together for the workday, however when she got home that night, she cried until her heart could take no more. She agonized over how to tell Jin. She finally managed to do so over a perfectly planned picnic in Victoria Park. He was equally heartbroken, but he didn't show it. He became very reflective and quiet. It was as if it was a fate he expected. Mei didn't understand his silence and lack of emotion."

"Couldn't he go with her to Shanghai?" Lily Rose asked urgently.

"No. Jin worked in the family business. His father wasn't well, so Jin was needed on a day to day basis to safeguard and perpetuate the family's legacy. His other two siblings were girls and girls were not considered for certain managerial jobs. Girls were lucky to get an education let alone meaningful work in the early 1960's. Of course, today all that has changed. Jin's family-owned several lucrative operations, one of which was an important gem business. That business was Jin's passion. He bought, sold and shipped quality gems all over the world."

"What kind of gems? Diamonds?" Lily Rose's eyes dilated and sparkled like stars.

"All kinds. They had the most beautiful green jade, I remember. They also owned two restaurants, one in Wan Chai, and one in Tsim Sha Tsui. I think one branch of the family also owned a fleet of ships in Hong Kong harbor. The Ho family was very influential and had many business interests. Jin couldn't leave his father in a lurch and Mei couldn't afford to give up her job. She didn't come from a wealthy family and needed her paycheck."

"Why didn't Jin just marry her?"

"That wasn't possible. Jin's family wouldn't have accepted Mei. She didn't meet the family's criteria as marriage material. The family would have made poor Jin's life miserable had he proposed to her. Family honor played a huge role in decision making and who you married was of strategic importance. Remember everything that Jin and Mei did together was secret. No one in the family knew about the depth of their friendship. Times were different back then, Lily Rose. We're talking early 60's here. Traditional, wealthy Chinese families had a lot of influence on who their children consorted with and eventually married."

"That sounds so unfair."

"It was unfair. Jin and Mei spent as much time as they could together those last few weeks. They snuck around to all the fun corners of the city and consoled and hugged each other. Mei did most of the crying and Jin comforted her as only he could. They were so in love and couldn't imagine a life without each other. They were truly soul mates."

"What's a soul mate, Grandma?"

"It's someone you love and connect with on many levels. Someone who shares your beliefs or temperament and accepts you the way you are. Someone who loves you without judging you; a person you hold dear in your heart for the rest of your life, no matter what happens."

"I see. Like you and me."

Marina smiled and nodded, her sun streaked hazelnut curls bobbing. "Exactly. Jin wanted to make Mei's last days in Hong Kong special. He treated her like a queen. Their last day together, he booked a luxury hotel room in the Oriental, now Mandarin Oriental and had a special feast delivered. They spent an exceptional day, sealing their friendship and love. Before leaving, Jin gave Mei a beautiful gift, a family heirloom he wanted her to have and remember him by. I know she treasured it forever."

Lily Rose perked up. "What was it?"

"It was an exquisitely carved jade gemstone pendant. It was beautiful, the color of a tropical forest after a rain shower."

"Did she ever see Jin again?"

"No, never."

"Didn't she visit or at least email him?"

"No. Back then, there was no email, only snail mail. She wrote to him many times, but he never replied to her letters."

"That's so sad. How do you know, Grandma? Didn't you leave Hong Kong too? And why didn't he answer?"

"I was in touch with Mei for a while, so I know. She was beyond sad. I can't imagine why he didn't respond."

"Did Grandpa know them, too?"

"No, they were my special friends, while he was at work. Grandpa traveled a lot, so I was alone much of the time. I met them through my job."

"I hope what happened to Mei and Jin never happens to me." Lily Rose's lids were starting to droop, sleep creeping in.

"It won't, lovey. You can marry whoever you like. Life today is different. I promise."

Chapter 1

Life's Curve Balls—
Fifteen years later

Lily Rose was late for work. The New York City subways were getting worse by the minute.

Lately, they were always dirty and overcrowded, but now they ran seriously behind schedule, too. She was ripe for a change, especially in her mode of transportation. For months she had been toying with the idea of putting in for a transfer to another city. She just couldn't summon the courage to actually go through with it. Leaving her mother, Ella May, and her grandmother, Marina, behind was unthinkable. Ella May worked a few blocks away and they often met for dinner, even if much of the time was spent disagreeing. Whenever Lily Rose had a long weekend, her grandmother would come to visit or she would hop on the Jitney bus to Sag Harbor to spend quality time with her. Marina was the glue that kept the three of them tight. With no siblings or father in the picture, Lily Rose valued her small family and her close circle of friends.

Working for a world-wide, luxury hotel chain had its benefits. The Hilton Hotel boasted properties in the most obscure and wonderful places and Lily Rose enjoyed the opportunity to visit a few of them for managerial meetings. When she and her family decided to go on a girls' vacation, she often benefited from a discounted rate.

Recently, on particularly frustrating work days, she had lingered on the Hilton website at night, dreaming about what it would be like to work in Miami, the Bahamas or in the New Orleans French quarter. Now that could be enticing! The options were endless. What was she waiting for? Where was her sense of adventure? What was holding her back from pulling the trigger? Surely her family would visit.

Arriving at the hotel in Times Square, after dodging indigenous, annoying cartoon characters who insisted on accosting her on a daily basis, she settled at her desk and checked her weekly calendar. She was relieved she made it from the subway to her desk without running into touchy, feely Spiderman again. Luckily the costumed characters shifted their location from day to day.

This weekend Lily Rose was working with her special events coordinator to make sure that a jewelry trade convention went off without a hitch. There wasn't a stagnant second in the hotel business. She loved the constantly changing landscape and the perpetually filled banquet rooms, but it was also stressful trying to keep it all running smoothly. She often thought about all the wonderful places people came from as they congregated in the Hilton event rooms. Lily Roses's private life needed a serious face lift. After working long hours, she came home exhausted with little energy left for anything fun. What was the point of living in New York City if you couldn't partake in some of the magic?

Glancing at her computer calendar, Lily Rose realized it was Friday the 13th.Not that she was superstitious, but she hoped she could sail through the day without too many fires to extinguish. She poured herself a cup of coffee and answered her most pressing emails. That done, she headed to the jewelry show, to make sure there were no hiccups or problems for the vendors. It was her job to make sure everyone was happy. Security was tight for these events. There had been incidents in the past-- thefts and the more predictable, vendors feuding over more desirable spaces. Lily Rose was often sent to diffuse the situation.

Once on the floor, she was greeted by a flurry of activity. The booths and their inhabitants were getting ready for the first day of business. Everyone was in different stages of the set up process. Posters were hung, trunks unpacked, and cases assembled and filled. As Lily Rose walked down the many aisles looking at the merchandise and chatting with people, she zeroed in on the section from Hong Kong. Her grandmother's many stories always ruminating in the back of her brain, Lily Rose was magically drawn to the exotic quality of these aisles. Gravitating toward the more unusual displays, she walked with her head down, eyes scanning the many treasures.

She vowed to travel to Hong Kong one day, hopefully with her grandmother, and visit all the places she had learned so much about. Her grandmother's love for the city had rubbed off. It would be infinitely exciting to see Victoria Park, Old Town Central, take the tram or visit Wong Tai Sin Temple, home to three religions, Buddhism, Taoism and Confucianism. Lily Rose was itching to see it all from Marina's story perspective. Some things might have changed, but the landmarks, she was certain, remained the same. She could picture them in her mind's eye. Walking past a particularly elaborate booth, she paused and took in the beautifully carved stones in bright translucent greens, purples, reds, oranges, and whites.

"Good morning. What are these stones here?" She tapped a delicate lavender manicured finger on the case.

"This is jade. These pieces are carved jadeite, which comes in many colors. Over here is nephrite. It's a less pricey jade." The young man studied her appearance with interest.

"I particularly love this apple green. It reminds me of springtime when everything is budding and lush." Lily Rose's face lit up as she looked through the glass separating her from the gems. She flipped her long blonde hair over her shoulder and bent down to examine the carvings more closely.

"Ah, you have exquisite taste. The stone you're looking at is imperial jade from the Quing dynasty. People often say the most prized and highest quality carvings are from that period. Imperial jade is the most important stone in the Chinese culture, you know. It's believed to bring good fortune and happiness to those who wear it."

"Interesting. Sounds like something I need to wear. Is the carved white stone jade too?"

"The white garden carving? Yes, that's called *mutton fat* and it's one of my finest translucent white stones. We debated on bringing it to New York. It's very valuable. It can run into five digits per carat."

"Amazing. I can totally appreciate its beauty, but I'm partial to the granny apple green. It reminds me of my love of nature. How much is it?"

"The amulet? It's sixty-five hundred. "

"Wow. I didn't expect that." Lily Rose's eyes widened as she looked up at the young salesman. He had a kind, pleasant face with straight black hair that angled sideways sweeping past his right eye. His sincere smile unexpectantly drew her in. Her glance wavered a few extra seconds as she took in his expression and features. He returned her look and smiled. "Natural, fine jade is more expensive than diamonds. We have some smaller, less intricately carved pieces that cost less. Here, let me show you. What's your name?"

"Hi. I'm Lily Rose Larsen, one of the special event managers here at the Hilton. I was actually just doing a quick tour of the show to make sure the vendors are happy and have everything they need. Do you?"

"Nice to meet you, Lily Rose. I'm Mingyu." He pointed to his name tag to help her with the pronunciation. "So far, we're happy. Our accommodations and our booth location are good. Hopefully our sales will be, too."

"Glad to hear that. Are you able to enjoy New York or are you working every day?"

"I've barely seen the outside of the hotel since I arrived, but I hope to have some time after the show."

"I know what you mean. I have many days like that." Not wanting to leave yet, she leaned down over the case again. "The imperial jade may be a bit too pricey for me. What's this stone here? I love the color."

"This is lavender jade. It's a cabochon cut with a sprinkle of diamonds in the band. Here, try it on." He handed her the ring capturing her attention. "It looks like it's a perfect fit for you."

"It is and I love it. This color is so vibrant! I'm scared to ask the price."

"It's a less intricate piece, so it has a smaller price." Mingyu turned to see if his father was occupied. Satisfied that he was, he turned back and whispered, "I can sell it to you for three-hundred-and-fifty dollars. Consider it a sweetheart deal. I can see you appreciate its beauty."

Mingyu smiled magnetically, his warm eyes eliciting a spark.

Lily Rose studied his handsome features and decided he was sincere. "I do."

"Right. Maybe I can turn you into a jade collector. This could be your starter piece." A strand of his straight, shiny black hair fell over one eye and he pushed it back. Lily Rose was captivated. "Shouldn't be that hard. I can't take my eyes off these gems. I'm in love with the colors. Can I think about the ring? Would you be able to hold it for a bit?" She asked, searching his face.

"Sure."

"Let me take your card and booth number. I better get back to work. I'll probably see you later. Can I take a picture of the ring?"

"Here, slip it on. I'll take the picture for you with your phone. Hold your hand up to the light." He gently positioned her hand toward the light source. A spark passed between them. Lily Rose felt warmth spread from his fingers through her body. When she looked up, their eyes met again. Embarrassed, she blushed and looked down at her hand.

"Thanks, Mingyu. I do love this ring. I might have to come back for it even if it means forfeiting a few meals," she joked. Slipping off the ring, she reluctantly returned it. Something about Mingyu's soft sales approach and information sharing made her want to stay and chat, but she had already exceeded her time limit and she had work piling up. A busy day threatened to swallow her time in monstrous gulps. She hoped to return later.

Continuing down the aisles, she passed the other vendors, stopping occasionally to ask if all was satisfactory. The Hilton crew had done a stellar job setting up the skeleton booths. Since this was a yearly trade show, they had the formula down, right to the champagne station near the restrooms. Peering down the many aisles and booths, she didn't see anything as striking as Mingyu's jade collection. His fabulous lavender jade ring stayed imprinted on her brain as she returned to her office. So did his silky black hair, warm chocolate eyes and compelling smile.

As anticipated, the rest of the day was spent organizing future events, while delegating all petty problems to her assistant. Before she knew it, the afternoon had slipped by and she was itching to get home. She thought of the ring, but knew Mingyu was already gone for the day. The jewelry show closed at five. She would have to purchase the ring tomorrow. Hopefully, he kept it on hold for her.

She fingered his business card on her night table and pictured him in her mind. That night she dreamt of Hong Kong as her grandmother's many stories sprung to life in the dark, only this time, they included Mingyu.

Chapter II

Jade Ignites Passion
Amongst True Aficionados

"Mingyu, why are you still holding this ring? The customer didn't come back yesterday." Cheng sounded irritated.

"I'm certain she'll be coming back. She works here in the hotel and probably got busy. She's the event manager. Keep it in the envelope." Mingyu could feel his father's grumbling skepticism and it annoyed him.

Sometimes his father could be so maddening. Nothing snuck past him either. Mingyu had purposely hidden the envelope for Lily Rose in the bottom of the hold box, quite confident she would reappear. When people responded to jade the way she had, they usually returned. He remembered how her sky-blue eyes had lit up when she delicately fingered the carvings. His father would spew fire if he knew the price he had given her. No matter. He would deal with it. His grandfather would understand. Mingyu had a good feeling about this girl. Hooking someone on jade, and recognizing their interest generally paid off. Long-term jade-inspired relationships made the best clients. His grandfather had taught him that, but clearly, this skill had skipped a generation. It annoyed Mingyu that his father was so near-sighted when it came to teaching new, potential clients about the beauty of jade. A genuine budding interest needed to be nurtured, like a bonsai plant or a peony flower.

Mingyu rifled through the earring section to see if they brought anything to compliment the ring. Negative. No problem, he could match the color with something else from stock and make a pair of delicate earrings when he got back to Hong Kong. He already secured Lily Rose's business card from the hotel's front desk and added her to his jewelry blog. He planned to be in touch whether she showed or not.

Something about this girl and her reaction to his prize pieces, resonated with him. Even at a trade show where hundreds of people stopped by his booth, it was possible to single out the true jade lovers, the people who understood and developed a deep appreciation for its authentic beauty. Only insiders and a select few newcomers understood this passion. Jade was all about color--the deeper the hue, the more exciting it was. Expert carving was an additional bonus. He was sure Lily Rose was a dormant insider, yet to be awoken.

As the day flew by, Mingyu kept busy. In rare free moments, he looked up and down the aisles, searching for Lily Rose, but there was no trace of her. Nonetheless, he kept the envelope with her ring hidden from his father, removing it from the hold box and slipping it into his pants pocket while willing the blonde beauty to return. Sadly, his wish remained just that-a wish. Lily Rose was a no-show. Two more days until they packed up and shipped the merchandise back to Hong Kong. Mingyu refused to give up.

In the meantime, he focused on what to do with his two extra days in New York. He mapped out a plan to visit famous landmarks. Tour groups were not his thing. He saw enough of them slogging around Hong Kong and he hated the idea of joining the fray. Luckily, his father would be tied up with business, leaving him to sightsee without restrictions. After working long days side by side, Mingyu was happy to escape. His father was intense and an insufferable workaholic. More so since his mother died.

At the end of each working day, Mingyu looked around the lobby hoping to catch a glimpse of Lily Rose. It appeared she had vanished into the hotel's many crevices. His heart wanted her to have his jade ring. He hoped to forge a connection with her. He wasn't sure why, but she had impressed him, left an imprint on his brain with her genuine curiosity and striking persona. Furthermore, he detected a common bond in her—that slumbering passion for jade. That passion needed to be jump-started and he was just the man to do it. Besides, the ring suited her. On the show's last day, Mingyu was still hording the envelope in his pants pocket. Every once in a while he fingered it, checking it was still there and hoping she would magically appear, but the aisles leading to his booth, although well-traveled, continued to remain devoid of her striking presence. When his father offered to go get lunch on their last day, Mingyu decided to take a break in his watch for Lily Rose.

"Let me go today. Write down what you want, or should I surprise you?"

"No surprises. I'll give you my order." Cheng barked with his usual frown.

When Mingyu exited the hotel and peered up and down the street, deciding which way to go, his phone pinged. He looked at the unrecognizable number on the screen.

"Hello?"

"Hi. It's Lily Rose. The events manager. Remember me?"

"Hi. Yes, I do." His heart took a leap. *It must be my lucky day.*

"Do you still have my lavender jade ring?"

"I do. It's in my pants pocket and I'm standing outside the hotel near the taxis."

"Oh good. Don't move. I was just leaving to grab some lunch. I'll be right there."

Minutes later she appeared, breathless. "I sprinted out before another problem grounded me in the office. These past few days have been nothing but trouble. I kept meaning to stop by your booth, but I've been crazy busy. Thanks for holding the ring. I dreamt about it, if you can believe that."

Mingyu looked pleased. "I knew you'd be back. This ring was meant to be yours. You make it shine." He pulled the envelope out of his pocket and handed it to her. He watched her face soften as she opened it and slid the ring on her finger.

"Thank you. What an incredibly nice thing to say. I love this stone and I agree, the ring is perfect for me. Here, I have cash because I suspect you gave me a super special price." She handed him an envelope and smiled. Mingyu peered inside, but didn't count the money.

Instead, he returned her smile and slid the money in his pants pocket.

"Aren't you going to count it?"

"No, I trust you. Thank you. Can I invite you for a quick lunch? I have cash." He tapped his pants pocket and laughed. Mingyu knew his father would blow a fuse, but he didn't care. Waiting an extra half an hour or so wouldn't kill the man and besides, it was the last day and traffic was slowing.

"I would love to, but I can't. My boss is out of the office, so I have to cover." She hesitated. "Are you free for dinner tonight or are you leaving right after the show?"

Mingyu's heart took another leap. *Yes!* "Dinner would be fine," he responded, hoping his eagerness wasn't over the top.

"I'm working until seven. I can meet you right here at seven fifteen. I would love to learn more about jade."

"I know. I sensed that. I'll be here at seven fifteen. See you then. Any lunch suggestions?"

"Try the deli on the next corner over there. They have a hot lunch buffet." She pointed to it and turned to go back inside. "See you later."

Mingyu couldn't stop grinning as he walked to get deli food he knew wouldn't please Cheng. It felt like nothing he did ever pleased his father, but right now he didn't care. He was happy he had left his father's scowling face at the show. Nobody was going to dampen his mood now.

Chapter III

First Date Jitters

Lily Rose and Mingyu were deep in conversation, seated in a restaurant on Grand Street in Chinatown. Upon arrival, she had deferred to him and let him order a cross-section of interesting dishes. She listened to Mingyu order, sipping a sweet Japanese plum wine while occasionally holding out her hand to admire the jade ring in the light. The color intrigued her as much as the man sitting across from her. "So what else can you tell me about jade that I should know, as a future collector?"

"Jade is comprised of two types of minerals, jadeite and nephrite. Your ring is jadeite. That's what you want to collect. Jadeite has a bigger range of colors, and it's a harder stone than nephrite. It doesn't crack or chip easily, but you still need to be careful. Store it in a soft pouch when you're not wearing it. I brought you one." He reached into his pants pocket and slid a beautifully embroidered silk pouch with gold threading across the table.

"Oh, how pretty! It's lavender! How thoughtful you are, Mingyu! Thank you."

"You're welcome."

"Tell me more."

"The stone's hardness makes it a good stone for carving. The most intricately carved stones, especially in the brighter, uniform colors, are the most expensive-- like the imperial jade you liked in my display. I have a collection of carved pieces I'll never sell, no matter what someone offers. My grandfather started the collection and over the years he's shared a few prize pieces with me. Since then, I've added to my collection. My grandfather taught me everything I know about the gem."

"Cool! Was that your father at the show?"

"Yes. He's strictly a business man with no special love for jade. Like many people, he favors the popular cut gems with lots of sparkle. He'd sell my grandfather's pieces, in the blink of an eye, if the price was right."

"I'm guessing you wouldn't let him. Where do you live in Hong Kong?"

"You're right. I live in West Kowloon, but my family lives on Hong Kong Island. Our business is in Tsim Sha Tsui. Have you ever been there?"

"No, but my grandparents lived in Hong Kong for four years. My grandfather's work took them there in the early 60's. He was an engineer for an architectural company. My grandmother loved life in Hong Kong and shared lots of stories. I feel like I know the city from pictures and anecdotes she shared during my childhood."

"You'll have to come visit and see it first-hand. I can show you my jade collection if you do."

"I would love that. I'd like to visit Hong Kong with my grandmother. We always talked about doing that one day."

"Don't wait. Do it while she's still able to travel. My grandfather no longer wants to make the trip to New York. That's why I came with my father."

"I'm happy you did." Her lips curled upward at the edges. "What do you like best about living in Hong Kong?"

Lily Rose studied his face as he spoke. His expressions were animated when he talked about his home, his grandfather or jade. She liked how his shiny, black hair kept slanting over his face, casting a shadow when he looked down. She studied the slope of his nose and his angular cheekbones. His smile was slow in coming, but when it arrived it was absolutely contagious. Conversation flowed easily throughout dinner and by the time they parted, Lily Rose knew a lot about jade, and a little more about Mingyu's family. She was pleased she had suggested dinner. Normally, she wasn't that bold, but something about this man intrigued her. He didn't talk excessively about himself, preferring to keep the focus on her, but he told her enough to rouse her interest. Over tea, they made plans for the following afternoon. Lily Rose had two days off after working the weekend. The timing was perfect.

That night as she slipped her ring into the delicate, lavender pouch, she reflected on her evening. She hadn't connected with anyone in a long time. Sadly, Mingyu didn't live in New York City. She was certain they would have seen more of each other had he stayed.

Chapter IV

Trans-Oceanic Seeds
Sprout and Grow

After breakfast, Mingyu and his father parted ways. He knew his dad would have liked his assistance for the remaining business calls, but Mingyu was promised two days off in New York, and he wasn't about to give them up. He was looking forward to seeing Lily Rose again. She had promised to take him around the city to all her favorite haunts, an offer he had no intention of refusing. His curiosity about her was mounting and he was dying to experience a day in her life and on her turf. Since they weren't meeting until after lunch, he spent the morning doing the touristy things he planned, just to say he did them when his family back home asked. He didn't share his afternoon plans with his father.

Dinner the night before had been a lovely, unexpected surprise. Their date had transitioned so easily from business to friendship over a common fascination with gems; he couldn't quite explain it. He enjoyed Lily Rose's inquisitive nature and thoughtful line of questioning. She didn't push the delicate areas about his family, the ones he preferred not to discuss, and yet he ended up telling her more than he shared with any outsider. She was so easy to open up to, so intuitive. He loved the way she flipped her long blonde hair over her shoulder or tucked loose strands behind her small, perfectly shaped ears. She wore minimal make-up, choosing to outline her bright blue eyes with a muted brown shadow and accentuating her plump, heart-shaped lips in a soft cherry color. He loved how her cheeks turned pink when she was embarrassed or excited, like when they talked about travel. She shared and quickly understood the things important to him which was a welcome eureka moment. Her clothing was just as subdued in palate as her persona. She reminded him of a dreamy seascape in the fog, all muted colors, beautifully blended. He wondered what it would be like to kiss her, make love to her, hold her in his arms.

After a quick lunch, he arrived at the Natural History Museum. Lily Rose was waiting on the steps, looking anxiously in all directions until she spotted him. Once she saw him, she visibly brightened and waved. He had detected her first and slowed to enjoy the sight. Her efforts to find him made him smile. He couldn't remember the last time someone cared about meeting him two days in a row with such enthusiasm.

She looked beautiful in a lavender flowing top over faded, fitted denim jeans and a tailored navy jacket cinched at the waist with tiny gold buttons edging down to her narrow hips. Her blue suede ballerina flats brought her down a notch, just below his eye-level.

"Hi. Did you have a good day so far? Where did you go?" Her smile was radiant and steamed his insides. *Am I falling for this girl? In New York?*

"I was a total tourist this morning. I started at the Statue of Liberty and worked my way up to Bryant Park. From there I walked up Sixth Avenue and took a bus here from Radio City. I prefer the city bus because you can see the landmarks and still get a sense of New York life. This morning it was standing room only, but when I came uptown, I got a window seat."

"Sounds like you covered a lot of ground in half a day. What time did you get up, sunrise?"

"I was on the first ferry to the Statue of Liberty at 8:30am this morning." Mingyu chuckled. "The island was pretty empty."

"Hope you aren't tired yet. We have tons of walking ahead."

"I'm ready. Comfortable sneakers." He pointed down his black torn jeans to the red-wine colored Sketchers. "My only purchase in New York so far. It was a clever one." He grinned.

He had carefully matched his t-shirt to his sneakers and added a black wool sweater with colored speckles. A black down jacket was scrunched in his backpack.

"Smart man. I have discount passes for us. We get them in the hotel. Prepare to be amazed at the gem collection here. We can skip the dinosaurs and taxidermy unless you're dying to see those too."

"A hard pass on the taxidermy, thank you. Lead the way."

Lily Rose nodded in agreement as she walked up a few steps ahead of him. "Ok, then. Follow me." She smiled over her shoulder and pointed upward toward the grand entrance.

He admired the curve of her behind as they climbed the many stairs. *Everything about this creature is beautiful.*

The Morgan Memorial Hall of Gems was impressive. Packed with rocks of all shapes and varieties, the museum offered samples of crystals ranging from large geodes to small, delicate cut gems. The exhibit was organized by mineral groups and featured a re-created gem pocket from Southern California.

"Wow, will you look at this. These crystals are incredible!" Lily Rose gushed.

"Truly."

They marveled over the Star of India, a 563-carat blue sapphire and drooled over the gem colors displayed in dizzying amounts. A kinship developed and deepened that afternoon. Bonding over their mutual fascination with gems, they left the museum satisfied and chatting animatedly. Walking through Central Park toward the *Metropolitan Museum of Art*, they enjoyed the mild fall weather. "I don't know how you feel about another museum, but this is our biggest art treasure. It houses pre-historic art all the way to present day exhibits. Any interest in going in?"

"One museum a day is enough for me. I need to let the gem exhibits sink in. Maybe I'll come here tomorrow. I have one more day to spend in the city."

"Ok, then. Let's take a selfie and hop on the Fifth Avenue bus. We can continue your city tour on wheels. We'll stop at Hudson Yards and walk the high line to the meat packing district. Trust me, it's more fun than it sounds. The bus ride will give you a chance to rest your feet."

"Sounds good. Let's get water for the ride." He strode over to one of the vending carts and purchased two bottles, handing one to her.

A few hours later, sitting overlooking the Hudson River, Mingyu turned to Lily Rose. "Thanks for the tour. You showed me places today I probably would have missed. To show my appreciation, can I take you to dinner one more time? You must be hungry. I'm starving."

"Sure, I'd love that. I'm definitely hungry and I don't think I can walk another step." She laughed stretching her legs out in front of her, lifting them from the knees straight out. "There are lots of good restaurants in the west village, close to this bench here."

"Good. I'll let you choose one."

"Are you super hungry, or can we sit for another minute? My feet are still recovering. I think I have a blister. Ouch."

"Rest. We'll go when you're ready. I'm enjoying the sights." He peered at her from underneath his slanted haircut, the corner of his eye capturing her spellbinding profile. He had never met anyone like her. She was fun, kind, smart and uncomplicated. Most women he knew were after something he had or they thought he had. They had an agenda. Here, far away from home, he felt like he could be himself--unguarded.

They concluded the day in a small French restaurant over a candlelight dinner and a few glasses of red wine. Mingyu didn't want the night to end. When they finally paid and left, he walked Lily Rose to her home in the west village. Lingering outside her door, he took her hand in his and turned to face her.

"Thanks for a wonderful day. It'll be my happiest memory of New York, when I'm back in Hong Kong." Maybe it was the wine or maybe it was the moonlight on her angelic face, but he couldn't resist. Leaning in, he kissed her on the lips. She felt soft and warm and tasted like red wine and mint tea. Her scent was inviting, a faint hint of roses-- he would have loved to explore, peel back the layers of fabric.

She smiled as if guessing his thoughts, and to his surprise she leaned in to kiss him again, bending slightly forward from the bottom stoop of her brownstone entrance. She wrapped her arms around him and gave him a snug hug. "You're welcome. I also have another day off. See you tomorrow?" Lily Rose locked into his dark, smoldering eyes, sure of his answer.

Pleased he was getting another chance to spend time with her, he replied quite happily, "Sure. Text me when you wake up." And with that he reluctantly turned, waved and floated to the nearest avenue to hail a cab. He was thrilled at the prospect of seeing her the next day, but disappointed to not be invited in. Seated in a taxi headed mid-town, a text appeared on his phone, *Thanks for dinner. REALLY FUN day. Air out your sneakers. You'll need them tomorrow.* It ended with a smiley emoji with heart-popping eyes and the gesture made his heart rate speed to double time.

Chapter V

Love in a New York Minute

The next morning Lily Rose awoke and reached for her phone. She looked at the pile of laundry on the floor of her closet, begging to be washed, and texted Mingyu from the comfort of her pillows.

Good morning. What would you like to do today? Anything special on your wish list?

Within seconds she had a reply. *Metropolitan Museum of Art? MOMA? Shopping and dinner in Soho? Am open to your suggestions.*

She texted back.

I can meet you on the steps of the MET at 10:30am.

A thumbs up emoji followed the text bubbles. She smiled and hopped out of bed.

In her robe, after a soothing shower, Lily Rose settled at her tiny kitchen café table for some granola and blueberries. Emptying the milk carton, she realized she needed to pick up some groceries for the upcoming work week. She was now officially out of skim milk, a basic morning necessity. Lunch and dinner food, she could forego, but life without breakfast wasn't conquerable.

She quickly straightened up, adding yesterday's clothes to her laundry basket, and made her bed. As she opened the dishwasher, a foul smell greeted her. Wrinkling her nose, she quickly placed her breakfast dishes inside and hit the start cycle. Surveying her tiny white cabinet kitchen with its steel appliances, she decided it was presentable. Her small living room was swallowed by a whale of violet velvet, a luxurious camel-backed sofa she absolutely had to have. The bamboo coffee table was cluttered with bills and papers that screamed for attention. Gathering them together into a neat pile, she stacked them on the small whitewashed wood desk by the window. The bills would have to wait. Dust bunnies were mercilessly congregating in every corner of her tiny space. The apartment was in need of a good wipe down, but that would have to wait until next weekend. She had places to go.

Walking to her closet, she agonized over what to wear. Planning a whole outfit around her ring was today's challenge. She fingered a few options, then discarded the first few grabs. She wanted to impress Mingyu. She decided on dark violet jeans, a loose cream-colored shirt and a red wine cashmere sweater with tiny black knot buttons. Applying a little make up, she looked in the mirror and studied her face. At 26, she looked the consummate professional when she went to work, but today, she wanted to entice. She swept her blonde hair into a loose bun, then undid it and pulled out her curling iron and plugged it in. Maybe a touch more femininity is what the day called for. After curling her locks, she added garnet drop earrings, a gift from her grandmother and a lilac pashmina scarf. She slipped on her new ring, the crowning of her outfit. Reaching for the black wool jacket on her coat rack, she studied her reflection in the mirror with satisfaction. She slid on comfortable black suede booties, then slammed the front door behind her. Lily Rose felt flutters of anticipation as she hopped on the subway for the long trek uptown for her third and final date with Mingyu. He was leaving the next day and she wanted to make the most of forming a lasting friendship.

As the train rattled through the tunnel, she pondered over the last few days. When she first asked Mingyu to dinner it had been on impulse, fueled by professional curiosity. That night he captured her attention with his passion and knowledge of jade, igniting an interest she didn't know existed. The fact that she found him attractive was a bonus. She wanted to get a sense of what he was about and what his life in Hong Kong was like. While at the Natural History Museum, he had impressed her with his vast knowledge and dedication to gemstones. Her opinion of him shifted from curiosity and a mild attraction to something more tangible. She was fascinated by his reserved manner and the ease in which he adapted from one moment to the next, whether in conversation, New York customs or their travels around the city. He was funny, kind and flexible, three attributes she realized she valued. He was different from the men she was used to, more refined, and she looked forward to spending another day with him even if it led nowhere because of distance. Meeting Mingyu felt like filling a gap in her education, an important multicultural one that exposed her to new worlds and infinite possibilities.

Arriving at the Met, she saw him seated in the center of the steps. He was staring, probing, unsmiling, making her feel self-conscious. Their eyes locked as she walked up the stairs to greet him. *What was he thinking? Did he like what he saw?*

"Hi there. I see you discarded your sneakers. I like a daring man," she teased.

"Hi. My feet needed a change of pace. These boots are made for walking," he joked.

He looked handsome in his faded blue jeans, black suede boots and emerald suede jacket. As he stood, he extended his hand to her. His expression warmed as she slid her hand into his. His skin was warm and his grip comfortable, as if they had done this a million times before. A good feeling invaded her insides.

"Nice jacket. I love the color." At the top of the stairs, she turned to him. "So, let's start at the information booth and see which exhibits float your boat. We can't see everything. This place is huge."

"I already looked. I got here early. I would love to see the American wing and the ancient jewelry exhibit. You?"

"Good choices. I'll get passes. You can pay whatever you want here. There's no set entrance fee."

"Thanks."

They started with the American Wing. Mingyu marveled at the Tiffany windows, the great hall, and the amazing pottery in the glass showcases in the breezeway, overlooking the park. As they walked around he kept her hand securely in his, using his other hand to gesture. A few times, she caught him peering at her from underneath his floppy hair, as if gauging her approval or reaction. She felt his warmth and good intentions and more importantly, she felt completely at ease. *He actually cares about what I think. How refreshing.*

Clearly, he wanted her to enjoy the visit as much as he did. When they got to the jewelry exhibit, she noticed his serious study of some of the gems. He pointed out their intricacies and the degree of difficulty in their carvings. She listened, letting him sweep her in his tidal wave of appreciation for exquisite craftsmanship.

Departing the Met, they took the Fifth Avenue bus down to the jewelry district. "New York's jewelry district encompasses one all-important block-- 47th street between Fifth and Sixth Avenue," she explained.

Perusing the blinding bling-loaded windows, Mingyu observed, "No jade anywhere."

No. It's hidden in the many offices in this block. There's also a jewelry district in Chinatown, if you want to look there."

"No. That's where my father is today."

Lily Rose noticed his tone of defiance and dropped the subject. Hopping back on the Fifth Avenue bus, they traveled down to Greenwich Village. Mingyu listened as Lily Rose talked, her hand firmly planted in his and resting on his lap. Getting off at Astor Place, the last stop, they found a suitable restaurant off Lafayette. Settling in a little bistro, they moved to more intimate subjects.

"Tell me about your parents and best friends. What are they like?" Lily Rose was curious.

Mingyu struggled for a moment. "My mother died a few years ago and my father is a workaholic. I have an older sister who is married. She just had a baby, so she's preoccupied. She runs one of the restaurants my family owns. My great aunt and her family runs another. The person I'm closest to in my family is my grandfather. My best friend? That's someone I went to school with, Bao. He's a journalist in Hong Kong for the *Oriental Daily News*. What about you?"

"I'm closest with my grandmother, Marina. I love my mom, but she doesn't understand me like my grandmother does. My father left when I was young. He has another family on the west coast, so I don't see him much. My best friends are Tina and Zoe. Tina works for a television network and Zoe dabbles in fashion. What do you like to do in your spare time?"

They discovered they both liked outdoor activities-- swimming at the beach, playing tennis, being out on the water in a kayak or sailboat.

"Lately, I've acquired a new hobby. My Grandfather is teaching me how to cook. We have *Dim Sum* on Sundays, sometimes in the restaurant, but recently, at his place. He prefers that because he can cook whatever he wants without my sister hovering."

"That sounds awesome. My grandma and I used to bake cookies when I spent summers with her. I'm not much of a cook. What do you make?"

"Pork buns, steamed dumplings, sausage rolls, sticky rice, stir fry. It's fun and it gives me leisure time with him. At work we can't chat about personal stuff; it's busy and there are always people around."

"I hope you'll cook for me when I come visit one day."

Mingyu didn't respond in words but she watched the corners of his lips twitch upward as he nodded. Lily Rose wondered if she had overstepped a boundary. Her training at the hotel had taught her that a home in Asia is considered a very private sanctuary. An invitation for a meal is reserved for family members and a select few friends. She blushed.

Further exploration revealed they both streamed some of the same pop artists. The more Lily Rose probed, the more she got Mingyu to open up. When the check came, she grabbed it.

"This one is on me."

"Thank you, but I'll only agree if you let me pay for dinner tonight." Mingyu countered politely. "You're sacrificing your only two days off from work. I know you must have tons of things to do."

He knew she had work in the morning and she suspected he was worried she would split after lunch. The realization made her smile. "It's ok. There's always next weekend."

He grinned, obviously pleased they would still have that time together.

"What would you like to do now? Explore downtown? A little shopping? Another museum? The Whitney Museum of American Art is close."

"Shopping sounds good. I need a few gifts."

"Perfect. We'll hit Broadway. It has great stores below Union Square."

That evening, they collapsed in a quaint Chinese restaurant on Bayard Street, their three-day friendship sealed after an intimate shopping experience. They had spent a fun, comfortable, collaborative day together. Maybe it was the plum wine that further accelerated familiarity, but Lily Rose didn't think so. By now, she sensed their connection was special, one in a million. A 'soulmate,' as Marina would say. Or was that description premature? How could a soulmate live so far away?

When Mingyu walked her home, their hands intertwined, she felt content. At the door, she turned toward him and leaned in. She wanted him to kiss her again. He didn't disappoint. It was a gentle kiss that could have easily escalated. She debated inviting him in, but it was late and she knew he was leaving early the next morning. Her place was a mess and she wanted to stay friends, given the distance between them. Sex would only complicate things. With some regret, she kissed him one more time and let go, stepping backwards.

"You have my email. I hope you'll stay in touch. Keep me on your company newsletter. When I buy another piece of jade, I would like it to be from you."

"Good to know." He laughed and pulled her in for another kiss. "I was educating you to hook you on jade, you know," he joked. "Did it work?"

"Really? Just jade? Well your strategy worked out well." Their eyes locked and lingered. "You might have hooked more than a jade interest," she teased. "Good Night, Mingyu." Her heart lurched. Debating once more whether she should invite him in, she decided his friendship was more important at this time. She didn't want things to be awkward the next time she saw him because she was definitely planning on seeing him again on a future visit to Hong Kong.

"It was great meeting you and spending time with you, Lily Rose. I hope our paths will cross again." He kissed her one last time, then backed up, keeping his eyes on her. When she was inside her door, he blew her a kiss and left.

Chapter VI

Life Changes Don't come Easy

Lily Rose woke early the next morning. Lounging in bed, she thought of Mingyu and Hong Kong. She had thoroughly enjoyed their brief time together, his warm smile and sideways glance still fresh in her mind. Something had changed in her life--a seed had been planted. She envisioned what fun it would be to travel and possibly see him again. Reluctantly unwrapping herself from the confines of her twisted comforter, she swung into action, showering, dressing and leaving for work. Regrettably, there was no milk for cereal when she peered into the fridge. *Damn.* She frowned, making a mental note to pick up some groceries after work. She would have to grab breakfast in the hotel. On the subway, she texted her grandmother.

Hi, would love to see you this week end. Do you want to come into the city and stay with me?

The reply came mid-morning.

Hi back. Come here as I've been a little under the weather. Nothing contagious.

I'm working Saturday, but I can come Sunday and Monday. Does that work?

Yes. LMK your arrival time and I will be there to pick you up.

The rest of the work week whizzed by. Lily Rose managed to catch up on the usual mundane chores. When she tackled her bills, she realized how much the ring had set her back. She glanced down at her hand and decided it was well worth it. She wore the ring every day and it reminded her of her short, but magical time with Mingyu. Saturday night she met Tina and Zoe for dinner. She was excited to share her news and let them swoon over her ring.

"The selfies of you two are cute. Any chance of seeing him again?" Zoe asked.

"He lives in Hong Kong, so not any time soon."

"You always talk about going to Hong Kong. Here's a perfect reason to expedite your visit." Zoe offered, grinning.

"The flight must be like twenty hours. It's in a completely different time zone," Tina added.

"There are direct flights that take sixteen hours on Cathay Pacific. I would love to go."

"Look at that. She researched flights already. Maybe you can meet half way in Hawaii?" Zoe teased.

"Yeah, but since it's completely out of my budget, especially after splurging on fabulous jewels, I won't worry about that right now." Lily Rose changed the subject. She didn't want to share her thoughts on transferring to Hong Kong, just yet. She had to be sure that was the right career move. Chasing a man, she just met across the world wasn't normally her style. But maybe she hadn't met the right man before?

Sunday morning, Lily Rose arrived at the Jitney stop a few minutes before her 9:15am bus to Bridgehampton. Marina had gotten her a paid ride in exchange for escorting a valuable shipment of truffles to a local restaurant. The guy delivering the goods to her was waiting when she arrived.

Getting off the bus in Bridgehampton, after a two-hour snooze, she spotted her grandmother and waved. The air was crisp, and a good ten degrees colder than the city, but the blinding sun added a few degrees of warmth through the car window. She was happy to be back. The house in Sag Harbor was home. Her New York City apartment was a convenient *pied a terre.*

"Hi, Grandma." She leaned over and pecked Marina on the cheek.

"Hi there. Let's drop the truffles first. Don't want them to spoil or get smushed. Are you in the mood for pizza? We can have an early lunch at World Pie."

"Always."

Lily Rose left the warm comfort of the car to drop the truffles, which were graciously received by chef Ari himself. He was standing at the bar of his restaurant, Summer Gardens, writing today's menu on a black board. "Thank you! How are you, Lily Rose?"

"Great. Happy to be out. What's on the menu that requires truffles?

"A vegetable risotto and a 'truffled' potato gratin for my lamb."

"Yummy. I'll let you know when I'm out again, in case you need anything from the city."

"Thanks. Always appreciated. Say hi to Marina."

"Will do."

Once settled in World Pie, Marina eyed her.

"So, what's on your mind, Lily Rose? How are you?"

"Good. I had the most incredible two days off last week. Remember I told you about the jewelry show at the hotel?"

"I do. What was so incredible?"

"I bought a lavender jade ring from one of the Hong Kong vendors." She stuck out her hand and flashed her ring. "He had the most amazing imperial jade collection, lavender jade and something called mutton jade. I fell in love with this lavender color."

"Mutton fat jade. That's an off-white colored jade. Sounds like you got a free lecture too.

"Your ring is beautiful. Totally suits you."

"Thanks. I did. My favorite colors are the apple green and lavender. The salesman gave me a special price. He was pretty cute, too." She batted her eyelashes, making Marina laugh. "I couldn't resist either one, so I bought the ring and ended up having dinner with the dealer three nights in a row. He gave me an abbreviated jade education in exchange for a guided tour around the city. I'm prepping for my next jewelry purchase. I may just become a jade collector."

"Not a bad investment. Or passion. Where did you take him?"

"All over. To the Natural History Museum. You used to take me there. Remember?"

"I do. They have a wonderful gem collection. What's your friend's name and how long is he staying?"

"Mingyu and he returned to Hong Kong. He was only here for the gem show."

"Too bad. There's always next year if he comes again. Was business good?"

"I think so. He mentioned being here in previous years."

Over lunch Lily Rose shared her new-found gem passion with enthusiasm. It surprised her how much Marina knew about jade. She also brought up her desire to transfer out of New York.

"I would only go for a few years. It would be great to travel while I'm young and unattached. Our hotel chain has so many great locations world-wide. I've been dreaming about working somewhere exotic with spectacular hotel grounds or in a new exciting city. What do you think?"

"I agree. Now is the best time to do it. Go for it. You'll learn and grow from the experience, but do your research first. Make a good choice."

"Would you and mom come visit?"

Marina nodded. "Of course, we would, budget permitting. Where are you looking?"

"What do you think about Hong Kong?"

Marina sat back in her chair and let out a burst of air. "Whew, I was thinking another domestic location, not clear across the world. Let me digest this for a second. Is your decision related to the boy you just met? Did you discuss this thought with your mother?"

"No, and of course not. I always discuss things with you first."

"Can I sleep on it? I'm hesitating because there's a lot of political tension in Hong Kong. It's also reeeally far away." Marina sighed. "Selfishly… I'd miss you so much."

"You did it. What's going on in Hong Kong?"

"I did but I was married at the time. You would be flying solo. You know that Hong Kong has fallen back under Chinese rule, right?"

"Vaguely."

"Hong Kong used to be a British colony and in 1997 it reverted back to Chinese sovereignty."

"Why?"

"According to an agreement made in the 1800's, the British monarchy was obligated to return Hong Kong to China after 99 years. A deal is a deal."

"Ok. So how does that change things?"

"Under British rule, Hong Kong grew from a sparse island into the powerful city it is today. I was there to see that growth in the early 1960's when factories were launched. Buildings shot up like bamboo shoots. Grandpa contributed to the new architecture. Unlike mainland China, Hong Kong has been exposed to Western culture and business practices for decades and once the genie is out of the bottle, you can't contain it, which is what China is trying to do. There've been massive protests periodically because the island would like complete autonomy from the mainland."

"How would that benefit the city?"

"Hong Kong is thriving. It's become an Asian metropolis and it's an important business center in the world arena, a gateway to Asia. The city is on a densely populated island, kind of like Manhattan and like here it's an international melting pot. The differences between mainland China and Hong Kong are substantial. Ever heard of the concept, 'One country, two systems'?"

"No."

"Hong Kong has its own governance and would like that to continue, but it appears China has other ideas. That's why the many people who flocked there in the past few decades and raised their families there are upset and leaving in droves. It pains me to read about it."

"What do you think is going to happen, politically?"

"Who knows? I don't have a crystal ball."

"What would you like see happen?"

"I don't follow all the details the way someone who lives there would, but from my vantage point, I think Hong Kong should be autonomous. Trying to make it fit into traditional China's mold is like squeezing a square peg into a round hole." Marina frowned.

"What will happen if the Chinese government gets more control?"

"Again, difficult to foresee. It depends what rules they implement. How it will affect commerce or human rights issues. Protestors are frowned upon and often mistreated. I just don't know, Lily Rose."

"I'll have to read up on this a bit more."

"Yes. It's a good idea to be informed before you ask for a transfer. You know I love Hong Kong, but things have changed so much since I was there. I just don't want to encourage you to travel to a place experiencing political unrest. Also, if China further restricts how the city does business, foreign investors will continue to disappear which means, the hotel business will be directly affected. It may not be safe to move there." Marina looked worried.

"I understand, but I would still be under the umbrella of the hotel."

"Hmmm. Are there any other hotel locations you had in mind?"

"Yes. I'll show you my list later. I have all the places I considered in a folder on my laptop."

"Good. I can't wait to see them. Let me think about Hong Kong, ok? Maybe you need to blaze your own trail elsewhere, instead of picking up mine."

Chapter VII

Hong Kong Fever Intensifies

Monday morning, over Marina's apple pancakes, Lily Rose felt compelled to resume her discussion on Hong Kong. "I did some reading last night and I'm up to speed on what's happening in Hong Kong."

"Good. What are your thoughts?" Marina poured some steamed milk into her coffee. The smell was intoxicating.

Her grandmother made the best coffee and served it in the nicest mugs. This one had a lotus design. "I think China needs to back off."

Marina laughed. "If only it were that simple. What made you focus on Hong Kong anyway? It's a big country and an even bigger world."

"Your stories, for one."

"And two?" Only Marina could get away with this kind of prodding and get an honest answer.

"Well, maybe Mingyu does have a little something to do with my choice, but honestly, I always wanted us to go to Hong Kong with you. If I transfer there, you and mom can visit and stay with me. I want you to show me all the places you shared in your stories. Think about it, Grandma. It would be so much fun for us to do this as a family."

"Yes, it certainly would." Marina sighed wistfully. "Do you know anything about this young man's life in Hong Kong? Maybe he has a steady girlfriend."

She poured milk into her coffee and watched her granddaughter spear an apple from her pancake. "No. Regardless, I've always wanted to go to Hong Kong. It was always my intention. We should have taken this trip a long time ago, but maybe now's as good a time as any." Lily Rose recited a few reasons supporting her plan and Marina listened without interrupting. When Lily Rose finished her pitch, Marina looked thoughtful.

"Which company sold you the jade?"

"Gem International Trading Company."

"What's Mingyu's last name?"

"Ho."

Lily Rose thought she saw her grandmother blanch. Marina got up quickly, stumbling as she walked her mug to the sink. When she turned back around after rinsing it, she asked, "Do you have a picture of your friend?"

"Yes, we took lots of selfies." She pulled out her phone and let Marina scroll through the pictures. Marina stopped at one taken on the steps of the Metropolitan Museum of Art. Heads almost touching, the picture revealed two happy faces, totally at ease with each other.

"He's very handsome. I like his trendy haircut."

Lily Rose was pleased when her grandmother reached for her glasses to get a closer look. The expression on Marina's face was soft, her eyes misting up.

"So do I," Lily Rose beamed.

"What else do you like about him? In three days, you get more than a first impression."

"He's kind and thoughtful. Generous, too. I like that he has a close relationship with his grandfather. They make dim sum together every Sunday at his grandfather's house on Hong Kong Island. He learned everything he knows about jade from him."

"Did his grandfather come to New York, too?"

"No. He came with his father, who appears to be a total grouch. His grandfather was minding the business in Hong Kong."

"Did his grandfather come in previous years?"

"Yes, but now that he's older, he travels less Mingyu said. The shows in New York are too strenuous."

"I can imagine. Do you have his card or do they have a website? I'm wondering where they're located."

"I don't have the card with me, but I can show you their website. Maybe you'll know it?"

"Pull it up on my computer and I'll look at it later. What shall we do this afternoon? What time are you headed back?"

"Let's go to town. My bus isn't until 5:30pm."

Marina and Lily Rose spent the afternoon browsing around the stores in town, chatting with friends. They had coffee and scones sitting on a bench overlooking the harbor and talked about travel. Imagining sailing away on one of the mega yachts frequently docked in Sag Harbor's deep sea harbor was one of their favorite pastimes. Lily Rose was surprised to discover that Marina still had an extensive travel bucket list. A few minutes before the Jitney bus was to arrive, Marina turned to Lily Rose. "I've been thinking about your Hong Kong decision. I think you should follow your heart. If you really want to live and work abroad, try it. If you don't like it, you simply come home. Now is the time in your life to take chances. Later, it gets harder."

"Thanks, Grandma. That means a lot." Lily Rose hugged Marina.

"Life is about taking risks. Some work out, some don't. Regardless how things play out, there's always a learning curve, a period of growth, even for unforeseen circumstances. If you decide to go, I'll support you, but I sure will miss you, kiddo."

Chapter VIII

The Unforeseen Becomes the Impetus

The next morning at work, Lily Rose received a text from her grandmother.

Did you know that Mingyu means 'bright jade'?

Lily Rose laughed out loud and texted back.

No, I didn't. How appropriate. Did you know that Lily is a symbol of purity and was used as the French Monarchy's emblem? Or that Marina means 'from the sea', she joked.

No way. I didn't realize we have such cool names. LOL

Cool names for cool people. See you soon?

You bet, Missy! Always happy to see you.

During lunch, Lily Rose stopped by human resources to secure a transfer request form. She would hold on to it until she was sure, then submit it. When she got back to her desk with her bag lunch, she checked her personal email. She perked up instantly when she discovered that Mingyu had contacted her. She devoured his email as she wolfed down her sandwich:

Hello Lily Rose,

I'm looking at some new merchandise we just bought, lavender jade carvings, and you came to mind. (pictures below)

How are you? The trip back to Hong Kong was long, but the memories are sweet. New York was fun. My next gem show will be here at the Convention Center in March. In the meantime, it's business as usual. I bought tickets to see the Gloomy Island Blues Festival with Bao. Too bad you can't join us. What's new in New York?

Warm Regards, Mingyu

She replied immediately:

Hi Mingyu,

So nice to hear from you!

The carvings are awesome! Thanks for sharing. I don't dare ask the price. I'm still in a hole. LOL Keep sending me pictures. I love seeing them. I was wondering if your grandfather had a say in naming you. I learned your name means 'bright jade'. He must have been clairvoyant .I've been crazy busy at work as we've had back-to-back shows. This coming weekend we're hosting a real estate convention. Ugh, not my favorite group.

No social plans for the moment other than a casual dinner with friends. Too busy to think, let alone plan outings. I've been wearing my ring every day and I love it. It reminds me of the special time we spent together.

XO, Lily Rose

Balling up her sandwich wrapper, she aimed for the trashcan and missed. Work was piling up by the minute. She felt constant pressure. She pressed send and moved on to a new set of problems to troubleshoot. The real estate convention wasn't her favorite because the crowd was demanding, expecting unreasonable perks. By the end of the day, she was spent and felt like a shredded crustacean after a shark attack.

The following weeks continued in the same fashion. Lily Rose worked, went home to rest, clean up and turned around to come back in the morning. She hadn't looked at the transfer forms since she picked them up weeks ago. In fact, the urge to make a change had dissipated, while trying to just stay afloat. Thanksgiving came and went. She and her mom, Ella May, spent it in Sag Harbor, cooking in Marina's kitchen. They argued over Lily Rose's wish to transfer. Her mother didn't see the value in leaving the country for a different work experience. "Really, Lily Rose. You don't have to travel that far for a change. Plenty of great places in this big country."

"You know I've always wanted to see Hong Kong with grandma. You could both come visit. It would break up the year and be so exciting."

"Have you been reading the news? They are having big problems over there."

"I would be working in an international hotel, Mom. That wouldn't affect me."

"Of course, it would. It affects everyone. Jump in anytime, Mom." Ella May glared at her mother. Marina shrugged and said nothing. Ella May frowned. Marina and Lily Rose were always on the same page, the one opposite her, and it frustrated her.

The only bright spot in Lily Rose's social life was her correspondence with Mingyu. She looked forward to his emails-

-hearing about his activities and seeing glimpses of his world. He filled her in on his new jade purchases, including detailed pictures, and he patiently answered her questions. Occasionally, he talked about events he attended or the protests in Hong Kong, steering clear of his political opinion. Even that sounded more exciting than being accosted by Elmo or Spiderman in Times Square every day. She noticed he didn't mention any personal relationships.

The pre-Christmas season in the hotel was hectic. Somehow Lily Rose could not get caught up in the season's magic. Just before Christmas, things got worse. While still at work one day, Lily Rose got a frantic phone call from her mother. "You need to come home right away. Grandma had a heart attack."

Chapter IX

Bad Egg in Hong Kong

Mingyu could sense the urgency in his grandfather's text. Jin wanted him to come for dinner after work to discuss something important. He had worked from his residence the last three days, which was unusual. Occasionally, Jin took a day here and there for outside appointments, but three days in a row?

Arriving at his grandfather's home on Stanley Village Drive, the other side of Hong Kong Island, he parked in front of the box like structure. Jin's home was across the harbor, in the opposite direction of his own home in West Kowloon and a good distance from work, but Mingyu never regretted the trip. The water view from his grandfather's deck was spectacular. Jin occupied one of the smaller homes on the street, but whatever it lacked in modernity and size, it made up for in character. Its unique bonsai rock garden surrounded by flowering tropical plants, large picture windows and patio, alone, were worth every penny in taxes. The house had been in their family for decades. Mingyu's father, Cheng, and his aunt, Chantao, were raised there. It was the chosen destination for all family gatherings on holidays if they weren't in his sister's restaurant. Mingyu loved Jin's home on the peninsula of Stanley. He used his key to let himself in the downstairs front door and sprinted up the steps, two at a time, to the living space, calling out, "Hello? *Ye Ye*, I'm here."

I'm in the kitchen." Jin's emerald jade-colored kitchen with its large bamboo counter top was open to the living room, a renovation he had completed after his wife died. The project had kept him busy during his grieving period and reignited his passion for cooking.

"Hi. Something smells delicious. I'm hungry."

"Good. I made fried rice with beef and vegetables. Pour yourself a glass of wine or do you want a Snow beer?

"I'll have a Tsingtao. You want one too? Shall I set the table on the terrace?"

"Yes to both. Turn on the heat lamp. How was work today?"

"We sold a few pieces. Nothing crazy. Why haven't you come in? Are you feeling ok?" Mingyu eyed his grandfather with concern.

"I'm fine. I've been doing some research and it was better completed here. Was your father in the office today?"

"Yes, this morning. He didn't come back after lunch. I think he had outside appointments. He didn't say."

"Hmmm." Jin nodded. "Dinner is ready. Let's eat."

They sat down and took a few bites to still their burning hunger. The silence between them was comfortable. When Jin finally spoke, he appeared to search for the right words.

Mingyu waited.

"I invited you tonight because there's something important I need to discuss. It can't wait until Sunday. It's been bothering me for a while, so I'll get straight to the point. I've been going over some business transactions with our accountant, and I think your father is making some bad choices with his gold company. I didn't want to tell you because I was afraid to alarm you, but I know you'd figure it out soon enough."

"What are you talking about?" Mingyu looked up from his nearly empty bowl.

"Your dad has been brokering gold deals of late. Not a bad thought, when the stone market slows, but the problem is, you have to know who your clients are and what their intentions may be. After some checking, I'm convinced he and Hu Fat are selling to the Yakuza."

"Whaaat? Why do you think that?" Mingyu's chopsticks slid through his fingers to the table.

"I think the *Yakuza* have infiltrated the Hu Feng Gold Bullion Corp. Your dad is doing deals with Hu Fat and has been for a few months. I've warned him over and over, but you know your father. When he smells money, he's very goal oriented and stubborn."

"Hu Fat is committing fraud?"

"Yes. Here is what I think is happening. Hu Fat and Cheng are selling the Yakuza gold as an Investment and issuing certificates for gold storage, but the storage facilities are empty and the gold is being smuggled into Japan without paying the required consumption tax. Since we don't tax gold here it's a very lucrative business, if you can get away with it. I suspect your father is using our family's shipping business to transfer the gold. I haven't spoken to your Uncle Huan yet. I wanted to be completely sure he is unaware. He is. I've been afraid of foul play since gold prices have escalated. There were whispers about these transactions Then I heard a confirmation from one of my more reliable sources." Jin paused waiting for a reaction.

Mingyu gulped. He knew not to ask Jin about his sources. His grandfather kept his relationships confidential. Mingyu's heart was beating double time. *Is this really happening? The family was doing fine, financially. Why would his father be so careless?*

Jin continued. "If your father wants to take risks with his International Gold Investments company, I can't do anything about it, but I will not let him taint or touch my gemstone business. I want him to get his own accountant for the gold business. We cannot share anymore. I need us to be on the same page, Minyu."

"I understand. Are you sure about this though? I mean… I know dad is business obsessed, but would he do this knowingly?"

"Yes, I'm afraid so. The only thing I'm not sure about is what kind of arrangement he has with Hu Fat. Your father refuses to discuss it. He told me to mind my own business. Well, that is exactly what we'll do. Mind our gem business. Moving forward, I want to make sure all our employees are committed to us, not facilitating Cheng. I can't trust my own son, but I know I can trust my grandson. Your father isn't thinking clearly and I can't reason with him. Are you with me on this?"

"Of course. I haven't noticed a thing. How can I help?"

"I don't want you to do anything. Definitely don't talk to Cheng about this. I need you to be observant and report back to me. Tell me if you hear or see anything suspicious. I'll be livid if your father is doing illicit business from our jewelry company. I have worked decades to build a good, honest trading company and I'll be damned if I let his greed ruin it for us."

Mingyu had never seen his grandfather so steamed. His demeanor was usually calm, Zen-like. It took a lot to ruffle Jin's feathers. Mingyu's stomach lurched. *Is this really happening?*

"And there's one more thing I want to clarify. My jade business goes to you and you alone, when I die. Your sister gets the restaurant and your dad can share the shipping business with Huan. I changed my will after your grandma died, and I just amended it recently. I haven't told anyone and I don't intend to. I'm of sound mind and the new copy is filed with my lawyer."

"Eric Wong?"

"Yes. Now, forget I told you until I keel over."

"I will because you're not dying anytime soon."

"I thank the Gods for you every day, Mingyu, because my son is a confused man. Very troubling. I'm so sorry. Buddha says, 'Prayer is the cure for a confused mind, a weary soul, and a broken heart.' I pray for my son."

Chapter X

Sag Harbor Blues

Lily Rose and Ella May were sitting in Marina's kitchen in Sag Harbor. Marina's funeral service had been beautifully simple, but emotionally draining nonetheless. As per Marina's request, delivered in person by her lawyer and trusted friend, a portion of her ashes were to be contained in a small urn with the intention of being scattered in the ocean on her March 24th birthday. Marina had the day planned out. She directed Ella May to organize a celebration of her life. The guests were handpicked by Marina. Ella May was instructed to organize a picnic on Captain Manny's boat with chilled beer, wine, prosecco and all her favorite foods. Her invited friends would be asked to prepare a vignette and remember Marina at her best. Only positive stories, NO GLOOM she had written in red capital letters. If the weather was inclement, an alternate date was acceptable.

Lily Rose was beside herself—she could barely eat, sleep or think straight. Her heart had suffered a terminal punch and her head was trapped in an unrelenting fog.

"Honey, eat a little something," Ella May coaxed her daughter.

Listlessly picking at her food, Lily Rose stared out the window at the darkened, gloomy bay. Rainclouds loomed, threatening to spill their contents on the barren winter grounds Marina had loved so much. Her normally radiant garden and her granddaughter looked dismal.

"Mom, I think I'm going to add a few vacation days to my personal days and stay here through Christmas. I just can't go back to work yet. I can't stomach the Christmas cheer right now."

"Are you sure? It may be good to keep your mind occupied. I can't stay with you. I've got to get back to work."

"Yes, I'm certain. I just need more time."

"I can come back next weekend if you like." Ella May looked at her daughter with concern.

"Let's see. We'll talk. Right now, I just want to be here. Alone."

After a miserable few weeks, Ella May and Lily Rose went to meet with Marina's lawyer. Seated in his office, they listened as he clarified Marina's last will and detailed instructions. To the women's surprise, Marina left her car, the house in Sag Harbor, its contents, and a sealed envelope to Lily Rose. He handed her the bulging envelope to be opened in private, when she felt up to it. No rush. Her mother received a good financial bonus, Marina's jewelry, and some stocks and gold coins, all of which were secured in a joint safety deposit box, locally. It appeared Marina had given her will a great deal of thought. Lily Rose was touched. Back at the house, the two women avoided talking about Marina's decisions. If her mom felt blind-sided, she didn't show it.

"Listen, Mom. If there's anything you want from the house, take it with you."

Ella May sighed. "I would like the seascape painting in the living room, if that's ok. I always loved that one."

"Sure. Take it."

"Can I take Grandma's blue cashmere wrap too?"

"Yes. It's yours. Any clothes you want, just take them."

"Thanks. I made a reservation on the five o'clock jitney. Will you drive me?" She sounded tired and Lily Rose leaned over to hug her.

"Of course."

The following morning Lily Rose awoke to bright sunshine pouring into her lilac and white bedroom. She turned to the window and lay looking at the tree tops swaying in the breeze. In happier days, there would have been a heavenly coffee scent escaping the kitchen and plumes of apple pancakes wafting up the stairs. The silence and lack of enticing fragrances was too much to bear. The house was eerily quiet except for a few groans from the pipes and whooshes from the heating vents. Still grieving, Lily Rose showered and trudged down the stairs to retrieve the car keys from the kitchen drawer. She would grab breakfast at Hamptons Coffee Choice, and pick up some groceries in Bridgehampton. Hopefully she wouldn't run into anyone.

She wasn't ready.

Finished unpacking groceries a while later, she slid on her Uggs by the kitchen door and walked to the garage. Retrieving logs to make a fire, Lily Rose piled them up on the front porch. She grabbed the three biggest and took them inside, dumping them in the fireplace with some smaller kindling wood. It took her a few tries to get the fire started, but watching Marina do it all these years seemed to trigger her memory. She congratulated herself on remembering to open the flue and close the metal curtain. Once the fire was roaring she made and poured white peony tea in Marina's favorite lotus mug and fetched the legal sized envelope Marina had left her. Settled comfortably in a plus sized armchair, she slid out the contents. A letter addressed to her accompanied numerous smaller envelopes. She read the letter first.

Dear Lily Rose,

So sorry I've left you so suddenly. I've been expecting it for some time, but that's unimportant now. What is important is that you carry on with your life as if I were there. You know what choices to make. Be bold in your decisions and follow your heart—if you are still thinking about transferring somewhere exotic for work, don't hold back. Now is the time. Your mother will be fine. She is not an adventurous spirit like you and I, but I have no doubt that she will visit you wherever you go.

I can't begin to tell you how much joy you've given me over the years. I always treasured our time together, especially our many summers. You have grown into a beautiful, capable woman and I'm happy to have been part of that journey. Please don't be sad. Remember our happy times together and let them be the fuel you need to blaze a new trail for yourself. I left you the cottage, so you will always have a home to come back to when you need to regroup, think or retreat from the world-- a safe place. You can rent it out in the summer, if you need to cover the yearly costs, but don't let it go. You will regret it if you do.

To get you started, I attached two envelopes. One is for your upcoming travels and the other is for maintaining your new/old home. I left a list of people who have serviced the house. They are all trustworthy.

Much love,

XO, Marina

Tears streamed down Lily Rose's cheeks as she refolded the letter and pushed it back into the envelope. She wiped her eyes with her sweatshirt sleeve. Needing to process Marina's words and feeling spent, she decided to check the other envelopes later. Looking for a mindless distraction, she flipped through the TV channels and settled on a romance movie. Curling up her legs, she swaddled a fleece blanket over herself, cuddling deeper into the armchair. Mid-movie, the fire crackling in the background, she drifted off into a deep slumber, dreaming of visiting Hong Kong with Marina. They were walking by the harbor, enjoying the lights and colorful floating *junks*. When she awoke, it was late afternoon and the phone was ringing. She reached for it. "Hello?"

"Hi there, how are you doing?" Zoe's voice was warm and caring.

"Hi Zoe. I'm sad. Heartbroken, really."

"That's to be expected. You two were close."

"I feel like I lost my best friend. No offense. You're right up there, too."

None taken. Are you still at the beach?"

"Yes. I decided to stay here through Christmas. My mom will come back for the holiday."

"That's good. Will you be in the city for New Years? I miss you."

"Yes. Thanks for coming to the funeral service. My grandmother loved you, you know."

"I know. I'll miss her, too."

"I'll call you when I get back. Right now I'm choosing to be unhappy here."

"I understand. I'm around when you need me. Tina, too. Call us anytime."

When Lily Rose hung up, she added another log to the fireplace and started an early dinner. Washing some mixed greens, she threw them into a bowl and added some olive oil and fig vinegar. Marina always kept quality basics in stock. She heated a comforting potato leek soup from the freezer to warm her frozen insides.

Fed, she wandered aimlessly through the small sunlit cottage. It was going to be dark shortly. Things always looked bleaker in the dark. In essence, she knew the contents of every corner and crevice of the house as she had searched for one thing or another in the many summers she spent with her grandmother. Nonetheless, she viewed the cottage with a new perspective. Now that Marina's house was hers, there was paperwork to take care of, utility bills to pay and phones to disconnect.

Early the next morning, she got to work. When she saw the tax bill for the house, she pulled out Marina's envelope and opened the one marked "house". It contained a bank statement with eighty-five thousand dollars in a joint account Marina had opened years ago for summer expenses and visits. Lily Rose had completely forgotten about it. It was now hers to use for house repairs. Feeling overwhelmed with gratitude, she reached for the other envelope marked "travel," and peered inside. It contained fifteen thousand dollars in cash. The money was wrapped in decorative paper with the amount noted on the wrapping.

"OMG," she uttered out loud. "I don't believe this." She wanted to call her mother and share the news, but she also didn't want to explain why Marina had left her travel cash. She would tell her at the right time.

Her head dizzy from paperwork and her stomach growling, Lily Rose prepared breakfast. Parked in the back of the refrigerator was the last of Marina's homemade granola. She threw a fistful into a bowl with skim milk and savored the taste. Pouring percolated coffee into her grandmother's favorite lotus mug, she leaned her elbows on the table and wept into her hands.

Later, still in an emotional state, Lily Rose headed to Marina's bedroom. The door had remained closed through the funeral week. Hesitating briefly, she pushed the squeaky door open and peered inside. It was tough entering, knowing her grandmother wasn't there. Everything looked the same. Plopping herself on the bed, she let her eyes travel around the sunlit space. It was neat, as if Marina had gone on vacation. Lily Rose walked towards the box on Marina's dresser, the one with all the costume jewelry. She picked up a bottle of her grandmother's favorite perfume, Chloe's rose fragrance and dabbed a little on her neck, and wrists, inhaling the scent. It screamed Marina and she loved it. She decided to adopt the scent as her own signature fragrance.

In Marina's night table, she found a book of poetry and a flowered journal that contained words of wisdom from philosophers, poets, celebrities and anyone else Marina deemed worthy. Leafing through the pages, a small curve forming at the corner of her lips. Her grandmother had transcribed whatever resonated with her and much of it spoke to Lily Rose. One saying in particular caught her eye. She could hear her grandmother's voice in her head.

There are only two mistakes one can make along the road to truth; not going all the way and not starting. –Buddha

Putting the book back, she walked into the closet. Marina's clothes hung neatly on three bars. Dresses to the left and pants and shirts on the right. The back wall was lined with shelves. Colorful hat boxes adorned the top shelves. Lily Rose grabbed the step stool and carefully looked through each box. She recognized most of Marina's pretty straw hats and remembered the occasions her grandmother wore them. Good memories flooded her brain and she couldn't help but smile at some of them. Behind one of the round hat boxes, she discovered a weathered green and white gingham box with a faded green silk ribbon around it. Curious, she lifted it down and brought it to the bed. Inside she discovered a stack of letters tied with a crimson ribbon. They were all addressed to Marina at her various New York addresses. The postmarks were from Hong Kong. There was no sender on the envelope. Another batch of letters with a golden ribbon had been returned to sender; the sender was Marina. The letters were addressed to a business in Hong Kong. Intrigued, but fatigued from crying, she took note of this discovery. She would circle back to them another day.

Underneath the letters was a small flat emerald green silk box. She jostled the top off and gasped at the contents, her eyes popping. *Oh my God! Could this be jade?*

On a small round-link, gold chain dangled the most exquisitely carved imperial jade dragon pendant. The pendant looked to be the same quality as Mingyu's showpieces. It was spectacular! The pendant was circular with a donut-like shape surrounding a yin yang symbol. Arched around the donut, heads meeting below it, were two fierce, roaring dragons, facing off. Between them was a half-round ball, possibly a world symbol? She was guessing. The stone was cold to the touch and it was an amazing apple green color. Given all she had learned from her brief education with Mingyu, she was certain this was authentic, magnificent jade. The real deal.

Next to the pendant were a pair of small, round jade disc earrings with a nail-head-sized diamond pave' button top. The discs circled carved peony flowers with delicate leaves. Lily Rose gently lifted them out of the box and walked to the dresser mirror, holding them up to her ears. She swiveled her head back and forth, watching the discs catch the light. Peonies were her grandmother's favorite flower. They bloomed magnificently in her front garden every June. The earrings' color was not as vivid as the pendant's, but still a nice shade of mottled green with a smooth, polished finish. Unbuttoning her blue cashmere sweater, she slipped the pendant over her head and studied it on her white t-shirt. It was simply magnificent. She closed the gingham box and put it back on a lower shelf. She felt compelled to research the meaning of the pendant's symbols on her laptop. Perhaps, Mingyu could shed some light, too. Racing to the kitchen table, she placed the pendant on a white linen dish towel and took a few pictures with her phone, but she didn't send them. She wasn't ready to talk about her grandmother's passing. She needed more time to share her loss.

The week before Christmas dragged as Lily Rose was stricken with estate tasks and a lingering cold. Hours escaped unnoticed when she explored Marina's inner sanctum while sipping tea with honey in Marina's distinctive mugs. When her mother arrived for Christmas, Lily Rose had completed the necessary estate paperwork with the lawyer's help, taken care of bills and explored every nook of the house. Marina, even in her absence, had made the house transfer easy. The two plus weeks alone in Marina's home had brought Lily Rose the solace and inner balance she needed to move forward. Over the Christmas holiday, the two women consoled each other and traded memories.

Marina's death left a gaping hole, but staying in the cottage had helped Lily Rose grieve properly. She began to understand why Marina had left the beach house to her. The house and its surroundings had healing powers. Her mother would have broken Lily Rose's heart all over again, had she inherited the cottage and sold it. Marina must have recognized that. She gave Ella May the cash and carry currency for a reason.

After Christmas, Lily Rose packed up her suitcase with a few extra mementos. Before leaving, she ran to Marina's night table and retrieved the journal with its proverbs. When Lily Rose got on the Jitney Sunday night, her mind was set. On Monday, she would hand in her transfer request for Hong Kong. She was finally ready to make her move. If she didn't make a change now, her dreary life would stay the same. Wasn't it Marina who always said, "If you aren't proactive to make a change, your life will stay the same." On the bus, she pulled out Marina's journal and flipped through the pages. In her grandmother's neat script, she read,

"You never know how strong you are until being strong is the only choice you have."—Bob Marley

Chapter XI

Trouble in the Ho Family

Mingyu arrived at work early and prepared the store for opening. Going about his morning rituals in silence, he methodically, opened the blinds, the large safe and watered the ficus trees near his grandfather's desk. He also made tea for Jin. Lingering in front of the radio on the polished bamboo shelving, he opted to leave it off. Melting into his leather swivel chair, he scanned through the pending papers on his impressive cherry wood desk, without really absorbing them. His concentration was shot. He leaned back and sipped his take-out coffee, staring into the office void. Shifting his gaze to the window behind his grandfather's desk, he let his eyes travel around the close-up prints of magnificently carved gemstones decorating their joint office and workshop walls. A glass-paned wall and door separated their two desks from the open workshop space.

Since his dinner with Jin, a week ago, Mingyu was anxious and distracted. He found it difficult to focus on anything. Often, he found himself scrutinizing their eight employees with a tinge of mistrust. He was fairly confident his grandfather's assistant and head gemologist, Hui, was above board, but Li, he was not so certain about. Li was his father's favorite go-to person. He was knowledgeable in all things jewelry and had a keen sense of business that bordered on overly aggressive, but he was also a good sales rep who created substantial revenues for the company. The silent type, Li offered little regarding his private life. Mingyu wondered if he had one.

The two women working the sales counter, Amber and Winnie, were pretty straightforward. They were not as vested in what happened in the office or workshop as they worked on a sales commission. The ladies were all about customer service, spending their days trying to connect with potential clients. Gossiping about clients was not out of their daily realm either.

Then there was the workshop. The company employed four jewelers in a small factory type setting on the second floor. Two men were metalsmiths, one was a CAD designer and mold maker and the fourth man worked as a setter. In a pinch, their skills could overlap. Most of the day, the workshop was busy, hustling to get things past Jin's stiff quality control. They had no time for illicit activity. Security was handled through an outside company whose employees were carefully vetted. The only possible weak link Mingyu could fathom was Li. Mingyu vowed to keep an eye on his father's quiet assistant.

Mingyu turned on his computer and smiled when he saw an email from Lily Rose. She calmed his soul with her upbeat notes. Lately they had been sharing tidbits about their past and how they got into their current professions. While in New York, they had focused on family dynamics and common interests. With general information out of the way, they were now on a discovery mission. Impressed with his knowledge, she wanted to know what his training had entailed. Inspired to respond, he started to write:

Hello Lily Rose,

Glad to hear from you. Hope your holiday went well. To answer some of your questions… I received a Graduate Gemologist degree at the Gemological Institute, (GIA) here in the Central District of Hong Kong. Post-degree, I worked for the GIA Laboratory for three years, evaluating submitted stones. I learned a lot and saw the most unusual merchandise. In college, I studied business. I wasn't sure if I wanted to work with gems at first. My grandfather convinced me to do the six-month course at the GIA and then decide. He paid for the opportunity. It strengthened my resolve to stay in my family's business. Smart man.

While working at the GIA, I decided to get my certification in Jewelry Design too. One year, I actually won a student award which totally surprised me. Jin was so excited he made the piece I designed in our workshop. It was a moment of celebration and pride for him, more so than for me. I understand the mechanics of design, but my heart is really with the carved jade and stone trade.

It was after my mother died, that my grandfather suggested I come work in the family business full time, so I left the Gem labs. Our company was growing and my family needed help. Jin lured me in with promises of travel and trade shows abroad. Overall, they were all good decisions. No regrets.

You asked when jade became China's imperial stone. Jade is a hard stone and therefore was used to make important weapons and tools over 7,000 years ago so our fascination with jade goes way back. It was carved into objects, figurines and furnishings for the imperial family's graves.

After that it took on a whole new meaning. Of course, everyone wants what the imperial family has, so now jade is mainstream and everyone has a few nice pieces in their family trove.

Tell me about your educational path and motivations.

M.

It was true, Mingyu never regretted his choice to work with his grandfather. He made a seamless transition from the GIA labs to the family business. A space was created in Jin's generous office landscape and Mingyu came to occupy the desk opposite Jin. The fact that he sat through Jin's phone calls and listened to his business meetings, allowed Mingyu to absorb the gem trade close up. In awe of his grandfather's approach to business and life in general, he thrived. Jin was infinitely knowledgeable and often sought out by other dealers for his expertise and expansive historical memory. He was a respected name in the industry and a world-wide authority on jade. Mingyu was a sponge, soaking it all in.

Cheng worked in an office down the hall, alone. Mingyu knew he preferred the distance, doing his own deals in a subsidiary gold company. Cheng clearly was happy to leave Mingyu's training to his father, regarding them as two kindred, softer spirits. He worked to live while they lived to work.

The workshop, connected to Jin's and Mingyu's space, separated only by the glass wall, allowed them to oversee all aspects of production. Grandfather and grandson spent as much time in the studio as they did at their desks arranging deals. Cheng stayed in his office more and more, rarely venturing out. Mingyu sensed a shift in Cheng and Jin's limited interactions. Hui and Li shared a section in the workshop, their desks facing each other. Since Li was on the road a lot, Hui had the luxury of spreading out across both desks. While the men had a good working relationship, they were not friends. Hui was clearly Jin's favorite so Li naturally gravitated towards the equally quiet Cheng. The arrangement worked.

Mingyu finished his email to Lily Rose, inquiring about her career path. While he knew what her job entailed, he was curious about her journey. Before signing off he attached a new jade purchase Hui had photographed the day before with a brief description, then pressed send. Lily Rose seemed to soak up everything he shared and often came back to him with intelligent questions. He thought about encouraging her to take a class at the GIA in New York, but refrained. He didn't want to appear pushy.

Employees at Jin's *Gem International Trading Company* generally stuck around for years. His grandfather treated his team with respect and if business was good, so were their bonuses. Mingyu was happy working there… until now. The unfamiliar tension between his father and Jin was taking a toll on him. He wondered if others noticed. Jin's demeanor never changed and Cheng hibernated in his office. If anything, Mingyu suspected he would be the clue that all was not well in the Ho family.

While others appeared oblivious, Mingyu couldn't help being pulled into the undertow. He thought about recruiting Hui as a scout, but until any suspicions were substantiated, he hesitated to disclose anything concrete to anyone. Family dissention was better handled internally. He closed his laptop and went downstairs to the sales floor.

As he moved around the cream-colored store, turning on lights and unlocking the downstairs safe, he looked around for any loose paperwork. He saw nothing unusual. Satisfied, he headed back upstairs, pausing briefly in the hallway. He heard some activity. Was his father in? He hadn't noticed anyone arriving. Treading silently toward his father's office, he heard another voice besides Cheng's. Was someone in his father's office or was Cheng on video chat? Mingyu froze and listened.

"Did they pay you yet?" His father's voice sounded impatient and tense.

"No, Akiyama was supposed to send a messenger with payment, but it hasn't happened yet."

"The ship is leaving the day after tomorrow. I finished the paperwork for the certificates, but if they don't pay in full, I'm not sending anything. Our shipping schedule doesn't bend for their business. We have other paying customers waiting for their freight and Huan will explode if I ask him to change his schedule. Not possible. You need to talk to them and explain that payment is due well before scheduling the shipping."

"I've told them more than once. When is your next ship going out if they miss this one?"

"Not for a week or so."

"They won't like that." The voice sounded anxious.

"I don't care. I'm not taking chances without compensation." Cheng's anger was real.

"The last time I rushed them, they pistol whipped me in the parking lot."

"Hu Fat, I'm not a charity. I only deliver to paying customers. Don't call me unless you have all the money. I don't work on credit."

Backing up soundlessly before his father noticed, Mingyu retreated to his own office, melting into his swivel chair. Rolling over to the bamboo shelving, he turned on the radio to announce his presence. *Who the hell was Akiyama?*

Chapter XII

Life is About Taking Chances

Without mentioning her intentions to her mother, Lily Rose put in her application for relocation with human resources. It was a long shot, but she needed to move forward in a meaningful way. Marina would have wanted her to. She decided she would share the news with her mother, if it actually materialized. Why fight now? Transfers did not happen overnight; openings had to be available. In the meantime, she would use the time to get her affairs in order. She didn't want to leave before Marina's birthday and life celebration in late March. However, just knowing the paperwork was in, gave her a rush.

When she sat in her boss's office the next morning to give Margo the news, she was nervous.

"Yesterday I handed in a transfer request. I've been toying with the idea of working on another Hilton property for a while now. Initially, I had a long list of choices I would have considered, but now, after doing extensive research and some soul-searching,

I narrowed it down to one place, Hong Kong. I would really like to work in Hong Kong."

As Lily Rose feared, her boss's initial response was negative.

"Are you kidding me? We've finally gotten to a place where I know I can fully rely on you. I fully count on you to appease disgruntled clients when I'm busy planning our next big money maker. I trained you for months to handle all situations like a pro. And now you want to leave? I thought you were happy here! I thought we were a good team!"

Anticipating Margo's reaction, Lily Rose was ready to explain. "This has nothing to do with you, Margo. We are a good team and I love working for you. I appreciate all you have taught me." She paused to search Margo's shocked face, then continued, "But....I'm going through a rough patch. As you know, I was very close to my grandmother and her death hit me hard, so changing up my life now would really help me move forward. I need to get out of New York for a while. It would totally lift my spirits. It's also a good time in my life to work abroad; I'm unattached. Later it may be harder. I hope you understand."

Margo steepled her red nails and peered at Lily Rose over the rim of her cobalt blue reading glasses. She looked like she was about to erupt, however, Lily Rose's pathetic expression and hunched over frame softened her demeanor. "Look, I get that you're sad. Losing a loved one is traumatic, for sure." She shut her eyes and emitted a controlled sigh. "Are you sure about this, Lily Rose? I mean, really sure?"

"I am. I've given it careful thought."

"I'm really disappointed, but alright then. I'll see what I can do. You do understand that you can't leave until you've trained someone for your position. I can't be left high and dry and I don't have the time to train someone myself. Again. I invested a lot in you."

"Of course. I didn't expect to leave today or tomorrow. I know how busy this office gets. If I started somewhere new in the Spring, that would be fine."

"Good. I'm glad that's clear, but I'm not making any promises. Out of curiosity, what other hotels were on your list?"

"I looked at Nashville, New Orleans and Miami, nationally. Worldwide, I was focused on Hong Kong, Sydney or London."

"Those are all nice choices, each completely different of course. Why Hong Kong?"

"It feels like the right choice for me. I've always been curious."

Margo waited, but Lily Rose offered nothing more. "Ok, let's get back to work. I have a really busy day. I'll keep you posted on any developments. You're absolutely sure about this, right? Because, once I start inquiries, I don't want to reverse gears."

"Yes, I am. Thank you, Margo. I really appreciate anything you can do to expedite my application." Lily Rose shot her boss a grateful smile. Relieved, she left the office as Margo turned her attention and red nails to the next fire.

<h1 style="text-align:center">Chapter XIII</h1>

<h1 style="text-align:center">Super Sleuthing</h1>

Mingyu spent the following weeks shadowing his father's assistant whenever possible, but his sleuthing turned up nothing. When he googled Akiyama, all he discovered was that he shared his name with Yoshihiro Akiyama, a famous mixed martial artist and judoka expert in Japan. Mingyu needed a first name or the name of a company. In addition, Li's laptop was password protected and he rarely made phone calls that were not directly related to the gem business, no matter how often Mingyu hovered to eavesdrop. To make his investigating nearly impossible, Li spent a good amount of time in Cheng's office with the door closed. Lately, Mingyu caught him in there even when his father was out. On a pretext, he went to canvass.

"Hi Li. Is my father out for the day?"

"Yes."

"Do you know where?"

"He's having lunch with a client in the *Kwun Tong* district, then he's meeting Hu Fat in the afternoon."

"Do you know who his lunch date is?"

"No, he didn't say." Li averted his eyes indicating he was done fielding unwelcome questions.

"Thanks." Mingyu shifted his feet and inched his way toward the door, purposely leaving it wide open.

Careful not to discuss anything relating to Cheng in the office, he and Jin compared notes every Sunday over dim sum. So far, their snooping hadn't amounted to much. Cheng did not leave paper trails and his computer was always locked. If they were going to find anything, they would need to hire a private eye. Frustrated, the two men deliberated on how to proceed.

"I can't ask our security company or my friend on the police force to run a check on my son. We need to find a trustworthy private investigator, someone who won't blackmail us or alert the police if Cheng is doing something illicit. I know a jewelry company that recently hired someone to trace stolen merchandise. Maybe that would be the route to take?"

Mingyu nodded. "Sure. Who lost jewelry recently?"

"Michael Chan. I believe he had success retrieving some stolen pieces. It was all handled quietly and no charges were filed. It even stayed out of the news. I could ask him for the investigator's name. He'll presume we're tracing merchandise, not your father."

"Ok, that sounds reasonable. If we wait until the next GIA lecture, we'll probably run into Michael. I always see him there."

"Good idea. Let me know when the next one happens and I'll come with you. For the record, there' s no 'we' here. I will speak to Michael alone. I don't want you involved. For your own protection, you understand. If I have a disagreement with Cheng so be it. I don't want you to have an awkward relationship with your father on account of me. Behind closed doors, we're a team of course."

"I understand. Thank you." Mingyu felt relieved. He looked up from his phone. "The next GIA lecture is in two weeks. Ironically, the lecture is called, 'Every day is a treasure hunt.'"

Chapter XIV

Sweet New Beginnings

Lily Rose was sitting in a staff meeting in Margo's office. She tried to focus on what Margo was saying, but found it redundant and tedious, a droning sound that lulled her into a trance. She hoped the others wouldn't notice her disconnect. As she glanced around the conference table, she saw only captivated expressions. Margo had the gift of persuasion. Normally, Lily Rose would have been right there with them, but today she counted bracelet links, tapped morse code on an empty notepad and arranged her wavy tresses with a dull pencil while staring at the gaping building cracks across the street. She hoped no one would see her fidgeting or notice her ennui, but the groups' attention hung on Margo's every word as if it was a gospel sermon. Lily Rose wondered how her boss kept her enthusiasm up for each new event. Perhaps she had her speeches memorized and functioned on auto-pilot at this stage in her career. Or maybe it had become second nature. The woman was so adept at thinking out of the box; every new problem was tackled and solved with a skill set that would make even the most senior executive blush. Margo fixed the unfixable without batting an eyelash or breaking a nail.

Since Marina died, Lily Rose was moving in warped time loop speed. It was as if she was encased in a bubble and everyone else bounced off the perimeter. She could hear and see them through a filtered saran-wrap fog, but she couldn't respond as they expected her to. She read the disappointment in her co-workers faces, but found it impossible to dig deep enough to muster her usual care. "Lily Rose, can you stay? I'd like to talk to you." Margo was looking straight at her as she dismissed the others with a wave of her manicured hand. Her red, full-lipped smile was brief as she stuck a long, pointed fingernail into her messy bun to keep it from tumbling. Neat diamond stud earrings sparkled in her ears, almost detracting from the perfect pearly whites in between. Margo was pleasant to look at and she exuded efficiency in her dark pants suit and the Apple power watch strapped to her wrist. Lily Rose guessed it kept track of her schedule, health regiment and probably her sex life too. She chuckled at the thought.

Startled, Lily Rose's attention shifted to the present as she gazed around the table. The meeting was adjourned and everyone was sprinting toward the door as if a swarm of bees was attacking. The queen bee had motivated her workers. Well … .most of them.

"Sure, Margo." Her eyes lethargically travelled back to her boss.

"Sit down. I have some interesting news to share. I heard from human resources today."

Lily Rose instantly perked up.

"There's a young lady in the special events office in Hong Kong who would love to change places with you for a year. She may be willing to swap apartments too from what I gather. She lives in West Kowloon, a nice area of Hong Kong. Her name is An. Sound interesting?"

Lily Rose felt the fog lifting. "That would be awesome, Margo! When? Same work I take it?"

"Well…most of our big shows are scheduled and on track, so you could take off end of March and start in the Hong Kong office April first. Same job. Will the timing work for you?"

"Yes! That would be incredible. It gives me enough time to take care of things in New York. Thank you, Margo. Thank you so much!"

"Ok, then. Let's meet with HR after lunch and get your new life moving. You can get An's email and work out the apartment logistics. I would guess the rents aren't too dissimilar."

Margo snapped her laptop shut. "And Lily Rose, please perk up. I want you to do me proud in Hong Kong. I trained you. My reputation is at stake. I know what you're capable of and these past few months you've been ….well shall we say, distracted?"

"Of course. I'm sorry, Margo. I've just been so depressed. I'll make you proud, I promise!"

Mid-day sunlight crept into the office and illuminated her boss's lined face with wrinkles. She would miss Margo, Lily Rose decided. She had learned so much from her. Margo was a tough but good boss. While she expected a crazy workload, she had her nice qualities, often randomly rewarding those who produced good work.

"You did what?" Ella May shouted in disbelief. "Are you out of your mind? Things are falling apart in Hong Kong. China just passed a new 'National Security Law' and international companies are relocating left, right and center. Even the New York Times moved half of their offices to Seoul recently. Hong Kong is changing…rapidly. Do you even follow the news? Or are you a total ostrich? Why do you still want to go?"

"I think… uh…." Lily Rose stumbled, trying to gather her thoughts. She hadn't expected such a vehement reaction. Nor did she expect her mother's political rant. Marina was usually the one who talked world politics. Ella May must have brushed up recently.

Ella May huffed, shaking her head in disgust. "The Hong Kong of your grandmother's youthful memories is long gone. Surely you get that? Marina won't be coming and I have no interest in visiting. Your head is in the clouds, Lily Rose. Caught in a nostalgic past that no longer exists. You're a dangerous dreamer."

Lily Rose could feel her mother's exasperation emanating across the room. She could also feel her own blood temperature rising with contempt. "This isn't about what you want, Mom. It's my life and I get to decide how to live it. This is what grandma would have wanted me to do and more importantly, what I want to do. Don't come visit, if you don't want to. I'll survive. See you in a year then." Lily Rose shot up from the murky red club chair, whose color she hated, and sprinted across the living room. She grabbed her handbag close to the door and slammed the front door to her mother's trendy, grey-hued apartment shut, tears flooding her eyes. The reference to Marina had stung and she wasn't going to let it pass unnoticed. She would never tell her mom about Mingyu, not now, maybe not ever.

Chapter XV

Feathering the Nest in Sag Harbor

Lily Rose assessed her New York city apartment over a calming glass of red wine and decided to make some adjustments. If a stranger was going to live in her space, she wanted her most prized possessions out. She would have to spend the next few weekends organizing her treasures. She had one month. Once they were assembled, she would rent a man with a van to take everything to Sag Harbor. She needed to empty her closets anyway, so An could use them. An had offered to do the same in Hong Kong, storing her personal belongings at her parents' home. Lily Rose hadn't spoken to her mother since their fight and besides, Ella May's apartment was way too small to store any extra baggage. Sag Harbor was the best and most cost effective way to safeguard her belongings.

When the van pulled up a couple weeks later, Lily Rose was ready. She intended to transfer all her clothes, her toiletries and her favorite dishes. She was also bringing her queen-sized bed with its new sheets, and covers, her spa seashell towels, a prized Lane white washed dresser and night table and her one-of-a- kind crushed violet velvet sofa to Sag Harbor. Everything else could stay. She already knew which of Marina's furniture pieces she would exchange--the extra-firm double bed from the guest room, a floral couch and matching armchair from the library alcove and two small side tables, one from the attic. Those pieces were of no consequence to her and would have gotten the heave-ho anyway. She wanted all her special belongings in Long Island and she liked the idea of an emptier house. She was in a de-cluttering mode. Her desk and chair were going to her neighbor for a small fee.

The beach house was getting an upgrade, a Lily-Rose infusion. Pleased about having all her favorite possessions safely in one permanent spot, she felt uplifted. She wasn't sure she wanted to come back to the New York apartment a year from now. She made sure she wouldn't miss anything she left behind. When the truck delivered her furniture and belongings to the beach, she loaded it up for the return trip, including some of Marina's gently used towels and linens. The next few weeks, before Lily Rose's departure, were hectic. A few times she had sat down at her laptop and drafted an email to Mingyu only to delete it again. She couldn't find the right words to announce her arrival. What if he had a girlfriend? What if he didn't care? Or worse, didn't want her to come? Perhaps he was too busy to bother with her beyond a polite welcome lunch. While his emails were warm and sharing, they weren't passionate. But then, neither were hers. She had consciously kept things on a friendship level, knowing the miles were too substantial for a long-distance romance. Not that she didn't think about him. God knows, she had nothing going on in New York. Regardless, she didn't want to jeopardize this important contact with assumptions or unwanted advances. She was counting on Mingyu's friendship and guidance, at least in the beginning, to help her get acclimated.

Regardless how things might go with him, she was thrilled to travel to Hong Kong. Her grandmother would be so proud of her courage. Tears crowded her eyes at the thought of Marina. Her grandmother's noticeable absence through this life-changing adventure would be hard to bear.

Lily Rose realized she needed to see her mother before she left. They had exchanged angry emails and left things unresolved. Ella May was not ok with the move and had called Lily Rose selfish. She knew her mother was scared for her and would be lonely without her, now that Marina was gone. On some level she understood her mother's reaction, but life was a journey and this was how she wanted to fly. The choices she made were hers to make. Her mother would come around eventually. Maybe even visit. She forwarded her mom her flight schedule with a conciliatory note. She was leaving in less than a week. That night she called her mom, wanting to part on better terms even if she didn't have Ella May's blessing.

"Hi, Mom. Did you get my flight information? I sent it today."

"Yes, I saw it. So, you're going, huh?" Ella May sounded tired.

"Yes. I'm switching positions with someone in the special events office in Hong Kong for a year. She'll come work for Margo and I'll take her assistant manager spot there. Equal footing. We'll trade our apartments too which makes things easy. I'll send you my new address before I leave."

"And Margo is ok with that?" Ella May sighed.

"She was upset, but you know Margo. She adapts quickly."

"You had such a great job with her. People would kill for that. Why are you giving it all up? You're being so foolish, Lily Rose. Very foolish."

"I disagree. I need a change and now is the time I can afford to make it. I'm excited to leave, so please don't dampen my mood again. Besides, my job is secure. In a year An and I will switch back. Gotta go. I have last minute packing to do. Please don't do Marina's burial without me."

"I won't. How will you take care of the Sag Harbor bills? Or do I have to do that too?" Her mother's weary tone was grating.

"I set up auto-pay. You don't have to do anything except occasionally check on the house. You have the key. Bring a friend and enjoy a beach weekend. Marina's neighbors have my email too. In case of an emergency."

"Ok. Please stay in touch and text me when you get there. Send lots of pictures."

"I will. Bye, Mom. Love you." She heard the line go dead.

In an earlier heated email exchange, Lily Rose and Ella May had decided to wait a year for Marina's burial at sea. Her grandmother's birthday had turned out to be a cold, stormy day and since they were both currently at odds, the sentiment and timing was off. Marina's ashes would be safely stored in an urn in Sag Harbor.

Lily Rose opened her laptop and started another email to Mingyu.

Hi.

I hope you're well… and around next week because I'm coming to Hong Kong! I decided I needed another hands-on lesson on the properties of jade from my favorite expert. What do you think?

She reread her first sentence and pressed delete. After a few more attempts, she saved a draft and thought about surprising

Mingyu when she got there. She didn't want her fear of rejection to overshadow her joy of going. A lot could have changed in six months.

When Lily Rose's plane approached Hong Kong, her heart was fluttering with excitement. The descent to the airport was stunning. It was a clear morning and she could see the many twisty waterways below. Boats dotted the blue haphazardly and the configuration of the islands was fascinating. She couldn't wait to explore. She was surprised to see the clusters of high rise buildings amidst the lush, green landscape. Wispy clouds were trapped around the hill tops like drunken crowns. The area was so populated she couldn't fathom where the plane would land. Every flat surface was spoken for. Then, magically, a runway appeared between the emerald hills, just beyond the water's edge. She had landed in her new home. *Wahoo, I'm finally here, Grandma.*

Chapter XVI

Life is Full of Surprises

Over Sunday dim sum, Mingyu filled Jin in on the phone call he overheard outside Cheng's office. "We need to figure out who dad and Hu Fat are doing business with. Then it won't be hard to ascertain their reputation. Those things are easily checked."

"If Hu Fat is involved, I'm not too hopeful. His ethics are questionable at best." Jin stroked his chin thoughtfully.

"Has he gotten into trouble before?"

"He's been caught with stolen merchandise more than once, but he's always managed to wiggle out of serious trouble. He has good lawyers."

"What has your private eye uncovered so far?"

"Nothing yet. Chase is wrapping up another case before he can be of use. I'm waiting for his first report. However, now that we know Huan is the shipper of choice, we have even more at stake. Not sure how I should handle this information. Any thoughts?"

"I think you have to tell him."

"I do. But timing is crucial. I think I'll wait for now."

Over another private dim sum, the following month, Jin confirmed Mingyu's fears. Kaito Akiyama had traceable ties to the Yakuza in Yokohama and Tokyo. It was unclear to Chase Wong where Akiyama's *oyabun* or boss was, but he assumed Akiyama might be a kobun for the yamaguchi-gumi gangsters. Chase couldn't follow the entire trail upward unless he traveled to Japan he explained to Jin, but his surveillance in Hong Kong revealed enough for Jin to be alarmed. Akiyama's veiled phone calls to middlemen in Yokohama were disturbing. It appeared that shipments of merchandise were being received in the Port of Yokohama by someone named Souta who represented GD Import/Export llc. That was all Chase could squeeze from his sources at Victoria Port."

"What's a kobun?" Mingyu inquired.

"A Yakuza warrior. You can sometimes tell who they are when you look at their right hand. Part of their initiation includes drinking boatloads of sake and sawing off half of their right, small finger. They also have distinct tattoos, but those are covered most of the time. Hu Fat is definitely entrenched in exporting gold to the Yakuza but the Yakuza are taking the bigger risk since they aren't paying the consumption tax in Japan. That would be on them. What concerns me is the fact that your father and Hu Fat may be disguising the shipments which would make them complicit. There is no need to send Chase to Japan. He'll only get himself killed if he snoops around. In the past, the Yakuza have made *egg foo young* from nosy reporters and investigators. People magically disappear, then reappear in body parts if at all. I don't want to field Chase's travel expense to Japan either. I only want to know what Cheng's involvement is. Either way, this cannot end well. I need to put a stop to this before it explodes in our faces."

"How are we going to do that?"

"For now, we'll quietly gather evidence and be watchful. When we have enough information I will confront Cheng, hopefully scare him. I'm not sure what else I can do without endangering your father. It isn't wise to upset the Yakuza or the 14k Triads."

"Do you think he'll listen?" Mingyu replied anxiously.

"I don't know, but we have to be hopeful that Cheng can be reasoned with. Jail is not an attractive option."

Mingyu shifted uncomfortably in his seat. *Jail? Body parts? How did we get here?* None of this sounded real.

"Under no circumstances are you to speak to your father about this. I don't want him to suspect we're investigating him. Do you understand? Do I have your word?"

"Yes."

Mingyu was seated in his office after-hours finishing up an appraisal for a client when he heard his father's voice. Cheng had returned from meetings out. His father's voice was agitated, angry. Thinking everyone had gone home, his office door was wide open, allowing Mingyu to listen in. Normally, the workshop machinery afforded privacy in the surrounding offices. To hear more clearly, Mingyu stood and lingered in his office doorway.

"What do you mean we can't ship? I promised the company their goods would arrive this week. Next week is not an option. Bump someone else's cargo."

His dad was speaking to his Uncle Huan, whose shipping fleet was known to operate on a precise schedule. Many companies relied on Huan's timely run business.

"No. This shipment can't wait till next week. Make it happen, Huan. Find room in a container." Cheng snarled and slammed the phone down on his desk with a thud. Mingyu shuddered but stayed in place. He listened to the next phone call too.

"Hu Fat, we have a problem. I just spoke to Huan and the ship is full. Can Akiyama wait a week? I breathed fire on Huan but I don't think he'll budge. He made promises to his regular clients and he's anal when it comes to keeping his word. Huan always delivers on time. You know that. Tell Akiyama he needs to respond quicker if he wants a timed delivery. I can't control the shipping schedule. That is strictly Huan's territory and he cannot be bought."

Irritation radiated in Cheng's voice as he waited for a reply. "I'll do whatever I can, but you need to be prepared for backlash. I want no part of that. I deliver what I'm paid for, no more, no less. Figure it out. He's your client." Cheng slammed his cellphone on his desk and cursed out loud. Mingyu tiptoed back into his office and silently shut the door. Frozen in his office chair, he waited for Cheng to leave. When he heard the door slam and the alarm being set, he mobilized. On his way home, he called his grandfather.

The next morning Mingyu arrived at the store early and checked his father's office. The desk was bare and his laptop, closed. Mingyu opened it to take a peek at what shipment was being discussed, but as expected, the log in page was locked. Closing the laptop, he went back to his desk to research the Yakuza's business practices. There was little to be found concerning legitimate businesses. Most descriptions stated the expected-gambling, prostitution, loansharking, extracting "protection" money. When employees began arriving, Mingyu closed the search window and deleted his google history.

Looking through his personal emails, he discovered one from Lily Rose. They hadn't spoken in a while. Delighted, he opened it.

Hi Mingyu,

I'm in Hong Kong—long story. It was a hectic departure from New York so I apologize for the lack of notice. I was wondering if you're free for lunch or dinner sometime? No rush. I'm here for a while. I would love to visit your shop and look at jade with you. Hope you're well.

Cheers, Lily-Rose

He grinned and reread the email, wondering what "a while" meant? A week? This was truly a welcome surprise. *What in the world is she doing here? And why didn't she tell me earlier?* Without much thought, he replied.

Neih Hau, Lily Rose,

What a surprise you're here! I'd love to see you. Where are you staying? Can I pick you up for dinner tomorrow night or do you prefer lunch and sight-seeing over the weekend?Saturday, maybe?

Best, M   95

He pressed send, got up and walked to the mirror. He desperately needed a haircut.

Chapter XVII

Acclimating to West Kowloon and the Conrad Hilton

The first three nights at the Conrad Hong Kong Hilton were comped for Lily Rose so she could meet her co-workers and set up her apartment stress-free. Work training would begin after the weekend, which gave her five days to explore and settle in. She spent the first two days wandering around the city, window shopping and enjoying the evening light show by the harbor. On Saturday after brunch, she moved into her new apartment in West Kowloon. An's building was called the *Arch* and it was located on Austin Street, in a nice area. The one- bedroom faced Victoria harbor and had a spectacular view. In contrast, her apartment in New York faced a dreary courtyard. She realized she was definitely not going to be happy there after living here. Poor An got the losing end of the real estate swap.

Lily Rose's new home was located near Austin Station half way between the West Kowloon Cultural District and the Jade Market. There were tons of young people around and the building's amenities were stellar-- an outdoor pool, a spa, table tennis, a roof garden and a billiards room. Surely, she would make friends here. She spent the first weekend exploring her surroundings and stocking up on supplies. She did a dry run to the hotel on public transportation to get an idea of direction and timing. It took less than a half hour door to door. Sunday night she laid out her clothes for her first day at work in the Hilton's special events office. She also drafted an email to Mingyu, but didn't send it. She couldn't find the right words.

Monday morning, she was introduced to the people she missed at her initial arrival at the hotel. She was surprised it was a larger team than Margo had in New York. Everyone was excruciatingly polite and seemed to eye her suspiciously as if she was sent there on an *Undercover Boss* mission. Assessing her surroundings, she was secretly amused by her co-workers' cautious approach to her. Once a major event hit the hotel, the usual pandemonium would surely take over and people would relax and be themselves as they worked tirelessly to make it a success. Pressure had a way of breaking down all barriers and pretexts.

Lily Rose was given a desk outside her boss's office in an open space she shared with another assistant manager, David Shen. In New York she had her own office and aid. After a brief tour of the premises, she was instructed to fill out tax forms and familiarize herself with the upcoming calendar. David, seated across from her, gave her a briefing. There were a slew of smaller, private events on the agenda, but nothing major in the following month. In New York she worked directly with Margo on back-to-back professional mega-sized conventions and trade shows that happened in a steady rotation. Private parties were peppered in between.

Things looked to be slightly different here. The parties on the calendar Lily Rose could handle with ease. She wondered if An would be able to stomach Margo's work load. She could just visualize Margo rolling her eyes with impatience. Margo had zero tolerance for incompetence.

She emailed An offering her assistance should she need it. She also marveled over the lovely apartment she now called home and gave An her mother's email should she need any referrals in New York. Ella May would be happy to help her daughter's counterpart. Anything to advance Lily Rose's career.

The next day, Lam Peng, her boss, assigned Lily Rose to an upcoming event. He passed by her desk periodically to check on her progress, a hovering drone orbiting its mark. As the week skipped by, he checked less and less, opting for an update on Friday afternoon. David assured her that was a very good sign. She had passed her first test.

"It took him at least a month, if not longer, to stop hovering over me. By week four I was ready to quit in a melt-down or have my doctor prescribe a strong sedative."

Lily Rose laughed. "I'm flattered." David was beginning to thaw. Extreme politeness turned into light humor.

Since she still had a few things to take care of in her apartment, Lily Rose decided to use her second weekend in Hong Kong to finish her set up and reboot. She accepted an invitation to join David and his friends for a Saturday night out. That proved to be a good decision. His friends were nice and the chatter around the table was insightful and eased her into life after dark in Hong Kong. She was secretly happy to have an ally and friend in the office after only one week. David had a sunny personality; he was kind and patient. Sunday, she spent playing table tennis with the neighbors in her building. Lily Rose was settling in.

That Sunday night she redrafted an email to Mingyu, but didn't send it. Instead, she planned her wardrobe for the following morning. By Wednesday night she had revised her email to Mingyu several more times, still anxious about his reply. Holding her breath, she finally pressed send and closed her laptop. Based on past correspondence, she didn't expect to hear from him immediately. Her heart palpitations were real. Would he reply at all now that she was here in his neck of the woods? Was he still interested on his turf? Or was New York just a fun interlude for him? Would he be too busy with his own life here? Lily Rose hoped he would be happy to hear from her.

The next morning, she checked her emails on her phone while lying in bed, curtains wide open so she could admire the harbor view. She was thrilled to discover that Mingyu had responded favorably. Emboldened, she replied:

Hi

Dinner Friday night sounds great. So does sightseeing on Saturday. Can we do both? Tell me where to meet you for dinner. I can magically appear around 8pm. LR

At work she felt grounded, the learning curve of her new job being mastered. She was operating on familiar territory with a larger team and less work. This fact was empowering. In New York she barely had time to breathe. Here she could go to the bathroom and reapply make-up without losing a client. Lily Rose realized she would actually have time to enjoy her new life. David and Mingyu's friendship, hopefully, would smooth her social transition. She wanted to succeed on all fronts in Hong Kong. So far, she was thrilled to be working in the city and over the moon to see Mingyu Ho again. Would they still have a connection?

Chapter XVIII

Work, Play and Holiday Teasers

Friday proved to be a busy day at work. Lam Peng called a meeting to brief his team on added upcoming events— a medical conference, a wedding and an office party for a mid-sized company. He distributed the workload so all would be busy, but him. Lily Rose seriously wondered what he handled himself. Lam Peng seemed to sail in and out of the office like a lost kite.

With Easter around the corner, a British mainstay, the hotel's restaurants were preparing special menus for the long weekend from Good Friday to Easter Monday. In-house luxury shops decorated their windows with colorful rites of Spring. The lobby and offices looked especially inviting with pastel displays of floral baskets and artfully colored eggs. Lily Rose basked in her cheerful surroundings. The thought of seeing Mingyu put an extra spring in her step.

Easter had always been Marina's favorite holiday. Her grandmother had loved March pansies popping up like bursts of color before her late March birthday, to mitigate the slate grey days of winter. The cold season always lasted way too long as far as Marina was concerned. She was happiest when she saw naked trees budding, bulbs sprouting pastel blooms and emerald shrubs rebirthing in her contained Sag Harbor garden, promising that summer's brightness was only a breath away. Lily Rose couldn't help but think of her grandmother as she moved around the hotel absorbing the holiday decorations.

She longed to share her current experiences with Marina, but Ella May would have to do. During lunchbreak at her desk, she shot her mother an email bringing her up to date on her first two weeks across the world. She included a few pictures of the hotel's artful holiday displays and a couple of her apartment with its spectacular view. She hadn't written to her mom since her safe arrival confirmation. She hadn't received any mail either.

As Lily Rose was getting ready to leave for dinner with Mingyu, Lam called her into his office. "It looks like you have the event planning down to a science from what I observed this past week. You'll be a good addition to my team, Lily Rose. Do you have any questions about anything?"

"Thank you for asking. I'm good for now. I think you briefed me well. David has been particularly helpful and your team made me feel appreciated and welcome."

"Good. Glad to hear that. This coming Sunday we have a small, important wedding. An influential Hong Kong family. I would like you to be here to observe and assist. I need you to come at 8am."

"Fine. Is there anything in particular you want me to do?"

"Help David oversee the set up. Be in touch with the bride and the bride's father if he needs anything. There is no mother present. I'll let you know if something else comes to mind. David will work closely with you. Check your email frequently. The wedding celebration begins at 2pm with the wedding party arriving for pre-party photos. Cocktails are served at four and dinner will begin at 6 pm."

"Wil you be here too?"

"I will."

"Great. See you then." She walked back to her desk as Lam breezed out of their suite, his feet barely touching the carpet.

David grinned. "He said he would be here Sunday? That means he'll come for five minutes, pose and smile for the client and leave when no one is looking,"

"Are you working the whole wedding?" Lily Rose shifted uncomfortably, not wanting to comment on her new boss.

"I work whenever Lam doesn't which is most of the time, especially on weekends. Last Saturday was a once-a-month weekend off."

"Well, thanks for including me in your once-a-month weekend. I'm honored. Your friends were great fun."

"You're welcome. I'll see you Sunday. I'm out of here before Lam comes back." David grabbed his backpack and sprinted to the exit.

Moments later, Lam returned. "Where's David?" He frowned.

"He just left a minute ago." Lily Rose smiled sweetly.

Lam grimaced, disappearing into his office. Lily Rose quietly packed up and left, following David's cue. She wanted time at home to get ready for her reunion with Mingyu.

When Lily Rose arrived at the restaurant, Mingyu was waiting at the bar. He looked good, even better than she remembered. His casual style and precision haircut immediately caught her attention and apparently that of the girls seated next to him too. She was glad he was her date for the evening and felt the girls' envy radiating her way.

"Hi, Mingyu. It's great to see you again." She gave him a little wave, unsure if a hug was welcome.

He slid off the barstool and took a step toward her, giving her a gentle hug. His eyes told her he was genuinely pleased to see her too. "Welcome to my city, Lily Rose. When did you arrive?"

"Ten days ago."

"Ouch! And you waited until now to email me? That hurts." He touched his heart.

Lily Rose laughed. "Don't be hurt. I was busy working. I'll fill you in over dinner."

"Right. Let's start with drinks. How about an Early Bird, a specialty cocktail here at the Envoy."

"What's in it?"

"Vodka, passionfruit, pineapple juice, a touch of vanilla….."

"Mmm….sounds delicious. Passionfruit….huh? Hit me up." She flashed him a smile which he readily returned from under his angled hair. A few sips and toasts later, they were chatting like old friends. Lily Rose sensed Mingyu's genuine interest and felt like a swaddled orchid. Why had she doubted his sincerity? Over exotic dinner dishes, she explained that she was part of a work exchange and would be here for a year.

Mingyu's eyes glistened. "Wow! How wonderful. I hope to see you often then."

"I'd like that. I was counting on your continued friendship. I don't know anyone here."

When she tried to stifle a deserved yawn, he paid and gently hustled her to his car. Dropping her at the Arch, he rolled down his window after she exited. "And remember, wear your walking shoes tomorrow. Isn't that what you told me in New York?" His smile was infectious. "I'll be here at noon so you can sleep in. Sound ok?"

"Very ok. Thank you for a fabulous welcome dinner. I feel so lucky to be here." Arms exuberantly stretched outward, she swiveled on her heels and waved over her shoulder. "See you tomorrow."

In that moment Lily Rose knew she had made the right decision to spend a year in Hong Kong. She was going to take her sweet time getting to know this incredible man. No rush. The chips would fall as they may. Friendship or lovers, either way, this promised to be a memorable year. She could feel it in her core.

The next morning, wrapped in a terrycloth robe, her hair in a towel, she rifled through her closet. She decided on embroidered jeans and a white flowing cotton blouse. Drying her hair and defying its irritating natural bounce, she attempted to straighten it. Make-up applied, she slipped on her lavender jade ring and her grandmother's green jade disc earrings. Pleased with her reflection, she pulled on a lavender sweater slightly shorter than her shirt and packed her favorite green leather handbag with the essentials, including a small gift for Mingyu. Comfortable white leather sneakers completed her ensemble. After a cereal breakfast, she skipped out the door, excited for the day ahead.

Mingyu arrived minutes later, dark eyes riveted on her as he approached on foot.

"Hello, don't you look nice," she beat him to the compliment.

"Thanks. Nice earrings. Pretty, like you." His eyes traveled to the peony discs, then to her raspberry lips. He held out his hand. "Ready?"

Happily, she slipped her hand into his, "That depends. Where are we going?"

"Today we'll do touristy things. I was thinking we could take the tram to Victoria peak to enjoy the view of downtown. You haven't done that yet, have you?"

"No. I was busy setting up my apartment and acclimating to work. And of course, I was waiting for you to show me around the city." She poked him in the ribs.

He shot her a sideways glance under his perpetually falling fringe and his lips tilted into a disarming smile. "Excellent. I'm the best tour guide this city has to offer. I know exactly how to please you."

"Yes, I've been noticing." Lily Rose felt a warm rush from his hand. *I still like this guy… a lot.*

The tram ride took roughly ten minutes once they reached the front of the line. The steep incline made Lily Rose's handbag slide to the base of the seat. She caught it with her feet. The views on the way up were stunning. She wedged the bag between her sneakers making sure her scented gift was still inside.

From the top, Mingyu pointed out all the major landmarks. It was a clear, sunny day so the view to downtown and Victoria Harbor was unobstructed. Lily Rose marveled at the scenery. Walking to the Lion's Pavilion, Mingyu asked her, "So… what did your family think about you leaving?"

"My mother is unhappy about the distance. She didn't want me to move so far from home, but my grandmother encouraged me before she died. She was more of a risk taker."

Mingyu stopped in his tracks. "Your grandmother died? You didn't tell me."

"She died just before Christmas. I wasn't in a very good place. She was my best friend. She's part of the reason why I'm here. I needed to get out of New York. Sometimes change is necessary for a fresh start, you know?"

"Yes. How do you know she wanted you to come here?"

"I'd been talking to her about transferring jobs for a while. We decided Hong Kong would be a good fit for me. At first, I was too nervous to commit, but after she died, I couldn't wait to."

"You didn't want to leave her. I understand."

"No, I guess not. I didn't realize it at the time, but I'm sure that played a part in my hesitation. So where are we headed now?" She needed to change the subject before tears sprung. Marina's passing was still an emotional soft spot.

"Now you have a choice. We can see *Tian Tan Buddha*, participate in a tea ceremony or I can take you to the Jade market and tell you what not to buy. We'll save the Star Ferry and Hong Kong Disney for warmer weather. In a couple weeks, it'll be perfect.

"Sounds good. Let's go to the Jade market. I guess I won't be spending any money, but I wouldn't mind looking."

"No. Save your money for better pieces. Looking there will be a good lesson in the lower qualities of jade. It's in Kowloon, near you. We can stop at the food market too and buy some groceries. I was thinking if you're free tonight, I would like to make you dinner. I live close to your apartment."

"You still cook? How nice! What would you make?" Being invited to Mingyu's home was an honor in Lily Rose's estimation.

"Do you like stir-fried rice with shrimp?"

"Love it. I do have to leave on the early side though. I'm working tomorrow and I have to be there at 8 am."

"No problem. I can have you home by nine or ten."

"Deal. I'll buy the wine. Plum for me and whatever you like to drink."

Mingyu winked and reached for her hand. The reconnect she was so worried about had happened seamlessly and she couldn't help but wonder where it would lead.

Chapter XIX

14K Family Wedding

"Good morning, Lily Rose. Walk to the ballroom with me. I'd like to explain how today's event needs to be set up. The bride's father is ver….rrry touchy and we're on a tight schedule. I still need to call the florist and talk to the kitchen." David seemed stressed, but he broke his stride to stop and admire her necklace. "Nice dragon pendent. Looks like jade."

"It is. Thanks. An heirloom from my grandmother. Who's getting married?" She threw her jacket over her office chair, stuffed her handbag in the desk drawer, then hustled to keep up with David as he scooted out the door.

He turned and eyed her. "What do you know about the 14K triads?"

"Triads?" Lily Rose searched her memory banks and came up with nothing.

"That's what I thought. This family is connected to the Hong Kong underworld. They import and export electronics and software, but the big money allegedly comes from their more 'private' dealings. Gambling and such. Anyway, Lam will never tell you this, but he's nervous and wants everything to go smoother than ice. The man's only daughter is getting married and he's sparing no expense, but he's worse than a bridezilla. The daughter says nothing, leaving everything up to him. Whatever it takes, we have to make the father happy."

"What's the family's name?"

"Wu. Carson Wu. His daughter is Alison. Here's the paper file."

"Noted. I briefly looked it over on Friday, so I have an idea of what they asked for. Do we have peach-colored tablecloths?"

"Yes. Look in our stock room. We have a rainbow of shades. Use the red table cloths for the buffet tables and tell staff to set up the table of fire sparklers at the end of the terrace. No firecrackers allowed, so the staff has to make sure the wedding party doesn't sneak them in. The floral centerpieces should arrive between nine and ten. I'll confirm that shortly. The tables have to be dressed by then so get the staff moving. The band brought gongs and drums which we'll put right inside the last terrace door close to the deejay. Most importantly, make sure the table place settings are correct or there'll be hellish consequences. You don't want to upset a 14K triad boss by placing rankings incorrectly."

"Ok. Got it. I see the table chart."

When David left, Lily Rose googled Carson Wu and his daughter Alison on her phone. Nothing on Carson but Alison loved her social media. Her Instagram was a fashion forward revelation. In the banquet room thirty-two tables of ten were being assembled. Red, peach, white and golden lanterns hung from the ceiling at varying heights, creating a garden ambiance amongst the small bamboo and fica trees. The gigantic origami chandeliers gave the room an opulent vibe while the plants and lanterns hinted at a magnificent Zen garden respite. Lily Rose looked through the extensive stock room and pointed to the long white tablecloths with gold trim. "Let's put these underneath the small red toppers on the banquet tables. It will look infinitely more regal with the red rose flower arrangements. She knew red was considered a good luck color. So were even numbers. She had researched the importance of *feng shui* over the weekend and knew how to set up the tables to create a pleasing balance in the room. The five elements of earth, fire, metal, water and wood had to be present in the decorations. Music, lighting and the buffet were arranged to accommodate a smooth traffic flow.

By the time the tables were covered, the florist arrived with a truck load of botany. Lily Rose felt lost in the forest. The additional plants were dispersed around the magnificent hall with its earth-toned carpeting and shiny, polished wood dance floor. Crisp white walls provided a neutral backdrop for Chinese paper cut-out decorations and a small fountain stood between the bar and buffet table.

Magnificent red rose centerpieces adorned with delicate white calla lilies and golden day lilies were bound with thick crimson and gold ribbon and placed on each table. Lily Rose and the florist arranged and artfully twisted each ribbon through the tableware. Elaborate white lily arrangements in golden-colored metal pots were placed on the banquet, bar and music tables, except for the main buffet which was embellished by a spectacular red rose and orchid arrangement . Each white dinner plate was adorned with a single, large-petal peach plumeria flower holding a fortune cookie placed in the center fold. It matched the peach tablecloths. There was no silverware—cherry stemmed bamboo chop sticks rested on each snow-white napkin and gold-trimmed place setting.

When all the tables were set, Lily Rose walked around with her seating chart and placed gold-embossed name cards next to each wine glass, double-checking each table twice. David's warning of getting it right was ringing in her ears. Next to the name card, every guest received a small white linen gift bag with a gold dragon stencil, their names attached with a red silk ribbon. Peeking inside, Lily Rose discovered polished natural stones with various Chinese symbols. She wondered what they meant and if they were personalized for each guest. She would have to ask David later.

Pausing to peruse the room, she took a few landscape pictures for her Instagram. Zeroing in on the wedding parties' tables, she aimed for perfection, straightening any slightly crooked item. Rechecking her file, she scanned every detail with a sweeping glance. Satisfied, she stood on a chair and snapped a few aerial views and shot a short video for her event portfolio. She knew Margo would see it.

"Wow, Lily Rose! The room looks beautiful. You sure know how to plan a party." David walked to her chair in the center of the dance floor and did a 360 swivel. "Perfect *feng shui.*"

"Thanks. I was just checking the file to see if I covered everything. The bar is being set up with all the premium brands and the bathrooms are decorated with white orchid plants. It smells like a perfume factory here. The deejay is setting up next to the band. Oh and I just noticed the red carpet is missing. Where do I find that?"

"Tell the men you want two of the long ones. You'll need the second coming in from the terrace where the instruments are. Then, we're done here. On to the reception area. We need to set up poster photos of the families and put out a sign-in book. Carson Wu was adamant about having that. We also need to finish setting up a digital slideshow of the happy couple to project on the screen behind the band. I already instructed the crew to do that. The guests will receive a glass of pink champagne with a strawberry when they arrive and sign in."

Lily Rose's head was spinning. "Ok. Let me get those carpets first. I'll meet you in the reception area."

Lam strolled into the reception hall as they finished hanging the last family picture. He hadn't been around all morning. "Everything looks good in the party room. Grab some lunch when you're done here. You have twenty minutes. The wedding party should be arriving shortly for photos. It'll be a very long day."

When Lam turned to leave, David grinned at her. "Not for him, it won't. Come, let's grab some food. I'm starving." Over lunch he showed Lily Rose the wedding menu.

"Fish roe soup, shark fin, abalone lobster? My, this is quite the banquet." Lily Rose took a bite of her grilled cheese as she fingered the elaborate gold embossed print. Careful not to get any grease stains on it, she handed it back to David.

"Traditionally, these food choices symbolize fertility." David chomped on his sesame chicken. "We have to put five menus in holders on each table."

"Fertility! Really? I'll have to remember that." Lily Rose smiled. She realized she was learning loads at her first social event.

At 1pm the wedding party arrived with two photographers. Lam reappeared from his extended lunch break just in time to meet and greet. After doing the honors, he called David and Lily Rose over to meet the bride's father. "Mr. Wu, these are my two assistant managers, Lily Rose and David. I have them both working today to be at your disposal. Please don't hesitate to tell them if anything is amiss."

Lily Rose tilted her head downward in greeting, then faced Carson Wu straight on. Fascinated, she studied his rugged features; he had hard facial creases, especially around the eyes, a flat wide nose that had seen a fist or two and his jaw line was razor sharp. He smiled without showing any teeth. His hair, laced with grey, was thicker and longer on top and he wore a black, shiny suit, a red textured tie with a gold dragon outline, some beaded bracelets, two of them jade, and a heavy gold dragon ring. Lily Rose saw nothing in particular that distinguished him as a dark figure, but all the details combined told an interesting story.

"Welcome, Mr. Wu. This is David Shen and I'm Lily Rose Larsen. Please let us know if there's anything you need. We are at your service." She extended her right hand.

Carson ignored it and nodded. He formed his fingers into a waving gun pointed at them and laughed. Before his eyes turned back to Lam, they lingered on the jade dragon pendant around Lily Rose's neck. It shone majestically on her white silk shirt, clearly capturing his attention.

"I want to see the party room. Are the name cards in place?"

"Yes, all is set," Lam bowed nervously. "There's also a list with corresponding table numbers posted near the champagne arrival. Come, I'll show you the room. We worked hard this morning to make it perfect. You can let me know if anything needs to be adjusted."

David turned to Lily Rose and rolled his eyes. "We?" he whispered behind Lam's back.

Once the photos of the blessed couple and the wedding party of eight were taken, the first guests trickled in. The bride disappeared. Two men from the wedding party stood centrally beside the champagne bar and collected the guests' envelopes. They also guarded the family photographs and sign in book. Each guest signed the elaborately dragon adorned book and admired the family picture wall. Lily Rose watched with interest how obediently the guests complied. No gifts were brought, only blood red envelopes.

When David reappeared, Lily Rose repositioned herself in the banquet hall to help direct people to their tables. Admiring the women's apparel, she noticed tastes ranged from traditional silks to designer dresses. The most beautiful silk cheongsams in vibrant shades were flitted and matched with dyed satin heels. Sequined, lace and organza dresses appeared to be popular among the younger ladies.

As Lily Rose stood at the red-carpet entrance she observed a man switching place cards. Waiting till he walked away, she consulted her chart and switched the cards back. From the corner of her eye, she noticed Carson Wu watching her as he spoke to a few of his guests She walked around the tables one more time with her chart, making sure all cards were in their proper place. As more people arrived, she watched for sneaky maneuvers. There was always at least one at every wedding.

She was relieved that David escorted the men with the money envelopes to Lam's office to lock them all in a safe during the event. The thought of missing envelopes made her shudder with fright. She wanted nothing to do with missing triad money. When David returned, he ushered the ladies and children to the terrace to stand on either side of the red carpet, handing each guest a lit sparkler. The men lined the inside red carpet holding gongs and drums, creating a steady beat. The bride and her family arrived amidst the sizzling wands waving above their heads, walking the length of the carpet from the terrace to where the groom's family stood waiting to receive them indoors. It reminded Lily Rose of a funeral procession in New Orleans. When the bride and groom were joined, the party was officially in full swing. The first dance was a father daughter dance to a traditional Chinese wedding song by Jay Chou.

When the band let loose with Chinese pop music, the dancing escalated and the first of six courses was served. The bride disappeared to change from her fitted white lace wedding gown into a hot red number with beaded bodice and spaghetti straps. Suit jackets were discarded, ties shed and sleeves rolled up to reveal a wealth of frightening tattoos. An impressive selection of gold chain necklaces featuring fierce looking dragon pendants made their appearance at the neckline of unbuttoned shirts.

Beneath the conventional white shirts shone ferocious dragons, skulls and triangular symbols expertly arranged around a blank V neck. Twisty dance moves revealed completely tattooed torsos. Raised pant legs paired with sagging socks confirmed that all remaining square footage was tattoo covered as well. Lily Rose gawked like a schoolgirl at a pop concert. This ink choices were way beyond a decorative sleeve or a pretty butterfly accenting a favored body part. Lily Rose couldn't help but stare at this visual affront.

After the main course was served, people shifted tables. Lily Rose noticed that the man who had switched name cards was now sitting where he wanted to be. He didn't switch for a young lady, but rather to sit with a man who he was in deep conversation with. The man was fat, rough-looking and had pierced ears and scraggly hair. Carson Wu kept one eye in their direction. He seemed to watch everyone.

To Lily Rose, the man who switched seats looked Japanese, not Chinese. She also noticed that he was missing half of his right pinkie and that he was one of the few whose tattoos extended to his hands. When he went to the men's room, she rechecked his name card. Keiko Akiyama was definitely a Japanese name. She checked her chart for the other man's name. It simply read Hu Fat. *Really?* Hu, she knew, meant 'wild' in Chinese, but the phonetics in English were hilarious and so fitting.

When she looked up, a grimacing Carson Wu caught her eye. He was holding court at his table, his back to the wall, near an exit.

Carson's view of the festivities was unobstructed. When the discussion around his table got heated, Lily Rose hurried over and interrupted. The men were arguing in Chinese and one had sprung to his feet, teeth clenched.

"Everything ok, gentlemen? Can I get anybody anything?" It was her attempt to keep things calm amidst record alcohol consumption and heated tempers. Looking around the table she smiled. She saw David watching, a pained expression on his face. Carson's beady eyes traveled to the dragon pendant around her neck and she felt a shiver down her spine.

"I have everything under control here," he growled keeping his eyes on the pendant. "Go check if the bride needs your assistance."

"Of course. That will be my pleasure." Lily Rose scampered toward Alison who was coming off the dance floor. "All good? Do you need anything?"

"Yes. Actually, I do. A safety pin. One of my straps is loose, ready to pop."

"Oh dear. We can't have that. Meet me in the ladies' room. I have a sewing kit in the office."

"Can I come to the office with you? Or is there another more private ladies' room?"

"Yes. Follow me." Lily Rose gestured with a flick of her wrist. "You look beautiful tonight. Both your gowns are exquisite. Who designed them if you don't mind my asking?"

"I designed the red one and Oscar de la Renta designed the white --the Lilith model. I got it at Trinity. They have the best selection. Why? Are you getting married?"

"No."

"Do you have a boyfriend?"

Lily Rose hesitated. "No, I just moved to Hong Kong from New York a few weeks ago."

"By yourself?" Alison's interest piqued, her inflection rising.

"Yes."

"That's brave."

"I guess. Look, I found some red thread. Our office bathroom is across the hall. Come. Let's see what the damage is. I might be able to stitch it on your body. Do you mind if I just unzip you half way?"

"No. Do you live in Hong Kong?"

"Yes, in West Kowloon. Where are you and your husband going to live?" Lily Rose unzipped the beaded bodice and started stitching the strap to the seam. She noticed Alison's most exquisite red lace undergarments, but refrained from asking where those were purchased. *Boy, do I need to go shopping if this is what the girls in Hong Kong wear.*

She couldn't help but ogle the elaborate tattoos along Alison's waist right up to her armpit. She had gorgeous budding red roses on one side and a curvy pink and white magnolia on the other. The flowers simulated beautiful watercolor paintings with soft bleeding edges. Lily Rose had never seen a tattoo like that.

"My father bought us a penthouse apartment in the Mong Kok area of Kowloon; it's our wedding gift."

"How nice. All done here. Your strap is secure. Go enjoy your spectacular wedding and congratulations. I'll get the wedding cake ready for cutting." She carefully zipped the dress back up and gently fixed Alison's hair over it. "I hope this isn't inappropriate, but your tattoos are incredibly beautiful. I've never seen such artful designs."

"Thank you. Chen Jie is the artist." Alison lingered for a moment as if she were going to say something else. Then she turned, shyness taking over, and left. Lily Rose looked in the mirror and unleashed her long blond tresses from the tight bun. She was feeling terribly ordinary in comparison and the weight of her hair was giving her a headache. Besides, her portion of the wedding was almost done. She wondered if Lam was coming back. Catching David in the office, she asked him.

"Fifty-fifty chance. With both of us here, he probably won't. You did good today. We're down the home stretch. The first few guests are leaving. Some quite drunk, I might add."

"Did you see those tattoos? It became quite a different picture when the dancing started and the jackets came off. From Red Hill suits to Mong Kok tats."

"Yeah, I know." David laughed. "I just pray we make it through the night with no incidents. I was worried for a minute, but you handled it well. There's no limit on the bar and these guys can really tuck the liquor away. No saying what could happen."

"Generous host. Who's the guy Alison is marrying?"

"Don't know anything about him other than his name, Chen Du. I think he's from the mainland."

"So, if she hyphenates her last name it will be Wu-Du? That's ominous." Lily Rose giggled. "Her father's wedding gift was an apartment in Kowloon, the Mong Kok area."

David laughed, shaking his head at her name reference. "Figures. Triad territory."

"When do they have to be out of the ballroom by?"

"Normally 11pm, but I don't think Lam will remind them. He left. I definitely won't."

After midnight, the last vestiges of the wedding were cleared. Carson Wu and a small group had stayed long after the bride and groom left. As Lily Rose visually swept the room after Carson's departure, she noticed a fabric gift bag on the floor. Someone had forgotten their keepsake. When she examined the pouch, she saw a polished stone with an engraving and a name card. The card read Keiko Akiyama. Lily Rose slipped it into her pants pocket and finished her sweep for lost items. All tables were bare and the band had packed up and left. She picked up one or two items people had forgotten and secured them in the office. David locked up and they both walked out of the hotel together around 1am, completely spent. Too tired to walk another step, she splurged on a taxi home. Collapsing into bed like a rag doll, she drifted off to sleep, wondering what Alison Wu's new life would be like.

Chapter XX

Sun Salutations Circle Mingyu

Ella May's emails to Lily Rose were starting to defrost. She included photos she knew her daughter would like--yellow and violet pansies she had planted in the majestic teal-glazed planters on the front porch in Sag Harbor and shots of Saks Fifth Avenue's Easter windows. Lily Rose felt a twinge of longing for springtime in New York, but it passed quickly. She was happy in Hong Kong. Her work week flew by rapidly and it was enjoyable, not riddled with endless problems like in New York. She looked forward to her weekends with Mingyu. This weekend he promised to take her to Lantau Island if the weather cooperated.

Saturday morning, he was waiting when Lily Rose emerged from her building. They had hit a jackpot day. The sun was shining and the temperature was rising steadily. Not a cloud in the sky.

"Hi, how was work? I see you survived and stayed." Mingyu's smile lasered straight through her heart.

"Hey. Yup, I'm still here. Anyway, I won't leave until you finish showing me all the sights. I'm having way too much fun." She wrinkled her nose at him.

"Well…then you'll have to stay a long time because I plan to keep coming up with must-see places. In fact, I have a list longer than a toilet roll."

Lily Rose laughed. "I'm ready and I'm wearing comfortable sneakers." She reached for his hand and kissed him on the cheek. She noticed he was wearing the cologne she had brought from New York and given him in Victoria park on their first outing. "Where are we off to, boss?"

Mingyu winked. "It's a beautiful day for Lantau. We'll stick with plan A."

Lily Rose looked through the clear glass bottom of the cable car. The ride was twenty minutes and extended over the lush hillside divided by scenic waterfalls. A spectacular view from the windows gave her a different perspective of the harbor. The water sparkled in the morning sun and yet bustled with activity. Pleasure boats dotted the blue expanse. "The scenery is magical," Lily Rose sighed.

"It's especially beautiful this time of day. I knew you'd appreciate it."

About two hundred and sixty steps later, they reached the massive Tian Tan Buddha, stopping to catch their breath a few times along the way.

"Am I really this out of shape or did I not eat enough protein for breakfast?" Lily Rose joked when she reached the top and bent over, clasping her sides, short-winded.

"You are not alone. Look around." Mingyu laughed. "We're working up an appetite for lunch." Overlooking the city, Mingyu pointed out various landmarks, some of which they had already visited together. Stepping closer to her, he wrapped his arm around her shoulders, gently drawing her in as he pointed. Encouraged, she threaded her arm around his waist and leaned her head in, feeling his strength and warmth.

"I know a good place for lunch, the Tai O village. It's close and has lots of options."

"Sure. Let's go."

A fifteen-minute boat ride and Tai O's uneven, rowed stilt houses looming over the water appeared. Lily Rose marveled at the fishing village's precarious architecture. Taking in the quaint surroundings, they opted for a fried fish lunch in the market. To aid digestion, they stopped at one of the venues overlooking the water for a traditional tea ceremony and chatted the afternoon away. On the way back, they stopped for dessert-mango moon cakes. At the ferry central terminal, Lily Rose suggested dinner in Kowloon, not wanting her day with Mingyu to end.

"I have nothing in the fridge. Maybe we can eat near home. My treat tonight. What do you think?" She looked at him, anticipation swimming in her eyes.

"I think that would be a good way to end a beautiful day. I love having a woman pay for my company," he teased.

Lily Rose punched his arm. "Watch out. I may slip something into your wine."

"I hope it's an aphrodisiac—I hear *red ginseng* works well."

"Ha! Good to know. I hear the element of surprise works even better."

After walking around the harbor area, they decided on a small intimate restaurant in Tsim Sha Tsui. Over dinner, Lily Rose told Mingyu about the Wu wedding. She made sure to mention the grandeur of it all in contrast to the tattoo display and fighting once the dancing began. He listened attentively, but commented only on the wedding customs, explaining whatever Lily Rose wasn't familiar with. Thankful for the information, she filed it away knowing it would come in handy for her next Chinese wedding event at the hotel. She pondered over his silence in regard to the Wu family. Maybe they weren't that known after all?

Sunday morning, Lily Rose decided to go lingerie shopping. She regretted not asking Alison where to go. Alison's steamy red lace garments had left an impression. Showered and sipping her coffee Lily Rose searched for suggestions on the internet.

At Blah Blah Bra, she found what she needed. She picked a beautiful nude silk and lace bra from La Perla, a paisley peach bra and panty set from Simone Perele and a strappy black number from Raven & Rose. The last one would make her mother blush. The bill made Lily Rose blush. On the way home, she wondered if Mingyu spent every Sunday morning with his grandfather.

Chapter XXI

Dim Sum a la Jin

Mingyu and Jin were fussing over their carefully orchestrated dim sum cooking collaboration. Mingyu's skill level was rising exponentially, notwithstanding a few outright flops like when his pork buns were undercooked and tasted like chewy bubble gum. With the addition of a blend of spices, he deferred to Jin to spice things up and time the oven. Instead, he preferred to make tea and set the table.

When the two chefs finally sat down, their masterpieces in front of them, he asked Jin, "Did you know that Carson Wu's daughter got married last weekend?"

Jin picked up his chopsticks. "Yes, in the Hilton, right? I saw an announcement somewhere. She married a man from the mainland."

"How many children does Carson have?"

"Legitimate? Only two I think. The girl who got married and an older boy. Illegitimate, who knows?"

"Has he bought anything recently? I don't remember."

"No. The last piece he bought he paid a fortune for—the apple jade dragon sculpture we secured at auction, remember?"

"Oh, yeah. That was a good one."

"Whenever I get something special in, I reach out to him. He prefers quality pieces with dragon motifs, his personal trademark. I generally know what he likes." Jin took a bite. "Have you overheard any more of your father's conversations with Hu Fat?"

"No, not since the one we talked about. This is delicious. Is Chase still shadowing them?"

"Yes, but all is quiet for the moment. Nothing new to report."

Mingyu nodded thoughtfully. "Remember the girl I met in New York?"

"Yes, Lily Rose? Have you heard from her again?"

"You could say that. She's currently in Hong Kong. She transferred here for a year in an organized work exchange."

"She worked for the Hilton, right?"

"Yes. As an event coordinator. She helped plan the Wu wedding." He could feel his grandfather's eyes fixed on him as he ate.

"You still like her, I'm guessing?" Jin casually dipped his chopsticks into his bowl and took a small bite.

"Yes. I like her a lot." Mingyu was slightly embarrassed by his admission.

"Did she come to Hong Kong for you? I'm guessing she could have transferred anywhere in the world, right?"

"I think she came here because of the memories she shared with her grandmother. Her grandmother talked fondly about her time in Hong Kong and as a result Lily Rose dreamed about visiting. When her grandmother died, she acted on it. "

"Marina died! When?" Jin shot up and walked to the kitchen counter leaning on it.

"Just before Christmas. How do you know her name?" Mingyu eyed him in shock.

"You must have mentioned it before. How did she die?" Jin looked pale.

"Heart attack. Lily Rose was devastated. I could tell she didn't want to talk about it. She teared up when she told me and quickly changed the subject."

Jin filled a glass of water and took a long sip. "I'm so sorry to hear that. I suppose we're all just mere mortals. When our time is up …." He cleared his half full bowl and started to make more tea, turning his back to Mingyu. His hands were shaking. "Tell me about Lily Rose. What do you like about her? What have you done together so far?"

"Well, she's only been here for a short time. I've spent the last two weekends taking her sight-seeing. She's fun and easy to talk to. I took her to Lantau yesterday, Victoria Peak, the Harbor, the Jade market, and Tsim Sha Tsui . We've shared a few meals. I like her outlook on life and how she relates to people. She's thoughtful and kind. I also like her curiosity about jade. She's genuinely interested."

"She sounds lovely. If you truly like her, take your time to really get to know her. If she's here for a year, there's no big rush."

"Tell that to my hormones."

Jin chuckled. "Good things can't be rushed. When are you seeing her again?"

"No plans yet. I was going to text her during the week. Any ideas?"

"When the weather is warmer, take her to Stanley beach. Pick a day during the week when she's off. Have dinner at the Boathouse."

"Good idea." Mingyu took another bite. "I'd like to have her come to the store when Dad isn't there."

"Pick a Saturday then. Or when Cheng is traveling. He's going away for a few days in two weeks, I think."

"He is? Ok, I'll wait."

"Where does she live?"

"In West Kowloon at the Arch. She traded apartments with the girl who took her job in New York. It was an easy exchange."

"Very nice. How lucky for both of them."

"Did you eat enough, *Ye Ye?*" Mingyu noticed that Jin had just picked at his food.

"Yes. I taste-tested too much while I was cooking. You eat. I'll have my tea."

"You have enough leftovers until next Sunday. Are you coming in to work tomorrow?"

"Of course! You take some of this home. Maybe we should invite someone for next dim sum? Lily Rose perhaps?"

Mingyu smiled gratefully. He knew Jin would be kind and welcoming. His father, not so much. Cheng was difficult, judgmental and opinionated.

Chapter XXII

Hong Kong's Different Shades

Work at the Hilton's event office was picking up. The more Lily Rose handled, the more Lam heaped on her desk. He had just given her another sizable project to organize.

"Welcome to the Hong Kong Hilton. You should have feigned incompetency a little longer," David laughed.

"It's ok. I like being busy."

"I'll remind you of that on one of our crazier days."

"Thanks, David. You really are a precious gift." She rolled her eyes playfully.

"I'm aware. Listen, I have this weekend off. There's nothing going on at the hotel. Do you want to get together Saturday night? A few of us are going to a Chinese movie with English subtitles and having dinner after."

Lily Rose hesitated. She hadn't heard from Mingyu and it was Thursday. "Sure. I'd love to. Which movie? Where?"

"*Mong Kok. Sin Tat Plaza.* I'll text you the movie and address before Saturday."

"Ok…sounds like fun! I'm in. Thanks."

When Lily Rose got home that night, she googled *Sin Tat Plaza* and discovered it was a popular shopping area. She resolved to go early and look around. Later, after getting ready for bed, she checked her phone and discovered a text from Mingyu.

Would you like to grab a drink after work on Friday?

Happy, she replied in the affirmative. They settled on a trendy rooftop bar close to the Hilton. Perking up, she straightened her bedroom. The living room was neat as she wasn't home much, but clothes sure did travel in her bedroom, especially if she didn't plan her outfits the night before. She carefully laid out her date gear for the next day and gave herself a rejuvenating facial while eating leftover *pad thai.*

Lily Rose got off the elevator and glanced around the place. To the right she saw a generous bar stocked with everything imaginable. Surrounding it were tables inside and out. The space looked like a tropical garden in the sky.

"Welcome to Ce La Vi. Do you prefer indoors or the terrace?" The hostess's trim black suit and fire red lips gave the venue an added air of sophistication.

"The terrace would be nice." She glanced around for Mingyu but didn't see him. Seated with a view to the harbor, she perused the drink menu and ordered a Jasmine Blossom. The ingredients were enticing- jasmine-infused vodka, honey, lime, apple juice and a splash of soda. Looking around, she studied the tourists and after work crowd. There was definitely a distinct difference between the two. It felt good to be counted with the Hong Kong professionals. Her sleek black pants, black suede pumps and pink flamingo silk t-shirt fit right in. A beaded black cashmere sweater was slung over her emerald bag, for the impending evening breeze.

When Mingyu approached, he wasn't alone. A slight, young woman with long black hair accompanied him. She was wearing a subdued, fitted, floral dress and sensible flats. On her arm, she sported a thick carved jade bangle. A dark jacket with a name tag was folded over her shoulder bag.

"Hello. Sorry I'm late. I ran into my cousin Victoria and invited her to join us for a drink. I hope that's ok."

"Of course. Nice to meet you, Victoria. I'm Lily Rose." She extended her hand.

"Hello. Pleased to meet you."

Mingyu jumped in. "Victoria works for HSBC, the Hong Kong Shanghai Banking Corporation."

"What brings you to Hong Kong?" Victoria had a deep, serious voice, belying her diminutive stature.

"I work for the Hilton corporation. I'm part of an exchange program from New York."

Victoria nodded. "Interesting. Why Hong Kong?"

"Why not? I've always wanted to visit."

Victoria eyed her suspiciously. While Mingyu ordered their drinks, the girls chatted politely. Lily Rose discovered he had two other cousins, Harlin and Elizabeth. Both worked in the family shipping business with their father, Huan, but Elizabeth sometimes moonlighted with Jin and Mingyu at trade shows. She loved gems too. Lily Rose was interested to hear that cousin Elizabeth was studying at the GIA. Mingyu had never mentioned his cousins.

When Victoria left, Mingyu and Lily Rose ordered appetizers and another round of drinks. She was relieved to finally be alone with him. Lily Rose felt dissected and judged by Victoria. She tried to focus on the positive. "Is Elizabeth thinking of switching to the gem business?"

"Yes, Jin has her brainwashed. We're waiting for her to finish her gemology degree and for an opening in the store. Right now we're fully staffed. You should try a few classes too."

"Tell me more. What class would you recommend first?"

"Start with a one day intensive and see how you like it." From there I would recommend taking the one-week intensive Diamond and Diamond Grading courses."

They chatted until Lily Rose got cold, even with her cashmere sweater on. Mingyu moved closer and put his arm around her. "Would you like my jacket?"

"No, I think I'm ready to go. I'm totally chilled."

In the subway, Mingyu inquired about her weekend plans. She could tell he was surprised she was busy Saturday night. When they parted, he lingered and held her chilled hands in his warm ones. "Maybe I'll see you next Saturday night?"

"Sure." She took a step closer.

Reassured, he leaned in and kissed her on the lips. When his train pulled in first, he sprinted to catch it, leaving her to stare after him. His kiss left her tingling from heart to toe and his lingering scent flooded her nostrils. She definitely liked him .... a lot. And his kiss had been worth waiting for. Mingyu's kiss tickled her lower belly chakra.

Lily Rose toured Sin Tat Plaza. She was happy she had dressed down in ripped jeans, a printed cotton shirt and stylish flats. The area had a fast-paced, sleazy vibe. She wedged her shoulder bag under her arm and squeezed tight as she walked. Men beckoned her into their shops, citing rock bottom prices, but she had little interest. For a brief reprieve, she ducked into a clothing store, but was totally underwhelmed. Continuing on her quest for something new, she discovered Sneaker Street, a shoe store specializing in all brands. A pair of purple Converse canvas sneakers with bright white laces caught her attention. *What a great color! I'm so getting these.*

Purchase in hand, Lily Rose continued browsing but was repeatedly accosted by salespeople stationed in front of their domains. When one in particular followed her for a few stores, she picked up her pace. Suddenly out of nowhere, a young woman appeared and loudly reprimanded the man in Chinese. Switching to English she snapped, "Leave my friend alone. Can't you see she's not interested?"

Shocked, Lily Rose gaped at how quickly he withdrew, head bowed, hand up in an apologetic stop signal. She turned to thank the woman. Recognition set in slowly. She looked different-- street stylish in tight, skinny jeans and navy platform shoes. A tight fitting cropped, crimson top completed her edgy ensemble.

"Hello, Lily Rose. What are you doing in this neighborhood?"

"Alison Wu! Thanks for saving me. I thought I would never get rid of him. I'm meeting friends for dinner and a movie. I thought I'd come early and check out the hood." She cringed the minute she said that. *Damn.*

Alison minced no words. "You stick out like a sore thumb here. When are you meeting your friends?"

"In an hour at the movie theater."

"Are you done shopping? What were you looking for?"

"Nothing, really. I was browsing."

"Come, have tea with me. I'll make sure you get to the theater unharmed. It will be dark soon."

Stunned, Lily Rose nodded, following Alison out of the mall and into a nearby alley. *Is this safe?*

They entered a small teahouse, unassuming from the outside, but quite elaborate on the inside, with honey colored wood and natural rice paper dividers. Alison nodded at the proprietor and he dispatched a waitress immediately. They seated themselves at a remote corner table and Alison ordered for them in Chinese. She turned to Lily Rose. "This neighborhood is ok during the day, but it's better you don't come here alone at night. Are your friends male or female?"

"Both, actually. You met David Shen. He works in the hotel with me. I'm meeting him and his friends, all local people."

"Not sure I remember him. My wedding was a crazy day. Where are you going for dinner?"

Lily Rose pulled out her phone and showed Alison the text. She didn't want to mispronounce the name of the restaurant. Alison intimidated her.

"Very good choice." Alison smiled, showing slightly crooked teeth. Pointing to the shopping bag she asked, "What did you buy at Sneakers Street? Can I see?"

Surprised at Alison's blatant curiosity, Lily Rose pulled out her violet sneakers. "I fell in love with the color. I was surprised to see Converse here."

"Why? They're made in China, you know. What will you wear them with?"

She wondered why Alison was so vested in her purchase. "Summer dresses, leggings and I have jeans the same color. Alison, your English is really good. What do you speak at home?"

"We speak Cantonese at home, but I went to schools that taught in English so I'm bi-lingual. Many in Hong Kong are. I also learned a little Mandarin which is the official language of China, but being born and raised in Hong Kong, I speak Cantonese with my family."

"Is Chen from Southern China? Does he speak Cantonese too?

"Yes."

The Oolong tea arrived on a beautifully arranged clay tray with a matching teapot and cups. After it was poured Alison tapped her forefinger on the table and nodded. The server smiled and withdrew. Lily Rose wondered if that was the correct way to say thank you. She had observed Mingyu do the same when they visited the Chinese teahouse in Tai O. Her eyes traveled over the intricately folded napkins and the patterned red and gold lanterns above. She liked the age-old Chinese tradition of sharing tea. The intimate quality of this practice resonated with her, made her feel welcome and reminded her of all the times she had sat in her grandmother's kitchen chatting over a cup of fragrant peony tea. She was beginning to grasp the importance of tea in the Chinese culture. It extended to discussing art, politics, current trends, and the act of sharing tea ensured quality time with the other person. She was fascinated to learn that inviting someone to tea could be an act of apology as well as friendship. The teahouse was the one place all social ranks in China were equal.

"This smells heavenly." Not knowing what else to say, she asked Alison, "How was your honeymoon?"

"Just got back. We went to the island of Sanya and to Japan. April and May are the best months to travel there. Not too hot yet."

"Where did you stay?"

"The Hilton's Sanya Yalong Bay Resort and Spa and the Ritz-Carlton in Tokyo."

"That sounds awesome. Glad you picked a Hilton resort. Did you enjoy it?" She always liked to get positive reviews on her place of business.

"Yes. The Sanya resort was beautiful. In Tokyo, Chen had to work so that was less fun. When he met business associates, I went shopping." She shrugged her shoulders.

Surprised at the answer, Lily Rose changed course.

I've never been to Tokyo. It must be a fabulous place to shop."

"Yes. It's a bigger city than Hong Kong. More choices. I got lost a few times, but I came home with beautiful clothes. One day, I'd like to visit New York, Paris and London too."

"Next trip." Lily Rose smiled.

"Tell me about New York. Do you go to Times Square?"

"Everyday. That's where I worked." Lily Rose launched into all her favorite things about New York; Broadway, the museums, her favorite department stores. Alison listened attentively, her features impassive. She was soaking up the information, but remained impenetrable. "Maybe I'll visit when you're back there." She flicked her long black hair over her shoulder and looked at her phone. Text messages were coming in at an alarming pace.

Lily Rose was surprised at her remark. It seemed Alison said whatever came into her head. Not knowing how to respond, Lily Rose changed the subject. "Tell me about yourself, Alison. What do you do?"

"I work in fashion … sometimes. I like to design clothes. One day I'd like to have my own business. I love jewelry too. Your ring is beautiful."

"Thanks. It was designed by a Hong Kong jeweler. Gem International Trading Company."

"The name sounds familiar. Do they deal in high grade jade?"

"Yes. I remember you saying you designed the red dress you wore at your wedding. Do you sew too?"

"No, I know how to design and cut patterns, but sewing is not my strong suit. Don't have the patience." Alison looked at her phone again. Lily Rose heard more texts ping.

"Let's go. I'll walk you to the movie theater." Alison jumped up, seemingly perturbed.

"We haven't paid yet."

"It's ok. I have an arrangement here. Let's go."

"Shall I leave a tip?"

"No. Can I get your cell phone number?" She slipped something to the waitress, not waiting for a reply.

"Yes. If you remind me who crafted your flower tattoos. I forgot the artist's name."

Alison smiled for the first time. "I'll text you her information and when you're ready, I'll take you there."

Lily Rose admired Alison's brazen style. Clearly, she was a woman who knew what she wanted. Her direct manner was disarming, but not without good intentions it seemed. In the presence of her father, at her wedding, she had been more soft spoken, docile even, but here she was definitely a woman in control. Was she though?

Chapter XXIII

Summer Escape to the Philippines

The summer heat was enveloping Hong Kong like a vice grip and the humidity made Lily Rose's clothes cling like a wetsuit. New York was bad in the summer, but the tropical weather in Hong Kong had it beat.

"May through September are consistently humid months, so you might as well get used to it. Bring a sweater to the office because the air-conditioning gets turned up. Lam wouldn't be caught dead with a sweat stain," David warned one morning when Lily Rose arrived particularly wilted.

"I noticed. I should just wear shorts and a t-shirt and bring my dress in a garment bag. You can't even tell I ironed it."

"I keep a few shirts in my desk for that reason. By the way, Lam put us on the schedule for this weekend. We have back-to-back events."

"Yeah, I saw. What days can we have off during the week?"

"I'm taking Monday and Tuesday. Doctor appointments. We can't both be out at the same time. Is that ok?"

"Sure. I'll take the following Thursday and Friday then."

"A long weekend. You should go somewhere." David sat on the edge of her desk, signaling his readiness to chat about destinations.

Lily Rose thought about his suggestion. "Good idea. I should, shouldn't I? Where do you suggest I go?"

"Why don't you look at a map of Hong Kong's surrounding areas and see what grabs you. That's what I do when I don't have a set destination. Macau is fun if you like gambling. Or Vietnam. It's a cheap vacation."

"Thanks for your suggestions. I'll do some research."

She picked up her phone and texted Mingyu.

I have a four-day weekend coming up. Thinking of traveling somewhere. Any ideas?

She waited for a response but none came. Maybe he was busy? She turned to her work, wondering how Mingyu would perceive her veiled invitation. Was it too soon? Too forward? She could dial it back by making it a casual friends trip. Busy all morning she checked her phone again before lunch. Mingyu had replied:

How about Macau, Taiwan or if you want to take the train through the Chinese countryside-- Shenzhen? Great shopping there. If you like the beach, consider flying to the Philippines. Do you want company? Was that an invitation to join you?

She grinned and typed:

I love the beach! Tired of shopping. Not a gambler. Yes, your company on this getaway would be welcome. Hilton in Manila looks nice. I'll check for a room. Can we share? It'll keep the cost down for both of us. Would you check flights? I can leave next Wednesday night. Must return late Sunday. Work for you?

A half hour later his reply was waiting.

Yes, that works fine. Our flights are reserved. Two hours direct to Manila. We have 24 hours to decide and pay. Sharing is fine. Totally up to you.

Enthusiastic, she answered.

I reserved us a room. Got a reduced employee rate. Let's talk tonight. Busy day.

That night Mingyu and Lily Rose finalized their travel plans. Excitement flooded through the phones. A long weekend at the beach was the perfect way to kick off the summer season and anything else that needed jump starting. To Lily Rose it felt like Memorial Day weekend. Unsure of what to do, she requested a hotel room with two queen-sized beds. Mingyu was hard to read and she didn't want to ruin a good friendship with assumptions and pressure. She would go with the flow. *But that last kiss….*She pulled out her suitcase and started throwing a few key things inside, a bikini, her favorite shorts, a sundress and her sexy new lingerie.

Ten days later, they were seated on an evening flight to Manila. Lily Rose was chatting like a newscaster before a storm, filling Mingyu in on her research about the Philippines. "The beaches are supposed to be incredible. Have you been to any of them?"

"Yes. We went on a family vacation once and stayed at a resort near Sombrero Island. I remember the beaches. They were beautiful. We spent two nights in Manila before returning to Hong Kong. I must have been ten or twelve at the time."

At the hotel, they checked in and were shown to their room. Spent, Lily Rose collapsed on one of the two beds. "I'm exhausted. I've worked ten very long days without a break. Do you mind if I wash up and go to sleep? I promise I'll be more fun tomorrow."

"That's fine. Relax. I'll go downstairs for a few minutes to gather some information for tomorrow and give you some privacy."

"Thanks. Can I have the bed by the window?" She spread out her arms and legs like a snow angel, rumpling the bedspread.

"Sure, it's yours."

The minute Mingyu left, Lily Rose showered, slathered herself in moisturizer, wrapped herself in a robe and pondered over her suitcase. The shower had made her drowsier, if that was even possible. Supreme comfort and the necessity of sleep overruled wanting to navigate a romantic interlude. She fingered her lingerie, but then slipped into an oversized t-shirt with cotton shorts, brushed her teeth, braided her hair and hopped into bed with a thin layer of night cream. She didn't want to scare the guy with a face full of goop. By the time Mingyu returned, she was fast asleep, snoring like a power boat, TV blaring in the background.

Chapter XXIV

Island Fever: Verde Island versus Corregidor Island

The next morning Mingyu woke Lily Rose after eight when the weighted room door accidentally slammed shut behind him. He was balancing two coffees and some tantalizing brochures. When she stirred, he dropped the leaflets on her bedcover."Good morning. Did you have a good rest?"

"Yes. You?" She yawned and turned towards him still swaddling her pillow, eyelashes fluttering open at a snail's pace.

"Yes. How do you feel about a beach day?"

"Pretty good. Mmm, that smells heavenly. I hope one of those is for me."

Mingyu grinned. "Only if you get out of bed. I've had my doubts. I rented us a car. We're spending the day on Verde Island. It's a bit of a drive, but I think it'll be worth it. The best beaches in the Philippines are on the outlying islands. Verde Island is known for awesome marine life too. Do you snorkel?"

"Yes! Used to do it in the Caribbean." Her eyes opened a tad more as he handed her one of the coffee cups. She swung her legs out of bed and took a big sip. "Ahh, so good. Just the way I like it. Thanks."

She hoped her loosened braid had prevented bed head. More than anything she wanted to get to the bathroom to brush her teeth. Mingyu looked so energetic and fresh while she felt like a crumpled brown paper bag.

"Good. I packed snorkeling gear for us. I'm ready to go. I'll be downstairs, waiting."

"What? No breakfast in bed?"

"No, that only works for two and you didn't invite me," he teased.

"Noted. In that case, why don't you go and have breakfast and just order me something good. I'll be down in a few minutes."

"Ok," he nodded. "Bring your beach bag. We'll leave after breakfast." Grabbing his backpack, he left the room.

Forty minutes later, they were traveling south to Verde Island. They briefly stopped at Laiya beach in the Batangas to marvel over the sights, then continued on to Tabangao Port to catch a private charter to Verde Island. The boat took them directly to one of the island's popular snorkeling spots. Once securely anchored, they hopped into the turquoise waters, snorkels and fins securely fitted.

Lily Rose popped her head out of the water and searched for Mingyu through her dripping, distorted goggles. He was right behind her. She tapped him on the head and he surfaced, disoriented. Removing her mouthpiece, she gushed, "This is incredible. I'm totally loving it! Did you see that yellow fish with the orange stripes? It reminded me of your shirt yesterday," she giggled.

"I did. Are you saying I looked like a tropical fish? For the record, that fish is emulating my striped shirt." He splashed her.

"Ha! Can't wait to see what else you packed to inspire the surrounding wild life."

"The only one I want to inspire is you, Lily Rose." He grabbed for her hand to pull her closer, but with one quick kick of her fins, she slipped away. Circling around, she grabbed his fins from behind. Her enthusiasm was catching and he let her tease him. When she was close, he grabbed her hand. "Keep that up and there'll be no lunch left for you."

"Oh no. I'll behave. I'm already hungry." She broke loose and gave him a thumbs up. Reinserting her mouthpiece, she popped her head back into the water. After a long while, they climbed back onto the anchored boat. Pulling off aqua shirts and gear, they sat down with their hotel-packed lunch boxes and water bottles while the captain continued his mid-day snooze.

"I'm famished. This was a brilliant idea. Thanks for arranging everything this morning. I know I haven't been much help for someone who works in event planning."

Mingyu grinned. "Yeah. I thought someone drugged you last night when I wasn't looking. I came back to the room and the TV decibels had the minibar dancing."

Lily Rose laughed. "I wanted to stay awake until you returned. Guess that didn't work out well."

"No, definitely not. Do you want to snorkel some more or should we do a tour of the island by boat?"

"Let's tour the island. I'm toast. Snorkeling drained my energy."

"Oh no. Not again." Mingyu laughed.

Lily Rose finished lunch and reapplied a high numbered sunscreen. The sun was broiling her sensitive skin. Wrapping a dry towel around herself, she snuggled in the rear of the boat, knees bent, feet tucked in, and marveled at the passing views. Mingyu instructed the captain to pull the anchor and circle. Then he came and sat next to her, putting his arm around her shoulders across the seat ledge. She leaned her head back and looked up to the sky. *This is heaven. I love it.*

The boat accelerated at a leisurely pace, lingering at the nicest spots along the coastline. The captain proudly pointed out the highlights. When he dropped the anchor at Sabang beach, he suggested having a cocktail at Angelyn's Dive Resort.

"What a great idea. Let's go, Mingyu."

Sipping cocktails in an idyllic setting created a mood. Together they dipped their feet into the infinity pool and watched all the scuba divers come back from a day of adventure. Lily Rose snuggled up to Mingyu wishing the day would never end. Hands touched, eyes sparkled, glasses clinked and sweet thoughts were exchanged in hushed whispers.

Back on the boat, they changed into dry clothes for the ride home and by six-thirty they were in their rental car.

"We can stop for dinner somewhere along the way unless you want to eat late in the hotel," Mingyu suggested.

"Along the way sounds good. If we wait till we get back to Manila, I might not make dinner."

"Oh no. Are you sure you're from New York? The city that never sleeps?"

"Very funny. It must be all this fresh air. My lungs aren't used to it. Give me smog and I thrive until the wee hours."

"Hmm." Mingyu laughed. "That's not what I remember."

When they arrived at the hotel, they took turns showering and plopped on their respective beds, eyeing each other. While recapping the high lights of the day, Mingyu threw out some ideas for the following morning too. Lily Rose listened as he researched and shared options, reading them out loud, but before they could settle on definite plans, his travel mate drifted into quiet nothingness. Once again, Lily Rose was fast asleep. Mingyu seriously wondered if she took melatonin with her tea.

Watching her and listening to her soft breathing, he tried to fall asleep, but ended up on his back staring at the ceiling. What was he doing wrong? Did he need to be more proactive? The next morning Mingyu woke first. He looked over to Lily Rose. She was facing him, her profile outlined on the pillow. He studied her fanned lashes and the curve of her nose. Her golden locks were tangled over the pillow and her hands were tucked under her chin at the bottom edge. She continued to sleep peacefully. He thought about their outing the day before. He enjoyed her company, her spontaneity and willingness to conquer. He suspected she wasn't quite ready for a romantic interlude and he was terrified of rushing her for fear of ruining everything. Striking out terrified him. He would let her initiate the next move. When she stirred, he sprinted to the shower in his gym shorts, needing to cool down with a cold rinse. Sharing a room was harder than he thought and not at all what he expected. Dressing quickly, he intended to slip out for coffee.

"Good morning," she purred. "What time is it?"

"Seven-thirty."

"Are you always up this early? What did we decide we're doing today? I forgot." She shifted her body and moaned.

"That's because you fell asleep before we decided."

"Really? In my defense, it was hard work kicking those fins yesterday. I'm feeling muscles I didn't know existed. Ouch. Ouch. Add cocktails and travel time--that's a proven recipe for being comatose. Aren't you sore?"

"No. Keeping your condition in mind, I'll plan a less strenuous activity. Today, we'll take the ferry from Manila to Corregidor Island and visit South Beach. Any objections?"

"None at all." Lily Rose swung her legs out of bed and groaned. "Owww. Hope we aren't doing anything that requires excessive legwork. Mine are out of commission." She grabbed a bathing suit out of her suitcase and ambled to the bathroom aware of her disheveled state.

When Lily Rose exited the suite's bathroom, Mingyu was gone. Was he a little grumpy this morning or was it her imagination? She arrived downstairs and found him sipping tea in the breakfast room. They ate and ordered lunch boxes for the beach. A taxi took them to the ferry.

"When we get there, we'll travel by jeep." Mingyu peered sideways from under his locks for her reaction.

"A jeep? Really? That sounds awesome. We can cruise to all the beaches in style. Is it a rag top?"

"It has no top. I thought you'd like that." He winked at her.

"Super cool." She reached over and playfully tipped his baseball cap downward.

Sitting in the sand, Lily Rose's arms were wrapped around her knees. Her eyes traveled over Mingyu who was sprawled on the towel next to hers, eyes closed behind sunglasses. She liked his lean, strong body, muscular arms and shoulders. His abs did not show an ounce of extra fat. She wondered if this was his natural build or if he worked at it. She only saw him on weekends and he was always relaxing then. Whenever they were together, he was a kind, caring and thoughtful friend. He was also patient and respectful. Was he waiting for her to make the first overture?

"Tell me about your last girlfriend. Are you dating anyone besides me?"

Mingyu lifted himself up on one elbow and faced her, dark sunglasses hiding his eyes. "If I had a girlfriend, I wouldn't be here with you." His expression was one of surprise. "My last girlfriend and I split about a year ago. I have no regrets."

"What was she like? Was she Chinese?"

"Yes. She worked at the same bank as my cousin. Victoria introduced us."

"Really? What was her name?"

"Fen."

"Why did you break up?"

"She wanted a serious commitment and I didn't," he replied, his face impassive.

"How do you feel about me?"

"I like you, Lily Rose," he answered without hesitation. "We have fun together."

"We do have fun, don't we?" She replied, trying to gauge his expression. *Am I going too far?*

"Yes." His face was serene, still showing no particular emotion, except for a slight curl in the corners of his lips.

"Are you curious about my past, too?" She was dying to squeeze more out of him. *Maybe if I share…*

"If you had a boyfriend, you wouldn't be in Hong Kong."

"Good guess."

"I'm ready for a swim. Coming?" He stood abruptly and extended his hand to pull her up.

He's purposely changing the subject. Am I making him uncomfortable? In the water, Lily Rose thought about how different he was from American men she had known. On second thought, she was glad he didn't ask about her last boyfriend, Kevin. *That cheating jerk. Ugh.* But…did he not care about her past? *Why isn't he curious?* She looked over to Mingyu, who was floating on his back. She put her hand on his abs and pushed down, folding him like a chair. Then she splashed him and raced away with Mingyu in hot pursuit.

A few hours on the beach coupled with playful dips in the water, their appetites surged. They devoured their box lunch and hopped in the jeep to explore the island. Fragrant ylang ylang trees filled their nostrils. Lily Rose enjoyed the adventure of it-- the warm breeze on her face, the sights, the sweet fragrances and the joy of sitting next to someone she felt safe with. She pulled out two water bottles and handed one to Mingyu. He smiled, gratefully. "Thanks."

When they stopped at a more secluded spot to enjoy the spectacular view, he surprised her by pulling her close and leaning his chin on top of her head. She wrapped an arm around his waist, then turned to face him. Emboldened by the information she had gathered on the beach, she lifted her chin and looked at him, probingly. Dense black lashes stretched across his dark eyes, assessing her intentions. After what seemed like an eternity to her, he leaned in and kissed her gently… passionately. It was a different kiss. Slower and more deliberate. She felt a strong connection, butterflies dancing in her belly. Their relationship was changing, becoming more deliberate. Was this his response to her inquisition on the beach? When he kissed her again she felt her world spin off its axis.

That night, after an intimate, candle light dinner in the hotel bar, Lily Rose dimmed the lights as they entered their room. She pulled Mingyu closer by inserting her slender fingers in- between his shirt buttons, caressing his abs. She undid a few buttons. "I'm not falling asleep early tonight," she whispered.

She was nervous. His softening expression and traveling hands encouraged her. She slid her other hand underneath his peach colored shirt and gently stroked his back. Responding, but letting her take the lead, he gazed at her in anticipation. She teased his lips with her tongue, then parted them for a more intimate kiss. Letting her fingers travel up, through his straight silky hair, she felt his heat against her. It was as if a nimbus of steam rose and circled them in a foggy swirl. The kiss unleashed a torrent of passion and bodies intertwined, creating a bubble of bliss. Within seconds clothes were flung through the air. Lilly Rose's carefully chosen lingerie purchases were superfluous. And just like that their relationship finally moved to deeper waters.

Chapter XXV

Island Fever from Mingyu's Perspective

Mingyu felt a shift in the way Lily Rose looked at him. It was as if the Philippian sun and leisure tropical location melted her armor in slow succession, reminiscent of a dripping *Salvatore Dali* timepiece. Each day, she visibly relaxed a bit more morphing into a malleable rag doll. He was loving the transformation. Her visible surrender empowered him. The fact that she enjoyed his activity choices felt like he had found the 'turn on' button for a treasured toy.

The protective wall she had built around herself and her reluctance to share certain personal information, thereby guarding her vulnerable heart, was crumbling, The wall was slowly being dismantled and Mingyu was thrilled. He guessed the trauma of Marina's death, Kevin's cheating and maybe a few other unfortunate experiences had held Lily Rose back from delving into uncharted territories sooner…from following her heart.

Heeding Jin's advice to be patient was paying off. His grandfather was truly a wise man and Lily Rose was proving to be worth the wait. She was a butterfly emerging from its cocoon. Anticipating the beauty of it all, took time. Metamorphosis couldn't be rushed. Mingyu's unyielding fascination with her was akin to discovering a rare blue diamond in the rough and painstakingly searching for the right lapidary approach.

He didn't take her falling asleep early the first two nights as a personal affront. He could see her exhaustion dissipate, feel her fatigue melt into calmness as time passed. Disappointed, when she faded on night two, he tried not to give in to frustration. She was recharging, returning to her true, unfettered persona, with every hour of unadulterated fun and subsequent rest. Intending to impress her with his ability to plan a memorable weekend, he was pleased to have hit it right. She was thrilled with his choices and deferred to him, pleased to not make decisions for a change. The woman who arranged everyone else's special days and nights needed a break from event planning. *Why does she work herself so hard?*

Recognizing this fact about Lily Rose was an epiphany of sorts and he knew exactly what to do. By day two, he resolved to give her a weekend she wouldn't forget. When he stopped to analyze and evaluate, he understood. He knew exactly how to unlock her, how to reel her in like a prized tuna. The line had to be loosened first before the relenting fish was reeled in. He was a man on a mission.

In the planning stages, before their trip to Corregidor Island, Mingyu was thrilled to discover the jeep option. He booked it without a second thought, knowing she would love it. The pictures the concierge shared convinced him, despite being costly. Giving Lily Rose what she asked for—an unencumbered beach vacation with no complications, no lengthy waits in lunch lines or annoying tourist transportation queues, was easy. He would deliver the much-needed beach break from her structured city life and the Hilton's hectic schedules. In short, he would lull her into submission with his strategic planning.

Their second morning, he let her sleep until she naturally awoke. Recognizing the day before that their fun activities had been way too strenuous for a first day of vacation, he slowed the pace down. The hour and a half ferry ride to Corregidor Island on day two was relaxing and he watched with satisfaction as she took in the sights. He loved watching her close her eyes and inhale the misting salt spray as they whipped through the waves. She thrived, letting the warm morning sun kiss her welcoming face. Mingyu was studying the world through Lily Rose's lenses and at Lily Rose's speed.

She had a joyous appreciation for nature and the simplest gestures. Her positive perspective anchored and hooked him. Once relaxed, she had the ability to adapt to her environment, soaking up all it had to offer. It was a gift he admired. Some people never got to that place. He supposed her openness to learning about jade, or anything new for that matter, was her ability to embrace and absorb. She was curious by nature and enjoyed exploring the new and unknown. Lily Rose awakened the passion to explore in him and Mingyu loved her for it. She made him feel things he had buried since childhood, since his mother had died.

"Look over there. I see the port." He pointed ahead to the long dock and lone building in the center. The surrounding areas were lush with green tropical plants and exotic trees. As they got closer, they could see clear across the island to the body of water on the other side, the South China Sea.

"It looks incredible. I'm really excited about the jeep. What a brilliant idea!" Lily Rose gushed.

Her enthusiasm warmed his soul. She looked particularly pretty this morning. Her blond waves were tied into a long ponytail and her feminine floral sundress made his eyes swim. Her funky purple sneakers complimented the softer colors in her dress. A sheer lilac cotton scarf hung loosely around her sun-kissed shoulders. He wondered what she had stashed in the huge decorative beach bag casually slung over one shoulder, besides the ribbon adorned straw hat that poked out.

As the ferry neared the port, he told her all about the military history of Corregidor. He had read the brochure. "Here's a little background for you. The island is in the shape of a tadpole and it's located directly across from Manila. Because of its location, it was considered an important military stronghold and used to protect the bay and city from foreign invaders. Manila is the most important harbor in the Philippines. When the Japanese invaded during WWII, the Americans and Philippines fought side by side to protect the city. Many soldiers died on and around this island. We can visit some of the ruins, but I have to warn you—it's said by many the ruins are haunted."

"What? Really? That's so creepy. It sounds darker than Pearl Harbor."

When they arrived at the island's port, they avoided the tour trollies and went straight to the jeep. Mingyu got directions and they drove to *South Beach*. They decided to do their exploring later in the day when it was cooler.

On the beach, they found a tree to sit under and spread out their towels. Lily Rose shed her flowered dress and he feasted his eyes on her floral two-piece. He loved the lanky, curves of her lithe figure and the grace of her fluid movements. They frolicked in the water and walked hand in hand on the beach before devouring their box lunches.

Just when he was drifting off for a brief snooze, she surprised him with relationship questions. Her probing was an eye-opener. *She's scared to commit! This is not a conversation I want to have here and now, in this Zen setting.* He reached for her hand and walked her into the warm waters, the perfect trajectory change.

Fed and cooled off, they rode around the island, first stopping at *Bloodstone Beach.* They marveled at the black sand and red spotted rocks. Mingyu picked one up with a large blotchy red stain and showed it to her. "The name of this beach comes from these unusual rocks. The lore says the sand is black because of all the bodies that were incinerated here during the war. The red marks on the rocks are symbolic of blood lost. This is the site of the largest mass suicide in history. Three thousand Japanese soldiers chose suicide over being captured."

"Yikes. That's so dark. If I take a blood rock home will I be saving a soul?"

Her comment made him smile. *How does she come up with these thoughts?*

"Good question. On the flip side, geologists have their own explanation why these rocks are stained with red."

"What do they say?" Her genuine interest amused him and he wanted to impress.

"Bloodstone is in the chalcedony family, sometimes jasper. It's usually green with red blotches. The rocks here are white with red blotches. Since this island sits on an extinct volcano, these rocks could be any kind of sediment mixture with iron concretions. That would be my guess."

"Listening to you makes me want to study gemology. I think I'll begin a rock collection, with pieces from around the world, starting with this crazy specimen." She picked up a stone rolling it around in the palm of her hand.

Mingyu smiled. He put his arm around Lily Rose and dropped his chin on her sun-warmed head. Before the jeep ride, she had switched from her straw hat to a white baseball cap, wearing it backwards.

"I'm glad I'm bearing witness to the beginning of a remarkable collection."

She laughed and pocketed the stone. When she turned toward him, tilting her chin upward he couldn't resist kissing her, unleashing all he felt. Her soft lips made his insides simmer. *She's mellowing-- finally loosening up.* He felt a seismic shift. It appeared their friendship was blossoming into a rare tropical bloom.

The rest of the day they looked at the sights: the lighthouse, the ghostly Malinta tunnel, the impressive mortar and gun barrel garrisons, the mile-long barrack ruins, the hospital shell shaped like a cross to avoid being bombed and the Japanese memorial site. Everything was in close proximity by jeep. The ferry ride home brought lots of talk about the paranormal vibe of the island. Their conversation was punctuated by sweet kisses and wandering hands.

"So, did you feel anything unusual at any of the sites?" Mingyu cocked his head at her.

"The Malinta tunnel definitely had an eerie vibe. I can't believe how heavily bombed those ruins were. There was definitely a sad vibe to the place. Spiritual."

"It's said that there are wandering ghosts in the Malinta tunnel. It was supposed to be a safe place, a bomb shelter, engineered by the US forces. When the hospital was bombed the hurt soldiers were brought to the tunnel, but they ended up dying there or were captured."

"Yes, it felt weird walking through it. Sad memories linger. I could feel it."

They sat in silence for the rest of the ferry ride. Lily Rose leaned her head on Mingyu's shoulder. He glanced down at their interlaced fingers and pondered what the night would behold. They had two nights left and he had high hopes after today's relaxed, reflective atmosphere. Lily Rose had finally responded to all his sensuous innuendos.

"Why don't we have dinner in the hotel bar tonight? We can get an early start tomorrow," Lily Rose suggested when they arrived at the dock in Manila.

"Anything special you want to do tomorrow?" he wondered.

"Look around Manila? Maybe hit the hotel pool in the afternoon? It looks really nice and we haven't been once."

"Sounds good."

During dinner, Lily Rose was back to her usual chatty self. Over dessert, she leaned in toward Mingyu, the candle shadowing her face in a favorable light. Her skin had a healthy glow and her natural waves framed her heart shaped face with its high cheekbones and tapered chin.

"Were you ever truly in love?" She looked at him unflinchingly.

After honest consideration, he replied. "Probably not."

She waited, but he didn't feel like elaborating. He was still sorting out his feelings. In his mind, he went through the list of women he dated for more than a night, but no one truly stuck out as a long-term goal. His fascination had always faded over time. Even his infatuation with Fen had fizzled after a few months. The extra six months he hung in were pure habit and a healthy sex drive. This felt different.

"Have you?" He studied her softening expression.

"I thought I was once, but it didn't last. Now, I think it was just a temporary obsession."

"How temporary?" He inquired.

"Two years."

"That isn't exactly a short relationship."

"No, I suppose not." She averted her gaze.

"What happened?" He hoped he wouldn't regret probing.

"We grew apart," Lily Rose explained, looking down into her wine glass. "He also cheated on me. Things were never the same after that. I lost trust and eventually broke up with him. It was harder on me than him, I think."

"I'm sorry."

"Don't be. I learned a lot along the way. He was the wrong man for me, but I didn't want to see that early on. There were clear signs that I stupidly ignored. In the end, he did me a favor. We didn't share enough common interests for it to have worked long term."

He nodded and thought about Fen and their fights about commitment. *We had no common interests besides sex.*

Mingyu swiped the key card and held the hotel door open for Lily Rose; he was surprised when she dimmed the lights and inserted her fingers through the button gaps in his shirt, pulling him close. Anticipation sprung in his heart and heat hit his lower regions or was it reversed? Before he could think about his next move, he felt her cool fingers slide over bare skin, sending a shiver up his spine. As she drew him in closer for a steamy kiss, he knew there was no stopping now.

Chapter XXVI

Transitioning from Manila back to Real Life

Last night made Lily Rose realize what a selfish lover her last boyfriend had really been. She woke up first, snuggled in Mingyu's arms, and absolutely relishing the sensation. If there were any lingering doubts about how he felt toward her, they had dissipated into the morning haze. She rolled over and slipped out of bed while he snoozed. Glancing back on her way to the shower, she thought how sweet he looked tangled in the sheets. Their relationship had taken a new turn and she was excited. No regrets. She hoped she wouldn't get hurt again, but some risks were worth taking, weren't they? When she emerged, refreshed and wrapped in a robe, Mingyu was propped against a pillow pile, checking his phone.

"Good morning. Did you get enough sleep?" She sat down on the edge of his bed to kiss him.

"Hardly, but no complaints here." He grinned. "Where shall we go, today?"

"While you shower, I'll check. We can make a final decision over breakfast."

He nodded, stretching. Hopping out of bed, he kissed her on the way to the bathroom. Her eyes followed him, taking in his strong back and firm behind. The memory of last night made her blush down to her hair roots. Mingyu had been an easy lover, sensitive to her needs as if he intuitively knew her body and soul. There was no initial awkwardness like there had been in past relationships.

She pulled her favorite sky blue skort and a white t-shirt out of her suitcase and got dressed. Slipping on barely-there white sweat socks and her purple canvas sneakers, she thought about their sensuous night and smiled. Studying her face in the mirror, she brushed and loosely braided her hair. The sun burned through the window, reminding her she needed to reapply her sunscreen more often. There were prominent red blotches across her nose and cheeks from previous beach days. She rubbed on the highest SPF moisturizer and threw the tube in her bag. On her phone she studied tourist destinations for Manila.

After breakfast, they took a *Grab Taxi,* which proved to be rather reasonable, and visited San Augustin, a Spanish colonial church in the oldest part of the city, in the Quiapo district. Walking around the quaint cobblestone streets, in the historic walled city, Intramuros, they decided to lunch in a Spanish buffet restaurant.

Tummies full, they viewed Manila Cathedral and headed to the market in downtown around Miranda Square and the Quiapo Basilica. They concluded their tourist day at San Sebastien, admiring the architecture.

Hot and tired, they deposited their souvenir bags in the hotel room, put on swim suits and strolled hand in hand to the pool for a cool down. Lingering in the water and eventually on a chaise, they chatted about the trip.

"Today was fun, but not as much fun as riding around in the jeep and snorkeling at Verde, my absolute favorite activities so far. Your planning was epic. You're hired as my personal tour guide." Lily Rose teased.

"My stand-out memory was last night." Mingyu reached for her hand and pressed it to his heart.

"Who knew you had such a flair for romance? I would have seduced you way earlier."

"And here I doubted your intentions and waited so patiently." He gave her a mock sigh.

"Well if you play your cards right, you might just get lucky tonight."

"At your service, honeybun."

Lily Rose smirked. "Since we don't leave until tomorrow night, do you want to go to the marine park in the morning? Or shall we hang by the pool until we have to leave?"

"I can do the park, the pool, both or just stay in bed," he teased raising his eyebrows. "Let me see if we can get late check out." He took her hand and placed it on his thigh enclosing it with his long fingers.

"Maybe I'll get breakfast in bed after all," Lily Rose countered.

"That can definitely be arranged. I hope they serve whipped cream with their pancakes." Mingyu raised his sunglasses and winked at her.

Back in Hong Kong, Lily Rose had a hard time concentrating on work. David was swamped and Lam was in a testy mood. *Surprising, since he delegates most of the office's work load. What reason could he possibly have?* She didn't want either to bring her down after her wonderful weekend, so she worked silently at her desk. From the schedule, she could see she was working both Friday night and Saturday. She hoped that Mingyu was free on Sunday. She missed him already. Maybe she would see him during the week now? What was he doing every day after work? At lunchtime, David stopped by her desk.

"How was your long weekend? I want to hear about it."

"Great. I hung on the beach in the Philippines. Did lots of sight-seeing and snorkeling."

"Damn, that sounds good. Things here were crazy. One emergency after another and Lam completely lost it. The set-up for the Saturday party was done wrong and the wedding cake disappeared out of the kitchen. No idea what happened to it. The bride was in tears and her mother had a major melt down. I've never seen Lam so apologetic and mad at the same time. Thank God he was here so I didn't have to deal with the backlash."

"How did he fix the problem?"

"Ice cream. Lots of ice cream. We sent out for extra flavors and garnished them with coconut, chocolate and peanut sprinkles. Lam also had to offer them a refund for the cake. The wedding party filed a complaint and management chewed Lam out."

"Well, that explains things. But it's not his fault the kitchen lost the cake. Someone probably dropped it or accidentally sat on it and was too scared to fess up."

David laughed. "True. But he's the manager. He should have double-checked everything. A last minute cake could have been bought and slathered with icing and *florettes*. I'm so glad I was working the other event. That one went fine. No major drama, only minor headaches."

"Whew." Lily Rose mock wiped her forehead.

"Yeah! Hey, do you want to go to the late movie on Saturday after work?"

"Sure. Sounds good." She knew by the end of Saturday she'd be toast. Chilling with David was perfect for a night like that.

That night Mingyu called. "Hi, How was your first day back?"

"Super busy. I miss lazing around with you."

"Yeah. Reality returns quickly. Would you like to come to the store on Saturday afternoon? We could have dinner after."

"Sounds lovely but I don't think I can. I'm working straight through until Saturday evening. That's the price I pay for a mini-vacation. I'm free for dinner on Sunday or Monday. Or one night this week maybe?" She cringed through his long pause. *I hope he doesn't ask about Saturday night. I'll be toast and just want to chill.*

"Ok. How about dim sum at my grandfather's on Sunday? We can hang out after.

"That sounds nice. Are any other family members coming?"

"No. They usually go to my sister's restaurant for dim sum. Jin and I started our own tradition because he likes a quiet Sunday. The restaurant gets crazy busy."

"I understand. What can I bring? What does grandpa like?"

"Five Spice Peanuts. He loves to sprinkle them on ice cream. It's his favorite treat."

"Done. Does your grandfather speak English?"

"Yes." Mingyu laughed. "Everyone in my family attended bilingual schools in Hong Kong. We use English on a daily basis in the store."

Lily Rose knew it was a big deal to be invited to his grandfather's home. Chinese people did not open their private sanctums easily. *He must have gotten his grandfather's approval to invite me.* She also noted it had taken him two months to extend an invitation to the family business. She wondered what she should wear. First impressions were so important and she was aiming to impress his favorite family member. When they finished chatting, she googled Chinese dining etiquette to refresh her memory. The list was longer than she remembered.

<h1>Chapter XXVII</h1>

<h1>Lost Dragon Pendant Rediscovered</h1>

Mingyu parked outside Lilly Rose's building on Sunday morning and waited. He was looking forward to seeing her. All week he had their holiday weekend together on replay in his head and he couldn't stop smiling. Their mini-vacation had truly been magical. Not seeing her for seven days was worse than a sugar withdrawal; it was exceedingly difficult. He had been extremely busy with two nights of rowing practice with Bao at the club, a mandatory dinner with his father, and a GIA lecture with colleagues. Saturday, he met Bao for dinner and tried to explain how he felt about Lily Rose. His best friend laughed and assured him he was officially down for the count.

"You have it bad this time, dude. I have to meet this girl."

When Lily Rose appeared Sunday morning, she evoked an English garden vision. Wearing a vanilla linen dress with large pink tea roses; she looked cheery and summer beautiful. Her golden strappy sandals and straw handbag with dangling gold streamers, interwoven with pastel-colored straps, completed the mood. Mingyu noticed her bag was filled to the brim and wondered about the contents. This girl did not travel light. Today, her hair was arranged in a partial up-do.

When she got into the car, he leaned over to kiss her hello. As he drew back, his eyes popped at the imperial jade pendant around her neck. *Wait. What? That pendant looks like top quality carved jade. Where did THAT come from?*

"You look beautiful today. Like you're ready for the Queen's garden party at Buckingham Palace," he joked.

"Thanks. Getting a dim sum invitation to your grandfather's home runs a close second."

Mingyu smiled. "Right. Don't think we invite just anyone to our private royal enclave. Usually, it's just the two of us and we like it that way."

"Way to not intimidate me. I already tried on ten different outfits for the occasion," she joked.

"Well, you got it right. You look beautiful. That amazing carved jade around your neck is more impressive than the crown jewels."

Lily Rose broke into a huge smile. "I know. This was my grandmother's pendant. Interestingly, she willed my mother all her jewelry, but this piece, she left hidden in the house, so that makes it mine. I was so happy when I discovered it. I love it."

"I would like to take a closer look when we get to Jin's place. It's quite impressive."

"Thanks! Sure. Maybe you and Jin can tell me a little about its history and iconography."

Arriving at Jin's home, Lily Rose was impressed by the beautifully kept garden. It was compact, but had the most amazing plant and rock arrangements. There were dogwood and orchid trees, azaleas, camellias and rhododendron and that only included the specimen she recognized. There was also a small rock garden. The house was one of the smaller ones on the street, but it was immaculate, like a precious jewel box in an opulent room. Mingyu used his key to let them both in. He bowed his head at the buddha statue set on a small fountain at the base of the stairs and reached for her hand, squeezing It reassuringly as they started to climb the steps to the main living space.

"Should I remove my shoes?" she asked, noticing several pair neatly lined up along one wall.

"No. We'll be eating on the terrace. In the kitchen area and on the terrace, we leave our shoes on for practical reasons. Everywhere else in the house, they come off."

At the top of the stairs, he called out, "Ye Ye, we're here."

Lily Rose looked around the open living space. There was a spacious kitchen with jade green cabinets to the left with a large bamboo prepping counter covered with bowls that gave off enticing scents. On the far side of the counter, near the glass sliding doors, she saw a traditional round Chinese rosewood dining set surrounded by six intricately fashioned chairs. Her eyes traveled to the right, around the living room. She observed a dark red lacquered sideboard, a seating area with a comfortable, modern couch and plush bamboo armchairs, all covered in soft golden fabrics. The side tables and coffee table were carved rosewood with mother of pearl inlay and in every spare corner stood majestic Asian patterned, porcelain flowerpots with luscious tropical plants. Grandpa definitely had a green thumb. A rosewood china cabinet graced the wall near the staircase, opposite the glass sliding doors. Across from the kitchen was an open arch that led into a smaller room that looked like a library or office. Beside it was a hallway that led to the bedrooms. The library had bookshelves along the length of the wall and an impressive scroll-footed elm wood desk.

Lily Rose sensed movement and her eyes spotted Jin. He appeared from behind the massive desk. Silently, he shuffled toward them in quilted black silk slippers. He was a wiry man of average height with wispy grey hair and a serene face. He was dressed in black and wore a simple gold ring with a beautiful cabochon jade stone.

"Welcome to my home, Lily Rose. So happy you could join us today." He smiled warmly as he studied his guest.

"Thank you for inviting me. I brought you some vanilla and mango ice cream and a bag of five spice peanuts. We should probably freeze the ice cream."

"Thank you. How did you know that's my favorite dessert?" He motioned to Mingyu to put the ice cream away.

"Your grandson might have hinted." She smiled shyly.

"Right. Come along then. I have some tea prepared on the terrace. Leave your shoes on." He motioned to the expansive outdoors that overlooked the water. He slipped into shoes that were parked by the sliding doors. "How do you take your tea?"

"With lots of milk, no sugar. Thank you. Your home is incredibly beautiful. Who takes care of all your plants and the garden?"

"Ahh. That is my weekend passion. I do have a little help though." He glanced at her, his eyes traveling down to the pendant around her neck. A flicker of recognition, then pleasure, crossed his face. His gaze rested on the pendant, appreciating its beauty as if rediscovering a long lost friend. "Tell me, what brings you to Hong Kong?"

Lily Rose noticed his fascination with Marina's pendant and it pleased her. He could barely unglue his eyes. She was flattered. "Work, mainly."

While Mingyu busied himself in the kitchen, Lily Rose told Jin about her life in New York and her decision to transfer. She briefly mentioned Marina's stories as a catalyst for her decision to come. Jin listened without interrupting, encouraging more nervous chatter.

When she finished, he offered his condolences. "I'm so sorry about your grandmother."

Lily Rose's face clouded. Not wanting to linger on a painful subject, he shifted gears, "I hear you and Mingyu took a nice trip together. Did you like the Philippines?"

She blushed. *How much does he know about this trip?*

"Yes. We had a wonderful time. Have you been?"

"Several times. Years ago. I don't travel much anymore."

Mingyu came out to join them. After an initial cup of tea, they decided to eat indoors after all. A tropical shower threatened. Mingyu set the table while Jin motioned Lily Rose to sit in a chair with a view. "Can I help with anything?" she asked.

"Usually, Mingyu and I prepare and cook our meal together, but today I prepared everything in advance, so we can relax and chat. Next time, you can participate, Lily Rose."

"I'd love to." *That's promising. He may invite me back.*

Mingyu carried a series of small, heated dishes to the table: steamed vegetable dumplings, pork buns, beef meatballs and eggplant. Lilly Rose was nervous about using her chop sticks properly, but instantly felt encouraged when Mingyu dropped a beef ball that splattered on his shirt. Unruffled, he went to wet a dishtowel with soap to clean the marks.

After lunch, they sat on the terrace sipping green tea and ate the dessert Lily Rose brought. Jin added some almond cookies. "These are from your sister's restaurant. So good."

"Delicious," Lily Rose politely agreed. She wondered if it was ok to dunk them in her tea, but decided not to.

Mingyu handled the clean up by himself so Jin could sit with Lily Rose. When Mingyu was done, he took her into the library, unlocking an apothecary cabinet that housed a collection of carved jade pieces, one in each small velvet-lined drawer. "These are all Jin's favorite pieces—the ones he'll never sell."

"They're incredible! How does he keep them so shiny and flawless?"

"Fine jade should be cleaned with a soft cloth and mild soapy water. Never soak it. Just wipe it gently. That will ensure its luster. Store the pieces individually in soft places. You have a pouch for your dragon pendant, don't you? It's exquisite."

She nodded and slipped it over her head. "What can you tell me about it?" She handed the pendant to Mingyu who held it with great care.

"It symbolizes the circle of life, your life, your world. See here, this is a yin yang symbol at the top. And this ball below it symbolizes the pearl of wisdom. The two dragons stretching around it are fighting over it."

"Cool. So, I'm protected whenever I wear it?"

"Yes." Jin walked into the room. "Your pendant is a particularly fine piece of imperial jade. The carving is done by an old master carver from the Quing dynasty. The quality is determined by the color of the jade and the depth and intricacy of the carving. Yours is top quality." He nodded for emphasis, then continued, "Dragons are meant to protect. In the Chinese culture, the dragon is associated with good things-- success, power, protection, strength, good luck. The Chinese dragon has a spiritual meaning whereas in other cultures, like Scandinavia for example, dragons are creatures to be afraid of. Not so in China. Our dragons come in two colors, green and brown. The green dragon of Buddhism is associated with springtime—rebirth, the season of new beginnings. Take good care of your pendant. It's a special one and very valuable."

"Thank you for the information. It belonged to my grand-mother. She must have gotten it when she lived in Hong Kong."

"My guess is someone who cared for her very deeply gave it to her. That's not the type of pendant you can easily find in the jade market or general marketplace. It's a collector's item."

Lily Rose nodded happily.

Jin continued tracing the pendant's lines with long, thin fin-gers. "A word of caution. Be careful where you wear it. In this part of the world, your pendant is considered a prized possession. Fine jade commands the same price here as diamonds do in New York. Here we say, 'Gold has a price, but jade is priceless.' Espe-cially, the expertly carved variety. Your pendant is irreplaceable."

When Lily Rose and Mingyu left Jin's home they drove around the beautiful neighborhood to admire the architecture. She noticed how proud Mingyu was of his roots: his family and their beautiful ancestral home. She understood his pride as she felt the same about her home in Sag Harbor. It was her special place. When Mingyu and Lily Rose returned to West Kowloon, they went back to Lily Rose's apartment to top off a perfect day with a night of blissful passion.

Chapter XXVIII

Mingyu's Professional World

When Mingyu arrived at work Monday morning, he peeked into his father's office. He was happy to discover that Cheng was still away on business. He knew his father wouldn't be as enthusiastic and welcoming to his new girlfriend as Jin had. Cheng had more traditional expectations. When his grandfather arrived Mingyu closed their office door for a private chat. He was still floating on a cloud following a night of sweet love making.

"Morning. So…what did you think of Lily Rose?" He stood in front of his grandfather's desk, his arms crossed, fingers tapping nervously.

"Good morning, Mingyu. She's lovely. You're a lucky young man." Jin sat down and started up his computer, but didn't look at the screen. Satisfied, Mingyu smiled and relaxed, uncrossing his arms. His grandfather's approval meant everything.

"Thanks for inviting her yesterday. She enjoyed it. We had a fabulous time in Manila. We totally connected. I never had this much fun with Fen or anyone else for that matter. Fen was so…difficult in comparison. So rigid. Lily Rose was easy to travel with and we enjoyed all the same activities: boating, snorkeling, swimming, exploring."

"How someone makes you feel is a good indication of their friendship. Buddha teaches that a good friend is someone who knows you well and still loves you for who you are."

"We're still getting to know each other, but I have a good feeling. She brightens my day whenever I see her."

"Mingyu, why don't you bring Lily Rose to the restaurant next week for the Dragon Boat Festival?"

"Maybe. Will dad be back?"

"I'm not sure, but does it matter? I think your sister and cousins would love to meet her, don't you? Has Bao met Lily Rose?"

"No. Only you and Victoria. I didn't want to bring her around the family yet. You know how opinionated they can be."

Jin nodded and smiled. "You mean your father. Listen, Mingyu. Follow your heart, regardless of what anyone else thinks. I didn't always do that and I regretted it."

"What do you mean? Was Grandma not your first choice?" Mingyu was shocked at his own unfiltered outburst.

Jin paused as if looking for the right words. "Your grandmother was a very good wife and woman… but no, she was not my first choice. I let my first choice slip through my fingers and I didn't realize what a big mistake I'd made until it was too late and she was gone."

Mingyu was astonished at Jin's admission. "Who was your first choice? What was she like?"

Jin sighed. "This is a conversation for another time. Over dim sum, maybe. Let's get to work."

Mingyu knew when he was being dismissed, so he respectfully withdrew to his desk.

Lily Rose entered the store and looked around. The space was small, but well organized and brightly lit, with counters on two sides and a seating area with wall displays to the right. The palette was neutral, natural cream tones. Beautiful rose wood counters offset by black lacquer surrounded the store with impressive fica tree accents on black flooring. Cream colored displays made the jewelry sparkle like glistening dew drops in a tropical forest. Two women greeted her, one moving in her direction.

"Good day. May I help you?"

"Hello, I'm meeting Mingyu. Can you tell him Lily Rose is here?"

The woman looked at her with renewed interest as she picked up the phone and called Mingyu's extension. Lily Rose felt eyes pierce her back as she perused the surrounding cases. When Mingyu came to collect her, he introduced Winnie and Amber. Winnie continued to stare as they exited the showroom to go upstairs, an area normally off limits to customers.

"So, you saw the retail section, now let me show you the workshop. This is where all the magic happens."

"The showroom is exquisite. Like a little jewel box." She noticed Mingyu smile with pride.

"Thank you. We renovated a few years ago. I hang out upstairs ninety percent of my day so I don't get to enjoy it as much as our sales ladies. Here is our workshop and in there, behind the glass wall, is my desk. I share an office with my grandfather. My father is down the hall but he's out right now."

"Nice set up." Her eyes swept the busy work stations. Soft music barely dampened the banging, sawing and torch hiss.

"Come. Let's say hi to Jin and then I'll show you some jewelry and jade carvings."

After exchanging a few pleasantries with Jin, Mingyu walked her around the workspace. Li seemed particularly curious about Lily Rose. He eyed the jade pendant around her neck, then spotted her lavender jade ring and half smiled. Lily Rose suspected he recognized their inventory. He hovered around Mingyu, assuming she was a special client.

"Li is our top salesperson. Half the success in sales is knowing your inventory and when to produce it. Li remembers every piece we ever made." Mingyu nodded at Li. The corners of Li's lips tilted slightly upward as he bowed once with humility and appreciation.

After meeting everyone in the workshop, Mingyu seated Lily Rose at his desk and pulled a few spectacular pieces out of the safe to dazzle her with while Li circled like a rooster in the hen house. It appeared he wanted to live up to his reputation and assist Mingyu with merchandise. Generally, Mingyu appreciated his attentiveness, but today it felt slightly oppressive. He waved Li away. "I got this. Thank you, Li."

Mingyu showed Lily Rose a few collection highlights and how the jewelry in production was being assembled. Then he directed her back downstairs to look at earrings to compliment her lavender jade ring. As they perused their options, the door chimed waking Winnie from her 'sleeping beauty' snooze. She rushed forward to greet the customer. Lily Rose could hear the reverence in her voice.

"Hello, Mr. Wu." Winnie bowed from the waist.

"Winnie." Carson nodded once." The boss, is he here?" Two fierce looking men positioned themselves by the door, hands crossed in front. The store's security guard eyed them with suspicion.

"Cheng is out of town. Jin is here." She bowed again.

"Perfect. I want to see jade." He tapped his fingers impatiently on the counter and looked over his shoulder. His eyes scanned past Mingyu and focused on Lily Rose. She turned to look at Mr. Wu and Mr. Wu turned to look at the dragon pendant around her neck. His eyes narrowed, forecasting trouble.

"I remember you. You work in the Hilton hotel. Did you buy that pendant here?" He gestured with his head toward Lily Rose's chest.

"No. This was my grandmother's. It's a family heirloom." Her hand flew to her pendant, fingering it defensively.

"Heirloom?"

"Yes."

"Are you selling your heirloom?" Wu barked, never taking his eyes off the pendant.

"No. I would never sell it. I love it."

"Too bad. I'd offer you a good price." Dark eyes veered to her face for a reaction. He got nothing but a blank stare and a side to side head shake.

When Jin appeared, Carson Wu shifted his attention and switched to Cantonese, ignoring Lily Rose. She and Mingyu returned to their gem exploration and quest for earrings. She pointed out a few designs she liked, but decided she needed time to think about it. It was hard to concentrate with Carson Wu hovering. He radiated danger and all she could think of was getting her pendant out of his sight. Mingyu picked up on her vibe.

"Would you like to think about it over coffee?"

"Yes. I'm not quick with expensive decisions as you know from New York."

"Of course. I'm going to run upstairs and get my jacket. Have a seat."

"Ok. Thanks." She sat down in the waiting area and studied Wu. He was dressed in black jeans, a white shirt unbuttoned at the neck and a royal blue suit jacket. All tattoos were conveniently hidden. Jin was showing him carved jade and Carson hunched over the jewelry tray, detonated questions that simulated a car backfiring. Lily Rose noted how patiently Jin replied. To a foreigner's ear it sounded like they spoke different languages. While she didn't understand Cantonese, Lily Rose could tell from Jin's calm demeanor that he was educating his client. She admired his sales style and soothing, Zen approach. He didn't seem in the least intimidated. Clearly, that was where Mingyu got his inspiration and patience. Outside a parked car, engine running, waited for Mr. Wu.

When Mingyu returned, they waved goodbye to Jin under Winnie's watchful eye. Carson Wu turned and cast a dark glance toward Lily Rose and the imperial jade dragon pendant leaving his field of vision.

Chapter XXIX

Dragon Boat Festival in Hong Kong

"The Dragon Boat festival is a big deal in the Chinese culture. It commemorates the death of the poet Qu Yuan, who killed himself by drowning. Dragon boats were launched to scare the fishes and save him, but they were too late and failed to find him alive. You haven't had breakfast yet, have you?" Mingyu raised an inquisitive eyebrow at Lily Rose. They had stopped at the top of the subway steps to get their bearing.

"No, you told me not to." She playfully poked him in the ribs.

"Right, I'm glad you paid attention because we're going to have *zongzi* down near the Aberdeen promenade and watch the races." He kissed her, took her hand and started walking.

"What are zongzi?"

"They're sticky rice dumplings wrapped in bamboo leaves. You don't have a peanut allergy, do you?"

"No. Why?"

"The traditional zongzi are made with glutinous rice and peanuts, wrapped in two bamboo leaves and served with a honey sauce sprinkled with more crushed peanuts. It's delicious but lethal for someone with a nut allergy."

"I'm safe."

"Good. I don't think I could date anyone who doesn't eat peanuts," Mingu joked. "Actually, I remember you ate peanut sprinkles at my grandfather's."

"I brought them, you goofball." She prodded his side again.

Mingyu smiled and continued. "Later today, I'd like to take you to my sister's restaurant. We'll have more zongzi, but the savory kind with meat and mushrooms or shrimp and chestnuts. They're topped with an incredible chili-mustard sauce--my grandmother's secret recipe. Myia makes the absolute best zongzi in Hong Kong. You better not be allergic to those either or the family will starve you."

"I'm starving now. Stop talking and feed me." Lily Rose rubbed her abs over her fitted pale lemon t-shirt. She wondered if she was dressed nice enough to meet Mingyu's entire family. *Why didn't he tell me?* She dug a fist into her loose-fitting capri jeans pocket and looked down at her emerald sandals and matching leather criss-cross bag. "Who else from your family will be there?"

"Probably everyone." He grinned.

Damn. At least I'm wearing my nice jade jewelry. "I noticed a lot of the stores are closed. Is this considered a national holiday?"

"Yes. A floating one, meaning it falls on different days every year. The dragon festival falls on the fifth day of the fifth month of the lunar year, so this year it is on the late side in mid-June. Sometimes it is as early as May."

"Lucky for us. Great weather. The hotel was booked solid this weekend. I suppose most people came for the dragon boat races."

"Probably. Big family day. Here we are. Grab those two seats. I'll get in line for food. It'll get crowded quickly."

"Ok." Lily Rose looked around at all the colorful decorations. Red and golden banners hung from every possible perch. When Mingyu returned, his hands were laden with goodies. "Here, iced milk *tea* and iced water for later. It'll get hot down by the harbor."

"Thanks."

"I know a number of people who are racing."

"Really? Who?"

"My cousin, Harlan. He's Victoria's brother, if you remember. My friend Bao is also racing and a few other friends you don't know."

"Cool. We'll cheer them on. Are they all on the same boat?"

"No. Harlan is on my uncle's company team and Bao is part of a club team with their own boat. I raced for a few years too, but now I prefer to cheer. I still train with them though."

Mingyu watched her unfold the leaves, look at the contents and take a bite, dipping the compact rice into the honey sauce. "So, what do you think?"

"Yum. Delicious. You're an awesome breakfast date." Lily Rose smiled. "Now I know why you're so muscular. When and why did you stop participating in the races?"

Mingyu smiled. "Maybe two years ago? No special reason. I got busy with work and classes, I guess. And Fen always complained that training took too much of my time."

"Really? I haven't noticed." Lily Rose lied. "You should get back into it."

"Maybe. I train twice a week after work. You're always working, so you wouldn't have noticed."

"I did wonder why I never see you during the week. Now I know."

Down by the harbor, they ran into Bao's family. Mingyu introduced Lily Rose and chatted with them briefly. They all turned to wave to Bao, who was already near boat number six, a fierce looking dragon boat with fifty paddlers. Lily Rose noticed a drummer sitting in the front of the boat. As if reading her mind, Mingyu explained.

"The drum is the heartbeat of the boat. The drummer keeps time with the strokes and incites the rowers to go quicker by increasing the beat."

"What is the drum made of?"

"Water buffalo skin and wood, so it growls like a dragon when pounded. My cousin Elizabeth is a drummer on my uncle's boat."

"Nice. I like the idea of a girl managing a boatload of men."

Mingyu laughed and squeezed her hand. "Look over there. An all-girl boat." Mingyu waved at them and about ten girls waved back. One in particular, stared back at them, the only one not smiling. Lily Rose was caught by surprise. "Do you know them?"

"Yes. I grew up here, remember?"

"I hardly ever run into anyone I grew up with in New York."

"See the dragon boat over there, with the men in black and red?"

"Yes. They look fierce. Who are they?"

"Carson Wu's crew. He sponsors his own team."

Lily Rose looked for familiar faces from Alison's wedding but recognized none. As the promenade got more crowded and the next group of racers lined up, Mingyu turned to her. "We can watch the races from my Uncle Huan's boat. It's docked over there." He pointed in the general direction. "Are you ok with that?"

"That's up to you. It might be nice to sit down." She was starting to feel slightly claustrophobic with the crowds inching around them like an inflatable vest. Her sense of personal space was totally invaded. She looked at the surrounding boats, dangerously crowded and wondered how they stayed afloat. People were watching the races from every possible perch.

As they weeded their way to the plank, Mingyu greeted tons of people. On the boat, he introduced her to his Uncle Huan and Aunt Chantao, his father's sister. Victoria came to greet them, eyeing Lily Rose with derision, like a prickly cactus bloom.

"Welcome, Mingyu. There's food inside. Harlan is racing shortly so find a good spot to watch from. Will you be at the restaurant later?"

Mingyu nodded. "Yes."

"Good. We can chat then. I want to secure my spot."

Lily Rose thought she detected a frosty undertone. They found a comfortable corner near the bow of the boat and settled in. The cheering from the pier was deafening and Lily Rose was happy to be seated comfortably and somewhat remotely.

After a long day of watching races and listening to drum performances, they arrived at Myia's crowded restaurant. It was configured in a large square with the kitchen and a party room in the back. The family was assembled around four large round tables in the heavily decorated party room. Mugwart leaves hung from the ceiling to ward off bad spirits and everyone sported bright, multicolored strings around their wrists, for added protection. One table was filled with children, who helped themselves to food from a centered Lazy Susan as they chirped excitedly. Jin presided over the table closest to the kitchen. He was seated with Mingyu's father and some older relatives. The other tables were all filled with young people, including Bao and his family. Mingyu greeted his grandfather first and introduced Lily Rose to his father and the other relatives. He immediately noticed Cheng's face cloud. His eyes focused on the dragon pendant around Lily Rose's neck. Mingyu's father was surprised to see her and it showed in his sour expression. After observing Jin's warm welcome, everyone else followed Jin's suit.

"Where's Myia?" Mingyu asked, wanting to escape his father's penetrating stare.

"Kitchen," Jin pointed with his head.

"Right. Come. Let me introduce you to my sister." He ushered Lily Rose into the bustling kitchen. Faces looked up from what they were doing and smiled at Mingyu. He greeted many by name. Huge vats of zongzi tied together by string were cooking. Some zongzi were hung to dry off ceiling racks. Myia was arranging a platter with the ones ready for consumption. When she looked up and spotted Mingyu, her face broke into a huge smile.

"There you are. I hear you watched from the boat today, accompanied by a beautiful woman. I'm glad you brought her to the restaurant so we can meet her too."

"Of course. We wouldn't miss your zongzi for anything." Mingyu was happy for his sister's comments. He hoped Lily Rose hadn't noticed his father's sour face.

Myia laughed and hugged her brother. Over his shoulder, her eyes dropped to the pendant around Lily Rose's neck.

"Myia this is my girlfriend, Lily Rose." He glanced back at Lily Rose for her reaction. He caught a flicker of surprise.

"Hello, Myia. Nice to meet you. Mingyu has been raving about your zongzi all day. He claims they're the best in Hong Kong."

Myia grinned. "Ha! He has to say that or the family would disown him. Nice to finally meet you. Did you enjoy the races?"

"Yes. Exciting day."

"Good. Now go sit down and eat. You must be hungry. I'll be out with more zongzi in a minute." Turning to Mingyu she added, "How did everyone do today? I hear Bao's team did better than Harlan's again."

"They did. Face it. The club team rules."

"How did Jun and the girls do?"

"Not bad. They were in the top ten."

"Oh, great! If you had helped, the club team might have won, or Huan might have at least tied with them."

"Yeah, yeah. They did fine without me." He laughed and took Lily Rose's hand. "Let's go eat. Can I take a bottle of plum wine out?"

"Sure. Glasses are on the table." Myia pointed and waved.

They seated themselves between Bao and Elizabeth who were already eating pork zongzi. Bao leaned over his plate. "Hi, Lily Rose. I'm Bao. Was this your first dragon boat race?"

"Yes. It was fun to watch. You did great. Did you hear us cheering?"

"Yes and no. Once we're on the boat, it's all noise. We're so focused on the drum rhythm and passing the other boats, the crowd disappears." Turning to Mingyu, he added. "I'll be so sore tomorrow. Pour us some plum wine so I can at least enjoy today. I hear if you have enough, you forget about all muscle aches tomorrow."

Mingyu laughed. "Yeah, you're focused on the hangover. No realgar wine for you then?"

"No, thanks. Some like it sweet."

"What's realgar wine?" Lily Rose asked.

"It's a Chinese wine made from cereal." Mingyu explained.

"And arsenic," Bao added. "It has some questionable ingredients, traditionally."

"Stop scaring my girlfriend." Mingyu warned, pouring the plum wine into Bao's glass.

"I think I'll stick with plum wine, too." Lily Rose smiled sweetly. While Mingyu and Bao talked about the race, she turned to Elizabeth and introduced herself. Inquiring about the drumming, they launched into a dialogue about the races, then gemology. It appeared they shared common interests. Elizabeth was friendlier than Victoria and fun to talk to, like Mingyu. When Mingyu and Lily Rose finally left the restaurant, she was pleasantly buzzed. On the subway platform she leaned in to kiss him and whispered, "I'm off tomorrow. Do you want to spend the night at my place?"

"I would. I do have to be in the office tomorrow, but I can go in a little late. Can we stop by my place first? I need some fresh clothes for the morning."

"Sure. I wouldn't want you to show up in the same sticky zongzi outfit," she teased. "You can teach me how to properly cast a spell tonight. Elizabeth told me that one of the holiday traditions is casting spells. I'm thinking of a love spell myself.

How about you?" She looked at the five-color string bracelet one of the children had tied around her wrist and waved the attached dangling perfumed zongzi shaped cloth bag in front of his face.

"I can go along with that. I have my own little spell in mind."

"Ohhh. You wicked man."

Mingyu was happy how the day had unfolded. Except for Cheng, everyone had responded well to his new girlfriend.

The next morning Lily Rose woke as Mingyu emerged from the shower. "I wish you could stay. Do you have time for breakfast?"

"No. I'll pick something up on the way. Stay where you are." He leaned over the bed and kissed her cheek. "I wish I could stay, too."

"Thanks for a fun day, yesterday. I had a blast." Lily Rose mumbled into her pillow. Mingyu grinned. "Me too. After last night, I'm completely under your spell and I like it. I'll call you later, witchy girl."

When she heard her front door slam shut, Lily Rose rolled over and fell back asleep for another hour, reveling in the fact that she was now officially Mingyu's girlfriend. She had heard him repeat it numerous times at the Dragon Boat Festival and it felt sooo right.

Chapter XXX

Family Backlash

When Mingyu got to the office, Jin was on the phone and his father was sitting at Mingyu's desk, sorting gems. He looked up.

"You're late." Cheng frowned as he spoke. "Good day yesterday?"

Mingyu looked at him, annoyed. *He's calling me out on being late? He's rarely here lately.*

"Very good. Thanks. How was your business trip? Where did you go?"

"I was buying and selling in Guangzhou, Shenzhen, and Wuhan."

"Wuhan? I thought the gold bars from Wuhan are actually gilded copper these days."

"I only deal with reputable dealers. Your friend, yesterday… isn't that the girl from New York? What is she doing here?" His dark, brooding eyes pierced his son.

"Yes, it is. She's working at the Hilton here."

"How long is she staying?"

"Not sure. Why?"

"I'm wondering why you're wasting time with her. She'll be leaving again."

Jin, who had finished his call, looked up.

"Why do you care if I spend time with her? She's an interesting girl." Mingyu could feel his temper rising.

"Because it isn't going to lead anywhere, and the nice Chinese girls who are always buzzing around you are going to lose interest."

"I'm not worried and I really don't care what you or the nice Chinese girls think. I like Lily Rose. She makes me happy." Mingyu was determined not to discuss this further. "What are you looking at?"

"Sapphires. I want your opinion. Let's put your education to work. Which one do you like best and why?"

Mingyu pulled out his loupe and studied the stones lined up on the grooved, white stone tray. "I like this oval. It has a good even color and not too many inclusions. What are the prices per carat?"

"All the same price. They're from the same lot."

"Definitely the oval then. Best value." He stood next to his desk waiting for his father to leave.

Cheng gathered up the stones in slow motion and wrapped the oval in a separate clear stone paper for weighing. "That dragon pendant your friend was wearing. Where did she get it?"

"It was her grandmother's. Why?"

"Where did her grandmother get it?"

"In Hong Kong, when she lived here years ago."

"It looks exactly like the one that was stolen from my grandmother. Did you notice that, Dad?"

"Yes. It is similar." Jin paused. "I'm surprised you remember the piece. The pendant disappeared before you were born, Cheng."

"Our missing pieces file is not very thick. Only a handful of items in it. I remember all of them. That was the most valuable one. I would love to compare it to the photo. Would she be interested in selling it?" Cheng put his hands on his hips.

"No. It means a lot to her. Don't you dare ask her." Mingyu was beyond annoyed now. "Can I get to work or do you have any other business at my desk?"

His father, looking slightly miffed, cleared Mingyu's desk and left for his office. When he was out of hearing distance, Jin cleared his throat. "Don't mind him. You do what your heart tells you. Lily Rose is enchanting. And…don't ever let her sell that pendant; it was meant for her. However, she may want to be more careful where she wears it. Too valuable for a street festival."

"I think she wore it yesterday because she was meeting the family," Mingyu fibbed. Bringing her to meet his entire family had been a spur of the moment decision.

"I understand. Everyone liked Lily Rose. Don't get side-tracked by your father. Cheng is difficult since your mother died. He's a lost soul."

"That's an understatement. He's always been difficult; he's just worse since mom passed. I have no intention of giving up Lily Rose to please him."

"He means well, even if it is hard to recognize. Remember, fighting only makes the situation persist. Ground yourself and 'conquer anger by non-anger' in the way of Buddha."

Chapter XXXI

The Wu Connection

When Lily Rose woke up, she languished in bed, looking out at the harbor dotted with the red-sailed junks. There was something peaceful and luxurious about watching sailboats from bed. She felt content, the view reinforcing her calmness. Reluctantly, she let her mind wander to the tasks of the day. Leisurely, she meandered to the kitchen to prepare her morning coffee. She needed the boost. Laundry was piling up and the usual dust bunny revolution threatened to take over her digs.

After throwing a dark load into the washer, she poured milk and cereal into a bowl. While slicing half a banana, her thoughts drifted to Mingyu's family. Except for his father, they all were polite and welcoming. Aunt Chantao and cousin Victoria appeared a bit frosty at first, but thawed a tad as the evening progressed. *Was it the liquor? Or did they take their cue from Jin?* She wondered what they really thought about her. His family was hard to read. She pulled out Marina's book of quotes and indulged in a couple while she ate.

Old friends pass away, new friends appear. It is just like the days. An old day passes, a new day arrives. The important thing is to make it meaningful: a meaningful friend – or a meaningful day. —Dalai Lama XIV

Love your friends from your heart, not from your need. —Unknown

Marina's quotes always started her day off on the right note. She finished her coffee and ran the dishwasher. Showered, she pulled on her purple jeans, a lilac t-shirt and stretched fresh sheets across the bed. Transferring the darks to the dryer, she started the whites and vacuumed while singing to the blasting radio. When the bathroom sparkled to her satisfaction, she slipped into her sneakers and reached for her jewelry box adding earrings and the dragon pendant to her outfit, admiring herself in the mirror. Grabbing her shopping bags on the console, she exited her apartment.

Outside, she bumped into Alison Wu looking fabulous in shades of hot pink. The girl definitely had her own style.

"Hello, Lily Rose. You live in the Arch? How nice!" Alison's eyes traveled over her, resting on the dragon pendant.

"Hello. Ah….yes." Lily Rose stuttered, surprised to see Carson Wu's daughter.

"It's Monday. Shouldn't you be at work?" Alison snipped as if it were her business.

Flummoxed, Lily Rose replied, "No. I worked Friday night and Saturday, so I have Sunday and Monday off this week. How are you?"

"Good. I see you're wearing the purple sneakers you bought when I last saw you. You're right. They do match your jeans perfectly."

"Thanks. I've worn them a lot." Not knowing what else to say, Lily Rose asked, "Did you go to the Dragon Boat Festival yesterday?"

"Yes. My father's boat ranked in the top three. Last year they won. Have you given the tattoo any thought?"

"Tattoo? No … not really. I've been too busy. If I decide to do it, I'll definitely call you though. I'm not even sure what image I would want. Probably a flower, like yours."

Alison nodded as if that were obvious. "Have you had lunch yet? I have time," she announced, eyes riveted on Lily Rose.

Taken aback by Alison's forwardness, Lily Rose thought about the offer. The girl definitely lacked social finesse, but her interest seemed genuine. "No. I was just going out to get groceries."

"I know a good place to eat near here. Want to go?" Alison tapped her foot nervously.

Lily Rose was curious. What harm would a lunch out in public do? "Sure, why not."

"Good. Come with me." Alison swiveled around and pointed into the direction she had just come from, her sheer top flowing in the breeze. Lily Rose fell into step beside her. From her side angle, she studied Alison's outfit—a gauzy patterned blouse over a soft pink tank topping slim fuchsia jeans and cobalt blue sandals. Alison looked great. *I wonder where she shops.*

They ordered won ton noodles at Chee Kee and talked fashion. Conversation flowed on this subject. Alison was curious what Lily Rose knew about New York's fashion world-- had she attended fashion week, what sample sales did she shop at and who were her favorite designers? Lily Rose filled her in with her limited knowledge. Over iced milk tea, she inquired,

"How's married life?"

Alison shrugged. "It's ok."

"Just ok? You're newly-weds!" Lily Rose wondered out loud. *Should I be asking this?*

"My husband works for my father. He's away a lot. When he's home, he's stressed and tired and not in a good mood. I get lonely sometimes." Alison looked around nervously.

"I'm sorry to hear that. Maybe you need to find your own niche. Keep busy with things you like to do. Start your own fashion business."

"I would love to do that."

"Do it. Don't get trapped with kids right away or you'll be stuck at home and even more bored and lonely."

Alison regarded her silently without answering, which made Lily Rose think she overstepped boundaries. She quickly switched to damage control and in a perky voice added, "Give it some time. Maybe things will change."

"And if they don't?" Alison's voice softened slightly.

"If they don't, you may need to have a serious talk with your husband. Express your concerns. If he loves you, he'll listen."

"I don't think so." Alison shook her head vigorously.

"Why?" *Yikes. Do I want to go here?*

"He's not that type of man." Alison kept shaking her head. "He only listens to other men."

Lily Rose couldn't stop herself. Having witnessed Alison's fairy tale wedding, she wanted to know more, "What attracted you to him in the first place?"

"He's handsome and generous."

"And?" *Ugh, I know I'm overstepping now.*

"And my father thought he would be a good match for me."

"For you or for his business?" Lily Rose shifted nervously. *Did I just say that?*

Alison stared and sighed. "I really don't know. My choices were limited. I don't think you understand how things work here. In my world, I mean."

"I probably don't, but I can tell you one thing for sure. You don't need to settle. This isn't the dark ages. You don't have to stay married if you made a mistake. Wait on kids if you aren't happy. Give yourself time to think this through. In the meantime, launch a business and become financially independent. It will empower you and enable you to think clearly. You have style, Alison, and a good eye for fashion. Don't waste your talent or wait for a man to adjust to your schedule. That will never happen. How old are you?"

"Twenty-five. How do you know? Are you divorced?" Alison scrutinized her.

"No. Just speaking from my limited experience and from what I've observed. Life in New York, you know?" She paused. " It's ok to realize you've made a mistake, but you need to be sure if that is indeed the case. Only you can decide that-- not your father, not your friends, not anyone. Follow your own heart, Alison." *That is exactly what Marina would say and it worked for me.*

Alison smiled wistfully. "Thanks. Maybe next time I can show you some of my designs?"

Next time? "Of course. I'd love to see them." Lily Rose reached out and patted Alison's hand. Suddenly, Alison appeared vulnerable and younger, despite her tough, unyielding exterior. *I can't believe I just said all that to a mobster's daughter. Will they string me up by my fingers?*

Alison stared at her, expressionless, then asked, "Are you off next Monday?"

Chapter XXXII

Cheng, Hu Fat and Li —Partners in Crime?

Cheng was sitting in his office, eyes squinting at the computer screen, when Mingyu walked in. "I have a customer interested in sapphires. Do you still have that oval?" Mingyu inquired.

His father looked up. "No. I sold it."

"That was quick. To whom?"

"A Japanese customer. Hu Fat brokered the sale."

"I thought your business with Hu Fat was limited to gold."

"Usually it is. This was a special request. Li returned all the other sapphires, so you'll have to look in Jin's stock or get something yourself." Cheng replied dismissively, eyes back on his computer screen.

Mingyu lingered for a moment, then retreated from his father's office. He stopped by Li's desk. "Do you still have the lot of sapphires the oval came from or did it go back to the dealer?"

"The oval your father just sold? Yes, that lot is still here. I was returning it today."

"Can I see it? I have a customer."

Li handed him the stone parcel.

"Can I see the bill of sale? Who bought the oval?"

"I don't have it. Your father handled it. It was bought by someone named Akiyama, Hu Fat's customer."

"Did it sell through us or my father's company?"

"Your father's. The stones didn't go through our inventory."

"When do you need to return them by?"

"No rush. Whenever you're done is fine. I'll let the supplier know."

"Thank you."

That night, Mingyu called Jin to chat. "Dad is selling stones to Akiyama. Li said they weren't entered into our inventory. Hu Fat brokered the deal. What do you think about that?"

"Not much. Who were the stones from?"

"They were on memo from a company in *Guangzhou*. Feng Gem Company."

"Never heard of them. I wish your father would stick to gold when it comes to Hu Fat. Stones are our business. However, if the client came from Hu Fat, it's just as well we didn't invoice it. Keep your ears and eyes open. I want something incriminating before I confront Cheng."

"Ok."

Mingyu sat back and thought about the implications. If his father did business with shady characters through his gold company that was his business, but jeopardizing the family business and all of their lives and livelihood was inexcusable.

When did his father start thinking off track? And how could Jin be so calm about it? Mingyu felt his own anger rise. He resolved to keep snooping around Li's desk. Tomorrow he would ask what other new stone dealers his father used. Realizing that he couldn't do anything but investigate, he resigned himself to silence. He fully trusted his grandfather's handling of the matter. Some things were out of his control.

Mingyu called Lily Rose and made plans for drinks on Friday after work. Hearing her cheerful voice calmed him instantly. Imagining her proximity made his pants bulge.

Chapter XXXIII

Bars and Company Secrets Don't Mix Well

Late Friday afternoon, Lily Rose was overseeing an event in the hotel's bar, a birthday party for one of Hong Kong's society ladies. Luckily, the spirited group was tucked in a private corner. As Lily Rose traversed the lobby, a substantial flower arrangement blocking her face, she noticed Winnie hurrying into the bar. Winnie's straight black hair was awkwardly curled and she sported a low cut, poppy red dress that made her cleavage ooze over the top like melted marshmallows between graham crackers. Her loud make-up and bold attire hinted at a hot date. *Who is she meeting here?*

The party Lily Rose was tending to was in full swing. The ladies were eating hor d'euves and sipping Happy Hour specials. The mood was festive, but creeping across the border toward tipsy. Lily Rose popped her head in after the first two rounds of drinks, to check on the birthday girl and their struggling server. Keeping an eye out for Winnie, she noticed the Ho's saleslady sitting by herself at a corner table. A folder of papers was neatly stacked in front of her and she was perusing the contents. Lily

Rose hovered on the opposite side of the room, tending her ladies, who were getting louder with each swig. She felt the waiter's pain, a young man, who was clearly overtaxed by the hefty influx of mature female hormones. Lily Rose needed to take control.

"How is everything, ladies? Can we get you any more appetizers?"

"We'll have another round of drinks before you bring the birthday cake," one lady voiced.

"And water," another quipped.

"And some napkins," a third added.

"We need fresh plates, too." said the birthday girl.

"Of course. Your server will take the drink orders. I'll be back with the rest." She winked at the waiter and caught his thankful look. Hiding behind the stack of plates and napkins piled high, she watched a vaguely familiar man approach Winnie. He was Chinese, chubby and had a scar on the left side of his face. His hair was longish, straggly even, and he wore black pants with a black windbreaker decorated with a prominent gold dragon emblem. Around his neck were numerous weighty gold necklaces and he wore earrings. It dawned on Lily Rose that she had seen him at Alison Wu's wedding. From the corner of her eye, she saw Winnie hand the man some papers. He browsed through them. When the waiter came he waved him away. Few words were exchanged. By the time Lily Rose had distributed all the plates and napkins, the man and the papers had disappeared. Winnie remained alone with her fancy drink. *Wow. She sure got dolled up for nothing.*

When Lily Rose had her party in a complacent lull, she hurried to the kitchen to check on the cake and champagne. She doublechecked the name on the pink frosting and made sure the champagne glasses were filled with iced strawberries, as requested. When she returned with the cake, Winnie was still there, her curled head slanted down over her phone. She was texting. While the rowdy women toasted the birthday girl and attacked the pre-sliced pink monstrosity, Lily Rose went to freshen up for her date. She was meeting Mingyu at their favorite roof garden bar, *Ce La Vie*. She splashed some water on her flushed face and undid her knotted bun, running her fingers through her hair. Pulling out her make-up bag, she freshened up her eye contours and lips. A spritz of *Allure* made her come alive again. Long, humid, demanding days could make any princess feel like a crashing kite.

Before leaving to meet Mingyu, she peeked into the bar. The waiter had brought the bill and the ladies were loudly discussing payment arrangements. Across the room at Winnie's table there were two empty glasses, but Winnie was gone. Lily Rose turned to leave when she saw Winnie and Cheng enter a hotel elevator. She back-stepped behind a column until the elevator doors closed, then, walked over to see which floor the elevator was stopping at. It was a floor with hotel rooms only. Passing by registration, she asked, "Has Cheng Ho checked in yet?"

"I have no one registered by that name," the girl at the desk answered after checking the hotel's guest list.

"Thank you." *Interesting. What's happening here?*

Hurrying to meet Mingyu, she wrestled with whether she should share what she saw. Should she ask him for Winnie's last name so she could check the registry again? When she spotted his happy face, she decided to keep the information filed away. Why ruin their night. His father's status was single and if he wanted to fraternize with the paid help, that was his business.

Chapter XXXIV

Summer Bliss Upended

In mid-June, Lily Rose met Alison for tea to see Alison's fashion design portfolio. Not knowing what to expect, she was surprised at the portfolio's content. The drawings were beautifully executed and included dresses of all styles and colors. Alison definitely had a dramatic flair for design in Lily Rose's lay opinion. "These drawings are amazing. Have you shown them to anyone in the industry?"

Alison smiled shyly. "No, I haven't shown them to anyone."

Lily Rose encouraged her friend. "You absolutely need to do something with this talent. It would be a shame to waste it. Honestly, If you want to be taken seriously and be viewed as a legitimate fashion force, you have to have physical samples of your designs. Get them sewn in China. Most of New York does."

"I've considered it. When I worked in fashion stores, I always thought about how I would improve the dresses I sold. Sometimes a small change of draping or a well-placed detail can make all the difference." She pointed to a dress cinched at the waist. "Like here."

"I see what you mean and I agree. I think you should make a few models and see where it takes you. Show them around at a trade show."

Alison nodded thoughtfully. "One of my teachers said the same, but my father always pushed business principles."

"Business knowledge is key for selling and marketing any product. If you have talent and business knowledge it's a win win. Try to make your beautiful illustrations come to life, Alison."

Inspired by Lily Rose's encouragement, Alison got to work. Over the summer months, she assembled five well-designed shift dresses. Three more samples were works-in-progress. Her goal was to produce a dozen and call it her first sample line. As it turned out, Alison was a force of nature when it came to the things she loved and fashion was her passion. Her husband Chen, less and less.

Lily Rose spent July and August in a lover's cocoon. The events office was slow despite the hotel being busy, so she and Mingyu spent wonderful, playful weekends at Stanley beach, at Jin's for Sunday brunch and gardening and at Disney with Mickey. They also managed to travel in between major tropical cyclones, spending romance-fueled weekends in Taiwan, frolicking on Fulong Beach and in Macao for a taste of decadent nightlife.

Lily Rose sent her mother lots of pictures and in return received shots of the Sag Harbor cottage. While Lily Rose missed her Long Island beach house, she still wasn't sure she could stand being there without Marina. Her heart wasn't ready. *Will it ever be? Would Mingyu visit?*

On the last weekend in August, summer bliss ended along with the height of typhoon season. While they had escaped damage from Tropical Depression Mun, Lily Rose had no idea what would hit her next.

An idyllic, peaceful Sunday morning was shattered by frantic banging on her apartment door. Mingyu had just left for dim sum at Jin's without her. She had stepped out of the shower and was leisurely sipping coffee wrapped in a floral waffle weave robe deciding what to do with her free day. Canvasing the peep hole first, she opened the door to a distraught Alison Wu. Lily Rose checked the hallway both ways, before closing the door behind her frazzled friend who flew in past her like a blue jay spotting a dangling gold chain.

Lily Rose caught sight of Alison's contorted face as she whizzed by. "What's wrong?"

"Chen destroyed my samples," Alison wailed as she threw herself on Lily Rose's couch, wiping away streaming tears with her sleeve. "Last night Chen came home angry and drunk. He wanted to pick a fight, so he destroyed my beautiful samples, tore them apart. I hate him. I worked so hard on perfecting them. All summer I've been working," she moaned.

"Wait. All five? But you still have the patterns, right? Why would he do that? Did you have a fight?"

"He's a mean man. I'm finding that out now. He doesn't want me to have a successful business. He's been fighting with me ever since I mentioned it. He's also mad that I'm not pregnant yet. His nosy family is messing with his head. He thinks I stopped taking the pill and that I'm not fertile."

Lily Rose looked at the shadows on Alison's face. She was wearing large sunglasses and a baseball cap pulled low. "You didn't?"

"No."

"Don't. This does not sound like a healthy relationship or a good environment for a baby. Are you sure you want a child with someone who hurts you?"

"I don't."

"Good, because things will only get more complicated. How did he destroy the samples?" Lily Rose was getting steamed, but trying to stay positive.

"He ripped them apart at the seams, yelling at me while destroying all my hard work."

"The seams? That's a good thing. That means they can be reassembled, right?

Alison stopped crying and looked at her thoughtfully. She took her sunglasses off and It was then that Lily Rose noticed the bruising.

"What happened to your face?" She eyed the colorful pattern emerging along Alison's right cheekbone and hairline.

"Chen pushed me away when I tried to stop him from touching my samples. I fell against the kitchen counter."

"Oh my God. Here, let me make you an ice bag." She filled a plastic baggie with ice chips and handed it to Alison who now sat at the counter. Sliding a tissue box in her direction, Lily Rose asked, "Would you like some coffee? I just brewed it. Or maybe a glass of wine to calm down?"

Ouch, ouch, tea please." she winced as she held the ice pack against her swelling cheek, clearly in pain.

"How did you find my apartment?" Lily Rose asked, curiosity mounting.

"I knew you lived at the Arch. I asked around. People know you. What do I do now?"

Lily Rose's thoughts wandered. *Who in the building would know where I live? The Arch is huge with over a thousand units.* She handed Alison a teacup, "Has he ever pushed you before?"

Alison nodded. "He gets mad over nothing. Later he's sorry."

"Alison, that's abuse. You don't deserve that. No one does. My God, you are half his size! And you haven't even been married for six months! This does not bode well for the future. Does your father know?"

"I haven't told anyone and no one has seen my bruises. I cover them up. I don't think my father would intervene. He wasn't kind to my mother. That's why she left."

"Where did she go?"

"To England. She left with her entire family. They've sent me pictures from different places, but I delete them right after I get them to protect her. If my mother had stayed in Hong Kong, my father would have forced her to come home. He sent someone after her, but she hid herself well. His guys couldn't find her. He gave up."

"So, he wouldn't support your asking for a divorce?"

"No chance."

"Shit. Listen. Chen is gone a lot, right? Next time he's out, get a lock and hide all your design materials in a closet he doesn't check, or better yet, store it in a work space somewhere outside the apartment. Pay cash for it. Are you sure your dad won't intervene? I would try that first. Your face looks convincing. He has to believe you. No father wants to see his daughter hurt."

Alison stopped sniffling. "I don't know. Maybe."

"Try it. You have nothing to lose and everything to gain. Chen works for your father. He won't want to be on Carson's bad side. Besides, after losing your mother, your father might not want to take the risk of losing you too. Play all your cards right."

Alison nodded thoughtfully. "My father might decide to do the opposite and keep a closer watch on me. He has the manpower. Until now I've always had a good amount of freedom, but Chen might convince him otherwise."

"Blood lines rule and I'm sure your father has better uses for his manpower than to have them traipsing after you. Talk to your dad. Today--while you still have a terrible bruise to show."

"Ok." Alison grabbed a few more tissues and dried her tears. "Chen was asleep when I left. I can go to my father's place now and still be back when he wakes up. He'll have a massive hangover. I never should have married him," she sighed. "It was a mistake, a big mistake."

"Were there any signs of his temper before you got married?"

"No. I didn't know him that well and I didn't see the true Chen until the honeymoon was over."

"Sorry to hear that, but it's not too late to fix it and start over. Just don't get pregnant! You can probably even get the marriage annulled. Listen, let me get a few pictures of this side of your face. As evidence should you need it later."

"Ok, but do it on your phone. Honestly, it's unlikely I'll ever use them."

"You won't speak to the authorities?"

Alison laughed. "No. They wouldn't help me, Carson Wu's daughter."

When Alison left, Lily Rose counted her blessings. If it had been one of her friends in New York, she would have marched her to a police station, but she wanted no part of scary Carson Wu, a leader of the 14K triads.

The fact that she had become friends with Alison had been a strange twist of fate. They bonded over common interests-- fashion and travel. Lily Rose also sensed Alison didn't have many real friends. She seemed lost in the wrong world, a world she was born into but didn't necessarily belong in.

Mingyu had warned her not to get too friendly with Wu's daughter. She remembered his exact words, "Keep those people at arm's length. You don't know what they're capable of. They're unpredictable. You don't understand, Lily Rose. They're dangerous." She had agreed with him, but in her heart, she knew that Alison was different. Alison needed a friend. Now her friend could potentially cause the first ripple in her otherwise smooth relationship with Mingyu. Would he be disappointed she didn't listen to him? Should she even tell him? She decided she couldn't turn her back on Alison Wu.

Chapter XXXV

September Crisis

When Mingyu came over Sunday night, he took one look at her and asked, "What's wrong?"

"Nothing," she answered turning her back to him as she stirred the contents of a pot on the stove. His intent gaze said he didn't believe her but he didn't push. They made small talk over dinner. Cleaning up later, he asked again. "Are you sure nothing is bothering you? I'm sensing something is wrong."

Still upset, she shared what had transpired. Keeping frightening secrets with no support system in place was difficult as is, but keeping secrets from the one person she trusted, felt wrong. Once she started, she couldn't stop until every detail had been spilled. She pulled out her phone and showed him the picture of Alison's bruise. "Her arm was bruised too. I couldn't turn her away. What kind of friend would I be?"

"Oh no. I wish you had come with me today. Don't give any more advice, Lily Rose. It could backfire in ways you can't foresee or imagine. Let's hope Alison doesn't disclose what you said to her people." Mingyu gave her a concerned look.

"I doubt it. I wish I had come to Jin's as well, but I wanted to give you two some quality alone time."

He wrapped his arms around her. "I know and I appreciate it. We had some important business to discuss. Lily Rose, this friendship with Alison concerns me, because you don't know if what you say to her stays confidential. Let this blow over and allow her to work out her own problems. No doubt, you gave her good advice. Now, let's see if she listens. In her world, they handle things their own way. The police don't get called."

"Yes, I gathered that."

Pleased that she could share her actions without incurring his displeasure, she burrowed into Mingyu's arms. His care and understanding felt good. She needed his support. Alison's problems had rattled her for sure.

The following week at work, Lily Rose was exceptionally busy, but her mind kept drifting back to Alison Wu. By Friday morning she still had not heard a peep from her friend and she was truly getting worried, so midday, thinking Chen would be out, she texted Alison.

How are you? Did you see your Dad? Been really busy with work this week, but thinking of you. Hope you're ok.

At lunchtime when she checked her phone, she had a reply.

Can you meet me for tea tomorrow?
No. I'm working. I can meet you on Monday. I'm off then.

Monday at noon? Chee Kee for lunch?
Yes. See you then. Stay safe.

On Monday, Lily Rose got to Chee Kee's first. She ordered green tea with honey and waited nervously. Alison arrived minutes later. What a difference a week made. "Hi. Your bruises are almost gone. You're back to being beautiful."

This solicited a faint smile. "Hi. The outside ones. Make-up helps." Alison sat down. "Let's order. I'm starving. I just had an intense work-out." She squinted, sweeping the restaurant, then flagged the waitress.

Lily Rose wondered what kind of work-out, but decided not to go off topic. *Better to listen.*

They put in their orders and waited for the waitress to leave. Alison got straight to the point. "When I left you on Sunday I went straight to my father's place. I showed him my bruises and told him everything. He was angry and promised to speak to Chen about not touching me. He did the next day. He told Chen if he ever saw me bruised like that again, he would give him a reminder he wouldn't forget. I'll spare you his exact words about missing digits."

Lily Rose shuddered. *Good. I have an idea.*

Alison looked around the restaurant, then continued. "He also looked at all my designs. I had them on my phone. He was surprised at what I've accomplished. He had no idea I was serious about making my fashion sketches come to life. He said he would back my business if I can get orders."

"That's great news."

Alison nodded, "That part worked out well, so thanks for pushing me to speak with him. My father is a business man, so if there is money to be made, he's interested."

"Ok. How involved would your father be, if he backed your business? Would he just put up the money like a silent partner or would he be hands on?"

"I'm not sure. I may need his support to start. The bad news is, my father was against divorce. He paid a fortune for the wedding and he doesn't want to lose Chen as a business associate. They have an understanding and unfortunately, I'm part of it now. He wants us to work it out. In China a traditional no-fault divorce is only possible if the husband agrees and writes an affirmation, giving his consent. Chen won't let me go. His pride wouldn't allow it. He would be too embarrassed if his wife left him. In his mind, he owns me. My father thinks the same way. He didn't let my mother go either. She had to flee with the help of her family when he wasn't looking."

"Well, two out of three problems are solved. That's a start. At least you can follow your fashion dream without being beaten up over it, but what are you going to do about Chen? You can't go through life being someone's property or punching bag. That's crazy."

"I don't have a choice. I'm stuck with him." Alison shrugged, her shoulders slumping.

"Stay focused on your business. Don't get pregnant. Have faith. You will get out of this bad union one way or another."

"Alive?"

Lily Rose felt a chill. "Of course, alive. What does Chen do for your father? Maybe their business relationship will change in the future. Does your father need him?"

"I can't talk about that. For your protection, it's better you don't know."

"Ok. Thanks for looking out for me. I'm only concerned about you." Lily Rose shivered as dark thoughts crossed her mind. She didn't want to find out what Carson Wu might do if she knew too much about his business.

Alison sighed deeply. "My life is complicated. Honestly, I wish I had your life, Lily Rose.

Chapter XXXVI

Hu Fat Sweats the Gold

Monday, after the store closed and all employees left, Jin and Cheng scheduled an uncomfortable, but long overdue business meeting. Mingyu knew what was on the agenda. Jin insisted he not be present.

"The less involved you are, the better. I need to speak to your father one on one. I'll call you after the meeting."

Mingyu left the office with a heavy heart and leaden steps. The worry for his grandfather, in his seventies and still putting in full days, was real. Exiting the subway, he picked up dinner on his way home. Mingyu felt like he was seated on a cactus, as he waited for Jin's call. When Lily Rose called, he let the call go to voicemail. He couldn't focus on anything but his family right now.

The night before, a very upset Huan had contacted Jin. A customs inspector in Yokohama discovered disguised gold bars in an electronics shipment, originating in Hong Kong. The gold had slipped through HKSAR customs, (Hong Kong Special Administrative Region) but was discovered by a customs official in Yokohama. Gold bars weren't accounted for on Huan's cargo ship and he was livid that someone dared to smuggle the precious metal without his knowledge. Huan ran a clean business.

The electronics were sent by Hu Fat and Cheng's client, a man named Keiko Akiyama, but the shipment was filed under a Japanese company name, GD Import/Export llc. Mr.Souta was the designated recipient. Allegedly, the company dealt in electronic equipment and software. Huan questioned Jin about the company's legitimacy.

"Do you know this company? Is Akiyama a client of yours?" Huan asked.

"No, he's not." Jin assured him. "I don't know who he is," he lied.

Apparently, Souta was held for questioning and had lawyered up immediately. Huan was doing his own investigation following a limited paper trail but not with too much luck. The papers looked to be in order.

"Do you think I need to hire a lawyer?" Huan asked.

"Not yet. Just cooperate with the authorities for now, but have a lawyer at hand, should you need him later."

Jin knew the paperwork for the gold bars would eventually be traced back to Hu Fat and Cheng's gold companies. He didn't clue Huan in on what his private eye, Chase, had uncovered, weeks earlier. He needed time to confront his son with Chase's damaging report, which had been sitting in his desk at home collecting dust. He wished he hadn't procrastinated so long. These things did not fix themselves. Jin guessed that the certificates and the smuggled gold was meant to be held in a safe in Hong Kong, as a financial investment for the Japanese company, a common practice.

Cheng's company IGI (International Gold Investments) and Hu Fat's, Hu Feng Gold Bullion Corp specialized in this type of business. The investigators would soon discover that Akiyama's safe was empty and a meaningless front for the smuggling operation. Jin was angry with himself for sitting on the explosive report. He had dreaded the confrontation with his son, but now he intended to give Cheng a long overdue tongue lashing. The information Chase had furnished over the past few months had confirmed his mounting suspicion.

"I need to talk to you, Cheng. Sit down. I got a very disturbing call from Huan last night. Disguised gold bars were found in an electronic shipment on his ship. They were sent by your client, Keiko Akiyama." Jin eyed his son for a reaction.

"He's not my client. He's Hu Fat's. So?" Cheng replied, clearly sitting on eggshells.

"You sold Akiyama an oval sapphire. That makes him your client too. I know you and Hu Fat have been selling him gold for investment purposes and that you arranged for shipping through Huan. The electronics are traced back to a 14K triad operation. That means the triads are working with the Yakuza in Yokohama. What in the world were you thinking?"

"I sold Akiyama gold. Yes. He asked for a shipping recommendation for his electronics business and I wanted to give Huan the business. What's wrong with that?"

"Really? That's your story?" Jin shoved Chase's report across his desk. "Based on my findings, you better get yourself a criminal lawyer really fast."

Cheng started reading and blanched. "How dare you investigate me."

"How dare you endanger our family business. Endanger my hard-earned reputation. Humiliate your son. Embarrass your family. I warned you months ago about doing business with Hu Fat. You lie with dogs, you'll get fleas. You will empty your desk immediately. Tonight. Take all your IGI files with you and work from your home office. I no longer want you associated with or working from my store. Is that clear?"

"You're kicking me out? I didn't do anything wrong. You can't do that." Cheng sniped.

"Yes, I can. This is still my business. Go pack up and leave. This will end poorly for you, if our name is associated with your illicit business practices. You brought shame on your family."

Cheng rose silently and went to his office. Jin followed to make sure he was packing up. "I strongly suggest you keep me up to date. I don't want to get my information from the news."

"Ok, but I'll be back." Cheng barked angrily.

"We shall see about that."

Jin gave his son a few more instructions and left him to pack. He stayed in his office until Cheng and his belongings were loaded in Cheng's car and gone.

Jin knew from his conversation with Huan that Huan would be cooperating with investigators. For the moment, Huan was clueless, but he wouldn't be for much longer. If he suspected Cheng's active part in this fiasco, it would create a rift in their tightly knit family and Jin was determined to not let that happen. He was seething at his son, cursing his stubborn streak and he felt bad for his son-in-law, who didn't deserve this headache. He also was worried about the effect this would have on Mingyu. Before things snowballed any further, he needed to do damage control. He hoped it wasn't too late.

Mingyu felt bad for his Uncle Huan and he was furious with his father. *What was he thinking? Why would he do this to us?*

When the call from Jin finally came, late Monday night, it was worse than he expected. "Your father will be hiring a criminal lawyer first thing tomorrow morning. I think I finally scared him enough to realize what a bad position he put himself in. We might be able to do some damage control, but I have no idea how we can minimize your father's ill-advised connection to Hu Fat. That in itself looks bad …very bad. I can only imagine what Hu Fat's client list looks like. Your father made a bad business choice and I want to distance our company as much as possible."

"What will happen now?" Mingyu held his breath and closed his eyes as he waited for a reply.

"First, I would like to keep our name out of the papers. I instructed Cheng to only use his gold company's name. Those transactions have nothing to do with our store. I told him to confirm that he ran his company separately from ours, out of his apartment office, which is partially true. I don't want him here in our company office until this is settled. He took his laptop and files with him last night. I made him clean out his desk. Tomorrow morning, I want to make sure nothing was forgotten."

"Ok. Should I come in early?" Mingyu offered.

"Yes. Even though I don't want you involved, I'll need your help. Let's do this search before the store opens. Meet me at 7am. We'll talk more then. I'm tired now. Good night, Mingyu. So sorry."

At 6:45am Mingyu entered the rear entrance of the store and found his grandfather busy in Cheng's office. Tea was brewed and hot Chinese milk bread rolls were set on a silver tray. "Morning. I found a few papers that need to disappear. I'm trying to decide if I should get them to Cheng or shred them."

"I can take them over to his apartment, later today," Mingyu offered.

"Absolutely not. You won't be dropping any incriminating papers. You are not to visit your father until this is handled. Neither will I. Maybe we should just shred them. I called Michael Wong last night. I have a meeting with him today."

"Will Dad be using him?"

"No. Your father needs to get his own lawyer, a good litigator. I'm keeping our business and my company lawyer completely separate."

"Makes sense. What should I do now?'

"Shred what I hand you and don't look at any of it. Shred it face down."

"Ok." Mingyu got to work, his mind racing. He couldn't control his trembling fingers as he fed the first few sheets into the machine's greedy jaw.

That same morning, Hu Fat's office was swarming with police investigators. Cheng called Jin to inform him of the ambush. He had received a heads-up text. Jin and Mingyu tried to focus on business as usual, but there was an impending doom permeating the air. By lunchtime, men in dark suits were asking for Cheng's whereabouts in the store. Jin handled it with grace, directing them to Cheng's apartment on Caine Road.

The store staff was speaking in hushed tones, wondering what was going on. Mingyu knew it was eating at Jin's insides. His grandfather loved his business, identified with it and ran it with great pride ever since his father died. It killed him that his own son would smudge their good name and unblemished business record. Mingyu's stomach remained in knots the remainder of the week as he silently prayed and went about his work. He kept a watchful eye over Jin and pampered him whenever he could.

They didn't talk about Cheng in the office, reserving all updates for private dinners after work. For once, Li's silence was greatly appreciated. Mingyu suspected he had an inkling of what was going on. Mingyu skipped all of his work outs and texts from friends to be at Jin's side. Even Lily Rose's calls continued to go to voicemail. The tension he felt was taking a toll as if his cozy bed had been short-sheeted and his lover left. *What is happening to my family?*

Chapter XXXVII

Paradise Lost?

Lily Rose was perplexed. Mingyu hadn't returned her phone calls or texts all week. Was something wrong? She decided to give him some space. Surely, he would reach out soon. Was he disappointed she didn't listen to him in regard to Alison? There was no news from Alison either. Lily Rose concentrated her efforts on work and gave her apartment a thorough cleaning. Following work one day, she treated herself to a small shopping spree. A little shopping therapy to feel better. She picked up a new summer dress, a fresh scent and another pair of canvas sneakers in snow white.

On a quiet Thursday in the office, Lily Rose searched Chen Jie's website. Her watercolor tattoos were absolutely stunning. Scrolling through all the images, she decided to take the plunge. Together with David, she discussed her options.

"Well if you like flowers, your name provides two beautiful possibilities. You can't go wrong with a lily or a rose. What colors would you choose?" David turned away from the screen to look at her.

"I like lavender, purples, blues, pinks, greens, peach. Look at this lotus leaf... ... and the birds. Or this butterfly—absolutely amazing!" She scrolled through all the images. "But, I think I like flowers best."

"Print the images you prefer and cut them out. You can hold them in place and decide. Where are you putting this tattoo? Or should I not ask?" His dancing eyebrows made Lily Rose laugh.

"I don't know. Definitely not on my arms or legs. Maybe my shoulder? Or side? Or maybe at the bikini line? Somewhere I can cover it up if I don't want it to show."

"Like the 14K triads."

"Funny, David." She rolled her eyes. "I think my mom will completely freak out if she sees a tattoo on me."

"Mine would too," David shared. "I would be disowned and cast out like common garbage."

Lam's office door opened and they scattered like moths on a screen. Lily Rose immediately closed *Chen Jie's* site on her computer and shuffled some papers.

"I just booked a party. A fiftieth birthday. Check your emails for the details. I'm going to lunch now." Lam scooted past them and out the door, not waiting for a reply.

David looked at his watch. "Two thirty. I thought he already had lunch. Where's he been all morning? He spent a half hour tops in his office today."

Lily Rose shrugged.

"He books one party and the man is exhausted. Let's bet what time he returns from lunch. I say four." David raised an eyebrow. "You?"

"I say not at all."

David laughed. Keeping tabs on Lam was virtually impossible. The man flitted around the hotel like a bee during pollination season.

By Friday morning, Lily Rose still hadn't heard from Mingyu. She was on an emotional roller coaster, but didn't want to leave another message. When David asked her to dinner the following night, she agreed. There was no sense in sitting at home waiting and wondering. They left work together and settled in a trendy bar/restaurant famous for its drinks. Red Sugar in the *Kerry Hotel* had a beautiful outdoor bar overlooking the harbor and an enticing selection of tasty dim sum bites.

"Cheers. So… how do you like life here so far? You've hit the half way mark, you know."

"I have, haven't I? Time flew by, so I guess I'm having fun. I'm enjoying work too….no regrets." Lily Rose smiled.

"Good. What are you going to do when your year is up? Stay or go back?"

"I don't know that I have a choice. I think An and I are supposed to switch back. Have you heard from her?"

"No way. An and I were not the best of friends." David made a face.

"Really? Why? You never told me. What was she like?" Lily Rose perked up. This was news to her. David, the diplomatic professional, had never shared this information before.

"She was very ….goal oriented, but in an annoying way. She always tried to make me look like the slacker in front of Lam." David took a sip of his fruity cocktail. "You know Lam. He does the bare minimum and tends to delegate. He liked the fact that An was competent, overzealous really. She pretty much handled his workload and treated me like an assistant even though we both had the same title."

"You're hardly a slacker, David."

"Thanks. I think that as much as Lam liked An's work ethic, he was also a little nervous about her intentions. She was gunning for his job."

"Well, then she met her match in New York. There's no way she's outgunning Margo. My old boss was the best at what she did. I learned a lot from her. She also knows how to put people in their place with a brilliant smile on her face. If An wants to move up in the ranks, it won't be to Margo's post unless Margo leaves."

"You're pretty competent yourself. You must have been paying attention back in New York. And guess what, I'm pretty certain Lam likes you better than An. If you asked, I bet he would let you stay."

"You think? I suppose I have a few months to think about it. I'm not sure what my plans are yet."

"Well for whatever it's worth—I hope you decide to stay." He patted her hand. "I like working with you."

"Thanks, David. The feeling is mutual."

Over the weekend, Lily Rose emailed An.

Hey An,

Haven't heard from you in a while. How are things in New York? Is Margo still treating you well? My assistant working out? I'm taking good care of your apartment and I'm enjoying the building's amenities whenever I can. I've used the pool and beat one or two neighbors in table tennis. Lost big-time playing pool though. Your neighbor in 7G says hello. She always asks about you.

David sends his regards. We had drinks after work yesterday at Red Sugar. Have you been?

Take care,

Lily Rose

Late Sunday afternoon, Mingyu finally called. Lily Rose was elated and relieved to hear his voice, but she was determined not to show it. She played it super cool. She couldn't help but notice how tired he sounded. "Hi, busy week?"

"Very. It was actually more stressful than busy. We had some business problems to deal with, but I think we have it under control now. Sorry I didn't call. My mind was occupied."

"What kind of problems?"

"It's complicated and I need a mental break from it."

"Want to tell me over dinner? "I'm making crab cakes and grilled veggies."

"Yes, to dinner, but no to talking about work. I'd rather forget my week happened."

"That bad huh? Fine with me. We can discuss our next outing. That's a good stress reliever. I hear sex works wonders too. See you around seven?" *I wonder if this has something to do with his father and Winnie?*

Mingyu laughed. "Sure, I like your remedies. I'll bring the wine and dessert."

"Great. See you later."

When she hung up, Lily Rose texted Alison.

Hi. You ok? Can we see Chen Jie on Monday? I'm off and I'm ready. The reply came quickly and it surprised Lily Rose. She had not noticed this information on the artist's website.

Chen Jie's business is located in Beijing. We'll have to plan a girls trip.

Chapter XXXVIII

Girls will be Girls

"How do you feel about aerial yoga?" Alison asked over Monday lunch, her previous problems on the back burner. Alison's elaborately embroidered, cropped ivory top and mid-rise jeans allowed her magnificent floral tattoos to be visible. Lily Rose couldn't help but admire them from her angle across the table. Her friend's shiny, dark hair, was held neatly in place by a mustard-yellow scarf around her head with an artfully tied knot. The scarf matched her new mustard *Converse* canvas sneakers. Lily Rose studied Alison's dangling gold earrings and mixed gold and jade bangle bracelets. She looked like a poster girl for hip street fashion.

"I've never tried it. I only did hatha yoga on a mat in New York. Hey, Did you get new sneakers? Those are nice."

"Same as yours. Different color. Do you want to try the yoga? I can reserve us a spot for Saturday morning. It's fun."

"Sure. I'll try it. So, tell me what to expect at *Chen Jie's.*"

"It's nothing to worry about. She's very professional. You can relax while she works. Figure on a couple of hours. What did you decide on?"

"A flower."

"Like mine?"

"Similar. Same flower but different colors and style. I'll surprise you."

"When can you go?"

"I can tack a personal day onto a weekend if you can make the appointment for me. Do you want to come? You don't have to."

"Of course, I'll come. I promised to take you. We have to plan it when Chen's traveling."

"Fun! A girl's trip! You look at Chen's schedule and I'll check my work schedule and hopefully we'll have an overlap."

"Ok. I'm going for a *cheongsam* fitting at Master Kan's store this afternoon. It's in the Mei Wah Sheug Wan shopping center. You should join me. It's an education in traditional Chinese couture." Alison laughed. "You won't believe his selection of fabrics."

"Remind me what exactly a cheongsam is."

"It's a dress that's custom-fitted to your curves. The cheongsam was banned during the cultural revolution. Now it's experiencing a resurgence for dressy occasions. It's really quite sexy." Alison explained.

"Are you getting it for an occasion?"

"Yes. Chen's cousin is getting married in a traditional wedding. I chose a violet satin cheongsam with a pink peony design. I would like your opinion if you have the time."

"Sounds beautiful. Now you have me curious. Yes, I'll come."

"Good. Let's pay and grab a taxi to Queens Road West. I can't be late. A little history--Master Kan's store has been there for three generations. It's an institution in Hong Kong. Even if you buy nothing, it's an experience you shouldn't miss. The fabrics alone are worth the trip, but maybe you'll get one too?"

"Maybe. I could benefit from a revamped sexy style."

Chapter XXXIX

Akiyama and Hu Fat
—Double Trouble

Mingyu and Jin sat in their office with the door shut. It was closed a lot these days as they worked in strained silence. Cheng continued to work from home, mainly with his lawyer. When he called, he grudgingly gave Jin updates, hating to admit to his father how badly he messed up. Today's update covered Hu Fat's status, partially gleaned from the man himself and partially from the press.

Hu Fat's lawyers were working diligently, spinning the usual web of deceit: no knowledge, no evidence of wrongdoing, no witnesses, no case. Meanwhile, the customs inspector in Yokohama who discovered the camouflaged gold bars and reported the smuggling incident was mysteriously brutalized and assassinated in one of the warehouse bathrooms, a single bullet lodged in his skull. Souta, now lawyered up, claimed he was only expecting an electronics shipment. The gold bars were a bonus he wasn't aware of. Were they shipped by accident? Or by someone else who intended to claim them in Japan? It couldn't have been anyone from his honorable organization. He had a clean business record.

Hearing this version of events, Jin coughed politely. "Who does he think he's fooling?"

Cheng ignored his father's response and continued to read from a news report. It stated that perhaps the licensed contacts in Hong Kong needed to be held accountable. The heat was currently on Keiko Akiyama, who bought gold and organized the shipment, but sadly, he was currently missing in action—completely off the grid.

"Off the record--before Akiyama disappeared, he gave Hu Fat a black eye reminder to keep his swollen lips sealed. A few cracked ribs later and a lengthy consultation with his lawyers convinced Hu Fat to do just that. "He knows his services are still needed or he would be a dead man," Cheng told Jin. "Maybe I shouldn't have done business with him," he conceded as an afterthought.

Jin made a disgruntled sound but said nothing. "Grrr…" *At least he is headed in the right direction.*

What Cheng failed to mention was that he also suffered a roughing up from a frightening visit by the *Yakuza*. They wanted to ensure his silence on his knowledge of Hu Fat's business practices with Akiyama. Jin noticed that Cheng's tone was shifting and he took a much more apologetic approach, although, no formal apology was forthcoming. He suspected Cheng was scared; it was apparent in his son's voice, and in his less aggressive demeanor, like when he crashed the family car as a teenager after he snuck out one night. Banking on the moment, Jin listened before he offered his thoughts.

"When this blows over, Hu Fat will continue business as usual. But not with your cooperation. Whatever profits you might have made will be eaten up by lawyers now. I hope you learned a lesson, that is, if you make it out of this dilemma with no jail time. Hu Fat's lawyers are probably covered by Akiyama or the triads, but you, you will pay your own fees. What a genius, you are."

Mingyu was horrified when he heard Jin's end of the conversation. *My father in jail?* He had a hard time stomaching what little Jin exposed him to. Most of the time, Jin and his father spoke in private before or after business hours. Jin then filled him in on the important stuff, on a need to know basis.

When the police investigators came back to question Li in the office, Mingyu broke into a cold sweat. The accompanying forensic suits pulled Li into Cheng's old space and closed the door. When he emerged, Li looked shaken. He didn't utter a word for the rest of the morning, going about his work as usual. After everyone in the workshop left for lunch, Jin pulled him aside. Mingyu listened from his desk, pretending to be busy with answering emails.

"What happened this morning? What did they ask you?" Jin wanted to know.

"They wanted to see transaction records for Cheng's company, whatever I had on my laptop. They copied everything that isn't on the cloud. The transactions for Cheng's company were all legitimate. I didn't do anything wrong. Cheng has all the same information on his computer, which they already have. I share all business transactions with him. I had no idea Keiko Akiyama was smuggling gold into Japan without paying the excise taxes. I thought it was being held in a vault as per the paperwork."

"As did Cheng," Jin lied.

Li nodded respectfully, but didn't look entirely convinced. Mingyu found it hard to read Li's poker face. *He seems so detached. I wonder if it's an act.*

"Thank you for your cooperation, Li. I'm sure Cheng will have this sorted out soon." Jin dismissed him with a reassuring pat on the back, but not before asking to see the transactions himself. They were, after all, on a company laptop he provided.

When they were alone again, Jin turned to Mingyu. "I believe him. He may have suspected something, but he's not complicit. Of that, I'm sure."

"How can you be so sure?" Mingyu quizzed his grandfather.

"I can't. I'm relying solely on my intuition and knowledge of human nature."

"Do you think anyone else here knows anything?" Mingyu shifted uncomfortably in his chair at the thought.

"Possibly, but I have no one in mind. Do you?"
"No, but bad pennies have a way of turning up eventually."

Chapter XL

Sharing Dreaded Secrets

Lily Rose and Mingyu were preparing dinner together at her apartment. Soft music played in the background. Filled wine glasses sat on the counter while the bottle chilled in an ice bucket. The setting sun cast a spell of colorful tinted light on the surrounding walls. Freshly lit candles smoothly transitioned the space from day to dusk. In spite of creating a relaxing setting, Lily Rose sensed the tension emanating from Mingyu whose food prepping efforts were engaging his body but not his mind. He was angrily chopping onions, until he yelped and cursed profusely in Chinese. He accidentally sliced his finger.

"Quick, hold your finger under cold water. I have a first aid kit." She rummaged in a kitchen drawer and pulled out some antibacterial ointment and a band-aid. Gently dabbing and wrapping his finger, she moved him to a counter stool and planted a kiss on his cheek. "Here, sit and have a sip of wine. Put your elbow on the counter and point your finger upward. I'll finish the onions."

Done chopping, she added them to a saucepan, stirring until they appeared translucent. She set the pot aside and turned off the flame. "Are you going to tell me what's really wrong? You've been absent all week and mentally unavailable. I know something is bothering you. Are we ok?"

Mingyu frowned and nodded. "It's work. I'm worried about the mess my father got himself into and the effect it's having on my grandfather."

"I don't mean to pry, but maybe you would feel better talking about it?"

Mingyu shifted uncomfortably. "Someone my father does business with is being investigated. My father had to help fill in some of the blanks. It's an ongoing investigation, but I hope we'll get it straightened out from our end. In the meantime, my grandfather is concerned about his unblemished business record being tarnished and my father is spending a fortune on lawyers."

"What did the business associate allegedly do?"

"It's complicated. He sold gold my father obtained for him to a Japanese business man who may have smuggled it into Japan without paying the necessary taxes. It was shipped on my uncle's fleet without his knowledge and he's very angry."

"Oh, wow. Was the Japanese man arrested?"

"No, he disappeared. His name is Akiyama."

"Keiko Akiyama? I know who that is. He was at Alison Wu's wedding. Wait." Lily Rose went to get the little gift pouch she had found and saved from the wedding and pulled out the inscribed stone. "What does this mean?"

Mingyu studied the Chinese lettering. "'If you pick up a hot coal with the intention to hurt someone, it is you who will get hurt.' It's a Buddhist saying that is often associated with business principles."

"Carson Wu gave this to Akiyama at Alison's wedding. Each guest received a personalized stone. Do you think it was intended as a personal message?" She held up the attached card with Keiko Akiyama's name.

"Carson Wu? Really? It might. He deals in electronics among other things, you know." Mingyu looked surprised for a split second, then his face reset.

"Think there's a connection?" Lily Rose glanced at him sideways as she added mushrooms, sprouts and beef to the onions to make a brown sauce. The rice was cooking itself in the pressure cooker.

Mingyu shrugged. "I don't know. Probably. The 14K triads have the market on illegal businesses."

"You know, I wasn't going to say anything because…. well, it's not my concern, but I saw one of your employees in our hotel bar meeting with a heavy-set Chinese man." Lily Rose described the man with the scar. When Mingyu didn't reply, she continued." I think the woman's name is Winnie. I met her in your store."

"Winnie?" Mingyu's eyebrows shot up. "She's one of our sales people."

"Yes…there's more." Lily Rose hesitated, hoping she was doing the right thing. "After the man left, your father came to meet Winnie. They both took the elevator upstairs."

Mingyu paled. His eyes narrowed and his hands clenched into white knuckled fists. "Damn him."

Chapter XLI

Girls Just Want to Have Fun
—in Beijing

"Hi, Lily Rose. How does your work schedule look for the next two weekends?" As usual, Alison got right to the point, her voice full of anticipation. "Chen is leaving for Japan and he'll be gone for two weeks. I say we finalize our long weekend trip to Beijing."

"Yes! Let me see if I can get an additional day or two. I should be able to squeeze out a long weekend; I've been working crazy hours."

"Let me know as soon as you can. I'll book flights for us and more importantly, Chen Jie."

"I'll try to get back to you by the end of today." Lily Rose disconnected her cell and pondered the offer. She had mixed feelings. *Was it safe to travel with Alison Wu? Would someone be watching them? And what should she tell Mingyu?*

Mingyu was very traditional in his ways. He had warned her about not getting too involved with Alison because of who she was. He probably would try to dissuade her from going on the trip. Perhaps he wouldn't condone or understand her desire for an artistic Chen Jie tattoo. She decided not to share the details of her trip.

A couple weeks later, on a rainy Thursday night, the two girls were seated on a plane. Alison had obtained a coveted appointment with Chen Jie for Monday morning. Until then, they would be tourists. That night they had dinner in the hotel bar, consuming a few celebratory drinks. Excitement permeated the air as they mapped out their weekend.

The following morning, the girls went sight-seeing, taking an architectural tour of the Forbidden City/Imperial palace, a relic from the 13th century *Yuan* Dynasty, and walked around the imperial gardens in Beihai Park. Lily Rose was dazzled by the Buddha statue in the Hall of Enlightenment carved from a single one-and-a-half-meter block of white jade. "Wow, this is incredible." She took pictures from every angle and sent a few to Mingyu and her mother.

"It's from the 12th century," Alison read from the signage.

Lily Rose expressed surprise that Alison had not visited these landmarks during her previous visit to Beijing.

"I was with my dad who was in business meetings the whole time, so I just walked around and went to stores near the hotel. One day, one of my father's guys took me to a few landmarks, but he wasn't very prolific or instructional. I was also younger and not as interested. Then I stumbled upon Chen Jie."

In the evening, the girls splurged on an expensive Beijing Duck dinner and a Kung Fu martial arts show Alison seemed excited about. "That was incredible," Lily Rose gushed afterwards. "Their body control boggles my mind. I could never be that flexible."

"Yes, you could, if you trained long enough. It's mind over matter and relentless discipline. I learned Wing Chun Kung Fu growing up, but later switched to *Wushu* training in high school. My father wanted me to be able to protect myself."

Without thinking, Lily Rose blurted, "That didn't work too well with Chen." *Yikes, why did I say that?*

Alison ignored the unfiltered comment and explained the facts. "Chen does *Xing Yi Quan*. He could easily overpower me."

"Does your father do martial arts too?"

"No. He's more of a street fighter turned businessman. He doesn't have the required level of discipline or patience."

"I see. How does your and Chen's training differ from Shaolin Kung Fu?"

"Well, Wing Chun was invented by a nun who was trained in a Shaolin monastery. That technique uses mainly the upper body. A habit can be cumbersome and restrictive after all. Xing Yi Quan uses the whole body and requires a strong core, skilled footwork and good sensory functions. So does Wushu. It's about flexibility and balance in space. Feel my core," Alison remarked barely cracking a smile.

Lily Rose poked a finger into Alison's middle. A brick. "Wow. One hard body you got there, girl."

Alison laughed. "It takes work, lots of hard work."

"So, do you still practice? Is that what you do in your workouts?" Lily Rose was surprised Alison had never mentioned it before. She assumed Alison took classes at the gym. Martial arts never entered her mind.

"Yes, of course. I train two or three times a week. I love Taijiquan or 'Tai chi as you probably know it, but Wushu Sanda is my favorite. Taolu Wushu too."

"What level are you?

"Second level."

"Cool. You have to teach me some moves." Lily Rose flung herself on the bed, ready to watch. "What makes wushu different from other martial arts like karate?"

Alison smiled benevolently. "I can show you a few moves, but the only way to learn is by experiencing a beginner's class with a master. Wushu is more than movement—Buddhist philosophy is a big part of it. The third and highest level is the spiritual level. I'm working to get there. To answer your question, wushu movements are circular while karate is linear." Alison did a few stances to show the difference.

"I study and train with Collin Chou. Look him up." Alison smiled mischievously.

"Cool. I will. I'm completely in awe." Lily Rose's eyes widened. Alison's body was small, but powerful, like many of the martial arts masters of Kung Fu. Lily Rose had assumed it was Alison's diet. Lying flat, ankles crossed, she paid attention when Alison stripped her t-shirt to put on silk pajamas. "What does the triangle and heart tattoo on your side mean? I never saw that one before." Lily Rose noticed it was placed above the waist, entwined by roses.

"This is a triad tattoo symbolizing the love between child, parent and adopted family."

"Oh." Lily Rose sputtered, stunned. She suddenly realized she had seen many variations of the same tattoo at Alison's wedding. The thought that Alison was branded like that, was simultaneously fascinating and shocking to her, especially when it dawned on her that the adopted family were organized gangsters.

The next day the girls visited Tiananmen Square, the Temple of Heaven, the Lama Temple and the Beijing Temple of Confucius. It was fitting to have a spiritual day after admiring the Shaolin warriors moves the night before. Lily Rose observed Alison's interactions in the temples. Alison bowed slightly before entering and dipped her hands in water. She then lit incense which each temple provided. She appeared introspective, an inner calm encircling her soul. *It must be her wushu training that makes her different than her father.*

After a colorful night in a nearby restaurant and bar, they chose the Great Wall over the Summer Palace, for their next day excursion. When Lily Rose and Alison arrived, after an hour and a half bus trip out of the city, they took the cable car up to the wall. The ride offered intoxicating views, but the final steep climb to the top nearly did her in. Alison, soldiered on, appearing fresh as a daisy with a morning dew sheen. Lily Rose, in comparison, was a hot, sweaty, panting mess ready to collapse in a hyperventilating heap. The steady, upward path, hot weather and uneven steps proved to be extremely challenging. She began to understand why the great wall was also a burial place. The five-minute toboggan run down the hill was a relaxing 1.6 kilometre thrill and a welcome cool down that ended way to fast.

Lily Rose realized they didn't have nearly enough time to see everything Beijing had to offer and it frustrated her. She knew she wouldn't make it back here. She had received a wonderful sampling of China's rich cultural past and it fascinated her. Taking lots of pictures, she had every intention of sharing them with her mother and close friends in New York, but the one person she would have loved to share her experience with the most was her grandmother. It hurt deeply that she couldn't send Marina her pictures.

That night, back in the hotel's vicinity, the two women hit the Hutong bars, the true hidden gems in Beijing that Mao couldn't destroy. Humans need a release after all and what better outlet is there than a little fun? In true Chinese fashion, the girls brought their take-out dinners to the first bar to refuel after a long day. Lily Rose noticed that Alison never drank more than a few sips of her liquor. Jumping from one bar to the next in the narrow streets, they were soon trailed by two annoying, young men. Lily Rose could sense Alison stiffen. When one of the men took her arm, Alison elbowed him in the solar plexus, causing him to double over. She kicked his counterpart with lightning speed, slamming him against a concrete wall. In a steely voice she snarled a warning. The men immediately backed away, disappearing into the alley's crevices. Lily Rose's jaw slacked in surprise as she cowered behind a huge red lantern. Alison certainly knew how to take care of herself.

Their last day in Beijing, they went to see Chen Jie, the crowning reason for their special weekend. Armed with flower print samples, Lily Rose was excited despite nerves kicking in, but

Alison's calming approach soon had her heart back in a normal rhythm. Alison assured her, "Stop worrying. Take a deep meditative breath and exhale until you have no more air left. Do it three times, like this." Alison demonstrated and encouraged Lily Rose to follow suit. "She's an incredibly gifted artist. I promise, she won't let you leave unhappy. It will be worth any discomfort."

A couple hours and a lot of soft groans later, the tattoo was done and Lily Rose was freed from any prolonged torture. "How did you manage to survive the tattoos on your sides? The skin there is so sensitive. I would have aborted and ended up with a stemless flower. I must be a total wimp," Lily Rose complained.

Alison merely laughed.

The final result yielded a beautiful lavender-blue rose accented with a wide range of pink and violet bleeding edges. The rose was prominently centered on Lily Rose's right shoulder blade. "I love it. It will be amazing once the redness and swelling subside," Alison promised. "I knew you would be happy. Soon you'll forget the pain."

"I doubt it. I have an elephant's memory when it comes to pain."

Over a delicious lunch of chive pancakes and steamed vegetable dumplings, the girls decided to spend the afternoon in the Dashanzi Art District/798 Art Zone. "You'll like it. It's a unique community of industrial complexes and warehouses reinvented as artists' quarters." Alison pulled up an image of the area on her phone. Lily Rose agreed. "Looks intriguing."

As they walked and shopped around the art galleries and stores, Alison's phone rang. Looking at the screen, her face transitioned from sunshine to a thundercloud. A brief conversation in Cantonese followed and the cloud darkened. When Alison disconnected the call, a string of noisy texts bombarded her and what had started as a tranquil day ended with a storm. The carefree spell of their girls' weekend had been breached.

"Everything ok?"

"Chen is home early. I think he had someone watching me. He's upset I'm not there."

"Oh no," Lily Rose gasped. "I thought it was acceptable for you to travel when he was gone. Will you be ok going home?" *Should I invite her to my place? Dare I?*

"I'll manage," Alison clipped. Every muscle in Alison's jaw visibly tightened.

Looking at her friend's expression, Lily Rose wasn't so sure. For the remainder of the day, Alison retreated into a shell, disengaging entirely. When they returned to the hotel Lily Rose washed with antibacterial soap, applied a soothing ointment to her wound and refreshed her bandage for the trip home. This would have to be repeated two or three times a day for the next two weeks. Her shoulder was raw, but she was ecstatic with the result. As they headed to the airport that afternoon, she vowed Chen Jie's magnificent rose would be her only body art. Getting tattoos bloody hurt. She couldn't help but wonder what Mingyu would think about her exquisite body art.

Chapter XLII

Greetings from the 14K Triads

Her first day back at work, Lily Rose was swamped. Lam wasted no time dropping a few new time-sensitive projects in their midst, so she and David worked diligently all morning. They had lunch at their desks and chatted briefly about the weekend, keeping their voices low so Lam wouldn't hear.

David eyed her shoulder. "When does the patch come off?"

She had discarded her sweater, revealing a floral sleeveless blouse. Her bandage peeked out at the edges. "Patience Mister. You'll be the first to see it, since you so kindly helped me narrow down the choices."

"Thanks. It's only fair. I have to look at it five days a week, occasionally six."

"Really? That's your reason? Not, Lily Rose, let me share in the beauty of your painted body?" Well, here's a hint. I hope you like looking at flowers."

"Hmm. Lily or rose? I'm guessing rose." He mock pondered the situation, tapping his forefinger on his lips, making her laugh.

"Guess you'll have to deal with the suspense a little longer. So sorry."

David bristled," Witchy woman."

Tired, at the end of a long day, Lily Rose picked up food on her way home. Enjoying the breezy evening air as she walked to her building, she jumped with fright when Alison's husband, Chen Du, fell into step beside her.

"You need to keep your distance from my wife," he snarled. "Ever since she met you, we've been having a difference of opinion and I don't like it. She leaves home behind my back to go on secret trips, she wants to be independent, run her own business, she lies … she doesn't act like a traditional Chinese wife should. Your western ideas are not welcome in my family. Stay out of our affairs. Stick to hotel work if you know what's good for you," he growled.

Lily Rose floundered in shock, then found weak footing. "Aaaa… I'm sorry. FFF… For the rrrecord, I didn't know Alison went to Beijing without telling you, but that's strictly between you and her." She noticed his facial features twitching and his teeth grinding into a frightening lopsided smile. Gaining a bit of courage, she added, "As for the business she wants to start— that's always been her dream. Don't you know that? I didn't put that thought into her head. It's been there."

Chen Du grunted, jaw tight.

"Alison is very talented. It would make her happy if you supported her. Don't you want your wife to be happy?" Lily Rose watched his features darken, eyebrows furrowed, lips thinning. Enraged, he grabbed her forearm in a vice grip. Lily Rose flinched, moving sideways, trying to escape.

"What… I… want is none of your business. Stay out of our lives if you don't want trouble. I can make your life in Hong Kong ver-ry difficult. Don't you forget that."

His hand moved up her arm, squeezing with such force, Lily Rose wanted to scream, but she was too frightened to make a sound. Instead, a wince escaped her lips. Chen leaned in closer, scaring her into submission. "One warning only. Pay attention," he hissed into her exposed ear. With that, he let go of Lily Rose's arm, leaving her confused and shaken. The violation took less than five minutes, but he had left an indelible impression.

Walking into a different direction, Chen Du joined two intimidating, waiting men with dark glasses, a few feet away. Lily Rose, rubbed the painful spot on her arm which was already beginning to turn a crimson color and hurried to her building. Over her shoulder, she noticed the three men disappear into a waiting, black car as she scurried toward the entrance portal. Badly shaken, she entered, pulling the door shut behind her. The sound of the lock clicking into place did nothing to appease her. When she arrived at her front door, key in hand, she noticed it was slightly ajar. Trembling, she pushed it open with her foot and listened. Deafening silence. A neighbor approached from down the hall, so she seized the opportunity to run in and do a quick sweep, leaving the front door wide open with one of her discarded shoes wedged underneath. Surely the neighbor would hear her scream if someone was lurking. She checked the entire apartment, then returned to slam the front door shut, locking it. Drawers, left half open, had been rummaged through and left in disarray. In the bedroom, they tumbled onto the floor. Bewildered, she called Mingyu first, who immediately contacted the police for her. While she waited for both to arrive, she checked for anything missing. Oddly, her laptop was still there. So were An's TV and radio in the living room. With lightning speed, she rushed to the bedroom closet to check the side pocket of her travel backpack. She fingered her grandmother's jewelry box, sighing with relief, but when she opened it for reassurance, she screamed. The dragon pendant was missing. Lily Rose sunk to her knees, "Oh my God, oh my God."

Somewhat thankful that she was wearing her lavender jade ring and Marina's jade earrings, she bemoaned the loss of her beloved dragon pendant, her most valuable possession. A handful of gold earrings had also disappeared— hoops, blue topaz lever backs, amethyst studs, dangling hearts and a tiny gold heart locket from her mother, a graduation gift. Even the box with her vintage costume pieces was gone. Absorbing the violation, Lily Rose crumbled in a heap. She could stomach the disappearance of her meaningless trinkets, but the theft of her grandmother's exquisite dragon pendant was beyond heart wrenching and too much to bear.

When Mingyu and the police arrived, she made a list of the missing items. It was short—only jewelry was taken and she didn't have that much. She had no cash in the apartment and the electronics were still in place. Lily Rose decided not to mention her encounter with Chen Du. She didn't see him in her building. He was waiting outside, but there was no doubt in her mind that the theft was part of his warning. Besides, she was scared of what he would do to her if she squealed. It dawned on her why Alison never considered a police report. It was pointless, unthinkable.

When the police left, she filled Mingyu in on her encounter and showed him her arm, which was starting to hint at a rainbow spectrum. Mingyu's eyes showed genuine concern. "Did he hurt your shoulder too?"

"What? No. That's my new tattoo." She searched his face, hoping he wouldn't disapprove.

"Tattoo?" His voice rose a pitch. "Why? What kind?"

His reaction made her eyes flood. "It's a rose. I got it in Beijing."

His face softened. "Really? Hmm. I didn't know you were even considering one." With a blank expression, he glided over the tattoo discovery to focus on the more urgent present. "Chen's warning was meant to hit you where it hurt. A girl's jewelry is special to her. It has meaning, and memories attached. I'm sure he intended to inflict pain. Be thankful he didn't opt for the physical variety. I'm certain he got what he wanted and won't be back unless you provoke him. I remember how Carson Wu coveted your pendant in the store. It wouldn't surprise me, if he requested it."

"Your grandfather was so right. I shouldn't have worn it around town so much," she wailed.

"No, Lily Rose. It's not your fault. Jewelry is meant to be worn. Otherwise, what's the point of owning it? You did nothing wrong. You just had the misfortune of crossing paths with Carson Wu and his people."

Lily Rose sniffled, draping herself over Mingyu's shoulder. His arms slid around her, careful not to touch the bandage or her bruised arm. She felt completely stripped of her security and her world was beginning to feel extraordinarily fragile. His warm comfort was just what she needed, what she craved, but it wasn't meant to last.

After Mingyu called a locksmith, they shared her dinner in strained silence. Mingyu broke the spell by trying to redirect her focus, "Can I see your tattoo?"

When she undid the bandage and stood before him, one arm slipped out of her blouse, he stared, a slight frown on his face. Finally, he spoke as Lily Rose was close to bursting into tears again. "It's a lavender rose! That's the most beautiful rose tattoo I've ever seen. It looks like a watercolor painting, a Georgia O Keefe masterpiece."

A small smile crossed her lips. Mingyu instinctively knew how to make her feel better and at that moment, she loved him for it. "Thanks," she replied, her relief showing.

While they waited for the locksmith, he asked her about her trip to Beijing. If he was surprised or angry she went to Beijing with Alison, he didn't show it. Feeling worse about her betrayal, her face flushed. She had purposely withheld information and now it felt wrong. She was ashamed. She knew he disapproved after all his prior warnings and yet he was tight lipped on the subject now making her feel worse. Once the door was fixed, Mingyu got ready to leave.

"I have to go. I need to be in the office early tomorrow. An important client is coming and I have to prepare. Lock the door behind me."

Astonished he wasn't staying, she nodded, then whispered, "I'll be ok. I'm just heartbroken." She gestured wearily, raising her arms half way, then letting them fall against her sides in resignation.

"I understand. I'm sorry. I doubt Chen Du will return. He got what he wanted and he scared you sufficiently to buy your silence, but now stay out of his way," Mingyu admonished.

"I will. I promise." She nodded meekly, hoping he would forgive her stupidity. She could tell he was disappointed in her and that hurt as much as losing her dragon pendant.

When Mingyu left, Lily Rose took a hot shower, avoiding her covered, sore shoulder. She cleaned up the mess in her bedroom then, lethargically, uncovered her bed and crawled beneath the sheets. From her night table she pulled out the batch of letters addressed to Marina. Up until now she hadn't had the fortitude to read them, but tonight she needed to feel close to her grandmother. The guilt of losing her magnificent inheritance was burdening her soul. Untying the red ribbon, she opened the first letter. As she read the script, she quickly realized this was a poetic love declaration, a letter filled with deep regret that Marina had left Hong Kong. Her heart twisted into knots. Marina had left a Chinese lover! She reread the letter twice before she arrived at the scribbled signature, trying to decipher it. Astonishment set in as she realized who the sender was.

Lily Rose gasped. The letter was signed by Jin Ho.

Chapter XLIII

Jin's Confession

The bomb Lily Rose dropped regarding his father's affair with Winnie still shook Mingyu to his core. So did her risky, veiled trip to Beijing, but he chalked the latter up to ignorance. *Traveling with Alison Wu—what was she thinking? What am I getting myself into here? I have enough trouble already.*

Between his father's downward spiraling life and the robbery in Lily Rose's home, Mingyu felt pressured. Why did those he loved choose foolish paths? Jin had warned his father about his business choices and he had warned Lily Rose about befriending Alison. It seemed everyone was destined to make their own mistakes. Mingyu needed a few days to process recent events. When he and Jin had dim sum the following Sunday, he unloaded his heart and thoughts. As always, Jin was a few steps ahead of him, fortified with sound strategies.

"It makes perfect sense to me now. I figured Cheng had help and I couldn't quite believe it was Li. He may be quiet, but he's always been very professional," Jin said as he poured black tea into their vintage rose medallion tea cups.

"Did Dad start an affair with Winnie to recruit her or was he having an affair and then got her involved?" Mingyu wondered out loud.

"Who knows. I can't say I noticed anything one way or another and Chase didn't mention her in his report, so it may be recent. Be that as it may, I will let her go tomorrow. I don't want any office affairs and if she's complicit with your father, she shouldn't be working under my roof. I have always trusted my employees. I can't say I trust her now." His words sped up as he became more agitated. "I'm disgusted and I don't want her to poison our other employees. There's only one team here and we work together. Let your father pay her salary from his gold business if they're so close."

"Agreed. I won't miss Winnie. Amber is infinitely more pleasant. What in the world was dad thinking? I can't stand to look at Winnie anymore. Glad we settled that problem. There's something else I wanted to share with you. Lily Rose's apartment was robbed."

"Oh dear." Jin looked concerned. "I hope she wasn't there."

"No, she was at work." Mingyu recounted the events, leaving out no detail. When he finished, he waited for Jin's thoughts, which were slow in coming. Finally, his grandfather spoke.

"Sounds like Carson Wu's people had a hand in it. Carson expressed great interest in the pendent when he was in the store the day Lily Rose visited. Told me to call him if she ever sold it. There's nothing we can do for her except register the pendant as stolen on the international art loss register and look out for it at auction, but if Carson has it, I'm afraid it will never resurface. He'll keep it in his private collection or trade up on the black market for a more desired piece. What a terrible shame." Jin shook his head side to side.

"She loved that pendant so much. I feel horrible for her. She was inconsolable after the robbery. Do you really think Carson ordered the theft or did Chen Du want to hurt her and have it for himself?"

"If it wasn't an outright request from Carson, Chen Du probably had his own agenda. He may use it as a bargaining chip or perhaps as a prized gift when he wants to fall into Carson's favor. Who knows? Either way, Carson Wu will find out about the theft. Nothing happens on his turf without him knowing. Why don't you invite Lily Rose for dim sum next Sunday? Maybe we can cheer her up a bit."

"Doubtful. She's really distraught." Mingyu replied with a grim expression. "But … I'll invite her."

"You know … I remember meeting Alison Wu once. She came into the store with Carson. She appeared to be of a different nature than her father, gentler, quietly observant, yet determined, with a different kind of inner strength. Not at all like the brash street urchin I would have expected from him. I recall being surprised they were related," Jin reflected.

They ate in silence, each lost in their own thoughts. Mingyu cleared the dishes and made green tea with honey which they shared on the terrace with some almond cookies. He wasn't ready to leave. Sitting in padded, comfortable chairs, like two old cronies, they chatted about possibly hiring cousin Elizabeth to work with Amber.

"I think I'll call Huan tonight and ask him if he can spare her. She's been wanting to work in our store. Asked me numerous times." Jin stroked his chin. "Maybe she can start with two or three days a week."

"Sounds good. It would be nice to have her. She must be almost done with her GIA (Gemological Institute of America) training by now." Mingyu liked the idea of having his younger cousin around on a daily basis. They got along well.

After a brief conversation lapse and feeling better about unburdening his mind, Mingyu shifted gears.

"Ye Ye, tell me about the woman before grandma, the one who got away." Mingyu looked out over the water, inhaling and holding his breath, then exhaling slowly as if measuring the silent beats. He wondered if Jin would answer.

After what seemed like ages, Jin finally spoke. "Yes, I've been thinking about her a lot lately, the woman who got away. She was American and she lived here in Hong Kong in the early 1960's, before the cultural revolution. She was a journalist. I was already working for my father and she came into our store for a watch repair. I thought she was so beautiful; I couldn't take my eyes off her. A short time later, by chance, I saw her again at a party we both were invited to. I'll never forget the dress she was wearing. It was a sleeveless white linen dress with Himalayan blue poppies that matched her eyes. She had satin brown hair and a sweet cherry smile. We struck up a conversation that night and chatted practically the whole evening until the waiters ushered us out. She was there by herself, but I discovered she was married. She wore a ruby ring, no wedding band. I found out later, she lost it. Her husband was an engineer based in Hong Kong, but he traveled frequently, leaving her alone for weeks at a time. At first, we met for coffee a few times under the guise of research for a story she was working on, but it was so much more than that.

I made excuses to see her. Later, we met on weekends when her husband was away. I escorted her, unofficially of course, to cultural activities and parties. At first our meetings were friendly and fun. She was bored and perhaps lonely in a strange city. Anyway, I found her company fascinating and I think we complimented each other in so many ways. She was well traveled and had a lot to share. I hadn't been anywhere. To me, she was like an exotic bird, always in flight. It was she who inspired me to travel in later years. I had never met anyone like her before and to be honest, I haven't met anyone quite like her since. She was fearless and so easy to talk to."

Jin paused and took a sip of tea. Mingyu held his breath again willing Jin to continue. He did.

"We became close friends, but after a few months of casual meetings, I fell hopelessly in love and we had an affair. We truly enjoyed so much of the same activities and thoughts, I knew we were soulmates. That kind of love doesn't come along often. I didn't have any life experiences back then to tell me so, but I realize how special that was now." He nodded and gazed out over the water. "She loved going to Stanley beach, I remember, so we went there often. She would have loved this view, my house and….my garden."

Mingyu sat stiffly and said nothing, lest his grandfather stop sharing.

Jin continued. "When my father realized what was happening, he was furious. He threatened to disown me if I didn't break it off, but I didn't. I couldn't. We became more secretive and took day trips out of Hong Kong, renting hotel rooms on the occasional weekend trip. After a couple years in Hong Kong, her husband was transferred. I was crushed. I should have asked her to leave him and stay with me. I believe she would have, but I didn't have the courage. If my father hadn't been ill, I might have left for New

York with her, but I couldn't abandon my family. I was needed in the business. It would have been an all or nothing decision, because I know she would have never been accepted by my parents. It's my biggest regret in life—letting her go. For many years I wrote to her, but I never heard back. It broke my heart, but I imagine she was disappointed, angry perhaps and I suppose she settled back into married life with her husband. People didn't get divorced so easily back then."

"Where was she from in the US?" Mingyu asked carefully.

"New York."

"Did her husband ever find out about your affair?"

"I didn't think so. We were very careful."

"You traveled to New York a few times. Did you not look for her?" Mingyu slurped his tea.

"No. She was married and I had let her go. Timing is everything in life and I realized I missed my opportunity. I secretly hoped she would come to the international jewelry shows, but she never did. Since she didn't answer my letters, I wasn't surprised our paths didn't cross again."

"What was her name?" Mingyu sucked in air. *I can't believe my grandfather has scandalous secrets. He always does the right thing.*

Jin hesitated as if he didn't want to let that last bit of information go. "I called her Mei, but her English name was Marina. She was Lily Rose's grandmother."

Chapter XLIV

Girlfriends No More?

Hi, do you have time for lunch? I have some news.

Lily Rose looked at Alison's text and pondered what to do. *Well, I don't have much more of value to steal anymore. Her husband already took my most treasured possession. But then again, I do value my bones intact.* Lily Rose debated how to respond. Not wanting to be victimized or turn up dead, floating with the fishes in Victoria Harbor, she decided to wait and think about it. Let some time pass.

Lily Rose wasn't in the mood to see anyone. The theft of Marina's dragon pendant had brought her to her knees as had Mingyu's surprising silence afterwards. It hurt. The robbery had been a shock to her system, a violation she couldn't get past that easily, but Mingyu's silence was unexplainable and heart wrenching. Was he turned off by her tattoo or was he mad she disregarded his warnings?

The pendant would never mean as much to the thief as it did to her. There were important memories attached to it, memories she felt every time she wore it. She wondered if Alison knew about the ambush. *Am I wrong about Alison? Was she complicit?*

So many people had admired her pendant, she couldn't be sure about who wanted it badly enough to steal it. And what about the love letter from Jin Ho to her grandmother. If that wasn't the most shocking discovery of all; how should she handle that? Life sure threw some curve balls at her. Lily Rose changed into her pajamas and crawled into bed with her laptop. She checked her emails and discovered one from her mother.

Hi Lily Rose,

Hope you're well and still enjoying Hong Kong. How's work? Is Lam still shirking his

responsibilities? How's David? Any other new friends? Zoe says hello. I ran into her a few days ago while shopping the sales. Things here are status quo. Nothing new to share.

Marina's house is fine other than the leak I told you about. All is fixed now.

I have vacation time accruing and I was thinking of coming to Hong Kong for Christmas. I could come for two weeks, stay in Hong Kong for one week and maybe travel with you for the second? Can you take some time off? Is there any place you'd like to visit? A girl's trip would be fun, don't you think?.

Looking forward to your reply,
XO, Mom

Her next email was from An.

Hi Lily Rose,

Sorry for not replying earlier, but Margo keeps me super busy. There are days I barely get a bathroom break, let alone a lunch break.

Thankfully, your assistant keeps me sane. You trained her well. Yes, I've been to Red Sugar. Great cocktails.

I have a favor to ask you. My cousin is getting married in mid-March and I wanted to be there for the wedding. Would you be agreeable to leaving early? Switching back on March 1ˢᵗ instead of April 1ˢᵗ?

Please let me know what you think.

Thanks, An

Lily Rose closed the mail window and placed her laptop on the night table. *Good Grief. Can things get any worse? No, I don't want to leave early. I'm not even sure I want to leave at all. And where can I go for a week with Mom? There goes my immersive gemology class. I can't deal with this right now.*

She slithered down her silk pillows and drew the covers over her head, closing her eyes and letting her mind wander. After a short reflection, she picked up the laptop again. Listlessly, she searched possible travel destinations. Thailand shot to the top of her list. Maybe, a travel week with her mom was just what she needed. It started to feel and sound better as she looked at the beautiful destinations—Bangkok, Chiang Mai, Khao Lak, Krabi, Phuket. She smiled at the thought. *Yes. A week with mom is what I need.*

Mingyu had not contacted her all week and she was in a funk. Between the missing pendant and his noticeable silence, she felt depressed. She couldn't talk to Alison, because she never shared anything about Mingyu or her intimate life. She was still insecure about Alison's intentions. In the past, she had always kept her different worlds separate, scared of possible repercussions--her work world, matters of the heart, casual social interactions. She missed Zoe, her go-to friend when life turned sour. Zoe always had her back. Realizing she didn't have any close girlfriends or family to confide in nearby, she shot Zoe an email. While she knew many nice people in Hong Kong, she was missing a close female connection she could entrust her heart to.

She scanned hotels in Bangkok and Patong Beach. The beautiful imagery lightened her mood. Travel always lifted her spirits. Yes, a planned vacation would definitely make her feel better. She emailed her mom back. Settling into bed, she pulled out Marina's letters again.

Chapter XLV

Life's Shocking Surprises

Mingyu left his grandfather's home in a daze. The secrets unraveling about his family were starting to choke him. It made him wonder what other surprises, hid beyond reach, were percolating beneath the familial surface. Until now his existence had been so pleasantly predictable. He may have been a touch complacent at times, but now he felt completely overwhelmed. The recent string of events was hard to process--his father having an affair with an employee and being deeply involved in illicit business practices that could land him in jail, his girlfriend becoming friends with a triad member whose husband most likely robbed her of her most prized family possession, and now finding out that his grandfather, his reliable rock, lusted after a married woman who it turns out was his girlfriend's grandmother. Could things get any more twisted than this? Arriving home, he showered and collapsed on his bed, instantly falling asleep, but the night was punctuated by bad dreams and he awoke more than once in a disoriented sweat.

At the office the next morning, Mingyu was anxious, a totally unfamiliar sensation for him. His family's business had always been a safe place, somewhere he felt completely at ease and successful, but now all that was changed. These days his stomach was in perpetual knots. Every morning he worried about what unknowns could surface and explode in his face. He wasn't sure, how much more upheaval he could absorb.

To sooth his soul, he made a pot of tea and checked his email. He hadn't heard from Lily Rose since the robbery other than a text exchange from work. She was busy, which was probably a good thing considering recent events. Sunday night, he had been so preoccupied after his grandfather's confession, he forgot to call her. The following days had bled by; he wondered if she felt neglected by him. Momentarily, he couldn't shake the sensation of feeling spent; he had nothing left to give. Was she ok? What could he say? *Should I tell her about Jin and Marina? How will that impact our relationship. I need time… time to think about this.*

In his mind he practiced his approach--*Your grandmother had an extramarital affair with my grandfather. Our grandparents fell madly in love and had an affair.* Ugh, it all *sounds so awkward and wrong.* Lost in thought, he jumped, dropping his teacup on the saucer with a clang, when he heard the workshop door slam.

Jin appeared. "Good Morning." He took a deep breath. "Oh good, you made tea," he said on an exhale. Pouring himself a cup, he eyed Mingyu at his desk and took a slow, savoring sip. "Ahhh, so good. Just what I needed." The outer edges of his mouth curled slightly upward as he walked over and stood opposite Mingyu, who was looking at his computer. "Have you spoken to Lily Rose yet?"

No." Mingyu looked up and then down again, his thoughts muddled.

"I was thinking, maybe I should be the one to tell her about my relationship with her grandmother. It may be … awkward for you."

He must be reading my mind. "That would be good. I was debating how to handle this information-- wondering if it should stay a secret or not."

"I think she deserves to know since you're in a relationship. Invite her to dim sum Sunday, before she makes other plans. There's also something unrelated I wanted to discuss with you. Let's go out for lunch today. I have a client appointment at noon, but we can have a late lunch right after."

"Sure," Mingyu shifted nervously in his chair. "Does this concern my father?"

"No. Don't look so worried. It's nothing bad. Listen, when Winnie comes in, send her up and stay downstairs to help Amber open. I'll handle firing Winnie myself."

"Oh….ok." Mingyu was happy to sit this one out. He hated confrontation.

"Open the safe first, will you? Today, I'm busy. I have back-to-back appointments this morning and we'll be short-handed now so you or Li might be needed on the sales floor.

Winnie spent fifteen minutes in Jin's office before she was back downstairs in tears, gathering up her belongings. The security guard, who had been alerted on his earpiece, escorted her out the door. Amber looked on in surprise. Mingyu confirmed her suspicions and assured Amber she had nothing to worry about.

The morning went smoothly with Li helping Amber out. By lunchtime, Jin was in better spirits. He had closed a few good deals.

"Let's go. Lunch is on me. Li, you're in charge until Mingyu and I get back."

Li broke into a rare smile and bowed his head. Having someone's trust was a wonderful thing.

Jin and Mingyu sat in the restaurant sipping tea, their food ordered. Jin leaned in over the table. "As you know, I keep a close watch on the news, locally and internationally. I was always concerned about Hong Kong's future when the British left, and lately I'm realizing we'll be in for a rougher ride than we thought. Foreign companies have moved their headquarters out of our city and many organizations have left China entirely, some to Seoul, some to Singapore. Hong Kong is changing; it's mutating from an international business city to a controlled Chinese suburb. Tourism is way down, almost twenty percent, which translates to a loss of business.

In our industry, quite a few companies are packing up and moving to London while they still have the option to do so with the BNO (*British National Overseas*) passport. Our business will keep changing, I'm afraid. Maybe not be as strong? I don't know. Time will tell. Therefore, thinking ahead I was wondering how you would feel about opening a London office for our company?" His eyes searched his grandson's astonished face.

Mingyu was incredulous. A flapping, flailing fish out of the sea, his mouth opening and closing soundlessly. "You want me to move to London?"

"The British Visa is good for five years. If you don't like London, you can come back. If you like it, you can apply for citizenship. By then we'll know if an office there will pay off or not." Many of our customers are in Europe. I don't know if they'll continue to come to Hong Kong in the future. Doubtful. We have a better chance of hanging on to them with an office in London. And here's another thought. Lily Rose is leaving soon, unless you know otherwise. In London, you would be closer to New York. Maybe she'll transfer to a London Hilton if you decide to stay in London. I'm assuming of course that you don't want to lose her. Correct me if I'm wrong."

"I don't, but I'm not sure I'm ready to commit to anything either. I need to think about this. What about dad? Does he know about your idea?"

"No. He's buried in his own problems. He can't see past the forest right now."

"I don't know, *Ye Ye*. This is my home. I've always been happy here. I never thought of living anywhere else in the world. I love to travel, but I always loved coming home more."

"Well...think about it and search your heart, but here's a thought. I won't live forever. If I'm gone and Lily Rose goes back to America, will you still be happy here? Will you enjoy working with your father?"

Mingyu gulped. He hadn't thought that far ahead.

"Think of this as an opportunity I'm offering you. I can set you up in London now. Later, it may no longer be possible. It's up to you of course. This is something you do when you're young. In later years, it becomes harder, if not impossible. I missed that opportunity, never had it, really."

"But your life turned out fine."

"It did. I'm not complaining. I'm just thinking about your future. Thinking globally for our company. The world is shrinking. Once the British Visa opportunity expires, it won't be so easy to leave China permanently; you can always come back. You have a Chinese passport and my house and business are yours. Give it some thought. No immediate rush to decide."

They finished their lunch in silence, Jin enjoying his tea and Mingyu experiencing indigestion.

After Jin paid, they hurried back to the office in the pouring rain.

Chapter XLVI

Dim Sum on Stanley Village Road

Mingyu sat in his car and waited patiently for Lily Rose to appear. He hadn't seen her all week and realized he missed her. After the week he had, he needed time to digest and process. Feeling like he was on a collision course and stretched to his limit, personal space had been a necessity for his mental health.

Lily Rose emerged in a white linen dress and colorful, strappy sandals adorned with a roped wedge. A honey-colored sweater was loosely slung over her shoulders and her straw handbag was filled to the brim. She was a welcome sight and instantly soothed his anxiety. He pointed to her straw tote. "Hi. What have you got in there? A small animal?"

"I brought some dessert and a few things I think Jin might like to see. How was your week? I missed you. In fact, I was worried you might be mad at me. You did absolutely nothing to dissuade that fear." She raised an eyebrow.

"Sorry. No, I'm not angry. Just exceptionally busy. I feel guilty I wasn't around much after your robbery, but I'm ready to make it up to you today and tomorrow. Would you like to have dinner tonight, just the two of us?"

"Dim sum… and dinner? I don't know. That might be attention overload after the draught."

"Fair enough. I deserved that. Were you ok in the apartment? I did think of you all week, I swear." He glanced sideways under his newly angled bangs.

Lily Rose melted. "It was a little creepy the first couple of nights. I won't lie. Your company would have been appreciated. I kept looking over my shoulder coming home from work, but I've been so busy and tired at the end of each work day, I didn't have the energy to obsess too much. I also bought mace. She pulled it out of her handbag and waved it back and forth in front of his face. "You better not aggravate or incite me."

"No such intention. By the way, carrying that in Hong Kong is against the law."

"Really? I got it on *Amazon*. Alison texted me, but I haven't responded yet. Do you think she knew?"

"I honestly doubt it and even if she did, she probably had no say in the matter." He noticed she was wearing her jade earrings and ring. *She's probably scared to leave them home now.* Feeling a wave of compassion, he squeezed her hand and placed it on his knee. They were stopped at a red light.

"Are you off tomorrow?"

"Yes. David is taking a few days off next week, so I'll be covering him then."

"I would like to take tomorrow off and spend the day with you. Yes?"

He could see a smile form at the corners of her raspberry lips. "Possibly. Let's see how today goes. I may get tired of you by dinner time. I got used to not having you around so be warned."

"Ouch. I'm noticing a rough edge this morning. I plan to make the day go smoother than ice." He glanced at her from the corner of his eye. She still looked a touch sad over the loss of her valuables, but it seemed acceptance had set in or was it resignation? He wasn't sure.

At Jin's house, he pulled into the driveway and turned off the car. When Lily Rose opened her door to exit, he stopped her by grabbing the arm closest to him.

"Wait. Again, I'm sorry about this week. I wanted to take you to dinner tonight because I was going to surprise you, but maybe now is a better time. He pulled a little brocade pouch out of his shirt pocket and handed it to her. "This won't make up for all you lost, but maybe it'll cheer you up and let you know I care." Eyes fixed on her face, he waited.

Lily Rose untied the string and pulled out an eighteen-inch, delicate 14kt gold link chain with a dangling carved rose. It was topped with a single snow-white cultured pearl.

"A lavender jade rose! It's beautiful, Mingyu. Thank you for the kind thought. I absolutely love it and …," she turned toward him, "I love you for thinking of me." She cupped his face and kissed him tenderly on the lips.

Feeling a rush of blood circulating, Mingyu changed positions in his seat. His awkward shift made his elbow hit the steering wheel and sound the horn in a loud succession. They both jumped and laughed. "Ok, now the whole neighborhood knows we're here. We might as well duck inside."

"Wait. Put the necklace on me first." She swiveled her legs out the car door and turned her back to him, holding the pendant in place. He secured the clasp and kissed the nape of her neck. Her skin felt soft and inviting and her signature scent crept up his nose, swirling around his brain matter. Her presence was intoxicating and he was pleased his gift had made her happy. Yes, he had definitely missed her.

When they climbed the stairs to Jin's living space, they found him busy in the kitchen. Soft jazz music filled the air as the sun streamed through the open windows and deck doors. A breeze off the water made the heat bearable. "Hello, come in. Welcome, Lily Rose. Lovely to see you. Mingyu, I have a few things in the oven. Can you check?

"Good Morning, Jin. Thanks for inviting me. I brought dessert." She pulled a few items from her trusty straw bag and placed them on the counter. "Your plants look wonderful," she marveled, her eyes circulating the green space. Walking out to the edge of the terrace, she took in the magnificent view. She never tired of its beauty. Returning inside, she put away her dessert and asked Jin, "Can I help with something?"

"Yes. Thanks. You can help Mingyu put food on the table. It's ready."

After they had eaten and had chatted idly about nothing in particular, Mingyu and Lily Rose cleared the dishes while Jin brewed a fresh pot of tea. The scent of the tea leaves felt familiar and soothing.

"Thank you for dessert, Lily Rose. Can you carry this tray to the outdoor table? "

"You're welcome. Sure."

Making a few trips, she set up the teacups and poured the tea, arranging them in front of everyone's favorite seat. Sitting down next to Mingyu she reached for his hand and placed it in her lap, interlacing her fingers with his. Leaning back, she closed her eyes and let the late September sun bounce off the glistening water and fondle her face. The last typhoon had passed in early September, but Jin's home seemed unphased.

Mingyu noticed tension in her tight grip. He lifted their intertwined hands out of her lap and kissed the back of her hand, squeezing her fingers lightly. Her eyes met his and she smiled. Being with Lily Rose calmed him. They definitely had a placating effect on each other.

When Jin reappeared, he was holding a small giftbox which he placed in front of Lily Rose. "It saddened me to hear about the loss of your grandmother's pendant. Mingyu told me what happened. I wanted to give you a present to lift your spirits, but also remind you that property is replaceable. The important thing is you weren't harmed."

"Thank you, Jin. I'm truly touched."

"There's a story that accompanies this present that you might enjoy. Go ahead and open it." Mingyu looked at his grandfather, then met Lily Rose's eyes and shrugged. He had no idea what was coming and was just as curious. Lily Rose untied the crimson ribbon and lifted the lid off the yellow papered box. She retrieved a thick satin pouch and peeked inside. "Oh my God. It's a jade pendant. You both think alike, don't you?" She winked at Mingyu.

Pulling out an exquisitely carved grass green jade buddha on a gold link chain, she laughed and held it up to examine it from all sides. It was substantially smaller than her dragon pendant, but it had a similar rich color. "It's beautiful ….and the color matches my dragon pendant. I don't know what to say." Her eyes were glistening, threatening to emit moisture any moment. "Thank you, Jin, for your extreme kindness and thoughtfulness." She got up and hugged him. "I can't wait to hear the story. I love that there is one. It adds value to the jewel."

Jin smiled and nodded. He cleared his throat. "This pendant was mine when I was your age. It was a gift from my mother and I wore it every day. Your grandmother, who I called Mei, and knew well when she lived in Hong Kong, had always admired it. She was a customer in our store back then. She bought gorgeous pearl earrings once, I remember. Anyway, she loved my pendent for its deep color; the vivid emerald green spoke to her. She said the color reminded her of the grassy beaches in Long Island. When she left Hong Kong because your grandfather was transferred, I intended to give it to her, but since the Buddha pendant had been given to me by my mother, and she would have noticed its absence around my neck, I gave Mei the dragon medallion instead. She loved it even more than the Buddha and I knew I had made the right choice. "Jin took a slow sip of his tea and continued, "I cared for Mei…. very much and was heartbroken when she left Hong Kong. I wanted her to remember our special bond and time together and it appears she did because she shared so many stories with you."

Mingyu looked from Jin to Lily Rose, who was fighting to hold back tears. Struggling to find her voice, she finally answered Jin. "I know how much you loved Marina." Both men looked at her with a surprised expression.

"You knew?" Mingyu croaked. "I just found out a few days ago."

Lily Rose looked at Jin. "I have something for you too." She went inside to retrieve a brown paper packet from her straw bag. When she returned she placed the packet tied with a satin emerald ribbon before him. "When my grandmother died, she left me her beach cottage. I always loved the place. I spent all my childhood summers there. It's my home. That's also where she shared most of her stories about Hong Kong. I think Marina was afraid my mother would sell the cottage and she wanted it to stay in the family--so she left it to me. Anyway, after the funeral service, I spent time alone there and I sifted through some of her more private belongings. That's when I found these letters postmarked from Hong Kong. I was too distraught to read them back then, but I kept them with me and brought them to Hong Kong to read when I was ready. I thought they would be easier to tackle if I was removed from Marina's environment. Only, once here, I forgot all about them." Lily Rose took a sip of tea to wet her tongue. "I didn't look at them until after the pendant was stolen. I read all your letters to Marina which she had saved in a hidden box in her closet, but I only opened one of the letters she wrote to you. I needed to be sure." Lily Rose pushed the bundled mail with the sealed letters toward Jin. "It looks like they were refused here in Hong Kong and sent back. They're all marked 'return to sender.' I'm guessing you never saw them?"

"No, never. It broke my heart when Mei left and I never heard from her again. I thought maybe she was mad at me for not stopping her from leaving or perhaps she was just too busy with her new life after moving. After all, she was married to your grandfather which complicated our genuine friendship and love. I'm guessing my father intercepted the mail and returned it. I still lived at home back then. Had I known he did that, I would have been furious."

"But Marina eventually received your letters. She knew you still cared. It's such a shame you never connected again. I know she would have loved to resume your friendship." Lily Rose offered as she patted Jin's hand affectionately.

It was Jin's turn to surprise everyone. "Oh, but we did reconnect." He poured himself another cup of tea, leaving the two youngsters in suspense, perched on the edge of their seats like gulls hovering over a fishing boat for scraps.

"You did? When?" Mingyu blurted, astounded. *Am I completely dense?*

"After you came home from New York last year, I received an email at work from Marina. She recognized the company name and emblem from the card you gave to Lily Rose at the trade show. She also thought you looked a lot like me when I was younger, Mingyu. I was overjoyed to hear from her. We were in contact until she died. We even spoke on the phone a few times. I didn't realize she died until you alerted me, Mingyu. I was surprised she lapsed in her emails, but people are busy..." His voice faltered with emotion. "She also told me she discovered my letters after her husband died. He had intercepted them and placed them in a locked box. She broke the lock after he passed, thinking it held insurance papers or stock certificates and such. I suspect my father alerted her husband, maybe even got him transferred back in the sixties. We'll never know for sure now."

Lilly Rose inhaled.

Mingyu chimed in, "I thought you acted strange when I mentioned Marina's death—as if you knew her."

Lily Rose exhaled. "That's some story! Incredible! She never said a word to me. She made me believe that Mei was a friend of hers who had to go back to mainland China." Lily Rose wiped a few escaping tears with the back of her hand. "I wish she had told me. I guess its fate that I'm here in Hong Kong."

She glanced at Mingyu, who was still processing knowledge acquired, his mouth agape.

"No. She did the right thing. It's good she didn't tell you. Coming here is your chosen karma. Karma and fate are not the same thing." Jin paused and looked at their questioning faces. "Fate is a defeatist approach. Karma is about acceptance and using it as a stepping stone; karma is positive energy…. uplifting. Fate is not. It's a form of resignation."

Lily Rose fingered her buddha pendant, pleased with the story attached to it. Jin's message was powerful. *I have a lot to learn about Buddhist beliefs. And… I cannot think of a wiser man, to learn these lessons from.*

Chapter XLVII

Hot, Humid and Emotionally Fraught —Cheung Chau Island

Lily Rose and Mingyu spent their Sunday night dinner rehashing the day's remarkable disclosures. They analyzed, sympathized and strategized how their grandparents could have handled things differently. It was a stark reminder how a few passing decades completely changed perspectives. Over dessert they agreed to switch their focus. They spent a magical night exploring their passion for each other.

Rummaging into someone else's past can have dire consequences. You never know what damaging or surprising information may hide beneath tranquil surfaces. Their grandparents' tragic love story might have been difficult baggage to navigate in the early stages of their long distance friendship and budding romance. They concluded Jin and Marina did good to keep their connection personal and under the radar. It felt right that Mingyu and Lily Rose were able to discover each other at their own pace without knowing their grandparents' difficult and turbulent history. Each gifted day was meant to be experienced with an open mind, an open aura and at their own leisure.

The next morning, they packed a bag for a day trip to Cheung Chau Island. Lily Rose had not yet been there and the weather was still beautiful and hot. The island was a forty-minute ferry ride from the harbor. There they could find peace at the beach, dine at one of the quaint harbor restaurants, stroll along the colorful pier and not think about anything serious unless they chose to.

"We can also visit some ancient temples and the mini great wall, "Mingyu offered as they sat on the ferry heading over to the island.

"Let's see how we feel. Right now, the beach sounds wonderful."

The beach was a perfect place to heal ones' wounds. That is where Lily Rose chose to go in Sag Harbor when she was feeling down or grappling with life's punches. As it turned out, they relaxed on *Kwun Yam Wan* beach, had a relaxed late lunch and decided to visit the mini great wall, but they skipped the other historical structures. Exploring along the harbor, at the end of the day, they looked at the many houseboats and Lily Rose wondered what life on a stationary boat was like.

"It must be terrifying in typhoon season," she remarked.

"They go to a typhoon shelter. Yau Ma Tei in Kowloon is one of them. The government built shelters after many boat people whose livelihood was fishing, lost their homes and livings at the same time. Today many of them work on land. You've been to that part of Mong Kok, haven't you?"

"Don't think so."

"You should see it. Boat people have their own subculture. Traditionally, they married within their community and their children rarely went to school."

"Did boat people intermingle for other things—like going to temples or buying necessities?"

"Not that much. Generally, they traded for what they needed at market. Generations of boat people prayed and left offerings to the Tin Hau shrine, asking for good weather and for their crop to be spared. They were pretty self-sufficient."Mingyu had Lily Rose's attention, so he continued, "However, change was imminent. They poured their waste into the water, polluting the harbor so much, the government finally cracked down because of the off-shore contamination. Also, crime was rampant and there were so many boat people that in the 1970's the government stepped in again. Some started to work on land and gained an education. In the 1980's many were given public housing."

"Wow. That's quite a history lesson. I can't image living like that."

On the ferry ride home, the sky exploded with torrential tropical showers. They huddled together under a single person umbrella on the boat deck, thankful the rain had waited until their departure. Lily Rose still found it odd to pack an umbrella in her beach bag, but summers in Hong Kong sprung leaks at the most inopportune moments.

Their day had been tranquil and neither had uttered a word about Marina or Jin. The subject had been exhausted the day before and the need to concentrate on their own relationship prevailed. Lily Rose nestled into the crook of Mingyu's neck and shoulder as he put his arm around her.

"Can you come home with me tonight? I don't want this day to end yet." The day's quiet reflections had resonated with both and put them in a peaceful mindset.

Mingyu nodded and planted a kiss on her nose. "I'd like that."

"Just grab some clothes and come over. We can shower at my place." Lily Rose offered. "In fact, bring clothes for a few days if you like. I can pick up some pad thai on the way home in case you get hungry later."

"Thanks." Mingyu smiled, his arm tightening around her. If anything, the delayed confession from his grandfather had strengthened their bond, made them grow closer and realize that what they had was remarkable. Jin's admission of love lost came at a time when it had more meaning. Mingyu wasn't sure he would have understood it months ago in the same way he did now. His love for Lily Rose had blossomed from mere infatuation to something much more meaningful. It scared him. Once he wrapped his head around his grandfather's regrets and condensed life choices, he realized how one important decision could change an entire future trajectory. The thought of losing Lily Rose was real and disturbing. Would considering the London venture change his future in a positive way? Or would it scar him? When the ferry docked, they both felt rested and ready to re-enter the bustling city.

Over a glass of wine, Lily Rose told Mingyu about An's request. His heart started to race. "Do you want to leave a month early?" he asked tentatively, not sure if he wanted to hear her answer.

"No. I don't even know if I want to leave at all."

His heart rate slowed. He didn't want to think about Lily Rose leaving and hadn't until Jin brought it up. "Have you spoken to Lam about any of this?"

"No. I think I'll run it past David first."

"I would be sad if you left early. Maybe I can help. Leave An's apartment a month early and live with me for your last month of work. An can take her vacation time in March, come home early and still start work April first as planned."

Lily Rose lifted her head and studied his face. She raised one eyebrow. "Are you sure you're ok with that?"

"Absolutely sure." He smiled reassuringly.

"I don't have that much stuff. I could probably leave one suitcase packed up for the last month. It could work. What if we break up before then?"

"Not a chance." He pulled her onto his lap, letting her lavender scented shampoo fill his nostrils. Her warmth flooded through him, strengthening his resolve to keep her close.

The next morning, they showered, shared milk tea and parted with a passionate kiss. Knowing they would see each other after work gave them both a warm, comforting rush. Lily Rose was thrilled to not come home to an empty apartment and Mingyu was happy to wrap his arms around his lover at night. However, he still couldn't decide what to do regarding their future together. Her Hong Kong expiration date was approaching fast and he was feeling the pressure.

When Lily Rose arrived at work, she cornered David. Hovering, she leaned over his desk, whispering, "I need to talk to you, privately. Can we have lunch out today?"

David looked up from his laptop. "Sure. What's up?"

"I'll explain later." She motioned with her head to Lam's open door.

David nodded. Lam had long ears given the opportunity. At times, he even seemed a bit jealous of their close working relationship.

When they were sitting across from each other in a nearby restaurant a few hours later, Lily Rose took her time gathering her thoughts. She speared a shrimp out of her wonton noodles and chewed with gusto as David waited impatiently.

"So … what's up? Don't keep me in suspense."

"I heard from An. She wants to come back a month early. Her cousin is getting married in March and she wants to be here."

"Noooo waaay. You're not doing that are you? I thought you might stay?" His eyes locked onto her face and he dropped his chopsticks.

"I've seriously thought about it. Should I talk to Lam? Or is it too early?"

"Way too early. Wait until after the holidays. Actually, I'm hoping he may leave before then. Ha ha."

Lily Rose smirked. "Doubtful. He's got a cushy deal with us working like beavers. Keep this quiet then."

"Of course. I have something to run past you, too. I was toying with the idea of applying for a British visa. China will be revoking our BNO passport at some point. I thought it would be fun to work for one of the Hilton properties in London for a year. You inspired me."

"That would be fabulous, David. You could come visit me in New York. But wait until I leave, please. We have to plan our exit together."

"I will. I have a few years to set it up before the opportunity is rescinded by the government. Lam will have a panic attack if we both leave at the same time."

"Not if trusty An is back. She'll be superwoman after a year with Margo." Lily Rose laughed. "How long does it take to get a visa?" She wondered out loud.

"About two or three weeks I think."

"You should go for it. Living abroad is a great experience."

Jin was sitting at his desk when Mingyu arrived in the office. "Good morning. Have you spoken to your father?"

"Morning, Ye Ye. Yes. A few days ago. Why?" Mingyu plopped his bag next to his chair and walked over to Jin's desk.

"He just called me. There's a bit of good news. His lawyers are doing a good job of separating him from Hu Fat's actions. We're somewhat hopeful he'll be vindicated."

"Finally, some good news." Mingyu sunk into his chair, exhaling. "I'll call him tonight." He looked through their inside office window and noticed the workshop coming to life. They were still very vigilant about not discussing anything 'Cheng' in the office, especially with the door open.

"How was the rest of your weekend? Was Lily Rose ok?"

"She's fine with everything, don't worry, Ye Ye. She likes you a lot and was touched with her gifts. It amused her that we both had the same idea."

"Good. I'm glad. She's a genuine, lovely person. Hold on to her. Have you thought about what I suggested?"

"I've given it some thought. It's consuming me, actually. What time is your first appointment today?"

"Now." Jin gathered up selected stone papers containing precious gems and carefully placed them on a tray. He was meeting a dealer in Cheng's old office.

Mingyu logged onto his computer and checked his emails, but his mind was on Lily Rose and traveling to London. When his grandfather left the office, he began researching visa applications.

Chapter XLVIII

Alison's Surprise

Lily Rose knew she owed Alison a reply. It had lingered in the back of her mind all weekend. She didn't like to let friends down, but her heart and mind were occupied elsewhere. After her lunch with David, she finally texted back,

Sorry about the delayed response. Work has been crazy busy. I'm working through this weekend. Can you meet after work? Or one day next week maybe? Want to hear your news. Delete this text after you read it. Chen threatened me to stay away from you.

Lily Rose reread the text and thought about deleting the part about Chen Du. Then she pressed send anyway. He had truly scared her and she felt it was better to be honest and warn Alison if she truly was in the dark. She wanted to avoid a repeat visit of Alison's husband at all costs. The reply was instant.

Whaaat? When? He's traveling end of the week. I can meet you after work then.

Ok. I'll let you know. Maybe Thursday? I'll text you.

Ok.

Her next communication was an email to her mother.

Hi Mom,

You're welcome to stay on my couch if you come for the holidays, or I can get you an employee discount at the hotel. LMK soon though. I would love to visit Thailand before I leave this part of the world, but I'm not sure about my vacation time yet. I'll need to check that with Lam. I was toying with the idea of taking a one-week intensive jewelry class, but I guess I can put that off. The GIA offers them in New York too.

Work is fine. Life in Hong Kong is good. Visited Cheung Chau Island last weekend. Nice Beach—very different than Sag Harbor. See attached pics. What did you think of the Beijing images I sent? Let me know what dates you're considering and I'll try to book something for us.

Love, LR

Since she was on a roll with pending mail, she emailed An too, politely suggesting they wait until after the holidays to decide on switching their jobs back a month early. She did suggest that An use her vacation time to come home for her cousin's wedding, promising she would be amenable to vacating the apartment a month early but not the job. Satisfied after rereading her response, she pressed send.

Thursday night she met Alison for happy hour. When she entered the bar, she looked around for any possible triad members, but saw no suspicious stand outs. She didn't really know what she was looking for anyway. She seated herself at a table near the end of the bar with her back angled against the wall. When Alison arrived, she checked for shadows but didn't notice any. *I feel like a bloody detective.*

As Alison approached, Lily Rose admired her sleek, stylish emerald dress paired with a flower- embroidered jeans jacket. The piece de resistance were her matte gold platform shoes. "Hi, you look nice. You're actually taller than me today."

"Thanks. It's one of my finished models. I wanted to show you." Alison smiled, her eyebrows raised in question.

"Take your jacket off. Let me see all of it."

Alison flung her bag and jeans jacket on the barstool and twirled in place, smiling self-consciously.

"Ver-ry nice. I like it. Nice swing." Lily Rose nodded enthusiastically. "How many dresses do you have done now?"

"Ten. I brought pictures. The last two are giving me problems, but I'll figure it out. Maybe you can help. First tell me what happened with Chen. He didn't say a word to me."

Lily Rose noticed Alison sat with her back to the bar so she too could see the entrance. "After our trip, he was waiting for me at the Arch when I came home from work. Basically, he threatened me to stay away from you. To mind my own business and stay out of your life."

All color drained from Alison's face. "How? What did he do?"

Lily Rose went into detail replaying the interaction in her head as she talked. It still gave her the chills, but less and less as time passed. When she told Alison about the loss of her pendant, her voice cracked. "I was beyond upset. That pendant from my grandmother meant the world to me."

Alison listened, but offered nothing concrete. "I'm sorry. Did you call the police?"

"Yes, but I didn't tell them about Chen. Should I have?"

Alison's answer was immediate. "No. It's better you didn't. It wouldn't have helped anyway. I'm really sorry this happened to you." Alison looked pale, all the previous excitement devoid from her face. Lily Rose realized she wasn't going to get any insights from her friend; fear had taken over. It was written all over Alison's face. Lily Rose changed the subject.

"What is your news? I hope it's better than mine."

"Yes. I'll be showing my line at the *Interstoff* Asia trade show in mid-October. My father helped me get a booth last minute. I'll be sharing it with a local shoe manufacturer."

"That's awesome, Alison."

"Thanks. I'll show my samples and if I'm lucky, get some orders. It's a start."

"It's a fabulous opportunity. A trade show is perfect for exposure and feedback. Congrats."

"It wouldn't have happened without you pushing me, Lily Rose. I'm happy you did, despite Chen's reaction." She shook her head in disgust.

They spent the rest of their meeting talking about fashion. Before they parted, Lily Rose brought up the possibility of obtaining a British visa, her conversation with David still fresh on her mind. "You should give it some thought. London is a big fashion center. Try it for a year. You could still manufacture in China.

You have all the right contacts." She purposely didn't mention Chen, wanting only to plant a positive seed. It was up to Alison to figure out how to nurture the idea, if at all. The last thing Lily Rose needed was for Chen to revisit her and blame her for influencing Alison with her 'western thoughts' and their incompatibility with the traditional Chinese woman's place. However, the thought of liberating Alison from Chen Du was enormously tempting.

Chapter XLIX

Wind Sand Chicken and Secrets

Mingyu and Lily Rose were preparing *Wind Sand Chicken* in her apartment. She was taking care of the sand portion by carefully chopping garlic into tiny pieces, while he coated the meat with panko, dipping it into hot sesame oil. The scent of garlic and exotic spices permeated the air.

Mingyu looked up. "Do you remember my cousin, Victoria? She's moving to London."

Lily Rose stopped what she was doing, in surprise. "She is? Same job?"

"Yes. Her bank is sending her abroad for a year. My aunt and uncle hate the idea, but Jin thinks it's smart."

"Why don't her parents like the idea?"

"Huan likes his chickens close to the coop."

"I suppose that makes sense. My mother hated the idea of me leaving New York. Did I tell you she's coming to visit in December?"

"No. I look forward to meeting her."

"Maybe." Lily Rose hedged. "We'll be traveling, so she's only going to be in Hong Kong for a few days. We're going to Thailand for the rest of her vacation." Lily Rose instantly regretted mentioning her mother. She wasn't sure if she wanted to introduce Ella May. She hadn't mentioned a word about Mingyu in any of her communications.

Mingyu dipped the last piece of coated chicken in the bubbling oil, keeping his back turned to her. His silence was unnerving. She didn't intend to hurt his feelings. Was he bothered about not meeting her mother? Changing the subject, she said, "I wrote to An and told her I wouldn't make any decisions about leaving Hong Kong early until after the holidays." She stared at Mingyu's back. He still wasn't responding. *Is he concentrating on the sizzling chicken or is he upset?*

She continued with a more volatile subject, "I saw Alison the other day when Chen was out of town. She wanted to show me her sample line. It's impressive. She's really good. She'll be introducing it at a trade show in October." She paused and waited for a response. Nothing. "I told her about Chen and the robbery, but she didn't say much… kind of like you right now. Did I say something wrong? Are you mad at me?"

Mingyu removed the pan from the flame and gave the pungent oyster sauce a stir. He remained silent. After a deep inhale, he put down the wooden spoon and slowly turned to face her. His face was impassive, his words controlled. "I won't touch the subject of Alison. You know what I think. I'm a little surprised you don't want me to meet your mother. Why is that?"

Lily Rose knew she needed to choose her words carefully. "It's not that I don't want you to meet my mother…I'm contemplating asking Lam if I can stay another year and my mother will automatically assume it's because of you."

"And that's a problem? Are you thinking of staying because of me?"

"I would be lying if I said it had nothing to do with you, but it's also because I don't feel like going back to New York yet. My life in New York was all work and very little play. It also revolved around my grandmother, who is no longer there. I'm not sure I can deal with that yet. I like my life here, with you, and I like that I have a more balanced schedule and a better quality of life. I'm simply not ready to leave."

"You're skirting my question, Lily Rose. I introduced you to my entire family, including my cousins, aunts and uncles. You don't think it's hurtful that you don't want me to meet your mother when she's here in Hong Kong?"

"I'm sorry. I just didn't want her to blame you for my decision to stay. It isn't meant the way you may think. If you really want to meet her, if it's that important to you, I'll introduce you. Look at it in the same light as you not bringing me to your father's house for dinner. Some relationships are just… more difficult. It really has nothing to do with you. It has to do with my relationship with her."

"Point made, but I would still like to meet her. And even though my father is difficult too, I chose not to hide you. I want you in my life regardless of what he thinks. It's my life, my decision."

"Ok, fair enough. Maybe I'm being immature about this."

"You haven't told your mother about me, have you?"

The heavenly sweetness of Mingyu's oyster sauce wafted up her nose. "No, I only discussed my love life with Marina."

Mingyu nodded and moved on. "What happens if Lam says no?" He turned back to stirring the oyster sauce, lowering the heat.

"I'll have to leave." She walked over to the stove and hugged him from behind, wrapping her arms around his waist and resting her head on his back. "But I don't want to leave you. I'm committed… … to our relationship."

He turned off the stove and turned back to her, kissing her gently on the lips. "I don't want to lose you either. My grandfather recently suggested something that I'm still digesting. I wasn't going to mention it yet because I'm still working it out in my own head, but maybe now is a good time."

"What's that?"

"Jin would like me to open a London office for our company. It would put me closer to New York on a world map, but we still wouldn't be on the same continent."

"Really?" Lily Rose could feel her heart accelerate. "How do you feel about leaving Hong Kong?"

"I have mixed feelings. This is home and I never thought about leaving. I would feel a lot better about relocating to London, if you transferred with me. What do you think about that?"

"Wow… … I think… … I think I would like that idea. London could be cool. I don't know if I could manage it directly from Hong Kong. I might have to go back to New York first."

"Why?"

"Well, for starters, I promised Margo I would be back. And then there's David. He wants to transfer to London with his BNO passport. I don't want to thwart his chance. I don't think we can both leave at the same time. Lam would have a melt-down."

"But you're scheduled to leave anyway. Why should he care if it's London or New York? Besides, it really depends on the hotel's needs. There could be two people in London dying to make a switch to New York or Hong Kong, Do your research. Maybe talk to people working in that office directly?"

"You don't understand. I have to go through human resources. They have a waiting list of possible transfers. Margo will be pissed if I put myself on the list again."

"Maybe not. Things change in a year. If you go back to work in New York, we may miss the mark completely. If the London office doesn't take off, I may come back here before you arrive there."

"I don't know if I can pull things together that quickly. I also was very fortunate with the living situation here. An and I just switched apartments and jobs. That was incredibly lucky. I like your idea though. I would definitely prefer London to New York. And I would love to be where you are."

"Perfect. We're on the same page then. Maybe we could live together? I could find us a nice apartment in London." He searched her face for a reaction. Lily Rose knew he was putting himself out there more than he was accustomed to, but these kind of life decisions needed careful thought.

"Maybe. Let me think about that." Lily Rose turned to the window and peered out over the darkening harbor. "If I come to London, I might still want my own space."

Chapter L

Jin's Gentle Prodding

Mingyu and Jin were cooking at home on Stanley Village Road, terrace doors flung wide open. It was a beautiful fall day. A tropical shower had just left a sheen of moisture on the large-petaled garden plants, making them sparkle like emerald gems in the shifting sunlight. Colorful boats dotted the water as their noisy inhabitants' voices echoed across the bay. Mingyu took in the scenery and thought about how much he would miss this view and the sensations the combined elements left on his soul. He enjoyed his leisure time with his grandfather in the home he loved. How would he fare without his family? He was close to his sister and cousins as well. They were a clan that supported each other, shared meals and spent most holidays together. He would miss that if he moved to London.

Jin checked the rice and his steamed shrimp rolls. "Have you given my proposal about a London office any further thought?"

"I have. I've also discussed it with Lily Rose and asked her if she would consider transferring there. She agreed, but she's not sure how quickly that could happen. She thinks she may have to go back to New York first."

Jin's lips curled upward ever so slightly. "Is that a problem for you? You could go first and concentrate on setting yourself up."

"Yes and no. Her coming would make the thought of going abroad so much more palatable. Together we would make the experience an adventure."

"I understand, but don't hinge your decisions on another person. It's an adventure, regardless."

Mingyu sighed. "Maybe. She also expressed concern about finding an apartment. Here in Hong Kong she was lucky to switch with a coworker. Housing in London is expensive and maybe more difficult to find?"

"Same as here or New York. That's a common big city concern. It's almost worse here since the government owns most of the housing. There it's private."

"When I suggested she live with me, she was tentative. She didn't exactly jump at the opportunity, which I have to admit, hurt a little. Maybe she's having second thoughts about us?"

"I see. Or maybe she just needs time to think? It's not a decision to jump into. I give her credit for not rushing into anything. However … there's a way to find out how she really feels and it will ensure her company and ongoing commitment." Jin said calmly, a smile threatening to spread.

"Tell me. How?"

"Propose."

Jin called Carson Wu to schedule a meeting. "I have a few fine jade artworks I'm selling from my private collection. I think you may be interested."

The reply was instant. "Yes, I am. When can I look?"

"Any afternoon this week is fine. Do you have a preference?"

"Is anyone else seeing them?" Carson asked with an edge.

"Yes."

"I'll come tomorrow at two."

Jin smiled. "Perfect. See you then." He had thrown out his hook and was satisfied Carson bit. After proposing his London office idea to Mingyu, Jin made the decision to part with a few gems to finance the operation and set Mingyu up for success. He considered it a strategic investment. After all, what good was his collection if he couldn't occasionally use it to finance bigger and better ventures. More than anything, he believed in Mingyu and wanted to ensure his grandson's future and happiness, even if it meant cutting him loose and sending him across the world. No doubt he would miss Mingyu terribly, but his next prodigy, Elizabeth, would fill the void.... somewhat. Jin believed in sharing his hard-earned knowledge, passing it down through his own family felt good. Knowledge was meant to be shared. But more than anything, he wanted Mingyu to be happy, successful and generate his own experiences. His mission to train his grandson was almost done. Now it was time for Mingyu to branch out. Lily Rose made Mingyu happy. Jin knew that in his heart and he hoped she would go to London too. He banked on it.

When Carson arrived, jin took him to Cheng's empty office, which now doubled as a private viewing room for dealers. Its location to the right of the stairs allowed for it to be separate from the workshop. The hallway at the top of the stairs offered no view of their very private inner sanctum, off to the left, an area Carson

Wu would never be privy to. He made sure that door was closed and would stay closed.

Once Jin had made up his mind to sell a few prize pieces, he called several of his most loyal collectors. Each had come to view the carved masterpieces and some had left sealed bids, but since Carson Wu had particularly deep pockets along with the necessary passion, Jin didn't want to exclude him. Furthermore, the opportunity to talk to Carson alone was too good to pass up.

When Carson arrived, Amber served tea. The security guard was posted by the office door while Carson's men remained downstairs in the shop. Li covered the downstairs with Amber. Mingyu was instructed to get the items from the safe and stay close to assist.

Jin leaned back in the padded leather chair, assuming control. He took a long sip of his tea and chose his words with care. He had rehearsed a dialogue in his mind and was prepared to direct the meeting. "I have three pieces for sale that you may like; you may buy one or all. I'm selling them to the highest bidder. They are being shown to a handful of collectors, my very best clients. The order in which they are shown doesn't matter, as I will give everyone a chance to see all the pieces and consider sending me their best offer. I believe that you have a high appreciation for fine jade, and will enjoy the opportunity to see these prize heirlooms even if you don't buy anything. Given your past purchases here, I owe you that opportunity and respect." He paused for emphasis and noticed that Carson had put his tea aside and was leaning forward. Jin knew he had Carson's full attention. He continued,

"These kinds of carvings rarely hit the open market. They're museum quality and extraordinarily valuable."

Carson bowed respectfully. "Thank you for your confidence."

Mingyu placed the three boxed carvings on the desk and Jin uncovered the first one as his grandson became invisible, retreating, back against the wall, fingers interlaced in front of him.

"The first piece is a small dragon sculpture carved by a master carver from the *Quing* Dynasty, the last imperial dynasty in China lasting from the mid 1600's to the early 1900's. It is an extraordinary piece of imperial jade. The stone's color is remarkably even. It has few imperfections despite its age. Pay attention to the fine detail in the carving." Jin pointed to a few intricate areas. Carson examined the specimen closely, his eyes laser-sharp, as Jin slowly turned the velvet cloth the sculpture rested on 360 degrees, to be viewed from all sides.

"Very nice," Carson muttered, visibly impressed. He touched the stones' smooth surfaces with the rough pillows of his fingertips and leaned in to eye the minute details.

Jin moved the sculpture to the side, placing it beside the box. "The second piece is a stylized, crouching tiger from the *Shang* dynasty, so the 12th century BC. It's a green/brown muddled jade, also with exquisite detailing. You can feel the power of this animal. Look at the muscular body contours—very naturalistic. What's remarkable is that it's also in mint condition." Again, he let Carson examine the piece as he turned it slowly to be viewed from every muscular angle.

"Incredible," Carson remarked impressed. "I'm very interested in this one. What offers did you get?"

"I can't tell you the offers made so far; they are sealed bids, but I can give you the estimated value you need to be near. Again,

I will not sell until everyone had a chance to examine the pieces and give their best offer, so don't worry about that. Let's move on to the third piece and then you can give me your thoughts. Mingyu will give you the accompanying paperwork with information about the piece and the estimate range."

Carson, clearly wasn't used to not being in charge and Jin could sense his bubbling frustration, but being the skilled salesperson he was, Jin used it to his advantage.

"The third piece comes from our private family collection. I'm willing to part with it for a generous offer. It's a fine example of imperial *Hetian* mutton fat nephrite jade. It's a vessel with elaborate carved bird and plant motifs from the *Zhou* Dynasty, 1122-255 BC." He, again, turned the velvet cloth in time loop speed, letting Carson look at and touch the piece. "This was in my father's collection so it has received the utmost care as you can imagine. All three pieces come with certification. "Mingyu, can you hand Mr. Wu the estimates?"

Carson studied the vessel, then the papers and Jin answered a few of his questions. Mingyu retreated back to the wall in awe of his grandfather's cool. When it appeared that Carson had finished his examination of everything, the last artwork was boxed and set aside on a tray, close to Mingyu.

"I'm interested in the dragon and the tiger. I think I'll pass on the vessel even though it's magnificent. I like the power and look of the first two sculptures. They appeal to me." Carson nodded without emotion.

"I understand. Both are excellent choices. Leave me your bid and a refundable deposit and I'll get back to you as soon as I hear from everyone."

"If someone bids higher than me, will you give me a chance to counter?" Carson asked fidgeting.

"Only if your bid is in the estimate range. If it is below, the highest sealed bid in the estimate range, gets the piece. Mingyu, please take the tray and put it back in the safe." Jin addressed the agency guard. "Accompany him."

When all pieces were boxed and both men were out of earshot, Jin leaned in closer to Carson and steepled his fingers on the edge of the bare, polished table. "There's something I wanted your help with."

Carson Wu waited silently, leaning back in his chair, his face still expressionless. Jin placed a close-up photo of a jade dragon pendant on the table, turning it and sliding it toward Carson. "A close friend of my grandson's was recently robbed of her jewelry, specifically a fine imperial jade dragon pendant she inherited from her grandmother. The pendant came from my shop fifty years ago, so I know it well. It was a devastating loss for the young lady. This is a detailed picture of it. I would like you to contact me if you come across it in your jade purchases or hear about its sale. It's registered as a stolen art piece in the international market. The person who stole it will not be able to sell it legally without attracting attention, nor will the pendant bring them much luck or protection. On the contrary-- stealing someone else's gifted necklace and family protection heirloom only ends in misfortune. Bad karma. Very bad karma."

Jin lied with conviction, twisting a Chinese superstition for his purposes. He added, "Provenance and intention are just as important as the carver and the subject. You know the unfortunate story about the Hope diamond, right? So sad." Jin shook his head and frowned.

Carson snatched the picture, looking closely, then put it down. "Hmm."

Jin spotted a hint of recognition, an involuntary twitch in the corner of Carson's eyes, but he didn't respond with more than a nod. After a minute, he added, "So sorry. Where was she robbed?"

"At her apartment in West Kowloon. She was at work. So unfortunate." Jin shook his head.

"Hmm." Carson said again, nodding. After a brief pause he got up. "I'll send you my bids. When will I hear your final decision?"

"Soon. In a week. Two, at most." Satisfied, Jin smiled cryptically. "Let me walk you downstairs." In his mind, even people like Carson Wu had their soft spots, similar to an armadillo's underbelly. A smart predator could strike at the right moment and in the right spot, thereby circumnavigating the tough exterior shell. Jin prayed he had penetrated Carson's armor with his phony folklore. He was banking on every bit of his almost fifty years of sales skills. If he was reading his customer right, Carson Wu would make it his business to investigate the story of the Hope diamond and realize the tragedy of its curse. If Carson had the dragon pendant, Jin had a chance at retrieval. Lily Rose did not.

Chapter LI

Mingyu's Reflections

Jin and Mingyu were chatting and looking at new stone inventory at Jin's desk. The sweet scent of jasmin tea permeated the air. Mingyu's chair was pulled up close along the workshop window side of Jin's desk, where the lighting was good. Stones sorted and priced, Jin motioned Mingyu to close the office door. Conversation shifted to Cheng and Jin switched to a hushed voice.

"Hu Fat is back at work. His lawyers were successful in getting him out of a pinch…once again. None of the charges stuck and the evidence was all circumstantial or tampered with. Akiyama disappeared, probably to Japan, or he's resting with the fishes. My guess is that harbor inspectors and police are being paid off or intimidated. If this is a collaboration with Carson Wu, the authorities are on his payroll, including Hu Fat. Terrible way to live and do business. It's hard to challenge and win against Black Society."

"Black Society?" Mingyu blinked.

"Organized crime. They do what they want. Not just here. It's no different in Macao, Taiwan, Yokohama, cities in the United States. The 14K triad's reach is global."

"I spoke with Dad last night. He's confident that he'll be cleared. I forgot to ask him about Winnie. Is she still working with him?"

"As far as I know. Haven't heard otherwise."

"He should dump her." Mingyu grimaced.

"Perhaps he will after this blows over. It's best for him not to rock the boat now. He doesn't want a vindictive lover to ruin his chances of being cleared. However, I'm not celebrating yet. Your father is not free until the investigation is completed. He has to pray he doesn't end up being the scapegoat in this action."

"But out of everyone, he's the least involved," Mingyu lamented.

"Doesn't matter. You never know how lawyers and police will spin things to show they've found the bad guy and met their quota or political goals. Let's hope this continues to be low profile in the press because once they get involved, the pressure escalates."

Jin sipped his tea, momentarily closing his eyes.

"Have you spoken to Carson Wu about the pieces you're selling?"

"No, not yet. I haven't heard back from the Sun brothers, my other interested clients."

"Are you sure you want to sell those pieces, Ye Ye?"

"Yes. They're not my most prized possessions. I can part with them if it means having money for more important endeavors. Sometimes it's better to have capital at hand. A smart investment pays off when you need it." Jin turned to his computer. "Ok, let's get back to work. Let me email a few clients."

Mingyu knew he was being dismissed. When Jin was done sharing, bulldozers couldn't change his course. Back at his desk,

Mingyu googled black societies. Among other groups, the triads came up. Jin's exhaustive knowledge about everything never ceased to surprise Mingyu. There certainly was a dark underworld he wasn't privy to and he was beginning to grasp how extensive their reach was. It made him appreciate how hard his family worked to make an honest living. He hoped his father wouldn't break the family mold.

Mingyu had become aware of the darker side of trade, when he attended business school—counterfeiting, gambling, human trafficking, and the Chinese opium trade. Much of it ran through Hong Kong, but it was all so remote from his immediate surroundings. Illegal trade was something he heard or read about in the news. Thinking of Carson Wu as anything other than a client who appreciated and collected jade was beyond his horizon. Was he maturing and seeing the world for what it really was?

Mingyu was beginning to follow his grandfather's way of thinking. Seizing opportunities when they presented themselves was like grabbing the golden ticket at the right moment. Why wait and possibly miss the chance to change your life? Wasn't that the mistake Jin had made when he stayed with the family business and let Marina go? Didn't he play it safe and lose love?

Jin's acquired worldly approach may have been a result of staying put, but it hadn't changed his growth or thirst for knowledge. It was his way of connecting by staying informed. Jin opened Mingyu's eyes to the possibilities outside of his small, safe bubble, as did Lily Rose. He was beginning to realize how fortunate he was that his grandfather recognized the need to expand beyond ones horizons. He was also grateful that Jin supported his love for Lily Rose. Jin's father hadn't done the same for him. Not only did he disapprove, but he meddled and ruined his son's chance of happiness with a foreigner. Different era. Maybe in order to grow as a person, you had to leave the cocoon and go out into the world and take a few shots in the dark. His thoughts traveled back to Lily Rose. Would he risk losing her if she decided against London and went back to New York? Or if she couldn't get a transfer? The idea unsettled him.

The rest of the day, Mingyu sent out promotional emails and answered clients' requests, but his mind was definitely elsewhere. He wanted to take another trip with Lily Rose. Wanting to recapture the fun they had in the Philippines, he texted her at lunch time. He suspected they both needed time to think about the future and relaxing together could possibly sway her in his direction. Diligence and patience had paid off so far.

Hi. Any long weekends coming up? It would be fun to take a trip—just the two of us.

He waited but no reply was forthcoming as he checked and rechecked his phone. Was she busy at work? At 4pm he pushed back his chair and stretched, then sprang into action. He shut down his computer and grabbed his gym bag. Exercise helped clear his head.

"I'm leaving early today. I have rowing practice with Bao and the team. I'll see you tomorrow." He waved to Jin, who was still on the phone, and sprinted out the door. Maybe boosting his endorphins would jump start his muddled brain to make a decision.

Chapter LII

Two Peas Who Belong in One Pod

Lily Rose saw Mingyu's text at the end of her workday and smiled. She relished the idea of another travel weekend, alone with him. They always managed to have a fabulous time together. She checked the event calendar for options, then asked David what his upcoming plans were. She knew she needed to save vacation days for her week in Thailand with mom and for the end of her stay in Hong Kong. She counted her vacation days and concluded she could spare a few. After speaking to Mingyu, she would clear it with Lam.

It looks like I can get a four-day weekend in mid-October. David and I checked the schedule. What and when do you have in mind? LMK before I approach Lam.

Ishigaki Island? I've never been. I hear the beaches and coral reefs are amazing for observing marine life. Or Bali? About 2.5 hours flying time for Ishigaki and 4.5 hours for Bali. When is flexible. Your thoughts?

Wow. Bali sounds awesome! There's a Conrad Hilton there. I just checked. I can probably get us an employee rate. Let me see if I can add another vacation day to make it five. I'll ask Lam about the second weekend in October tomorrow. Would that work for you? Let's confirm tonight.

Totally works for me.

When Lily Rose arrived home from the office, she got a call from Alison. "Hi, what are you doing?"

"I literally just walked in the door, so nothing yet."

"Are you free for dinner? Chen is out."

Lily Rose hesitated. "I don't know. I don't think I can handle another surprise visit from Chen."

"Don't worry. He's in Japan and he's already forgotten about you. Trust me, he has bigger problems to take care of right now."

"I won't even ask. Ok, if you think I'm safe, I'll meet you. I have nothing edible in the fridge and I'm too tired to cook. Give me time to shower and change out of my work clothes. They're literally sticking to me."

"Good. I'll text you when I get to your building. We can eat in your neighborhood."

Forty minutes later, they were seated in a nearby restaurant at a private table with cocktails and menus. Lily Rose sipped her tropical drink. "So, how are you? How is the collection coming along?"

"I'm stressed, but the dresses are finished. I have all twelve samples ready to show, along with a collection of printed scarves. The scarves are easy to reproduce and could be a quick seller."

"Is the one you're wearing one of them? It's beautiful." Lily Rose admired the sheer cotton fabric imprinted with a medley of soft pink, pastel yellow and lime paisley patterns. It was loosely draped around Alison's narrow shoulders enhancing a rocking, hot pink tailored dress.

"Yes. This is one of the scarves. I picked sheer fabrics that work as scarves or beach wraps. This one is for you. Your colors. Look at my logo tag." She handed Lily Rose the scarf off her shoulders and proudly held out the label sewn in one of the tasseled ends. Lily Rose leaned in to read it. Centered on the tag was a white lotus flower with a lemon center and delicate soft pink edges. On one of the petals was the letter 'A.', prominently displayed in coconut brown. Underneath the flower she read Alison W. Designs.

"I love it, Alison. It's beautiful. Will that be your company name?"

"Maybe." Alison smiled. "My logo is the lotus flower with the letter 'A."

"That should get Chen's ire. What did he say?"

"He's silently stewing because my father is supporting me."

"Well, good. Let him stew. You go, girl."

"Thanks." She grinned. "I was going to ask you to work at the show, but I think Chen may come around."

"Well, I would have offered, but honestly, I'm too nervous. Chen makes me queasy."

"I know. He makes everyone queasy, including me. Are you still happy with your tattoo? I regret not getting another one in Beijing. Chen Jie is the best."

"Very happy. No regrets. What would you have gotten?"

"I've been thinking of covering the triad symbol with another flower. I like the idea of a small Buddha too."

"Really? Well, couldn't you just cover the triad symbol with a Buddha?"

"No. You don't put the image of Buddha below the waist. It's disrespectful."

"I see. What kind of tattoos does Chen have?"

"He has double dragons that cover his entire back and a tiger, three triad symbols and his ranking on his chest. Nothing on his arms and legs."

"Ranking?"

"His triad ranking-426. The triads have inked number rankings that show their place in the organization."

"Really?" Lily Rose wondered if that was too much information, but nonetheless, she made a mental note of the number. She would google triad rankings when she got home to see where Chen stood in Carson's group. She wondered what happened when someone moved up a rank. Did they ink over the old number? "Did your mother have tattoos?"

"No. Mainstream Chinese people see tattoos as defamation of the body. She never wanted one. No one in her family was inked. It bothered my father that she refused. I got my tattoos after she left."

Lily Rose was beginning to sense why Alison's mother took flight. She wondered how a woman who clearly wasn't from the triad culture would have married into it. It did explain why Alison didn't exactly fit the gangster girl mold, whatever that required. Alison definitely had a softer side to her when she let you in. Her affiliation wasn't by choice Lily Rose reminded herself. despite having the identifying ink. Perhaps Alison wasn't fully triad indoctrinated?

They chatted a while longer, then parted ways. Alison had ten days to prepare for her debut and she was nervous, but in essence she was mentally and physically prepared. Lily Rose felt bad she couldn't support her friend in person, but she hoped to be in Bali that weekend…nowhere near Chen Du.

Chapter LIII

Bali is a Blast

Lily Rose and Mingyu were cuddling in bed in Nusa Dua, their first night in the *Conrad Hilton Bali Resort*. They hadn't seen all that much in their twelve-mile ride from the airport because it was dark when they landed, but at first glance, the lit hotel grounds appeared promising. A quick walk around the premises offered an impressive array of lush tropical gardens and the suggestion of a beach from here to infinity. If they never left the hotel it would still be a memorable stay.

Lily Rose awoke when Mingyu's protective arm around her waist shifted. Opening her eyes, she watched him slide on his silk boxers and open the curtains to reveal a tropical paradise. Large diamond-shaped leaves surrounded a small, private patio. Mingyu cracked the sliding doors and Lily Rose felt a moist breeze creep in and cling to her. The sweet fragrance of orchids invaded her nostrils. They were in a ground floor room with pool access. On the patio, she observed a café table with two chairs and a double-seated, padded chaise.

Surrounding palm trees offered plenty of shady options. Inspired to explore, she slithered out of bed and pulled an oversized t-shirt over her naked body. Poking her head outside, she took in the tantalizing scent of fresh coffee wafting over the screened divide from the terrace next door.

"Mmm…coffee. Shall we get some and take a beach walk? We can come back and have breakfast later."

"Ok. I'll get it while you finish getting dressed. Oh…and use bottled water to brush your teeth. You don't want to get Bali belly."

"Bali belly?" Lily Rose quizzed.

"The water isn't safe here. We need to stick with bottled water and cooked foods."

"Ok. No salad for lunch then."

"No. Not recommended. Shall we stay on the premises for the day and do an island tour tomorrow? I seem to remember you needing down time the first day of vacation."

Lily Rose laughed. "Yes, that would be great. I could use a day to decompress."

Mingyu smiled. "I thought so."

When he returned with coffee for her and tea for himself, they set off toward the beach. It was hot and humid, but still bearable at this early hour. The hotel was slowly coming alive as curtains and doors slid open, revealing happy vacationers. On the beach, they stuck their toes into the water and took in the peaceful ocean view. In the distance, surfers waited for the big wave to glide in on.

Strolling past a triangular glass structure in the sand, with two open sides, Mingyu stopped.

"I wonder what this is for?"

"I bet it's for beach weddings and parties." Lily Rose gushed. "Let's check it out."

The glass house was big enough for a small standing group, but not much more.

They stepped through the opening at the garden side, stopping at the other open end, facing the ocean. "This is ingenious. It keeps the wedding party dry during monsoon season. I would love to have a beach wedding. Wouldn't you? How romantic. I can't think of a nicer venue."

"Ahh...I don't know. Haven't thought about it much." Mingyu shifted his feet awkwardly.

Lily Rose looked at him. "You never once imagined what your wedding would look like?"

"No. I guess I assumed it would be in a Buddhist temple in Hong Kong." Mingyu shrugged.

"Regardless of who you might marry? What if the person isn't religious or of a different religion?"

"Is this a trick question?" He asked, eyebrows wrinkling.

Lily Rose watched him squirm and decided to change direction.

"What does a Buddhist wedding ceremony look like? What are your traditions? We've only had receptions at the hotel." She reached out and touched the glass with her hand. It felt warm.

"Marriage is not considered a sacred ceremony in Buddhism. It's more of a social event where the two families and their friends come together and meet. The ceremony takes a half hour tops and it's led either by a priest in the temple or a friend or civil servant, if it isn't."

"Do you say vows?" Lily Rose wondered.

"Yes. They're based on promises to maintain a harmonious and spiritually centered relationship." Mingyu took a step toward the exit, then stopped when she didn't move.

"Cool. That sounds beautiful. What are the customs for the celebration?"

"They vary depending on your culture. In China, we exchange gifts. Traditionally, the night before the wedding, nine monks meet with the couple and honor the bride's ancestors. They chant and pray together. The couple says their vows and their heads or wrists are joined by a sacred thread symbolizing their union."

"That sounds intriguing. Go on…"

"In temple a candle is lit and water poured into a bowl for the ceremony the next day. Holy water. Most people choose to light incense and make flower offerings to Buddha. The next morning the couple is blessed in the shrine room where they remove their shoes. Buddhist weddings are simple, but joyous."

"What happens after the ceremony?" Lily Rose took a big sip of coffee as she waited in place for his reply.

"There's a reception with traditional, regional food, depending on which part of Asia you're from."

"What do people wear?"

"At my sister's wedding, she wore a red wedding dress and my brother-in-law wore a dark suit and red tie."

"Do women always wear red wedding dresses?"

"No. When one of my friends got married in the summer, he wore a white suit with a red tie and the bride wore a white dress." Mingyu finished his tea and crushed the paper cup, his knuckles turning white from the pressure.

"At Alison's wedding she wore white and changed into a red dress for the reception. I know because they took lots of pictures in the hotel. Chen wore a dark suit and red silk tie with a dragon print, but the groomsmen wore red, a *changshan* with dragon motifs."

"Hmm." Mingyu took another step toward the ocean-side exit and looked out, his back to Lily Rose.

She kept talking. "They had a wedding cake and a pop band too. I noticed that guests don't bring gifts. They give red money envelopes."

"And I bet you each denomination ended in one. Numbers ending in zero signify the end, while one symbolizes a positive beginning," he explained over his shoulder as he stepped out of the structure. He was sweating profusely.

"I didn't know that. I never looked inside the envelopes," Lily Rose giggled.

"Whew, it's getting hot. Ready for breakfast?" Mingyu wiped sweat beads from his forehead with the back of his hand. He walked toward the water and dipped both hands in, splashing his face. Lily Rose wondered if the sun-heated glass made him sweat or the threatening subject of marriage. She pondered in silence, as they walked hand in hand to the breakfast room. The rest of the morning was spent in and out of the Indian ocean.

They opted for a late lunch on the terrace. While enjoying a fruity drink, exotic, colorful birds chattered and swooped around them.

"What shall we do tomorrow?" Lily Rose asked.

"We can go on an island tour. There's a museum and some galleries and markets to explore. Then there are a few temples and other beaches to discover. We can also go to Komodo National Park and see a komodo dragon lizard or two."

"An art and crafts tour sounds like fun. I think a temple might put you over the edge."

Mingyu stared at her in surprise. "What?"

"I had the impression I scared you silly with all my questions about weddings this morning. I was just curious. No ulterior motives. Relax." She leaned over and held his hand reassuringly. "Lily Rose. You surprised me, but not in the way you may think." He took her hand in his and looked at her, his expression serious. "This morning surprised me because when I thought about it, I could truly see myself sharing a future with you. It scared me because whenever I think of you leaving, I worry about not being able to sustain a long-distance relationship until we're ready and know what we want. I don't want to lose you, like Jin lost Marina." His warm eyes focused on her trying to gauge if he might have revealed too much.

"Really? That's what's on your mind?" His quiet demeanor was obviously misleading. "I didn't plan to just fly back to New York and forget about you, you know. I figured when I have to leave, we'll make some kind of arrangement if we want to stay together. I care about you, Mingyu. We'll figure us out, if we both want to. This isn't the 1960s."

Mingyu exhaled audibly. "I always thought I'd live in Hong Kong forever. Now, I'm not sure about so many things. Life has become more complicated and unpredictable. I'm trying to acclimate to the thought of possibly moving and I'm weighing my options. I may be confused about my direction, but not how I feel about you."

"I understand…honestly. Look, I never thought I'd be living in Hong Kong by myself, but here I am and I haven't regretted a single day. I've traveled to places I never would have imagined traveling to and I had the opportunity to see you again after our chance meeting in New York. How cool is that? I consider myself lucky and I know I've grown as a person from the experience. Sometimes you have to take risks. Knowing which ones to take are key, but then again, it takes mistakes to get things right. Even if we parted, I would never regret the time we had together. Marina never forgot Jin or her time abroad. Besides, if you were going to play it safe, you could have married Fen, but you didn't. So…. I think you're ready for something more complicated even if you don't realize it."

"If it involves you, I think you're right. You inspire me to re-evaluate my direction, my goals."

"Thanks. I'm not leaving until the end of March. That's five months from now. Let's see how things unfold. There's plenty of time to plan ahead. And there's always the possibility that you may completely change your mind and dump me by then," she laughed.

"No chance." He winked at her.

"Oh look, here comes our food. Let's ask the waiter where we should snorkel."

The next day, they took the organized art tour. Discovering Balinese arts and Indonesian wood carving was educational and eye-opening. At the market, Lily Rose bought a Balinese beaded straw basket with a cover in dreamy shades of ocean blue and bright pink and aqua edging. Mingyu bought a palm-sized intricately carved buddha statue.

At a jewelry store, Lily Rose admired filigree gold hoops called *Chand ball* earrings.

"I'll think about these. My gold jewelry is gone, so I wouldn't mind splurging on a nice pair of hoops. My new jewelry collection will no longer include costume pieces. I'm so past the junk." Continuing her search, she fingered carved sterling silver ball earrings with a faint bell sound and smiled. "These are cute too. No sneaking around with these on."

The salesperson came over to offer a smile and an encouraging discount. "Those are traditional *Bali ball* earrings. The ball is believed to capture your dreams."

"Cool. I might need a bigger ball than that." Turning to Mingyu, she whispered, "What do you think? Are the prices ok?"

"Yes. They're both nice and reasonably priced."

"Maybe." To Mingyu she whispered, "We can always come back on our last day. I may still find something I like better."

"Ok. Just know that these are unique to Bali. I can't make these for you in our workshop."

"Hmm… I'll wait anyway. I have their card."

Before returning to the hotel in the late afternoon, they watched a Balinese stick dancing performance and listened to some synchronized chants around a fire pit, enjoying the cultural overtones.

After a refreshing swim at the hotel, they settled on the couple's chaise outside their room. Lily Rose spread a large beach towel over them and cuddled up to Mingyu. The late afternoon sun warmed her limbs and she could feel Mingyu's body heat transfer to her. She leaned her head on his shoulder and snoozed, while he read world news on his phone. When a tropical shower cleared the pool area, she awoke from the sound of raindrops on the edge of their terrace. Feeling frisky, she slid her hand over Mingyu's abs and snuggled closer, planting butterfly kisses on his neck. The covered porch sheltered them from the torrential downpour while the plush towel hid her exploring hand. When her fingers traveled south under his waistband, he dropped his phone and sucked in air. Lily Rose smiled deviously as she circled a sensitive area. Inspired, his hand gently moved behind her neck and loosened her bikini top. Skillful fingertips explored and teased her.

"People in Bali frown on public displays of intimacy. Let's go inside..... your forwardness has my complete attention. Right now, I'd follow you to Mars."

She breathed in his ear. "So, there'll be no lovemaking on the beach after dark tonight?"

"I highly discourage it, unless you want to see the inside of a Balinese jail."

"Hard pass. Mars, huh? Follow me." She held her top in place as she got up and stepped inside the sliding door, then flung the scant material over the nearest chair. Mingyu locked the sliding doors and drew the curtains before he pulled her close. Merging tongues coupled with warm damp skin quickly escalated into volcanic heat.

"Mars, now," she mumbled, hot breath escaping for the launch.

Chapter LIV

Alison Soars

Lily Rose's first night back from Bali was anticlimactic. After a romantic getaway with Mingyu who admitted he loved her and saw a future including her, she couldn't focus on much else. The memories of that weekend left her breathless. Their conversation ruminated in her brain. London and the possibility of moving there was discussed again.

Lily Rose wondered if Margo would let her go for another year. It was doubtful Lam would orchestrate a transfer for her. Should she even ask? There was no payoff for him and Lam rarely did anything without considering his benefit. She decided to wait until after the holidays to address any life-altering changes, An's request included. For now, she just wanted to enjoy the holiday season with Mingyu and her mother.

Lily Rose was at peace with Mingyu and her mother meeting. She was happy to reconnect with Ella May. Space and time apart had eased their tension. The timing felt right. Their last email exchange had been pleasant and light, both looking forward to their trip to Thailand.

The last trip they took together had included Marina and felt like eons ago. It had been so fun and joyful—boating and snorkeling in the British Virgin Islands, a wonderful but very distant memory now. Lily Rose was worlds removed, but she knew in her heart that her grandmother would be proud of her recent decisions and travels.

During her lunchbreak she texted Alison.

How was the show? Did Chen behave? Do you have time to meet or are you too busy filling orders?

When she checked her phone again a while later, she saw Alison's reply.

Show went well. Lots of interest and a few orders. Can you meet this week for further details? Chen is in China.

When they met a few nights later over tropical drinks, Alison was lit. Her success at the show had given her the push she needed to expand her world; the girl who had once only felt secure in *Mong Kok* now talked about traveling to cities across the globe. Hearing that made Lily Rose happy.

"What about Chen? How is he handling your success? Did he come to the show?"

"Yes, he came. He's taking a hands-off approach, because my father told him to, but he can't help making comments to dissuade me. He thinks my business will ultimately fail. He wants me to fail so he can wave it in my face."

"That isn't very encouraging. He should be your cheer-leader."

"No….never. You are my only cheerleader. And my mother would be, if she knew."

"Who helped you at the show?"

"One of my friends from school. She's between jobs and was happy for the extra cash."

"Where are your orders going to?"

"London, New York, Shanghai and locally, thanks to my father. I hope to hear from a few more interested parties. I had a good launch and I'm satisfied. It's more than I hoped for."

"That's wonderful, Alison! I want to put in an order for two dresses as well. I'll make one my mom's holiday gift. The other is for me."

"Oh, good. Thank you. You can advertise for me in New York when you wear it."

"I plan to. I'm a fan. One of my closest friends in New York works in fashion. Perhaps she can help too. Give me whatever promotional material you have and I'll forward it."

"Thanks." Alison smiled. "Text me the models and sizes you want. I can come over with a few samples and you and your mum can try them on. The workshop is a hot mess."

"Sounds good. I also wanted to get a cheongsam before I leave. Maybe you can come with me to Master Kan's and help me choose the right fabric?"

"Of course. Let's go after the holidays. He's probably swamped now. He'll need a few weeks to perfect it, so don't expect it quickly, but it will be ready before you leave."

"Great."

Friday night Mingyu came over for dinner. While sipping wine, they prepared their food, 'Dragon balls'--finely chopped shrimp, kneaded into balls, then dipped into bread crumbs and deep-fried--were on the menu. Lily Rose was mixing a sweet and sour sauce with chives and assembling a salad to add the healthy component. As Mingyu dipped the balls into the sizzling oil, her phone rang. It was Lam.

"Lily Rose, I'm sorry for the short notice, but I need you to come in tomorrow morning. David is sick and we have that damned convention that has caused so many problems. Please be here at eight."

"Sure, Lam. See you then." She had barely replied when the connection went dead. She rolled her eyes at Mingyu. "That was Lam. I have to work tomorrow. David is sick."

"Sorry. Dinner is almost ready. We'll make it an early night. Will you have to work late?"

"No, the convention ends at five. I should be out by six."

"Great I'll plan something relaxing for us."

"Ok." Lily Rose appreciated the thought. "What?"

"Don't know yet—it'll be a surprise." He placed the shrimp balls on a paper towel, one by one.

"I love your surprises. They're the best." She snuck up behind him and slid her arms around his waist.

Mingyu grinned. "Good. It makes me want to come up with something spectacular. This is ready. Let's eat."

When Lily Rose came home from work, Mingyu was waiting in her apartment. He had let himself in with a spare key.

Hi. Change into something comfortable and put your hair in a ponytail. We have a seven o'clock appointment."

"Where?"

"If I tell you, it's not a surprise. Do you really want to know?" Mingyu raised an eyebrow, his shiny black hair creating a shadow over one eye.

"Surprise me."

"Ok then. Move it. And bring your bathing suit."

"Ohh… I like the sound of this already."

Soon they were seated in a hot tub at the Spa in the Arch.

"This was a brilliant idea. Just what my aching body needed." Lily Rose stretched in the warm water, letting her pink-skinned, lilac-manicured toes surface. She seated herself in front of a jet and let the warm stream hit her lower back. It did wonders for aching joints after a long day on her feet.

"Knowing what a mermaid you are, I thought you might enjoy this." Mingyu glanced at the clock overhead.

"Mermaid? I guess I do love being submerged." She moved across the hot tub to sit closer to him. "You sure know how to surprise a girl."

They sat entwined, enjoying the sea of bubbles exploding around them.

"Ok, Ariel, your twenty minutes are up. Time to move on to surprise number two. Follow me." Mingyu motioned with his head to the steps.

"There's more?"

"There is. The night is just starting. I have at least three surprises, maybe more."

"I hope the third one involves food. I'm working up an appetite."

"It does, but it won't be served in the conventional way. I'll let your imagination work on that one."

"Hmmm."

As they moved down the corridor in their plush robes, they entered a room overlooking Victoria Harbor.

"Welcome. Please take a few minutes to get comfortable and positioned on the tables. We'll be back for your massages," the attendants handed Mingyu two sheets and folded towels. Soft music filled the space and a wonderful peony scent traveled up their nostrils.

Lying on their tummies they reached across the space between the two massage tables and held hands. "I feel like a mermaid princess." Lily Rose muffled into her sheet.

You are …. but for one night only. My catered dinner will be the crowning. At midnight, all cast spells dissolve into darkness, complete nothingness."

"Sounds dangerous. I like it."

Chapter LV

The Holiday Spirit Prevails

The weeks preceding Ella May's arrival were hectic at the hotel. The conventions had let up, but there were holiday parties, weddings and large family gatherings. Sometimes these smaller intimate events were more demanding than the larger corporate ones. The conventions generally had a set formula, but dealing with people's personal expectations was a whole other story.

In an attempt to cash in on the pre-holiday festivities, Mingyu got tickets to the Gloomy Island Blues Festival. Lily Rose was thrilled. The two day event was pricey, but Bao had gotten a press ticket plus one, so Mingyu shared the price of her ticket. The event took place at Green Lohas. Pitching a tent, and the three of them stayed overnight. While the sleeping arrangements weren't ideal, the blues culture was phenomenal. It encompassed a lifestyle that worked for two fun-filled days, including yoga classes, workshops and informal jam sessions. The music was incredible—Tommy Chung, Tomii Chan, Ram Blues Trio and more.

When Ella May arrived three days before Christmas, Lily Rose was ready for a break from work. Luckily, Ella May had opted to stay in the hotel at an employee rate rather than sleep on Lily Rose's sofa. Lily Rose was thankful. The first couple of nights, they met for drinks and dinner, sharing updates on New York, work life and touristy explorations. Ella May enjoyed exploring Hong Kong with her daughter's suggestions in hand while Lily Rose smiled at her reports. The elephant between them was Marina. Neither daughter or mother wanted to acknowledge her painful absence, lest the mood changed.

Christmas Eve the women exchanged gifts in Lily Rose's apartment and shared a catered gourmet meal. The dress Lily Rose had purchased for her mother, a cobalt blue square neck, fitted number matched her mother's cornflower eyes and was received with enthusiasm. The fit was perfect. "I absolutely love this dress!"

"It's also available in black and emerald. Let me show you." Lily Rose pulled up Alison's website. "This is the one I have. She pointed to another model. Mine is violet. What do you think?"

"I like mine, but I wouldn't mind getting another style. Can I buy your model in black?"

"Let me check." Lily Rose sent Alison a text.

Hi. Mom loves her dress. Fit is fine. She would like my model in black. Is it available? We're leaving Tuesday night.

Yes. I can drop it Monday evening. Ok?

Perfect. See you then.

Saturday night, Lily Rose and Ella May met Mingyu for dinner. Lily Rose hadn't told her mother much about her boyfriend, so her nerves kicked into high gear when she picked Ella May up in the hotel. She was pleased to see her mother was wearing Alison's blue dress.

"Wow, the dress looks spectacular, Mom. Better than I imagined. I like the black suede pumps and sweater with it too."

"Thanks. So, tell me a little about who we're meeting for dinner."

"Mingyu is the man I've sort of been seeing for the past few months. He's looking forward to meeting you, so be nice. I've met his entire family and they've been extremely kind and welcoming to me." It stood to reason that sharing this information would indicate how serious Lily Rose was about her guy. Her mother caught the intended message.

"Why haven't I heard about him if you're that seriously involved?"

"We were just friends for the first few months I was here. Things changed recently." A small fib wouldn't matter, if it spared her mother's feelings.

"Tell me about him. Is he British?"

"No, Chinese."

Lily Rose gave her mother some details about Mingyu and his family's business. She also mentioned their travels together.

"So, all those trips you took were with him?" Ella May's head tilted, one eyebrow shooting upward.

"Not all. I went to Beijing with a girlfriend. My friend, Alison, the dress designer. I also hang out with David, who you met in the hotel, and his friends." Her mother would faint on the spot if she knew who Alison's family was. No way would she share that tidbit. In fact, the thought of introducing her mother to Carson Wu made her squelch a good laugh.

"It sounds like you're socially active."

"Enough to keep me happy and busy after work. Socializing here has been easier than in New York. It's a smaller city, the people are friendly and there are great places to go."

When they got to the restaurant, Mingyu was waiting at the bar. He greeted Ella May warmly, but with reserved caution. Signaling the hostess that his party was complete, they were seated in a private corner. Mingyu turned to Ella May, attempting polite conversation. "How has your stay in Hong Kong been so far? What have you done?"

After their first glass of wine, Lily Rose noticed her mother relax. By the end of dinner, they all chatted amicably. Before Mingyu bid his good byes after driving them back to the hotel, he invited them to Stanley Village Road for brunch the next day. "My grandfather was wondering if you both would like to come for an authentic dim sum tomorrow morning? Around eleven?"

Ella May turned to Lily Rose with a questioning expression. "Don't we have plans?" Lily Rose guessed her mother wanted out of this engagement, but she wanted Ella May to meet Jin and see his stunning home. It mattered to her.

"No, we would love to come. Should we meet you there?"

Mingyu's reply was guarded. "No. I'll come collect you both."

"Ok. Thanks."

After dropping Ella May, Lily Rose and Mingyu drove to Mingyu's apartment. Lily Rose had his holiday gift and her overnight bag in the boot of his car. Sharing a cup of tea, they exchanged gifts and avoided talking about the evening. Lily Rose hoped Jin could thaw her mother.

Lily Rose's gift to Mingyu was a peridot Egyptian cotton shirt and an emerald cashmere V neck sweater, which he seemed to genuinely appreciate. She knew he liked green but had nonetheless labored over her choices. Mingyu handed her a small carved box.

"What's this? This box looks Balinese." She glanced up at him, then untied the red silk ribbon.

"It is."

When she opened it, she discovered the filigree gold hoop earrings she had admired on their Indonesia trip.

"Oh my God! The Bali Chand Ball hoops. They're sooo beautiful. When did you buy them?"

"When you weren't looking."

"I so regretted not going back to the store."

"I bought them while you were busy trying on silver earrings. You were so immersed, a bomb could have dropped beside you and your focus wouldn't have shifted."

Lily Rose laughed at his description. "I love them. Thank you." She walked to the mirror and tried them on. "So beautiful!"

Lily Rose flung her arms around Mingyu, who was sitting on the bed. "You're the best boyfriend—always kind, forever thoughtful and you're super cute. A win win for me."

"I've never been described that way." He joked. "I think I'm pretty lucky too. You're pretty, you cook and you get us good rates on hotels."

"Let me show you how lucky."

Arriving at Jin's the next day, Lily Rose greeted him and unpacked her straw tote, plopping all goodies on the counter before putting them away. She let Jin take her mother out to the terrace for tea hoping Ella May would mellow. Clearly uncomfortable and not wanting to give up a day in Hong Kong to visit Mingyu's family, her mother had been fidgeting silently in the car. She also seemed nervous about driving on the wrong side of the road. Lily Rose could tell she was happy to get out of the car.

Once there, Lily Rose gave Jin some space to talk about his garden and put her mother at ease while she and Mingyu navigated the kitchen. She could feel her mother's eyes follow her movements, probably wondering at her comfort here.

Mingyu checked on their food. The table was set. Lily Rose noticed Jin had used different dishes today. It was a fancy set with a gorgeous Chinese garden pattern. She turned to Mingyu, "I haven't told her anything about Jin and Marina's history. I don't want to bombard her with too much at once. She's unpredictable."

"There's no need to tell her anything, if you prefer not to. Marina and Jin's history can remain private. In our case, it made sense to know."

"True. Marina was her mother. I don't know how she would take the news that her mother had an affair."

"My lips are sealed and I guarantee you Jin's are too. We never told my father. It's up to you how to handle it in your family."

"Thanks. I appreciate that."

Over dim sum, Ella May relaxed. She chatted about life in general and asked what she and Lily Rose should see in Thailand. As usual, Jin was a wealth of information. He had traveled in Thailand extensively over the years. Their meal ended on a positive, friendly note and Lily Rose sighed, relieved.

That night Lily Rose and Ella May had a light dinner in the hotel bar.

"The house on Stanley Village Road was quite the gem -- those gardens and the spectacular view over Victoria Harbor from the terrace. Incredible! Where do Mingyu's parents live?"

"His father has a condo on Caine Road, not far away. I've never been there. His mother died and his older sister is married, has two small children and runs the family restaurant. She lives nearby too. The restaurant is a popular family hang out. The food there is good. Mingyu's uncle has a shipping business and two of the cousins work there. The third cousin works in a bank."

"A very entrepreneurial family. Mingyu seems like a nice young man. What will happen when you leave? Have you thought about that?"

"I don't know. I still have a few months. I'll cross that bridge when I get there."

"Three months. They'll pass quickly." Ella May paused. "You're coming home, aren't you?"

Lily Rose noticed the edge in her mother's voice. "That's the plan." There was no point in discussing her unknown future. Chances were she would have to go home to New York for a while anyway which would give them plenty of time to argue. If she decided to go to London, she would deal with telling her mom then. She saw no benefit in fueling the fire now when they were leaving for Thailand in two days. She wanted the vacation to be fun and healing.

Monday night Ella May was cleaning up after dinner while Lily Rose finished packing her suitcase. Her mom was bringing her luggage to the hotel so they could leave directly to the airport after work the next day. As she threw the last few items in, the doorbell chimed. "That must be Alison with your dress." Lily Rose opened the door to a heavily laden Alison. She had two large garment bags, one tucked under each arm.

"Help, grab one of these. My arms are about to break off."

Lily Rose clasped one of her bags and threw it over the back of the couch. "My goodness. How many dresses did you bring?"

"I had a sales appointment before stopping here. Hello, Lily Rose's mother," she smiled, her eyes traveling over Ella May.

"Nice to meet you, Alison. Please, call me Ella May. I absolutely love my blue dress. I've already worn it."

"Happy to hear that. I brought the black one you asked for. You can try it on."

"Let's see the others too," Lily Rose chimed in.

When it came to talking fashion, Alison's insecurities and hard edge disappeared. She pulled out one dress after another, elaborating on the detail work. When all was done, Ella May had purchased two more dresses and a scarf. "These are perfect for work. Your designs are beautiful, Alison. I love the natural fabrics and fluid feel. I wish you lots of luck with your new business."

"Thank you. One client at a time." She looked at Lily Rose. "So glad my load going home is lighter."

When Lily Rose walked her to the door, Alison rolled her eyes." Wish I could stay for a drink, but Chen expects dinner. He knows I had an appointment at four and will be wondering where I am. Call me when you get back, Lily Rose, and have a wonderful trip."

"I will, I promise. I'll be needing multiple drinks by then." She whispered, winking at her friend.

Chapter LVI

New Year, New Plans

Mingyu and Lily Rose met for cocktails in their favorite roof top garden overlooking Victoria Harbor. Enjoying the play of color from the *Symphony of Lights* on the surrounding buildings, they sipped deliciously decadent tropical concoctions.

"Wow, that light show is more colorful than BTS hair styles. They should change the music," Lily Rose gestured with a speared pineapple.

"Write a letter. When one country, two systems crash, this may be a thing of the past. I see lots of changes ahead." Mingyu complained with a sour face.

He didn't usually complain or talk politics, so Lily Rose took note. "That's just sad. It's stealing autonomy from the peninsula. Have you been hanging out with Bao?"

"Yes. It all worries me." His face brightened a little. "I want to hear about your trip. How did Jin's recommendations work out? I also have some good news to share."

"You first."

"My father was cleared of all charges."

"What? That's fantastic! Jin must be thrilled. I'm so happy for you." She clinked his glass splashing a little liquid on his trousers. "Sorry. Tell me more."

He dabbed the spot with a wet cocktail napkin. "There wasn't any compelling evidence to show that he knew what Akiyama was doing. Akiyama disappearing into the wind didn't hurt either. It's a relief for the whole family. The legacy is restored… even if it is slightly tarnished. I don't want to get into all the details. Water under the bridge now and I just as soon forget the tension it caused my family…"

She noticed his hesitation. "But?"

"But, in the industry, it's still a black mark. People don't forget so quickly. Our field operates on trust."

"I understand that. It takes time to regain that status." She wondered if that was the only thing bothering him. She knew his father's misstep was an open wound. *He's clamming up. I won't pry.*

Mingyu abruptly changed the subject. "Chinese New Year is around the corner, on February fifth. It's a huge celebration in my sister's restaurant. Are you off that day?" He reached for her hand.

"I doubt it. Maybe I can join you after work?"

He nodded and motioned for her to move closer. She slid around the corner to his part of the bench and he put his arm around her shoulders, leaning his head against hers.

"What's going on? You seem a little… blue tonight." She placed their joined hands on his knee and glanced at his profile against the bright, exploding lights.

"I was thinking about you leaving next month. What have you decided with An?"

"I'm not leaving early if that's what you're worried about. I offered to vacate her apartment, but not the job. And she still has to pay March rent in my New York apartment."

He perked up a bit. "So, you'll stay with me for the month of March?"

"Yes. If your offer still stands."

"Of course." Mingyu nodded, his smile returning. "Let's hear about your vacation with mum."

In her mind, living with Mingyu was a trial run for…she wasn't sure. "One more thing. I wanted to take the intensive diamond course at the GIA in March, but I think it'll have to wait until I'm back in New York now. I don't have enough vacation time left."

"You can always take it remotely. Start here and finish there."

"Really? That's an option? Cool." Lily Rose smiled. "So, my trip with mom."

At work, the next morning, David plopped himself on the edge of Lily Rose's desk.

"I'm going to speak to Lam today about possibly transferring to London."

"Already? Shall we do this together? I might want to ask him too. "

"Wait. Are you seriously saying you're interested in London too? Don't mess up my chances unless you're serious."

"I am and I don't think it will hurt your request. It might make the trade easier."

"How do you figure?"

"There could be two friends in London who are dying to spend a year in Hong Kong, together, like us."

David smirked. "Unlikely."

"Look, Lam already knows I'm leaving, so nothing new there. Why would he care if it's London or New York for me? Gone is gone."

David looked surprised. "You are sure about this, right?"

"Yup," she lied.

After further discussion over lunch, they marched into Lam's office. Lam leaned back in his chair and listened to the onslaught. When they finished their pitch, he replied, "Funny you should ask that. I just got an email from Margo. An is coming to Hong Kong in March for a visit and a wedding, but she wants to return to New York. I was going to ask you, Lily Rose, if you wanted to stay. If not, that would leave me with no assistant managers." He made an ugly face. "I can't be left with no adequate help. However, I've been receiving requests from other applicants to come here so maybe we can work something out."

"Of course, we wouldn't leave you in a lurch. Anyone from London?" Lily Rose asked.

"No. Anyway, I'll need to check with human resources and get back to you on all of this. Why do you both want London? Are you leaving Hong Kong for good, David?" Lily Rose saw David flounder and jumped to the rescue.

"David would like to try London and I don't want to go back to New York yet, but wouldn't mind being closer to home. It would be fun to go together."

"I suppose your mother added a little heat when she was here? I ran into her again on Saturday. She looked fabulous in a royal blue dress. I think she had a dinner date." Lam was fishing.

"Yes, with me." Lily Rose replied quickly. She had no intention of elaborating on her private life. *Ugh, he is so nosy.*

"You know, if An wants to stay in New York and I get a spot in London, she can stay in my apartment. The rent is reasonable."

"Not my worry. You all can figure those logistics out amongst yourselves." Lam turned to his computer.

The following week, Lam called them both into his office. "I have some news. There's one position open in London starting April 1st. I am recommending David. I want to hire someone from Singapore to fill David's spot and I would like you, Lily Rose, to train him for a couple months."

Lily Rose sighed and Lam swiveled a full circle in his chair. When he stopped, he continued with an authoritative tone. "In September, there may be a second opening in London, because someone there is making a switch to I don't remember where. I can recommend you for that, Lily Rose but frankly, I wish you would consider staying in Hong Kong. Any chance of that?"

"The thought has crossed my mind, but if there's a possible spot in London for September first, I would like a shot at it."

Lam frowned. "Ok. If the employee from Singapore is trained and I find a good replacement for you, it's possible. Does that work for everyone? I hope so because all this change is giving me a migraine. Talk to whoever you need to and let me know by tomorrow or at least by the end of this week."

David looked at Lily Rose, then Lam. "I'm good. April first works for me." His face broke into a huge smile. "Thank you, Lam."

"When will you know about my position?" Lily Rose asked cautiously. "I'll need time to work out living arrangements here and where ever I go." She wasn't sure if this was good news or not. Lam wasn't committing. Clearly, he was happy to replace David. *But will he let me go? And where am I going to live come March? Can I stay with Mingyu that long? Is London the right move?*

"Not for a while. That reminds me. Margo mentioned An would love to take over your lease in New York. She'll email you directly." Lam added.

"Does that mean I can stay in her apartment until I leave in August?"

"You girls need to work that out. I don't do housing." Lam stood and walked away his hands up in surrender mode.

"Ok, thanks, Lam."

When she got to her desk, Lily Rose emailed An and Margo. Then she wrote to her contact at human resources and expressed interest in the London position.

That night Mingyu came over with take-out dinner. Lily Rose was eager to share her news. After pouring him a glass of wine, she started. "I have something to share. Are you ready?"

"Always."

"I spoke to Lam about transferring to London. There's some good and bad news."

"Ok, I'm listening." His attention and eyes were focused on Lily Rose, as he sipped and savored the alcohol, a pleasing, sweet aroma.

"David got a spot in London for April first and there's possibly a spot for me starting September first. That's the good news. The bad news is Lam wants me to stay here through the summer to train some new people and he's hinging his decision on him having the right help so that leaves me in limbo for a while. I also have nowhere to live."

"That's great." Mingyu's smile was radiant. "I didn't hear any bad news really."

"An wants to take over my lease, but I'm not sure I can stay in her apartment. That means I need a rental for five or six months and you know how hard that is. Most housing contracts are for a year."

"Stay with me and save money." He put his hands on both her shoulders. "Housing in Hong Kong is difficult. The government owns half of it and people don't leave their apartments if they have a decent one. When I go to London, I'll probably sublet my apartment so I don't lose it. An will most likely want to do the same."

"What if we live together until summer and it doesn't work out? And what if I give up my New York apartment and don't get the London job? I'm the one taking the risks here. You aren't going to back out of London, are you?"

"Lily Rose, relax. There's no risk. We'll plan this right. Wait and see what An says. My guess is that she'll want to sublet. If that doesn't work, I would love to have you stay with me for the last few months. Why don't you just do that? I don't need you to pay half the rent."

"Ok, I'll cover expenses and food but let's see what An says first."

The next morning, they had their answer. An wanted Lily Rose out by March first. She was subletting her apartment to her cousin and her new husband after the wedding.

Chapter LVII

Chinese New Year:
Triumph or Bust?

Chinese New Year was unusually cold with temperatures dipping below fifty degrees. Despite a chill gripping the city with uncommon fierceness, the mid-day sunshine balanced the scales, allowing its inhabitants to enjoy their family gatherings and revered holiday with a touch of brightness. Cold weather could not dampen celebratory spirits, however the political undertones emanating from mainland China certainly could.

The hot topic on everyone's minds, while languishing over meals of fish and *nin gou,* sweet, glutinous rice cakes, was Hong Kong's political direction. While China was publicly agreeing to the peninsula's autonomy, there was a strong undercurrent of fear, protest and outrage over veiled threats to overhaul Hong Kong's government. As a result, thousands of citizens were contemplating emigration and international businesses were leaving without much fanfare or warning. Was the city's democracy being threatened? Would Hong Kong be at Beijing's mercy?

Lily Rose listened to the dialogue around her and felt the tension. In the hotel, their international convention schedule was lighter than in past years and some events, previously blockbusters, were now poorly attended. Marina had lived through the vibrant transition years in the early to mid 60's, but Lily Rose was witnessing a political change of a different nature. Her grandmother thrived through the economic growth years prior to the cultural revolution in 1966, while Lily Rose was witnessing the city's decline as an international hub. This stark contrast was not wasted on Lily Rose.

She was well aware that over a million people died during the Cultural Revolution and many more in the ten-year period after, until Mao's death in 1976. Marina had schooled her well on China's and Hong Kong's history. *What is going to happen to Hong Kong now, in 2019?* During her lunch break, Lily Rose ventured out to the streets to see the parade of painted faces, the dancers, the marching groups making music and to receive some goodie bags launched into the waiting crowds. The festivities brightened her dark thoughts. When a red bag flew in her direction, she caught it with both hands before it smacked her in the face. After checking it's generic snack content, she handed it over to the short, innocent face beside her who accepted it with glee.

Walking further, she stopped to watch an elaborate lion dance--*Gu* drums beating, the bronze gong of the *luo*, tail wagging, confetti flying and crowds clapping. She wondered how many people were hidden beneath the dragon that followed. Red costumes, floats and dragon processions filled every square inch of cobblestone. However, the feeling of political deceit breezed through the streets like an icy gust.

Later, when she finished work, Lily Rose fought the crowds to get to Mingyu at his family's restaurant. The sun had vanished and it was starting to sprinkle. Running late, she decided to skip going back for the umbrella in her office desk. She needed to escape Lam's clutches. He loved to assign last minute tasks. The streets were mobbed, but she forged ahead like Captain Hook in a raging storm at sea.

China's 4000-year-old New Year's tradition was taken seriously in Hong Kong and earmarked for a spectacular firework display over Victoria Harbor. As Lily Rose hurried along the crowded streets, her gaze traveled over the predominant gold and red decorations and the pig images floating before her. The year of the pig in the Chinese zodiac was a symbol of wealth. People born under this sign allegedly displayed enthusiasm, energy and warmth toward others.

Myia's restaurant was as crowded as the street festivities. The atmosphere was festive with decorations covering every square inch of space. In the center of the main room, a small dance floor had been cleared and a dragon dance was in progress. Lily Rose pushed her way through the crowds, looking for Mingyu. She spotted him in the smaller party room, reserved for family and close friends. He was seated amongst his cousins and Bao's family. An attractive Chinese girl stood near him, flirting shamelessly, her fingers playfully twisting her shoulder length black hair into instantly dissolving corkscrew curls while smiling from here to Bejing. Mingyu looked fully invested. When the girl reached out and touched Mingyu, Lily Rose momentarily held her breath. *What the hell.* He looked so comfortable with the girl, so utterly at ease and familiar, it made Lily Rose wonder. She called out to him, but the drums drowned her voice out as she struggled to get to his table. When he saw her, Bao motioned Mingyu to turn around. When Mingyu spotted her, his face broke into a warm smile. He rose to greet her with a hug. The girl's face transformed into an ugly frown. Clearly, Lily Rose had interrupted her agenda.

"You made it. I was beginning to worry. I hope you're hungry,"

"I'm starved. It was a battle getting here." She eyed the girl whose dark stare penetrated her with inquisitive, cold eyes. Having lost Mingyu's attention, she silently retreated.

Mingyu pointed. "Look, I saved you a seat. Let me tell you today's menu. We have stuffed fish, pulled pork, or crispy duck for the main dish. There's steamed shrimp tofu puffs and a vegetable stew with bean curd and oysters to start. I waited to eat the main meal with you, but I couldn't resist a few appetizers. We should get our order in."

"Thanks, I'm impressed with your restraint. Steamed shrimp and duck sound fabulous. What are you drinking?"

"Red wine." Mingyu pointed to his glass, lost in the sea of others.

"Perfect, I'll join you."

He looked for a clean glass, poured the wine and handed it to her. She noticed he was a bit tipsy.

"Thanks. Let me say hello to your family." Lily Rose made her way over to Jin, but it was difficult to talk over the drum beat and loud chatter. She blew him a kiss instead, which clearly surprised Cheng seated next to him, eliciting a critical or was it an 'evil eye'? She waved at him, too, but got no recognizable response. *Is he ever going to like me? Even holidays don't soften his grouchy demeanor.*

When she returned to her seat, the girl who Mingyu had been talking to was back. She leaned over suggestively and whispered in his ear, making him laugh. Something about her irritated Lily

Rose. When she approached them, the girl scooted off to a seat, a few tables away.

She had a clear view of Mingyu and looked over frequently. *Could that be Fen?* When Mingyu went into the kitchen to check on their order, she leaned over and asked Bao. Bao shook his head. "No, Fen isn't here. That's Jun, a friend we went to school with."

Lily Rose swallowed her next question because Mingyu was on his way back with her shrimp order. She noticed his balance was challenged. *How much did he drink?* He placed the dish on the table with a clang, tripping over a chair leg.

"Looks delicious. Thanks." She dug into her shrimp with gusto as Mingyu chatted with Bao. Hunger pangs stilled, Lily Rose caught up with Elizabeth, but whenever her eyes traveled in Jun's direction, the girl was staring at her. It was really beginning to unnerve her. *Damn, she's after my boyfriend!*

For dessert, Mingyu brought rice cakes to the table. Lily Rose opted for ice cream with peanut sprinkles, Jin's favorite. Time passed slowly while Mingyu continued to chat with everyone, including Jun, who circled like a vulture. Lily Rose was tired and not feeling overly sociable as dessert wrapped. The crowds, the noise and Mingyu's lack of attention was irritating after a long, hectic day at the office. She leaned over to Mingyu and whispered close to his ear, "Are you ready to leave soon?" *If I hear one more gong, my head is going to explode.*

"Soon," he answered, swaying in his chair.

Mingyu, in a stellar mood, was clearly not itching to leave. She, on the other hand, felt a massive headache coming on. *Is it the red wine, the luo or Jun?* Finally, they said their good byes and were out the door. By this time her head was throbbing. The rain was torrential and she regretted not bringing her umbrella. Within minutes she was soaked and shivering.

"Are you coming to my place?" Mingyu asked, putting his leaden arm around her.

"I can't. *Why do drunk people always feel like dead weight? Ugh.* "I need fresh clothes for the morning. "*And I'm not interested in sex with someone who may pass out mid act.*

He looked disappointed and Lily Rose couldn't fathom why. Surely, he remembered she had work the next day? His shop was closed, but there were no paid holidays in the hotel industry. You worked the hardest when everyone else was off.

"When is your free day this week?" His speech was slightly slurred.

"Saturday. I'm working Friday night and Sunday. I told you."

"I'll see you Saturday then. I have family stuff the next few days and I probably should sleep in tomorrow. I celebrated a bit too much." He waved his hand in a haphazard way.

No shit. "Does your family stuff include Jun?"

Lily Rose knew she shouldn't go there, but she was feeling pissy about his obvious connection with Jun and his sloppy state. Tipsy men were ok but drunk men were a turn off; she had dealt with her fair share in the hotel business. She also couldn't forget how Jun had looked at him and he seemed to be enjoying it. No amount of rain could quench her bubbling anger.

Mingyu looked astonished. "Yes…why? She belongs to the rowing club. They're having a New Years' celebration that I attend every year, but you'll be at work or I would have invited you." His words were elongated and unfocused.

"So, you do remember I'm working." Lily Rose snipped. "Does that mean you see Jun every week at the club? You never mentioned her before."

"Yes, I do. She's an old friend. Part of my group." Mingyu answered patiently.

"That is not what I saw tonight. I saw a girl who is seriously interested in you, even though she knows you have a girlfriend. A friend would have been curious to meet your girlfriend. And… maybe you should have introduced your 'friend.' Just to be polite, perhaps?" She knew she should let it go, but she couldn't stop her frothing anger. When he didn't respond, she was ready to explode. Not wanting to make things worse, but losing all control anyway, she barked, "Happy New Year, Mingyu. Enjoy your parties with Jun. I'll see you when you're sober… maybe." And with that she picked up her pace, expertly weaving through the crowds in the pouring rain. She sprinted down the nearby steps to the subway platform. She heard Mingyu calling her name, but didn't want him to see her welling tears, so she didn't stop. Luckily, her train pulled in immediately and she hopped on before the doors closed, relieved he didn't catch up with her in his drunken state. Steamed on the inside, drenched on the outside and seriously spent, she slumped into a vacant seat amidst the happy revelers. A pity puddle formed around her feet.

Chapter LVIII

Alison Drops a Bomb

Lily Rose was still in shock when she awoke with a wounded heart the next morning and remembered the botched New Year's celebration. At least her headache was gone. She felt bad about her first serious squabble with Mingyu and it left her with a rancid taste. Last night she had taken migraine medicine and silenced her phone before bed to block out her failed night, but when she turned on her phone in the morning, a flurry of messages flooded her screen. On the way to the shower, she scrolled through them. Most were from Mingyu. They showed his initial anger at her leaving, but then morphed into a more apologetic tone. However, Lily Rose couldn't get over feeling blind-sided, so she didn't respond. She needed space to cool down.

Lily Rose knew there had to have been other women in Mingyu's life, but he had always kept his romantic past vague, rarely volunteering details. How did Jun pop up out of nowhere? Had he seen her on club nights and week nights when they weren't together? All her old fears of Kevin cheating resurfaced.

Getting ready for work, she paid extra attention to looking stylish. Alison's sleek, violet dress made her feel pretty and professional. She paired it with sexy, crimson suede pumps.

Marina always told her looking good makes you feel better too. When Lily Rose looked in the mirror, she agreed.

David was a welcome breath of fresh air. He was back after two days off and full of interesting chatter. The man had a social circle of a charmed prince. It never ended. She wondered how he would fare in London, not knowing anyone. As she listened to him, her phone pinged. Thinking it would be Mingyu, she dropped it into her desk drawer and slammed it shut. She wasn't in the mood and she certainly wasn't ready to deal with her jealousy. Last night hadn't been her finest moment. But….did she overreact? She wondered.

Mid-morning David turned to her. "Listen, Lily Rose, if you have no plans tonight, come with me to see the fireworks by the harbor. They were postponed because of the rain last night. You know all my friends. We have dinner plans before the display and I can easily add one more person to the reservation."

The invitation's timing was perfect for lifting her spirits. David to the rescue. "That sounds great, David. I'd love to go."

"Good. It's settled then." He smiled radiantly. "We'll have fun."

David's inclusion of her felt like a warm, fuzzy blanket. He was so busy chatting, he hadn't picked up on her sour mood. She would miss him when he left for London next month. Her phone pinged again from inside her desk. She ignored it and got to work, her stomach growling.

Just before lunch the front desk called her and announced a visitor.

"Who? I'm not expecting anyone." *Could that be Mingyu?*

"The name is Sue. Claims to be a friend of yours."

"Sue?" *Did they mean Mingyu? Oh God.* "Send him back," she instructed.

Two minutes later, Alison Wu appeared in what looked like a disguise.

"Sue? Is everything ok?" Her friend's unscheduled appearance in her place of business was disconcerting, but infinitely better than Mingyu showing up after a fight. She worked hard to keep her private life private. Nervous about Chen Du, Lily Rose checked the length of the hallway. All clear. Why did Alison feel the need to use an alias here?

"Sorry to ambush you at work. I need to talk to you and it can't wait. I tried calling and texting numerous times last night and this morning, but you didn't respond." Alison looked around Lily Rose's shoulder at David, who was now completely captivated.

Alison was dressed in black with a sheer flowing, red floral top over a black bra. A trendy black wool jacket with multiple pleats and pockets and black ankle boots completed her ensemble. One of her beautiful printed scarves was loosely draped around her shoulders. Her long hair, tucked into a black captain's cap, was in hiding. Generous dark sunglasses resting on the edge of her nose, offered a nice contrast to expertly contoured red lips. Lily Rose sensed Alison's apprehension with David in earshot. "I was just going for lunch. Do you want to join me?"

"Can we eat in the hotel? Somewhere private?" Alison whispered still eyeing David, who was now pretending to be occupied. Lily Rose knew his mock busy look. He was as curious as a ferret.

"Yes. The bar is quiet at lunch time. Let me grab my bag." She threw her phone into her handbag, lest it ring while she was out. She didn't put it past David to be tempted.

In the bar, they sat at a quiet corner table. When the waiter came over, Lily Rose ordered her favorite salad and an ice tea. Alison ordered green tea.

"Order some food. My treat. Aren't you hungry?" Lily Rose urged her friend.

"Ok, thanks. I'll have today's soup," Alison informed the waiter, dismissing him by shoving the closed menus into his hands. When he was out of hearing range, she leaned over and started talking in a hushed voice. "I don't have much time. I'm on my way to the airport. The past few weeks I've been preparing to leave town."

Lily Rose's gaze swept the bar for intruding eyes. "How are your orders coming along? Is this a business trip?"

"Yes and no. I'm leaving Chen and I'm going to run my clothing business from elsewhere."

"What? Where? He doesn't know you're leaving?" Lily Rose put down her water glass, her stomach doing a succession of summersaults.

"No. He can't know. He's away on business. There's something I need you to do for me."

"Wait. Does your father know?" Lily Rose looked around the bar area, bewildered and nervous about what she was getting herself into by being complicit.

"Lily Rose, the less you know, the better. Listen to me carefully. I don't know where I'll be staying, so you can't reach me. I left my personal cell phone at home so don't text me.

Tracking. I'll be in touch with you at work. Can I get your business email?"

Lily Rose nervously rummaged through her purse. "Of course. Here, my card."

"I have some trunks that are ready for shipping. Here are copies of the shipper's receipts. I'll email you once I know where I can best retrieve them. You'll need to call the freight company with the address and have them shipped immediately after you hear from me. The shipper knows you'll be calling him. Everything is prepaid. I tipped him well. Can you do this?"

"Yes, of course. I call the shipper once I hear from you on my work email and tell him to ship immediately. I got it. I have some news for you too. I have to move out of my apartment at the end of this month and I'm not sure where I'm going. 'My work email stays the same until the summer. My stay in Hong Kong got extended by a few months because I have to train a new employee. Long story. Let me give you my New York address as well. 'll be there after I leave Hong Kong before I decide where to go next. It may be London."

She thought she saw Alison's mouth twitch at this information, but Alison's lips stayed pressed together. The food arrived and Alison took a few sips of her soup holding the deep bowl with both hands, inhaling the aroma, eyes closed as if she was trying to savor the scent of home. Alison asked her no questions. *Is she going to London too? Applying for citizenship? Looking for her mother?*

Alison opened her eyes and rested her half empty soup bowl on the saucer. She looked up. "Lots of changes ahead, but our paths will cross again. I'm certain of that. I know how to find people. I'll find you," Alison assured her. Lily Rose felt no need to question her methods.

Alison looked at her watch. "I wanted to thank you, Lily Rose--for being my friend, for giving me good advice, and for being there when I needed someone to be smart. You opened my eyes to new possibilities I never would have dreamt of." She pulled a rumpled brown paper package out of her handbag and slid it across the table. "Don't open this now or in the office. Open it at home, tonight ….in private. Consider it my parting gift, my 'ultimate sacrifice' for a good friend. I'm sorry we never made it back to Master Kan's for your cheongsam fitting, but I picked out some fabrics that will work with your coloring and style. He's expecting you. Go see him on your next free Monday."

"Thank you, Alison. For everything. I'm sure I'll treasure whatever this is." Lily Rose pointed at the roughly wrapped gift. "I bet I'll love the fabrics you picked too." She was touched her friend took the time to gift her, despite being under such duress. A rush of emotion passed through her and her eyes moistened, a stray tear escaping "I'll wait to hear from you when you're settled. Stay safe. I'll miss you, but I'm certain you're doing the right thing and I believe in your choices. I believe in you."

"Thank you. I hope I am. Your support means plenty. Promise me you'll go see Master Kan." Alison looked a little misty too, despite her usual hardened poker demeanor.

"I promise. It won't be as much fun without you though." Lily Rose confessed, hand over her heart.

Alison half smiled. "It will. I assure you."

Lest she burst into tears, Lily Rose changed the subject. "David Shen, the other assistant manager you met at your wedding and just now in my office, will also know where to find me. He's transferring to a London Hilton in March. You can always contact him. He's a good guy and a close friend. I plan to stay in touch with him … always."

"Good to know. Do you have his card on you?" Alison finished her soup with one big gulp.

"No, but I'll get it in the office before you leave." Lily Rose stared at the phone Alison pulled out. *A burner phone? Why isn't she sharing that number?*

Alison glanced at the screen. "I have to go." She picked up her handbag and grabbed the oversized hand luggage she had clung to. "My suitcase is with the concierge. Stay and finish your lunch."

"Ok. Wait. Let me give you David's full name and current email addresses. His personal one won't change. I want you to take it with you. You never know when it may come in handy. "She scribbled the information on another of her business cards. "I love you, Alison. Safe travels and stay strong. You can contact me on my Instagram. Message me in code." She hugged her friend, then watched her disappear like a ghost on a foggy night. *It must be scary to live on the edge. Did she get Carson's blessing? Hope I don't hear from him or worse, Chen Du.* A cold shiver crept up her spine.

Lily Rose finished her salad, paid the bill, and checked her phone. She saw numerous missed calls and texts from Alison's personal cell phone, the one she left behind. There was only one text from Mingyu asking for a call back. *Well, well. Look who's awake and hopefully sober. I wonder if he's seeing Jun today. I don't trust that girl.*

Stuffing the brown package into her handbag, she trudged back to the office, feeling like crap.

Chapter LIX

David Shen's Parting Gift
Pales Compared to Alison's

When Lily Rose returned from lunch, David stopped what he was doing and looked up at her.

"Everything ok?"

"Fine. My friend is taking an extended trip. I'll miss her."

"Too bad. I was going to quiz you about her. I thought her edgy style would be a good match for me," David joked. He followed his comment with an exaggerated wink, but she wasn't in the mood.

Lily Rose realized that David hadn't recognized Alison. *Good. Just as well.* She decided not to remind him that he had worked tirelessly with her father to organize her wedding. She changed the subject, hoping to prevent any further thoughts in that arena.

"I'm getting depressed that you're leaving next month. All my favorite people are abandoning me. I hope the new guy from Singapore is fun."

"I don't know about that. His name is Adriel. How much fun can he be?" David guffawed, trying to cheer her up.

"How do you know his name?" She laughed in spite of herself. David had that effect.

"I overheard Lam talking to him on the phone. Adriel this and Adriel that." David did a perfect imitation of Lam's voice, making Lily Rose laugh more.

"Well, I think his name is … interesting, you mean man." She shook her finger at David.

"Harumph." David rolled his eyes. "We'll see about that. Judging from Lam's end of the conversation, the guy sounds like an insecure wreck."

Before leaving work, Lily Rose went to the bathroom to primp. She switched from her red work pumps to stylish silver flats and sighed with relief at the immediate comfort. She pulled out a basic black sweater and a black cashmere slouchy hat she kept in her desk for colder days. She would need them on a February evening outdoors. Since Lam wasn't around, they left work twenty minutes early, hoping the boss wouldn't call to check.

"No way, he's drunk by now," David assured her. "The man loves a good celebration."

Like Mingyu? She shoved all thoughts of her boyfriend out of her mind, but they kept creeping back. Bottom line. She missed him.

At the restaurant, David's group sat indoors, close to the windowed terrace from which they would watch the fireworks. They were a lively group of seven and Lily Rose was happy she came. She needed the distraction. Yes, she was definitely content to be surrounded by joyful chatter. They laughed, shared good food and toasted the new year, purposely leaving politics behind for a night. Lily Rose suspected there might be divided political opinions at the table and David, schooled in diplomacy and problem solving, knew how to circumnavigate the differencesby skillfully redirecting the conversation. Her mind began to drift to darker thoughts. *Mingyu is probably watching the fireworks with Jun. Ugh. Did I push him right into her tentacles?*

When the first colorful explosions were launched, everyone rushed outside to enjoy the spectacular display over Victoria Harbor. David took Lily Rose's hand and guided her away from the others to another part of the terrace for a better view. She was aware of his body heat and close proximity behind her as they watched the orgasm of colors merge in the dark sky amongst "oohs" and "ahhs." She noticed David's strong signature cologne because close-up she got a generous whiff in the evening breeze. It smelled good—familiar and comforting. When the fireworks ended, she turned to face him and before she realized what was happening, he pulled her close, wrapping his arms around her waist and kissed her on the lips. It was a gentle kiss and she responded in kind. Lost in the moment, the attention felt good. When they parted, she squinted at him, "Are you drunk?"

"Tipsy maybe? I thought I seized the perfect moment. Couldn't resist. Now, that I'm leaving in a few weeks..." He looked flustered at her reaction and searched her face when she didn't reply. "Am I wrong? I thought the feeling was mutual."

"I'm flattered, David. Really, I am, but I see you as a close friend and colleague. Also...I've kind of been seeing someone. Not sure where that's going lately, but...." She shrugged, not wanting to share more.

"I'm sorry. I didn't know. I got swept up in the beauty of the occasion. Let's forget this happened and go back to where we were, ok? My honest mistake."

"Yes, that might be best, especially if we end up working together in London. No harm done. No worries." She smiled, her fondness apparent.

The thought of staying in Hong Kong indefinitely, without David, or Alison, or her spectacular harbor view apartment, and possibly without Mingyu, was unthinkable. It put her in a melancholy mood on the way home. David's kiss was sweet, but nothing more. Her heart ached for Mingyu's touch.

At home, after getting ready for bed, Lily Rose sat on her plush duvet and pulled out Alison's brown paper package and unwrapped it. Inside was a violet, fine leather jewelry box with gold-colored hinges, lock and key. She slid her hand over the smooth leather exterior and smiled. *Nice. Love the color.* She opened it not expecting anything inside. She admired the rectangular black velvet tray with its many small compartments. All empty. Lifting the tray, she peered underneath and discovered a wad of delicate lilac tissue paper. Gently probing it with her slender fingers, she realized it was safeguarding something. Carefully peeling back the layers, her heart began to beat faster. The outline felt familiar. Once the piece was uncovered, she gasped at the contents.

"Oh my God! Oh…my…God!" Jumping up, dancing in place, she gently lifted the spectacular carving out of the box and examined it from all sides. It was perfectly intact. Hidden beneath the tray was her grandmother's imperial jade dragon pendant, Alison's 'ultimate sacrifice' coming full circle.

Chapter LX

Reconciliation is Sweet

The next morning things in the office were back to normal. Lam was delegating the day's tasks while David made comical gestures behind his back. Relieved, Lily Rose turned on her computer, unpacked her bag and went to get coffee while Lam exchanged his morning pleasantries with David and the assistants. When she returned, she handed David his cup just the way he liked it.

"Hey. I had a nice time last night. Thanks for including me. We're totally good, right?"

David rushed to assure her, "Totally. Sorry for the mixed signals."

"They weren't that mixed, David. It's just wrong circumstances and bad timing. I'm recently involved." If it spared his feelings, a little fibbing was justified. She knew his intentions were sincere even if they weren't fully reciprocal on her end.

After work Lily Rose walked home from the subway, her feet dragging. It felt like a long work day. Normally she looked forward to seeing or at least talking to Mingyu which made the day go by quickly. The thought of not interacting with him and the memory of their fight, depressed her. Was it time to reach out? He had left numerous messages. Looking ahead but not really seeing, she turned the corner to her street and collided with a disgruntled, elderly neighbor who dropped his grocery bag, oranges rolling out. He barked at her to watch where she was going. Mortified, Lily Rose helped him pick up his escaped fruits, apologizing profusely. Her eyes swimming, she looked up and spotted a familiar silhouette near her building entrance. She stopped and squinted, trying to collect herself. *Oh no. What should I say?*

Mingyu was pacing outside the front entrance. The sight of him made her heart flutter, as only he could do. After a brief hesitation, she sped up and raced right into his opening arms. For a moment, neither spoke. His scent and strength felt wonderful. She realized he elicited a much stronger response than David's kiss.

"I'm sorry," he whispered into her hair. "I should have introduced you….and told you not to assume anything. I know how it must have looked to you. Jun likes me, but we've never been more than friends. I don't feel anything other than friendship for her. Besides, we don't think alike. Her family is from the mainland and pro-Beijing. It would never work between us."

"Wow, I knew she was scary." Lily Rose joked, then paused. "I just wish you would have been more transparent. Given my romantic past, which I shared with you despite you sharing very little of yours, I jumped to conclusions," Lily Rose muffled into the fabric of his shoulder, happy his arms were still wrapped tightly around her.

"Well, don't. Trust me. You should know you can by now," he assured her. "My past is exactly that…. the past. I missed you last night. What did you do?"

Lily Rose swallowed. "Ahh… I went to see the fireworks after work…. with David and some of his friends. How about you?"

"I was at the club party. Then some of us went to see the fireworks from Uncle Huan's boat. I tried to invite you, but you didn't answer your phone."

"Sorry. I was busy at work and still angry at you."

"Too bad. Well… old news now. Can we move on?"

She nodded, relieved he was so forgiving. She hated fighting with him.

His glance traveled downward at her unraveling scarf and stopped at her neck. Staring in disbelief, he blurted, "Is that your grandmother's dragon pendant?"

A sprouting smile curled her bottom lip. "Yes."

"How did you get it back? A new 14K triad boyfriend?" He snarked incredulously.

She laughed. "Long, boring story," she teased.

"I love those kinds of stories. Will you invite me in? I brought a peace offering--plum wine."

"Is it the brand I like?"

"Yes, it is. Tough lady."

"You have no idea." She grabbed him by the front of his jacket and pulled him in for a passionate kiss.

Lily Rose floated into the office after a night of making amends aided by small amounts of premium plum wine. She stopped short when she noticed Lam's door was shut. Mornings were when his door was wide open to all, as he delegated and monitored the work load. Hushed whispers suggested a private visitor in his enclave. David was off so she settled at her desk with a cup of coffee and checked her inbox, wondering who would surface from Lam's office. Not a day went by when she didn't check for news from Alison, worrying about how her friend was faring.

When Lam's office door finally swung open, she was struck speechless. Lam emerged behind Carson Wu who was preceded by two men dressed in black, their eyes shaded by aviator sun glasses. Lily Rose's body turned to pudding and her expression could have scared a crow. *Damn, what the hell is Carson Wu doing here?*

"Good Morning, Lily Rose. You remember Mr. Wu." Lam coaxed her. She mustered a nod, not able to stand. Her legs were liquid. Lam looked at her with a pained expression, "Mr. Wu is planning a small, private gathering at the hotel. We will use the small party room off the bar. It's a birthday celebration for one of his associates. Can you sit with him and get the details squared away? The event is planned for next Friday."

"Ahhh, s sure, Lam. G Good Morning, Mr. Wu." Lily Rose croaked.

"Morning. Can we talk in the bar? I have a few thoughts regarding the set up. Bring your phone." Carson squinted at her, then nodded at Lam, dismissing him. "Mr. Peng."

"SSure." Hesitating, she reached for her phone and tablet and reluctantly left the safety of her office, fully aware that Carson Wu was following her tentative, trembling gait. Carson's men stayed a few steps behind him.

Seated in a quiet corner of the bar with his protection two tables away, she asked Carson the customary questions for event planning. When she had all the details she needed, she rose with the intention of excusing herself. She could barely keep her thoughts on track. "If there's anything you would like to add, just call the office." She stuck out her hand.

Carson ignored her outstretched gesture and brusquely instructed her, "Sit down. I'm not done."

Lily Rose sunk back into her seat, her heart beating wildly. Carson spoke in a soft steely voice that made her skin crawl and her mind switch to overdrive.

"Meddling in someone else's life can have serious consequences, Miss Larsen. You don't have all the facts. So.... you can't possibly know what's good for the person. I don't think you considered that when you gave your advice so freely to my daughter, Alison." Carson grimaced, his dark eyes riveted on her.

Lily Rose nodded, her features frozen. She felt like passing out.

"Chen Du is angry with you. Ver-ry angry. Alison left him and right now, I'm your protection, the only barrier between you and his wrath. Do you understand?"

"Yes. Thhh-ank you, no harm intended." she whispered truthfully, head hanging.

"Your intentions don't matter. You created problems in my family. You embarrassed Chen. You caused me to lose my only daughter and you put a target on Alison's back. I can no longer protect her from my business rivals if they choose to use her as bait to get to me."

"So sorry," she mouthed inaudibly, her mouth feeling like the Sahara.

"You're the last person Alison called, "Carson barked. "Five times!"

"Yes, she called me, but I never spoke to her. I was working and didn't hear the phone."

Technically, she wasn't lying about the calls. Lily Rose could barely breathe. Carson Wu's intense stare inspired a trickle of sweat to wander down her spine. Her armpits were moist and her trembling fingers could barely grip the tablet as she squirmed at the edge of her chair. She looked around the room and saw people, but only Carsen was watching her. His men were preoccupied, conversing quietly. *He can't hurt me here! There are people around.*

"I see. Hand me your phone and unlock it."

"What? Why?" With trembling hands, she did as he asked and handed over her phone. While Carson scrolled through her recent calls and messages, she sat frozen, shocked that her privacy was being violated in her place of employment no less. However, she didn't dare complain.

"I have no clue where she is. I swear. She hasn't told me anything."

"I hope you're telling the truth."

It appeared he was enjoying her obvious discomfort which angered Lily Rose. After an uncomfortable few minutes, Carson handed back her phone and released her with a dismissive wave. "I'll see you next Friday. Make sure you do your job as well as giving unsolicited advice. I suggest you stay clear of my personal business or I will unleash Chen. Do you understand." He snapped his fingers at the mention of Chen.

"I shall. I promise. Th...Thank you." She rose unsteadily feeling like molten wax. Set free, she made a beeline for the door akin to Peter Rabbit escaping an irate Mr. Mc Gregor in his vegetable garden, but Carson's unwavering voice forced her to retract like a whip. Without turning, he held up his card.

"Here's my card. If you hear from Alison, I'll be expecting your call. This is not a request."

"Understood," she whispered meekly turning back to retrieve the card. Overcome by a wave of nausea, Lily Rose hurried out of the bar and raced into the nearest bathroom. The rest of the day was shot. She couldn't focus because her mind was set on instant replay.

For Valentine's Day, Mingyu took Lily Rose on a sunset cruise. Daylight's last rays danced off the water, as romance permeated the air. The sun sinking in a fiery blaze, steamed up the rear of the boat, where the two love birds sat enjoying the mild night and each other. Thankfully, the storm clouds had dried up since New Year's, allowing them to find pleasure in an idyllic setting. Disembarking in Aberdeen, they transferred to a large floating dock restaurant for tropical drinks. Lily Rose was thankful for the crowds, but couldn't help looking over her shoulder periodically. Her mind wandered to Alison and Chen Du. *Wonder what he's doing for Valentine's Day.*

Mingyu was oblivious. "You have to experience this place at least once before you leave. I know it's commercial, and in the past, I smirked at the venue, but being here with you makes it fun." Mingyu searched for her reaction, peering sideways from under his freshy angled bangs.

"Thanks. Are we eating here?" A drink certainly would calm her jitters. So far Carson had kept his word and she had kept hers. She hadn't heard from Alison.

"No. We're having a late dinner in a more intimate setting. It'll get cold soon anyway."

"Sounds good." Lily Rose glanced around the crowd.

The first few sips of liquor went down smoothly. It was just what she needed to refocus on Mingyu, who was going through great lengths to make the night special.

The restaurant he ultimately picked wasn't glamorous in terms of décor, but the food was scrumptious—pink radish salad with soy dressing, stir-fried noodles with chanterelles and duck, spicy crayfish and for dessert, almond floats. They ordered another round of cocktails and chatted about their future plans around Hong Kong.

"Day trips are fine with me," Lily Rose offered, feeling comfortable after another drink in a much smaller setting.

"Yeah, but weekend ones are more fun," Mingyu countered.

"True, but I don't have that many vacation days left. I'll have to play with my days off to squeeze out a three- or four-day weekend."

"That'll do."

They circled around the more distant future. Mingyu still waffled when the conversation turned to London and pinpointing a departure date. Lily Rose decided she needed to make decisions for herself, regardless. Her London plan was still in place and now that David was going to be there, she found the idea compelling. At least she would have him and possibly Alison, if Mingyu backed out last minute. She also guessed that if she changed course and decided to stay in Hong Kong, Lam wouldn't say no. He liked her work ethic, depended on it. Remembering how long it took her to decide to come to Hong Kong, she didn't push Mingyu. She gave him the space he needed because she understood it was a life-changing decision. Besides, she was an independent woman. Come what may, she could craft her own happiness. It wasn't contingent on anyone, even Mingyu. *Sigh, but I sure hope he chooses to come.*

That night she dabbed on her favorite perfume, Chloe's rose scent, as she got ready for bed. Before leaving the bathroom, she made sure her dragon pendant was still in its hiding place. She wasn't wearing it these days. Chen lurked in the back of her mind on a daily basis. Feeling empowered wearing her black *Raven & Rose* lingerie hidden under a short, pink terry robe, she dimmed the lights as she exited the bathroom. Mingyu was waiting. On her pillow, she noticed a small gift box.

"What's this?" She asked as she crawled onto the bed in Mingyu's direction.

"Open it, Valentine." He smiled. "It's an early birthday gift too. I'm covering both occasions." She tugged at the red silk ribbon and opened the lid. Inside, she found a velvet pouch with gold lever-back earrings, set with a lavender jade center, offset by tiny micro diamonds. The earrings matched her ring in style and flavor.

"These are amazing, Mingyu." She held one up to her ear. "I think I'm glad Chen stole all my crappy jewelry. I'm building an incredible collection now."

Mingyu smiled. "Glad I got it right. You know you can exchange them."

"Why would I want to? I love them … truly. They're perfect," she gushed.

Mingyu smiled and tugged at her robe tie, pulling her closer. As her robe slid open, his eyes widened with appreciation. "Wow. Are you wearing my gift?"

Lily Rose gave him her best seductive smile. "Nope. Yours is under your pillow."

Chapter LXI

March Madness

Lily Rose moved into Mingyu's flat the first weekend in March. Two trips in his car and the job was done. She was pleased to see he had cleared space in his closet and emptied a dresser drawer for her belongings. He also lined up a few baskets for random things and cleared a space at the counter for her computer. A set of new plush lilac towels, for her use only, were waiting on the bed. His initial efforts impressed her and made her feel welcome. How things would evolve was up for grabs, but so far, the move felt right. Time would tell if the cultural differences and dynamics would work. The hard part was cleaning An's apartment and leaving the building she so enjoyed living in. Mingyu's apartment was adequate, but it didn't have as many amenities as the Arch. Nor did it have the same spectacular view over the harbor.

Days later, Alison sent her shipping address. Lily Rose wasted no time contacting the shipper and sending the crates. She replied to Alison's obscure email address and confirmed the crates' departure. As she expected, Alison was in the UK. The thought of contacting Carson Wu didn't enter her mind until all was done. She hadn't heard from him or his crew. Silence was golden. His threat nagged at her, but her loyalty to her friend was stronger. She had to take the risk. She wanted Alison to succeed. *Wu probably sniffed things out on his own by now.*

Lily Rose took the opportunity to get shipping quotes for sending her own belongings to London and New York. She wondered if David could hold a box or two; she'd have to ask him first. Chen Du's extended silence gave her a huge sense of relief. He must have been embarrassed —saving face and all that. Lily Rose suspected that Carson Wu did control his actions and she prayed he would keep his protection promise, even if she hadn't kept hers. Secretly, she racked her brain why Carson would protect her to begin with. Carson Wu did not do anything without purpose she guessed.

Lily Rose dreaded Wu's private party at the hotel. That Friday night she set everything up to perfection, not missing a single detail. She made sure her full staff worked the shift. Staying on site, but monitoring from afar in her office, she delegated every action. She couldn't bear to face Chen Du. On camera, the dinner looked like a *Who's Who* of all the top ranked triads from Carson's group. Lily Rose recognized some of the faces from Alison's wedding. It made her shiver with fright.

Thankfully, Carson was busy having a good time and didn't ask for her. She guessed he also didn't want to remind Chen Du of love lost. No point in triggering a loose cannon. When the night was coming to a close, one of her assistants handed her a message. "Mr. Wu wanted me to give this to you. "In the closed envelope was a folded paper that read, *I'm still watching you. CW*

Lily Rose blanched and immediately ordered car service to take her home. Once the night passed without further incident and she no longer lived alone in the Arch, she felt less nervous about another confrontation, but in reality, that was silly and a false sense of security because if Chen Du or Carson Wu wanted to find her, they would in a heartbeat.

The next week, Mingyu was incredibly busy at the *Hong Kong International Diamond, Gem & Pearl Show* with Jin and Li. Deals were being made everywhere—on the exhibit floor, in hotel suites, in hotel bars over drinks, over long dinners. International gem dealers were a tightly knit group and as often as not, brokering deals was as lucrative as selling your own merchandise. It all depended on who the client was and how badly they wanted what you had. Lily Rose visited the show to look around, but Mingyu had no time to spend with her. He was slammed and working hard to build new European contacts. This encouraging fact convinced Lily Rose that her lover was indeed serious about following her to London. She left the show reassured, a warm halo around her heart.

In the third week of March, An and David missed crossing paths by a hair. David left for London after a lukewarm farewell party hosted by Lam, while An marched into the office two days later. It was apparent she came to fawn over Lam and sniff out her competition.

"Nice to finally meet you in person, Lily Rose. I came to say hello. Margo sends her regards." An ogled her with appraising interest—like a prized rooster before a cock fight.

"Oh, hi, An. Thanks. How was your cousin's wedding?" An looked exactly as David had described her--short, squat, with probing, coal eyes and straight black hair in an Anna Wintour bob. Her clothes were dark and conservative. The only spray of color were her fire red fingernails. They reminded Lily Rose of Margo. *Must be a 'woman in power' thing.*

"It was lovely. I'm glad I could attend. Thanks for leaving the apartment neat and in a timely fashion. My relatives will be moving in after their honeymoon. I trust you found a place to live?"

"I did, thanks. I'll be staying with a friend. Oh, here's Lam." She had no interest in sharing her private living arrangement with An or Lam. "It's a shame you missed David. He left two days ago." As soon as she verbalized it, it dawned on Lily Rose, that was by design. An didn't want to see David. She came to schmooze with Lam behind David's back.

An's voice rose to a sweet-as-saccharine pitch. "Hello, Lam. How wonderful to see you. I hear David left for London already?"

"Yes, you missed him. Welcome home, An. How's life in New York?" He motioned her into his office.

"Busy, busy…but fun. I've learned a lot from Margo."

"I bet," Lily Rose mumbled under her breath. She watched Lam close the door behind An. *Gossip time.* She now understood why David was happy when she arrived. Working with An and Lam would be no picnic for anyone. She could imagine how excluded David must have felt with that sneaky duo. *Guess that's how Lam feels with David and me. He seems so chipper now that David is gone, always stopping by my desk to chat.* She chuckled to herself and wondered what Adriel would be like. Inspired, Lily Rose sat down at her computer and sent David an email.

Hi there,

How's London? Hating the weather yet? Any good apartments? An is here today visiting with Lam, behind closed doors. She's exactly as you described her. You were so on point I had to be careful not to lol. She was wearing what looked like a Mao jacket. Adriel arrives next week. For now, I fly solo with the assistants. I miss your smiling face. Write when you can,

Miss you, LR

p.s. Can I send two boxes to your apartment once you're settled? I'd like to ship my stuff directly to London for my September arrival.

The reply came a day later,

Hi LR,

Success. I found an apartment and I'm officially starting work April 1ˢᵗ. No joke. I popped into the office this week to say hello and was impressed with the space. I think I'll like it here. On my way out, I was given an envelope that was hand delivered for me. Imagine my surprise when I read a message from 'your friend', Alison? She wants to meet for drinks. Did you set this up?

An must be a distant relative of Chairman Mao—maybe she inherited the family's wardrobe? Ha ha. Glad I missed her sour face and syrupy voice. Beware of her red claws.

BTW- Feel free to set me up with any other London friends that come to mind. I'm available for fun. Below is my new address—for your two boxes.

XO, David

Chapter LXII

Office Dynamics Slump
and Home Dynamics Soar

April first, Adriel arrived in the office, starched and pressed, with an eternal question mark lingering over his head. Only a few years older than Lily Rose, he shadowed her like a Velcro attachment. His desire to please was welcome at first, but incredibly tedious by day three. Lily Rose missed David more than she wanted to admit. David was quick to laugh and a creative problem solver. He could easily think beyond blurred lines and smooth over any bad situation with kind words and convincing solutions. It was his gift of gab and ability to make decisions under duress that made him an ideal partner in a fast-moving office.

Adriel, on the other hand, was annoyingly careful, tentative at best and had a tendency to over-analyze the simplest problems with a demeanor so serious, Lily Rose thought his head would explode. Adriel strictly played by the rules and if he didn't know them, he was lost, relying on Lily Rose for direction.

In some ways she appreciated that, since there was less to correct, but in other ways he came across as needy, showing a complete lack of initiative. To make matters worse, Lam deferred

Adriel's training solely to her. Lam chose not to hover the way he had with David and her. In fact, Lam couldn't be bothered with training his new assistant manager and he cleverly spin-doctored the situation by making a big deal of trusting Lily Rose's ability to direct and train Adriel in all matters. It was tiring to say the least.

At the end of Adriel's first week, Lily Rose took him to lunch. She was spent and close to losing her mind. Chatting amicably over grilled shrimp, she figured out that Adriel wasn't shy or purposely holding back. After some prodding, she realized he was just terrified of making mistakes. Squeezing Adriel for information about his previous boss, she learned that his former boss was in the habit of hanging Adriel out to dry whenever things got sticky, which happened frequently. As a result, Adriel's guard was perpetually up. He needed and wanted a fresh start with a clean record. *Did his boss give him a good recommendation to get rid of him?*

After hearing this, Lily Rose hoped Adriel would eventually adjust to her and Lam's pace, and with some patience and understanding, rise to the occasion. More importantly, she wanted Adriel to relax and to trust his abilities and training. He was a work in progress and after their lunch, she was somewhat hopeful he would turn out ok. She assured him, she had his back.

"We work as a team here, Adriel. Communication is key."

With Mingyu's encouragement, Lily Rose began her remote class with the Gemological Institute. The assignments weren't difficult, but they did require concentration, not an easy feat after a long day with Adriel. After each completed chapter there was a test and at the end of each course there were comprehensive exams. Lily Rose was happy to have Mingyu there to answer questions and quiz her, but she couldn't help but stress over the final, which summarized all components. She didn't want to disappoint Mingyu…. or Jin. This realization made her more tolerant of Adriel and his bumbling ways.

Life with Mingyu was easy and fun. Most nights when they were home, they cooked together, an activity they both seemed to enjoy. The nights she worked late or Mingyu went to his club for strength training, they picked up food or ate leftovers. They quickly fell into a comfortable rhythm. On weekends, she was content to wake up snuggled next to him. Lily Rose still missed the Arch and An's glorious view, however, spending quality time with Mingyu trumped all. Their living styles seemed to mesh.

Saturday was their fun day together, unless work beckoned. Sunday mornings Lily Rose had alone time to primp, as Mingyu continued to have dim sum with his grandfather, a tradition she didn't want him to forfeit. She was happy for those mornings to herself. Once a month, she joined them.

Spending time with Jin was always a learning experience. His Buddhist approach to life broadened her horizons and shed light on whatever issue she presented. Their gem discussions added depth to her studies in ways her lessons didn't. Jin appeared to be pleased she was studying at the GIA and often included her in his and Mingyu's gem buying considerations. She absorbed so much, soaking in his vast knowledge of the market. She realized how complex the gem field was.

Occasionally, Mingyu and Lily Rose managed to squeeze in a few day trips--Guangzhou and Shaiman Island, Shenzen to shop, Xiaomeisha Beach, Zhuhai, Macao, Ocean Park, Shek O Beach and Tang Wan Beach with its view of Tsing Ma Bridge. Marina was always present in her mind on these excursions. She recognized the names from Marina's story list and she often wondered how they had changed since the sixties. Sometimes she googled the images to compare.

With the tropical shower season in full swing, Lily Rose kept a pocket umbrella in her handbag and beach bag at all times. It was crazy how sporadic the skies clouded over without warning and in nanoseconds dumped buckets of water. Mingyu took it in stride, running for cover, but Lily Rose refused to get side-lined or soaked after her infamous New Year's drenching. Thankfully, those negative vibes were in her rear-view mirror now.

One Saturday morning while lazing in bed with coffee, Mingyu surprised her. "Do you think you could get Monday off and take a three-day weekend May 10th?"

"A three-day weekend? Do you have a travel destination in mind?"

"Yes." He stared at her without elaborating, his bangs dropping down, shading his expression.

"I can try. It's harder with Adriel. He can't be left alone yet. I'll check with Lam on Monday. Where do you want to go?" She boxed her pillow and sunk back into it, sipping her brew.

"*Cheung Chau* Island? *Lamma Island? Jeju* Island? *Ho Chi Minh City? Ho Tram?*" Mingyu looked at her expectantly.

"Wait… what? Are you trying to trick me? *Chueng Chau* and *Lamma* Island we could take a ferry to. *Ho Chi Minh City* is Vietnam, isn't it?" She sat back up.

He grinned. "Good catch. I was wondering if you were paying attention."

Is three days enough time for *Saigon*? Where are the other two places?"

"*Jeju* is South Korea and *Ho Tram* is close to *Ho Chi Minh City*. Three-hour flight."

"Wow. Have you ever been?"

"No. That's why I'm suggesting it."

"Which neighboring countries have you been to?"

"Besides China? Japan, South Korea, Cambodia, Indonesia, India, Burma, Thailand, the Philippines, Malaysia and a different part of Vietnam."

"And outside Asia?"

"Only the United States."

"Wow. I didn't realize." Lily Rose stared at him, her mind processing. "So, going to London for you will be like coming to Hong Kong for me."

"Yes. Where have you traveled?" Mingyu asked.

"All over the Caribbean, Europe, Canada, Mexico and the US. Plus, the countries we traveled to together.

"Where in Europe?"

"France, Germany, Italy, Spain, Portugal, Greece, Holland, Switzerland, Austria and England."

"Nice. Did you travel with your family?"

"Yes. And also, with friends. I went backpacking with a girlfriend one summer and a boyfriend another summer."

"Kevin?"

"Yes. Tell me about your travels over breakfast. I'm hungry. Pancakes?"

Mingyu leaned over and straddled her. "Now or in ten minutes?"

When Lily Rose arrived at work one day, Lam was waiting with his office door open. "Good Morning, Lily Rose. Come into my office, please."

"Morning, Lam. Be right there." She put her handbag into her desk drawer and brought her computer to life, then entered Lam's office.

"Close the door and have a seat." Lam steepled his fingers, elbows on his desk. He leaned forward. "How is Adriel doing?"

"He's coming along. Why? Did he do something wrong?" Lily Rose wondered where Lam was going with this.

"No. I just don't see him excelling. He seems to rely on you a lot."

"He does sometimes, but I think he's getting more comfortable." Or so she hoped, but she wasn't about to verbalize any reservations about his hire.

"There has been a change of plan with your replacement. I'm hiring a girl from London and it appears she'll be coming to Hong Kong earlier than anticipated, in mid-May instead of August. I can't say I'm happy about this as I wanted you to have more time to train Adriel, but she's too good to pass up. The other candidates paled in comparison. It also leaves the door open for you to switch back in a year. I would like you to have that option."

"Thank you, Lam. I would too. I've truly enjoyed my time here."

"Glad to hear that. Here's the problem. If she starts June first, I can't keep you through August. My budget won't allow it, especially in the slow months. Would you be amenable to leaving in June?"

"When would my job in London begin?"

"Still September first. The good news is you would have the summer off to reorganize yourself at home in New York."

"Without pay, I take it?"

"Yes, but we'll pay for your moving expenses, your travel to New York and London and of course, your health insurance."

"I see. Do I have a choice?"

"Yes. If it's a financial burden, Margo will be happy to have you back in the New York office for the three months. I checked. Your choice."

"Thanks, Lam. Can I think about it and let you know? I need to check my finances and …. well, I gave up my lease in New York to An so I currently have no apartment in the city."

"Of course. Give it some thought and let me know as soon as you can. Later this week would be good."

"Ok. I'll try."

When Lily Rose got home, Mingyu was prepping dinner, liberally pouring *Shaoxing* wine into a marinade with ginger, molasses, oyster sauce and soy. "Hi, I'm making grilled beef with broccoli." He looked up. "What's wrong? You look bothered."

"Lam called me into his office this morning. My replacement from London is coming two months early and he wants me to leave work by June first." She plopped onto a counter chair and rested her chin on propped hands. "They're offering me a choice—either three unpaid months or three paid months, working in the New York office, which I don't really want to do. Margo and An? No way. Also, I'd have to live with my mom or find a temporary place. Both undesirable. Rent would gobble up most of my salary."

"So, don't. Consider it a wonderful opportunity to travel and reorganize yourself in Sag Harbor. You can stay here as long as you want, rent-free. The money you save in rent should carry you through, no? And you can work on your gemology degree." He searched her face.

Lily Rose perked up. "Maybe. Let me think about this. I still have to pay for the house in Long Island. I can't rent it out because I'll have nowhere to stay and besides, I was looking forward to spending at least part of the summer in Sag Harbor with you."

"Three months is not that long. It'll fly by. I think it's a good thing, a blessing, really."

"I definitely won't be able to travel to Vietnam. I have to save my pennies now. Lam caught me off guard. I was so stunned I forgot to ask him about the travel dates anyway. It's just as well. Dinner smells really good. I'm starving."

"It's almost ready. Pour us a glass of wine. We'll strategize later. Don't worry. We'll figure this out … together."

Chapter LXIII

Alison's Surprise in Absentia

Lily Rose took one night to decide she would grab the three summer months unpaid. Not having to pay rent while staying with Mingyu had fattened her bank account. She was at peace with her decision and now looked forward to her final days of work. She began to think about her leisure time in Sag Harbor, however, the thought was bitter sweet. Not seeing Marina was still a sore spot. She would make the best of it…maybe start a home improvement project, one that wouldn't break the bank. The cottage needed a fresh coat of paint. *How much could that cost?*

On her next Monday off, Lily Rose finally went to visit Master Kan to view the fabrics Alison had set aside for her.

"Hello, young lady. I was beginning to wonder if you were coming. Let me find the fabrics Miss Wu picked for you." He disappeared into a back room while Lily Rose looked around. There were fabrics stacked everywhere. When Master Kan returned, he had four rolls, two under each arm, which he plopped onto the counter. One was a cream floral lace, the second, a soft lilac silk with small pale blue and green flower clusters, another, a fuchsia raw silk with large violet tropical blooms and the last was a textured black brocade with dark red embroidered roses.

"Wow! These are beautiful. Did Alison pick a dress style for me?"

"No, that she left up to you. She only picked the fabrics. I remember she spent an eternity narrowing it down. Come look at the dress styles. Do you want a long or short *quipao*?"

"Short. I like this short-sleeved style with the stand-up collar and flare skirt. The black fabric with the red roses has my name on it. I think I'll go with that."

"Good choice. Miss Wu predicted you would pick that one. Which other one do you like?"

"I can only afford one—how much will the tailoring cost?"

"Nothing. Miss Wu prepaid for two dresses. You may pick one more."

Lily Rose looked at the man incredulously. "She paid for them?"

"Yes. Didn't she tell you? She said you helped her with something important. This is a thank you gift from Miss Wu."

"Are you sure? I had no idea. What a generous gift." Lily Rose froze in place, staring at the man. "She already repaid me, I thought."

Master Kan smiled patiently, uncomprehending. "Yes, I am sure. I have her money."

When she regained her equilibrium, Lily Rose asked, "I love the ivory lace; what style do you recommend for that?"

"That's a light weight fabric. Perhaps a longer, sleeveless dress with a key hole neck and a slit on the side? Like this one." He held up a fitted, sleek and sexy sample.

"I love it." Lily Rose nodded with enthusiasm.

"What's your favorite color?" He asked, one eyebrow shooting upward.

"Lilac or sky blue. Why?"

"We can make the silk slip underneath the lace that color and match the piping. Or you can stay neutral, all ivory. This one here, has pink piping." He held up his sample. "What do you think?" Lily Rose examined the dress. The piping looked nice she decided. "I think I'll pick a very pale blue silk lining and a slightly brighter sky blue for the piping. Does that work?"

"Very nicely. Let's get you measured." He motioned her over to a pedestal and pulled out his well-worn tape. As he began spitting out the numbers, an assistant materialized and wrote them down.

"For the black fabric with the roses--do you want the flowers running down the center or concentrated on the sides of the dress?"

Lily Rose thought of Alison's tattoos. "Down the side. Also, I like the dresses a little looser—not too form-fitted. Which fabrics did Alison pick for herself?"

"Hmm … I think she picked the same ivory lace as you, but a different dress style with black piping. She also chose a red brocade with white lilies and a violet silk with golden lotus flowers. She has exquisite taste, I remember."

"Yes. She does. I like all the fabrics she picked for me, but I think these will work best in New York."

As the man measured her, Lily Rose's eyes traveled over the bolts of material piled around her. The piles extended up to the ceiling and had the most enticing colors and patterns. Nothing jumped out as a better choice. She truly loved Alison's picks for her.

When Master Kan finished measuring, she wandered around the store. A pastel green linen with slightly darker, embroidered bamboo stalks adorned with dainty leaves captured her attention. Not missing a beat, Master Kan held up a sleeveless, flared dress, tapered at the waist with matching fabric buttons down the front.

"The linens work well with this style. You can make it any length." He held the dress up and swung the skirt to and fro. "Not too expensive. Linen is cheaper than silk." He pointed to the price tag.

"I'd like one with this fabric. It's perfect for summer in New York. How much is it?" He pointed to the sign. "Same price. I'll have your measurements on file. If you decide to order more later, just call or email me. Here's the linen section. See if there's anything else you like." Lily Rose picked out two more linens. A white, flower embroidered design and a coral fabric with hibiscus flowers in a darker tone.

"Can you hold these two fabrics for me? I may order one or two more dresses. I need a gift. Here is my business card for when the dresses are ready."

Not giving up, Master Kan gestured to a stack of silks. "We also make silk scarves." "They make excellent gifts." His crooked smile was convincing.

When Mingyu came home, Lily Rose was cooking American food.

"Hi. I hope you're in the mood for honey mustard chicken and baked sweet potato with molasses. I was in the mood for comfort food."

"You went grocery shopping? Thank you. It smells good. What spices are you using?" Mingyu looked skeptical.

"I did. We're good for the next few days. Would you like a glass of wine? I got that too." She ignored his spice question. She barely used any.

"Sure." He sat at the counter and watched her. "My father came to the store today. He and Winnie are no longer dating."

"That's good, right?" She opened the bottle and poured two glasses, handing him one. Not waiting for his reply, she took the baked potatoes out of the oven and slid them onto waiting plates. Slitting them open, she put a dab of butter in each and a teaspoon of molasses.

"Yeah. I'm glad he dropped Winnie. I'm not sure about him returning to the store though. Jin and I are discussing it."

"He made a mistake. Hopefully he's learned from it. Don't you think?"

"I'm sure he did, but that doesn't mean we trust him. There's a part of me that's still deeply disappointed in him."

"Understandable. How does Jin feel?" Lily Rose opened the oven and poked a fork into the chicken.

"Hard to tell. I'll find out over dim sum." Mingyu took a sip of his wine and picked at his potato as if it were an unknown foreign lab specimen. He grabbed the five-spice powder and sprinkled some over the top. "Carson Wu came into the store today. He bought a gift for his son-in-law. A watch."

"Really? Was there an occasion?"

"Not that I know of."

"Sounds like a bribe. Dinner is ready. Go wash your hands and top off the wine." She watched him scuffle to the bathroom, shoulders slumped, then put the salad bowls on the table, adding his favorite ginger dressing. She eyed his potato and smiled. Her man needed a little pampering tonight. Between his dad and a dinner he wasn't keen on, she felt for him. She sprinkled some five-spice powder on his chicken, just in case. A skimpy after-dinner distraction wouldn't hurt. She knew exactly how to shift his focus. When he returned from the bathroom and poured more wine, she changed the trajectory with her feel-good story.

"I went to Master Kan's today. You wouldn't believe what Alison did."

Mingyu listened to her story and frowned. "Do you think it's wise to accept her gift? You'll be indebted to a triad."

Chapter LXIV

Mingyu's Perfect Afternoon

The weekend Mingyu and Lily Rose planned to be in Vietnam had arrived and Lily Rose was particularly sad they weren't going. After Mingyu encouraged her to review her finances, she realized it made sense to forego the expense. Nonetheless, she couldn't help but feel blue. She wasn't optimistic about going after her last day of work either. She needed to save money for the summer months.

Except for her splurge at Master Kan's, Lily Rose watched her budget like a kingpin. To cheer her up after watching her mope all weekend, Mingyu promised to leave work at noon and organize a Monday afternoon outing to jump start the week on a positive note. She appreciated his effort and perked up at the suggestion.

With savings in mind, she spent the morning preparing an elaborate picnic basket. When Mingyu texted her to meet at the Victoria Peak tram at noon, she packed it up and scooted out the door. Lily Rose hadn't been to Victoria park since her arrival in Hong Kong. She was looking forward to revisiting her grandmother's old stomping grounds.

Sitting on the subway, she reflected on her whirlwind year. It had been a better experience than she ever would have dreamed.

Taking the leap to live abroad was the right decision; she had no regrets. To her surprise, when she arrived at the tram, Mingyu was waiting with a cooler bag slung over his shoulder.

She kissed him on the lips, happy to see him. "Hi. Did you bring lunch too? I made us crab salad sandwiches with mango slices. What did you bring?"

"Perfect. I brought drinks and dessert."

"Wow. We really are in sync. This'll be quite the luxurious lunch for a boring Monday."

Mingyu grinned, peering sideways from under his fringe. His eyes twinkled. "There'll be nothing boring about this Monday, I promise."

She loved when he looked at her like that. It was usually a precursor to something good. Seated side by side, basket and cooler bag wedged between their feet, the tram slanted upwards toward the peak. Lily Rose rested her head on Mingyu's shoulder and looked out the window.

It was a gorgeous day and she was blissfully happy. Regular tropical showers had left a carpet of luscious green. Spring flowers arched toward the sun, sprouting shoots in every possible direction and the trees, green globes lining the ascent, stood like erect sentries welcoming them into their magical kingdom in the clouds.

At the top, they stopped to take in the magnificent harbor view, with its red-sailed junk boats. Mingyu wrapped his arm around her shoulder, and inhaled deeply, releasing his breath in measured spurts. He cleared his throat. "This is where I first fell in love with you." He paused. "In New York, you sparked my interest, but you were out of reach, literally. When you came to

Hong Kong to stay, it blew my mind. I couldn't believe my luck. I didn't know what to expect, but when I saw you again, I knew for sure that I wanted you in my life—as a valued client, a friend or a lover. Anything. I was ready for whatever you offered. And now, a year later, we're living together. I still can hardly believe it."

"I know. This morning I was thinking what a good year it's been." Lily Rose looked at the sparkling water. "I wasn't even sure if you still liked me when I first got to Hong Kong. I was so nervous about contacting you, I rewrote my first email no less than five times. But…. when you took me sight-seeing after our first dinner, I felt like our friendship from New York was cemented and it made me happy. I needed and wanted a friend in Hong Kong and I'm so glad it was you."

"Thanks. The beautiful thing about a slow-growing friendship is that you can take your time falling in love….and we did. When you asked me to join you on the trip to the Philippines, I was surprised but ready for anything. And then you made me wait … …and wait." Mingyu laughed at the memory.

Lily Rose wrinkled her nose. "I guess that worked to my advantage, didn't it?"

"I wasn't giving up, no matter how long it took."

"It didn't take all that long. I just needed some reassurance that you weren't messing with me."

"I wasn't. I was committed from the moment we stood up here last Spring, a year ago."

Lily Rose tightened her arm around his waist and leaned her head against him. They were still facing the harbor view as they talked. It made baring the soul so much easier. Mingyu turned toward her and tenderly placed his hands on either side of her face. He leaned over and kissed her lips softly. When they parted, Lily Rose rattled her basket. "Hmmm. All these confessions are making me hungry. You?"

Mingyu laughed. "Let's eat in the gardens. The view south and west from there is spectacular."

They settled on a straw mat, under a shady tree and unwrapped their sandwiches. With their bodies intertwined like familiar tree roots, they sipped the cooled green tea with honey and talked about travel-- all the places they wanted to go... together. When Mingyu stood and reached for her hand, she purred. "Do we have to? I don't want to leave yet."

No one was around, a rare moment for this popular tourist attraction. "We aren't. Come with me."

He walked her to the gazebo on the lawn. Stopping in the center, he reached for both her hands. "I've given London a lot of thought in the past couple months and I'm finally at peace with leaving here and giving it a shot. When Jin first asked me, I thought, no way, I'm never leaving Hong Kong. It's my forever home. But.... after watching you and how bravely you came here and thrived... I'm open to trying something new. You inspire me, Lily Rose. In more ways than one."

"I do?" She cocked her head, wondering where this was going but liking the feeling.

"Yes." He nodded. "I'm also thinking about you leaving soon and I hate the idea. In a very short time, I've become so accustomed to having you in my life on a daily basis; I don't want to come home to an empty apartment anymore."

"Whew, I thought you were getting ready to give me the boot. I really don't want to leave Hong Kong without you next month.

Can you come to New York for part of the summer? Before we go to London?"

"That depends." He dropped her hands and dug one hand into his jeans pocket.

"On what? You can stay with me in Sag Harbor. Rent free. For two months." She smiled and winked.

"Thanks. You'll still owe me one month, you know," he joked.

"And…. if I get an apartment first in London, you can stay with me there. Then we're even."

"About that…" Mingyu got down on one knee and pulled the ring box out of his pocket. "I was hoping we could continue living together on a more permanent basis. Lily Rose….I love you. Will you marry me?" A strand of hair fell over his eye as he nervously held the ring out in front of her, his fingers trembling slightly.

"Oh my God. Are you sure? I mean…. yes! Yes, I'll marry you. I love you." She danced in place.

"Stand still for a second, you wiggle worm." He slipped the ring on her finger and took her into his arms. "You make me happy….and I don't want to repeat Jin's mistake. Live a life with regrets."

"I can't believe this! I thought you were acting a little nostalgic today. It worried me, for a second. But I never expected a proposal," Lily Rose chatted excitedly. "You've never mentioned marriage before. Damn, I wasn't even sure you were really coming to London. Now you have to come." She held out her hand, wiggling her fingers. "This ring is beautiful, Mingyu. I love the oval diamond. So cool. And it fits me perfectly. Look!

Am I talking too much?"

"Never. If you have another style in mind, we can swap it. I want you to love the ring you'll wear forever."

"Are you kidding me? Noooo, I already love this one. I'm so keeping it." She glanced down at the sparkling diamond, moving her hand back and forth to catch the refractive light. The stone, perched on a thin white gold pave'-set band, glittered in the sunlight. "I can't stop looking at it. Are you sure this is mine now?"

"Absolutely sure." He smiled, amused. "The stone comes with a certificate. I have it at home."

"Am I dreaming? You're not going to take this beauty back when I'm sleeping?"

"Nope. It's yours. Forever."

"Good. Because I love it as much as the dragon pendant and that is going nowhere…ever. You know, Victoria Park is where Marina told Jin that she was leaving Hong Kong. They were having a picnic. Did you hear that story?"

"No. We've come full circle haven't we? Tell me the story."

She beamed at him. "We certainly have. First things first. What's for dessert? Are you keeping that a secret too?"

"Wait here." He sprinted across the lawn and grabbed his cooler bag. Striding back, he placed it on the bench and pulled out a champagne bottle and two flutes. Popping a noisy cork, he let the champagne fizzle and waterfall into their glasses. "A toast. To us. To our future. May it be as fun and joyful as our past and present." He handed her a clear plastic flute with a scrolled, gold design.

"To us," Lily Rose echoed. "I love you."

"And I love you. To us," he echoed. They clinked glasses and sipped the bubbly. "Ready for strawberry cheesecake? That's my other surprise."

"Oh my God, I thought you'd never ask." Lily Rose clapped once. "Where in the world did you find it? That's my favorite."

"I've got sources." Mingyu winked. He sliced the cake and slid it onto a clear plastic plate with gold trim, feeding her the first bite.

"Mmm...so good. Your sources rock. I'm in heaven. In fact, this whole day feels other-worldly."

"Don't get too carried away. Tomorrow you're back at work and making dinner," he joked.

"Ugh. That's tomorrow. Let me have this moment. One more bite please and don't forget the strawberry. I'll take another glass of bubbly too. Just today, I'm a fairy princess floating on air."

Chapter LXV

Let the Good Times Roll

The next morning, when Lily Rose's eyes fluttered open, she reached for her ring and slipped it on. Still swaddled in a cotton blanket, she extended her hand high in the air admiring the sparkle, then looked over at Mingyu stretched beside her. He was watching her with a lazy smile. She was deliriously happy. "Morning. I had to see if it was still there…..on my night table. Does your family know?"

"Only Jin." He moved closer and kissed her cheekbone, working his way down her neck.

"I'm surprised you proposed to me on May 13th. That isn't a lucky number in the Chinese tradition, is it?" She propped herself up on one elbow, curious for his reply.

"We met in September, on Friday the 13th. It's a lucky number for me. Thirteen isn't a bad number in Chinese numerology, only in the United States. It has a Christian origin I think. Judas was the 13th guest at the last supper and he turned out to be a traitor. In China there are worse numbers, like four, or five. We can pick different numbers for our wedding day."

"I don't know the Christian origin, but then I don't pay much attention to numbers or religion. I'll let you pick the wedding date."

"Good. Fixing a date takes intense strategizing in China." Mingyu kissed the soft area between her breasts.

Lily Rose giggled, then realized he was serious about Chinese numerology. *Oh boy. I better watch it.,* Giving into his exploration of her body, she relaxed and sunk back into the pillows wearing nothing but her ring.

When Mingyu came home Tuesday night, he was glowing. "Hi. I shared the news with my family. My sister wants to throw us an engagement party at the restaurant."

"Really? How nice! How can I help?"

"You don't have to do anything. We just need to decide how many people we want to invite. Jin, Myia and I will pay for it."

"Well…considering that I have no one on my side coming on such short notice, it's really a question of what you want." Lily Rose hedged in her seat and glanced back down at the computer, not sure how to react. She didn't want to upset him.

"Do you want a party? You don't seem terribly excited." Mingyu moved closer.

"I'm fine with it. Maybe you should sit down and make a guest list. This sounds like a big expense and we're trying to save money for our move." Lily Rose felt her nerves kick in. She shifted uncomfortably, wondering if she was saying the wrong things. *Kind of a lop-sided party, but if it makes him happy…*

"I don't want to offend my family, but if I'm honest, I don't want a big party either. We might as well wait until the wedding."

"My thoughts exactly. Then here's what I suggest. Why don't we have a lunch or dinner celebration with your immediate family at your sister's restaurant and go out to dinner with your closest friends before we leave. You can tell them we got engaged and say goodbye at the same time. No pressure." She looked up at Mingyu, who was now hovering over her. He seemed to be weighing her suggestion.

"That sounds like a perfectly good idea. I like it." His face brightened. "We can do the same for your family and friends in New York." He paused. "I hope my sister won't be too disappointed."

"With all due respect, she had her engagement festivities and wedding. We get to plan ours the way we want, don't we?"

"And what do you want, Lily Rose?" Mingyu's voice softened. He moved closer.

"I really don't know. What I do know is that I don't want a lot of stress during our last few weeks in Hong Kong. Let's keep things intimate and manageable. This way we'll enjoy our engagement and our limited time, before leaving. The rest, the wedding decisions, will fall into place, later. When the time comes, we'll know what we want to do."

"How did you become so wise?" He rested his hands on her shoulders as if needing the support.

"I plan a lot of weddings, remember? I know how stressful they are. Look at Alison. She truly had a fairy tale wedding that, in the end, meant nothing. And…it cost a fortune. I saw the invoice. Maybe my needs are different because of what I do for a living. Or maybe it's because I have a small circle. I don't know." She paused and looked up at him. "Do you want a big wedding? In Hong Kong?"

"Maybe. I'd like my family at our wedding and I guess a Hong Kong wedding would be nice since my family has a lot of older members who don't travel. We can celebrate in two places if you like."

"With enough notice, I'm sure my mom and my close friends will come to Hong Kong. We don't have to decide this today, do we?"

"Absolutely not. Tomorrow works too," he joked, taking her into his arms. "What are we making for dinner?"

Lily Rose was on cloud nine. She was engaged to the man she loved and she had passed her *Diamonds* gemology course with flying colors. The next academic step was *Diamond Grading*, a practical course entailing serious lab work. She hoped to complete diamond grading over the summer. That would seal her certification in diamonds. When Mingyu came home that night and heard the news he encouraged her. "I'm proud of you. One step at a time."

"Thanks. Don't tell Jin, ok? I want to tell him myself." Her face was lit.

"Sure." The edges of Mingyu's lips curled upward. Her success pleased him, but the fact that she was eager to share her accomplishment with Jin made his heart smile.

The Saturday of their engagement dinner at Myia's restaurant crept up slowly. Luckily, Master Kan delivered the new dresses just in time. Lily Rose chose to wear the ivory lace *cheongsam* with the pale blue slip to the party. The fit was perfect; Master Kan had done a masterful job. Lily Rose was so pleased with everything, she put in another order for two more linen dresses, a white on white embroidered one for herself and the peach one, intended as a peace offering for her mother for not immediately sharing the engagement news. Hopefully Ella May would be delighted with her gift and get over the latter.

So far, Ella May had only expressed fear that Lily Rose would stay in Hong Kong, but she assured her mother that she and Mingyu were planning on moving closer. It was a good time to share their London plans, merely a six-hour flight from New York, same distance as California. Ella May was not appeased or pleased.

"London! Really? Does Margo know? What about your house in Sag Harbor?"

"Margo already got over it. She and An have bonded and An is staying. I'll be in Sag Harbor for most of the summer to reorganize. Maybe I can rent the house out for September to cover costs? I plan to ship my belongings directly to London and the rest I'll store in Sag Harbor. By the way, I gave up my apartment in the city so that expense is gone too." Her last statement was met with a gasp, then silent static. She knew her mother wouldn't understand giving up her apartment in Manhattan. Ella May was a practical soul who understood the value of prime real estate even if it was the size of a postage stamp.

When Lily Rose and Mingyu arrived at the restaurant, they were greeted by inquisitive, smiling faces eager to meet the bride,

Cheng being the exception. His lips were drawn into a thin horizontal line and his arms tightly crossed his chest like a squished pretzel. His sister, Chantao, seated next to him, initially echoed his demeanor, but softened when she saw Mingyu's joy. Lily Rose wondered if cousin Victoria took her cue from her mother as she mimicked her to a fault. Lily Rose seated herself between Mingyu and cousin Elizabeth, far away from the Cheng supporters. Harlan and Elizabeth were a delight and Lily Rose was thrilled to join the more congenial half of the family.

Lily Rose, her golden hair flowing over her shoulders, was wearing soft natural make up accentuated with a coral lipstick that brightened her smile in Taylor Swift fashion. She had no intention of letting Cheng ruin her mood or spoil their special celebration so, she sported her smile like a badge of honor. Glancing around the long, rectangular table, she discovered a few unfamiliar relatives. Her confidence grew as Mingyu grabbed her hand and proudly introduced her to each auntie and distant cousin as they worked their way around the spread, collecting kind congratulations and warm wishes for the future along the way. Mingyu's joy was infectious and soon she felt comfortable chatting with relatives she hadn't yet met. She noticed Mingyu was well-liked in his family. Cheng not so much. Maybe Cheng's recent brush with the law had soured their view of him. Or maybe relations had always been strained?

Hearing the commotion, Myia came out of the kitchen in her apron to greet and congratulate the couple. "Welcome and Congratulations! I'm happy you agreed to a family dinner. This occasion needs to be celebrated. I understand your reasons for not wanting a big event. The timing isn't right. But…. I hope to be dancing at your wedding...maybe here?" She smiled warmly at Mingyu and Lily Rose.

"And you shall," Mingyu promised her with a hug. "We have no wedding plans yet, so let's just enjoy today," he announced loudly enough for all to hear. He had warned Lily Rose not to discuss wedding plans if they didn't want to be locked into any firm commitments publicly. "My family has the memory of an elephant." Lily Rose relaxed after his announcement and chatted with whoever engaged her.

When all were seated, before dinner was served, Jin stood and cleared his throat. Tapping his glass with chopsticks, he commanded everyone's attention, getting it instantly. "I would like to congratulate my grandson, Mingyu and his bride, Lily Rose, on their engagement. Over the past year, I've watched their friendship unfold and their love grow and I'm very happy with their decision. It is the right one. Lily Rose, you have added another layer of happiness and meaning to my grandson's life. Now you both will embark on a new chapter in your lives where your diversity will be a milestone to be conquered in unfamiliar territories. You've already done a fabulous job of bridging any cultural differences. Remember to honor, listen and understand each other to maintain a tranquil life. Marriage should not be subject to religious restrictions or be a vehicle to compromise your identity, but rather an invitation to flourish with respect and support for each other. I wish you both good health, success and prosperity and most importantly, peace in your journey. Welcome to the Ho family, Lily Rose. My arms and doors are always open to you."

Lily Rose stood and bowed her head. "Thank you, Jin. I feel blessed to have met Mingyu and to have gained such a wonderful, extended family." She raised her wine glass and circled it around the table, nodding collectively at everyone. When her eyes passed Cheng, she noticed his expression hadn't changed. He avoided her gaze and still looked like he had sucked rotting lemons with his black tea.

Over dessert, Lily Rose changed seats with Mingyu to share her gemology news with Jin. Jin put on his reading glasses and perused the letter she handed him.

"Congratulations on your success, Lily Rose. Soon you'll move on to the more difficult part of gemology—colored stones. I hope you'll email me whenever you have questions."

"Thanks, Jin. Why do you say more difficult?"

"Diamonds have a very clear grading system. Colored stones are more complicated. Often, they're harder to identify correctly and their popularity and value can change depending on current trends. One thing to remember though, is top quality always retains its value."

Mingyu chimed in. "The gem identification test is more challenging too. There's so much more to remember and you have to name every stone correctly to pass. Some people in my group had to retake it to graduate, because they missed one answer."

"Way to scare me," Lily Rose teased.

"But you have us as reference tools," Jin assured her, patting her hand. "You'll be fine."

When it was time to say goodnight, Lily Rose noticed Mingyu's underlying sadness. While his words were upbeat, he couldn't hide his upset heart as he said his goodbyes to his extended family members. He wouldn't see some of them again before he left and he was close to many. She realized they would have to seriously consider having their wedding in Hong Kong to make this close-knit family happy. She was totally fine with that because more than anything, she wanted to make Mingyu happy. The few people she cared deeply about would come to Hong Kong for her nuptials and the rest, well….they didn't matter.

Chapter LXVI

Tying Up Loose Ends in Hong Kong

April and May were tense times in Hong Kong. Lily Rose and Mingyu followed the news with dread. Protestors gathered almost daily to protest an extradition bill they wanted withdrawn. The bill would have allowed people accused of an offense to be sent and sentenced in mainland China. Fear of this bill, jeopardized Hong Kong's right to govern itself and encouraged many outspoken international companies to relocate to Singapore, Seoul and other neighboring cities and countries. News agencies, business groups, legal eagles, and foreign offices felt threatened and simply packed up before the government relented months later, but the damage was done. Hong Kong lost a lot of its international business in the spring and summer of 2019. Mingyu was painfully aware of these changes and it rattled him to his core.

The celebration dinner with Bao and all of Mingyu's close friends, amidst the political unrest, was a guarded experience, overshadowed by political rhetoric. The group drank *gunners* and shared favorite foods and memories. Jun dialed back her political opinions, but not her obsession with Mingyu. It appeared as if she accepted one battle was lost, but maybe not the war. Her brooding eyes were still fixated on Mingyu as if she could will him to change his mind. Lily Rose had the sneaky suspicion the minute there was a ripple in her and Mingyu's relationship, Jun would pop up like a scary jack-in-the-box.

Mingyu's friends were shocked to hear about the engagement and their friend's impending move to London. He was the last person they expected to relocate. His close friends knew how connected he was to his family and home. Their comments made Lily Rose realize how hard the transition to London would be for him. She vowed to be as supportive as possible; she didn't want him to ever regret his choices. Since she did not have the same attachment to her former life in New York City, she felt a tinge of jealousy too. She envied his deep roots and close family ties, something she didn't have.

Sag Harbor was different. Marina's way of life and her special connection with her grandmother was preserved there and Lily Rose held onto her fond memories with closed fists. Never had she been homesick for New York City while in Hong Kong, but Sag Harbor was close to her heart. For Lily Rose, home was about people, not places, Sag Harbor being the exception. As sad as she was to leave Hong Kong, she was excited about new beginnings with Mingyu. The thought of seeing Alison and working with David again, added an extra allure. She was pleased not to have to go back to her job and dingy city apartment. Somewhere along the way, she had outgrown both and moved on professionally and spiritually. She looked forward to the challenge of another international transfer, having mastered the first one so brilliantly. Visiting New York would be fun, but living and working in New York City was intense wear and tear she no longer wanted. *Been there, done with that.*

She worried that London would be overwhelming after Hong Kong by sheer size. The Hong Kong office had been such a positive and intimate experience. She had excelled and enjoyed the staff, feeling protected in their office cocoon. Could that be repeated?

One Sunday while Mingyu brunched with Jin, she sat down and calculated her finances. So far so good, but the trip to Vietnam rescheduled for when her job ended was still out of the question, if she wanted to give Sag Harbor a facelift. She decided the renovation was more important to her. She wanted Mingyu to love her home, too.

When Mingyu returned from work that evening, she shared her thoughts. "I think we should shelf the trip to Vietnam for another vacation. It's not the right time for me to be splurging. We'll be back here to see your family, so let's plan a side trip to Vietnam then. What do you think?"

"That's fine. I wouldn't mind the extra time here before I leave. The protests are unsettling and I'm worried about my family's future."

"I understand. I was hoping we could leave for New York a bit earlier. The beginning of next month maybe?" Lily Rose asked tentatively.

"In June?" Mingyu looked alarmed.

"June and July are beautiful in Sag Harbor. We could make that our summer vacation. What do you think?"

"Yes, but that would mean leaving in a few weeks. I need more time to pack up and prepare. Listen, why don't you go back in June and give me the last few weeks alone to organize and empty out my apartment. I discussed the move with Jin and he offered to let me store whatever I'm not taking with him. I've decided to give up my apartment and I'm sure if I ask around, I'll be able to find someone to take over the lease for August. Should we come back to Hong Kong in the future, we'd want a bigger space anyway."

"But you're coming to New York before August, right? Shouldn't I stay and help you?"

"No. You go. I'll come in July. You can help me now by sorting through my clothes and setting aside what I should take to London. The movers will handle the rest. Jin and I will pick what I need to ship for the office. I'll be up to my eyeballs in boxes going to different locations after you leave. You should do the same in New York so we can enjoy our free time when I come."

"Ok, I guess.' Lily Rose made a face. "When in July would you come? And what are you keeping? I love the carved wood piece over the dining room table. Please don't get rid of that."

"I won't. It was my mother's. I'll come as early as I can. I need to leave things in good order here and at work. I can't burden my grandfather and I won't ask my father for help."

"Understood, but I hate leaving before you. What if the protests get worse and you can't leave?"

"The protests will get worse. That's why I want you out. I'll be fine." Mingyu pulled her into his arms. He nuzzled her hair and kissed her, offering his assurances. "I'll come no matter what happens. I promise."

The next morning Mingyu encouraged Lily Rose to rummage through his closet. "Put aside two or three boxes for London. I'll check them tonight. Remember, I'm meeting my father for dinner after work, so you're on your own this evening."

"Got it. I feel like Cinderella. Good luck later. I hope you have a good reunion." Mingyu laughed as he headed out the door. "Thanks, Cinderella. I promise there's a ball in your future."

Mingyu's father was still working from his apartment on Caine Road, so seeing him was something that had to be arranged in advance. It was strange not having him around in the store every day, but Jin had been adamant, "Trust has to be earned." With Jin, all actions had consequences.

That night Mingyu and his father met at a fancy new restaurant in Cheng's neighborhood. Mingyu was surprised at the choice. He assumed it was Cheng's meager attempt at reconciliation. They usually ate well, but rarely splurged. After drinks and pleasantries were exchanged, Cheng wanted information. They ordered and waited till the waitress left to get into things.

"Your grandfather was vague about what he wanted you to do in London. I'm curious to hear things from your perspective.

How do you feel about relocating? And giving up your desk to cousin Elizabeth?"

"A bit nervous, I suppose, but I would like to give it a try. I think Elizabeth will do fine."

"What are your immediate goals and do you have any office leads?"

"I'll work shows to start, sell loose goods around Europe to increase our client base. I have no solid office leads yet, but Jin ferreted some contacts for me at the last show. I'll contact them before I leave."

"Are you leaving because of the girl? Did she want you to do this?"

Mingyu felt his temper flare. "No. Jin did. It was a business decision. And the girl has a name. Lily Rose. She's my fiancée. I asked her to join me in London because I love her and would like to build a future with her."

"A business decision Jin never discussed with me," he spat resentfully. "I thought you and Jun would make a nice couple."

"And before that you thought Fen and I made a nice couple. But the problem is, you never asked me how I felt. They're both perfectly nice women, but they would never make me happy."

"And you think this girl will?" Cheng sounded skeptical.

Mingyu glared at his father. "I know she will." *Should I bother staying if this is where the conversation is going? He's purposely pushing my buttons.*

The waitress arrived with their food, placing it between them. They silently waited till she was done, tension filling the space between them.

"If that is truly the case, I wish you both the best of luck. I didn't ask you to dinner to create more problems between us. I wanted to apologize for the stress I caused you and the family.

I made a terrible mistake. Jin has forgiven me. I hope you will too." Without waiting for a response, Cheng served himself. It was typical for him to get right to the point and hope to move on without discussions or repercussions. He had a way of confronting what needed to be, but then brushing it under the rug once he said his piece, but this time, Mingyu wasn't having it. Mingyu locked eyes with his father, then took a big swig of his drink trying to cool his rising heat. "Not remembering my fiancé's name and being antagonistic toward her doesn't exactly build bridges."

"I only want what's best for you." Cheng averted his gaze and started eating.

"Then you'll support my choices. And for the record, I'm not as forgiving as my grandfather. Why did you put him in that embarrassing position anyway? You know how hard he works and how proud he is of the business he's built. His name, his reputation means everything to him. What were you thinking? A one-line apology with no explanation isn't going to excuse the past year of daily stress and shame, you inflicted on all of us."

Cheng studied his dinnerplate, grappling to assemble a reply, but Mingyu wasn't done. "And what about Winnie, Dad? That was your carefully chosen relationship choice? In all of Hong Kong? Do you really think you should be giving me love advice? Where is Winnie now? Will she come back to bite your arse? Or did you pay her off?" Mingyu's anger was escalating. He felt like walking out before he said worse, but he needed and wanted to hear his father's reply.

"Winnie was another mistake. She was flirty and I've been lonely since your mother died. I merely took the bait. The relationship meant nothing."

"I hope she knows that." Minyu shot back. "Are there any other mistakes you would like to disclose? Now would be the time to come clean. Let's air it all, so we can start fresh."

"No, I have nothing more to add." Cheng frowned not wishing to prolong his embarrassment. "Please, eat. The food is getting cold."

"You haven't really explained yourself. Or told me why you digressed with Hu Fat, who everyone knows is shady. I'm not ready to forgive you. Ye Ye's strong Buddist beliefs, his age, his wisdom and kind disposition may make him a bigger, more forgiving person than me. I may follow, however, I'm not there yet, especially in light of how you treat my fiancée. Don't think I didn't notice your sour face at Miya's party for us. Besides, you not only hurt your father and embarrassed our whole family, but you also tarnished our brand. Maybe that's another reason I decided to leave for a while—or why grandpa decided to expand the business without you. Did that ever occur to you?" He glared at his father who shifted uncomfortably in his seat, looking around for who might be overhearing his son's outburst.

"I hear your anger, but when it comes to women, don't confuse my actions with your choice to start a life and family with an outsider. I think you're making a bad match, but it's your choice. I think we should both think about things and not jump into an uncertain future. As far as my business digression goes, I've apologized. You are disrespecting me now." Cheng continued eating.

"I feel confident about my choices. I think you should concentrate on yours, business and otherwise," Mingyu barked.

To curb the explosive tension, Mingyu put some food on his plate. The mingled scents of anise, chili powder, cloves, garlic and saffron teased his nose. He took a bite. This action, sent Cheng the message that his son was staying for the meal. Mingyu saw him visibly sigh. His father appeared to realize he had amends to make and that it would take time, more time than the duration of a fancy dinner. Mingyu was hungry. Now that he had said his piece, he took a few bites and chewed thoughtfully. His silence expanded in the air, letting the restaurant noises take over.

"Look, I'm sorry, Mingyu. People make mistakes. Parents aren't perfect. We do our best." Cheng's head hung over his plate like a curved lamppost, his humiliation apparent.

Mingyu thought about his grandfather's mistakes. Falling in love with a married foreigner. Then letting her leave without speaking up, thereby breaking her heart and his own. *I suppose people do make mistakes. But ye ye would never do shady business. And he stayed in Hong Kong because his father was ill and needed him. Ultimately, grandpa did the right thing, hard as it was. He didn't desert his family when they needed him. He also saved them the embarrassment of traipsing across the world after a married woman who it turns out, was pregnant with her husband's child. That in itself must have been an excruciating nine months.*

The two men ate in silence, each lost in their own grumbling thoughts. When the waitress returned, they both decided to skip tea and dessert, opting to call it a night. Everything that needed to be said, had been, and now they needed time to heal. Mingyu knew his father wouldn't shed more light on his actions and inner thoughts, but he was confident time would help heal their relationship. Mingyu wasn't ready to share this realization yet. He wanted his father to suffer a little longer, like Jin and he had this past year. Mingyu wasn't past his disappointment and maybe he never would be, but over time his Buddhist beliefs would soften his demeanor and compel him to extend forgiveness. He was a work in progress. *Aren't we all?*

When Mingyu got home, the living room looked like a flea market. His clothes were folded in neat piles all over the furniture. As if clairvoyant, Lily Rose had set up an iced bucket with chilled prosecco and bowls for ice cream. She looked up from her puttering when he entered and smiled. From his expression, she could tell it had been a difficult night.

"I'm guessing you didn't stay for dessert," she asked softly.

"No. It was a painful evening."

"In the U.S. we think ice cream makes everything better. Would you like some? I even have topping choices."

Mingyu smiled. "What a novel solution. I'm going to like living in the U.S." Exhausted and mentally drained, he dropped his work bag and walked over to hug her, holding her tight, propping his chin against her head. She smelled good—comforting. "Thanks."

Lily Rose felt his tense muscles. She massaged his back. "I missed you this evening. Let's have a relaxing night and make you feel better. You don't have to talk about the dinner if you don't want to."

She poured him a glass of bubbly and handed it to him. "Would you rather something stronger? A *baijiu?*"

"No. This is perfect."

"Strawberry or Vanilla?"

"Vanilla."

"Chocolate sprinkles or five spice peanuts?"

"Both. Tough night."

Chapter LXVII

Jin's Final Confession

Mingyu and Lily Rose followed the local news closely. The anti-extradition protests in Hong Kong were escalating daily; politics was all people talked about. You couldn't move about freely on the streets without being confronted. To make matters worse, Carrie Lam, the city's leader, stuck by her controversial bill. The streets were on fire with peaceful, but vehement protests during the day, that escalated into violence after dark.

While Mingyu and Lily Rose sympathized with the protesters, they didn't participate. Mingyu didn't want to expose Lily Rose to possibly being arrested as a foreigner and deported, or worse, sent to mainland China for a minor infraction. She didn't need a police record to impede her reentry in the future.

The protesters were afraid the contentious bill would fully erode the city's judicial independence. Extradition to mainland China was a threat most British colony survivors hoped to avoid at all costs. The thought of being subject to the Chinese legal system, with all its flaws, terrified most Hong Kong residents, especially the press, foreign and local.

Most nights Mingyu and Lily Rose stayed home, watching the bedlam on the news, discussing the issues over creative dinners they prepared together. Their personal goal as a newly minted couple was to save money for their summer in Sag Harbor and the move to London in September, so dinners out and costly entertainment were consciously scrapped. Lily Rose and Mingyu were busy cooking and making love, not war.

Lily Rose was glad she wasn't working in the hotel anymore. Hong Kong's hotels were affected by the daily protests. Hundreds of thousands of people were marching on the streets, blocking roads and skirting tear gas. She had left the office at a good time. On her last day, Lam surprised her by bringing a small chocolate cake and a bottle of champagne to share. He presented her with a parting gift, a luxury key chain from Gucci. "For your new apartment and office keys in London," he said. "Stay in touch, Lily Rose. You can always come back. The door is open for your return. "His kind gesture had touched her. He hadn't extended that offer to David as far as she knew.

On the first Sunday in June, Lily Rose and Mingyu were invited to Jin's so she could say her goodbyes. It was a bittersweet invitation because of his advanced age. Having lost Marina so unexpectedly, she was well aware of the possibility of not seeing Jin again. Of course, she kept this fear to herself, but it floated in the air between them all.

She had taken extra care shopping for Jin's favorite dessert. This time she varied the flavors, buying papaya and vanilla ice cream and two different brands of five spice peanuts. She also made an almond jelly pudding to share, a recipe she gleaned from Miya with her own additions. Wearing her new green linen dress, embroidered with bamboo shoots, paired with gold sandals, she looked traditionally pretty and garden fresh. Mingyu's appreciative eyes told her so.

"I love this dress. I wish I had gotten one more in lilac linen. Remind me to do that, next trip." Mingyu smiled and made a humming sound, not answering, his thoughts drifting judging by his expression. The idea of being able to say 'next trip' made her looming departure less hurtful and final. Once they married, she would have an extended family in Hong Kong who cared about her. She considered herself very lucky, coming from a small, fractured family.

When Mingyu and Lily Rose arrived at Jin's, they parked on the street and wandered through the garden first. "I have to see what's blooming," Lily Rose remarked with nostalgia. She walked past the small rock garden and fountain at the entrance to where the more serious plants were lined along the building sides and in the back yard. The wonderful fragrant scents of jasmine, peony and sandalwood wafted up her nose. She breathed in and closed her eyes. "Mmm…I wish I could bottle this and take it with me."

"It will be a fond memory and another reason to come back. You can remember the scent when you meditate."

"Is that what you do? Mingyu, look, Jin has peonies! Those were my grandma's favorite."

"I bet he knew that." Mingyu's glance followed her around the garden as he waited patiently while she sniffed all the newly blooming flowers. Watching her delight, he smiled.

Satisfied that she had seen and captured everything in her mind's eye and on her phone, she walked back to the front door with Mingyu at her heels. He kissed her before unlocking the door with his key set. Inside, Lily Rose noticed fresh flowers from the garden by the Buddha statue. She slipped off her shoes and carried them upstairs.

Jin was cooking in his emerald kitchen like a mad scientist. "Hello you two. "A different tantalizing scent teased her nose, one with ginger, soy and garlic. Lily Rose greeted Jin warmly and put the ice cream in the freezer. Washing her hands, she remarked, "What smells so wonderful?"

"Glad you're here, Lily Rose. This is my own special version of spare ribs. My mother's recipe. I marinated them overnight with hoisin sauce, honey and spices."

"That smells heavenly. I'm going to miss this kitchen. Good memories here. How can I help?"

Mingyu gave his grandfather a rare hug and started setting the table outside.

"Stir the fried rice and make sure it doesn't burn to the wok. I still have to add the shrimp."

Jin finished rinsing the peeled shrimp and threw them in a handful at a time. "You're always welcome to come back, Lily Rose. You're family now. Did you have a hard time getting here with all the protestors?"

"No. I think they're still sleeping. It'll be worse going home," Mingyu answered.

"Probably so. Thank you for braving them. I'll miss seeing you both in the coming months. My Sundays won't be the same. I'll probably start going to the restaurant again so I don't get lonely."

"Maybe we can make a phone date for Sundays. Have Mingyu set up *Zoom* on your computer before he leaves. It's easy. Or I can do it today, if you like."

Jin perked up. "Would you? I'd like that. You can show me how it works after we eat."

Once they were seated, they chatted about the protests, Mingyu's plan of action in London and finally, about Mingyu's dinner with Cheng. Jin listened as did Lily Rose. Over dessert and tea, he became reflective. " In regard to your father, let me quote Buddha—*a mind beyond judgements watches and understands.* No doubt, Cheng has made mistakes, but the sooner we forgive and move on, the better for all concerned. When I first found out that my father had returned all of Marina's letters, I was furious and disappointed in him. Even after all these years! But I soon realized, he did it out of fear of losing me. He was sick and didn't want me to go—he couldn't bear it. Was it selfish? Controlling? Perhaps, but I know he did his best. He was ill and had a business to run."

Lily Rose and Mingyu looked at each other but stayed silent, sipping their tea.

Jin continued," When I spoke to Marina before she died, she confided to me that my father had contacted your grandfather's boss about our affair. My father asked his boss to transfer your grandparents out of Hong Kong. Your grandfather, Lily Rose, was the bigger man. He left a lucrative job he enjoyed to save his marriage. He never said a word to Marina. She found out years later. Again, I was angry with my father, but I turned to Buddha's teachings for guidance. *With gentleness, overcome anger. With generosity, overcome meanness. With truth, overcome delusion."* Jin paused. "Before you leave, forgive your father, Mingyu. Let go of your anger, and you'll find peace. You never know what may happen while you're away."

Mingyu frowned. "I'll work on it. Communication from London works too. I'll call him when I'm ready. I'm not ready yet."

When the time came for Lily Rose and Mingyu to leave Jin's home, Lily Rose became emotional. Jin had touched her heart and soul. His Buddhist and worldly approach had resonated with her, and in many ways, brought Marina back to life. She could see why her grandmother fell for him. She had to work hard to hold back her tears when she hugged Jin as they parted. It was like saying goodbye to Marina all over again. When she and Mingyu left, the floodgates burst open in the car. He pulled over and let her sob in his arms.

On Friday June 7th, amidst roaring protests in the streets, Mingyu took Lily Rose to the airport. Her extended year in Hong Kong had come to a close. Emotional, amidst the chaos, she bid her lover an extended goodbye. Promises were made with every intention of keeping them. After Mingyu dropped her and helped her check in at the airport, he left. Traffic was horrendous due to escalating protests.

At the airport terminal, Lily Rose spotted Chen Du in the crowd. She gasped when he approached her with his two wingmen. *What is he doing here?* He had her full attention when he stopped about ten feet away. Eyeballs locked, he pointed his forefinger under one eye, then pointed to Lily Rose. Stunned, she stared at him, unable to move. Chen Du crossed his muscled arms and stood in a motionless stance, feet planted like tree roots. Taking a deep breath, Lily Rose regained her mobility and hurried to the security line, seeking comfort in the strangers around her and in the fact that she may be secure on the other side of the checkpoint. Looking over her shoulder, Chen Du stayed in place until she was out of sight. *What message is he sending me? Is he going to hurt Mingyu? Because Carson protected me?* She hadn't told Mingyu about her brush with Carson at the hotel. Nor about the written message at the party. Once through security, she planted herself at the departure gate. It was definitely time to leave. She could do without the threat of Chen Du and without second guessing Carson Wu's protection. To calm herself, she pulled Marina's book of quotes out of her handbag and randomly leafed through it for comfort. She paused at a quote from Buddha. It read, *"The blade need not be long, only sharp."* She shuddered. When she was finally airborne, she looked down at Hong Kong's many waterways, remembering her arrival over a year ago. She prayed that Mingyu would make it out safely... soon.

Chapter LXVIII

Restless in New York

Two days later, on Sunday, June 9th, 2019 more than one million people marched in Hong Kong to block officials from entering the government building to sign the contentious extradition bill. Lily Rose was following the daily news with apprehension and concern. It was the largest demonstration in Hong Kong's history, including people of all ages and backgrounds. Many wore white to represent justice. The protests were a stark reminder of the *Umbrella Revolution of 2014* when pro-democracy protestors took to the streets using umbrellas as shields against police brutality. Mingyu and Bao were among the people who marched.

Lily Rose arrived in New York exhausted and emotionally spent. Her plane's arrival was greeted with a much-needed wave of good weather. The previous days had been fraught with torrential showers, not of the short tropical kind, but rather of the dreary all-day New York gloomy kind. On the plus side, it gave the vegetation in Marina's garden a natural post-trauma facelift. The blossoming peonies in her front yard were recovering from the pelting and slowly returning to a full bloom, heads-up position. Those that survived.

Exhausted, Lily Rose dragged her suitcase up the few porch steps and wheeled it into the living room. She pulled up all the shades and opened the windows to get a cross-breeze circulating. The house was stuffy, but looked the same as she had left it. Only she was different. She had grown as a person--become worldlier. She had also shed her anxiety and tapped into a healthy dose of Jin's Zen approach to everything. She hoped she could keep that vibe going. Pleased to be home, she texted Mingyu to let him know she was safe and sound in Eastern Long Island.

Looking around, she was relieved to see her mother had not changed or moved a thing. Everything was neat and tucked in its proper place, waiting to be rearranged by Lily Rose. That was her prerogative now. She did a quick walk through of the downstairs, checking for leaks or other unpleasant surprises, but thankfully, there were none, other than a slew of dead bugs. Even the leak her mother had taken care of was not detectable. Ella May had done a stellar job of fixing the problem and painting over it.

Satisfied, Lily Rose climbed the creaky stairs, lingering at the top, before placing her backpack in the guest room, the room that had always been hers. She walked into Marina's bedroom and did a 360 turn. All of her grandmother's clothes still hung in the open walk-in closet as if she was coming back. While it hurt not to see her, her grandmother's presence was felt … in a good way. Marina was here, in her heart, as was Jin.

Maybe now she would be able to tackle weeding out whatever her mother and she didn't want to keep. Redoing the master bedroom would be her first home project, before Mingyu arrived. She wanted to make the bedroom theirs, transform it while she stayed in the guest room. Lily Rose went back downstairs and checked for the car keys. As expected, they were in the same kitchen drawer. She ventured out to check the car battery. It worked. *Bless your heart, Mom.* While she still had a small reserve of energy, she decided to get a few groceries for the morning. She needed coffee and she was craving granola, a blueberry muffin and Justin's honey peanut butter. Her mother was coming for the weekend.

The next morning, Lily Rose was up early. The sun steamed up her bedsheets as she lay coddled in her soft quilted blanket. She rolled over to face the window and watch the tree tops sway. Reaching for her phone, she checked for emails or messages from Mingyu. There were none.

After breakfast, she conferenced Tina and Zoe and invited them for the following weekend. She hopped into the car and went to the hardware store to get paint samples, swatches and a new broom. On her way back, she picked up more groceries and her mom at the bus stop. "Hey, Mom." She hugged her mother and swung the small weekend case into the car." Want to have lunch in town or at home? I bought groceries."

"Welcome home, Lily Rose. I was so worried with all those protests; it looked frightening in the news. So glad you're back. How does it feel?"

"Good. Different. I had a wonderful year. It was hard to leave, but it's also great to be back. Yes, the news is scary. The protestors have taken over the streets. It was crazy when I left."

"Tell me all about it over lunch. *World Pie?*" Ella May suggested. "We can save the groceries for tonight."

"Sure. I missed their pizza. My groceries should be fine. I used cooler bags."

"Let me see your ring. Wow.... it's beautiful, Lily Rose. Congratulations. May it bring you and Mingyu good fortune and a happy life together."

"I know, right? Thanks."

In the restaurant, Lily Rose talked about her love of Hong Kong, its people and the wonderful places she visited. She shared her many pictures and memories. All talk about the future was set aside. Both women wanted to enjoy the moment without controversy. For the next few months, Lily Rose was home. They had time.

By the end of the weekend, they had caught up on time missed and sorted and packed three garbage bags of Marina's clothes for donation. Ella May had a bag of her own to take when Lily Rose dropped her at the bus stop Sunday night. As nice as it was to spend quality time with her mom, Lily Rose was itching to roll up her sleeves and get to work revamping Marina's bedroom.

She waited until her mother left to tape all her paint swatches to the wall, not wanting any input. She wanted to make her own decisions. One sample was a warm off-white, the other a soothing sand color. Not loving either in Marina's bright natural lighting, she decided to go back to the paint store in the morning. She wanted the room to be perfect.

Perusing colors the next day, Lily Rose picked up three small paint samples and a hot young handyman between jobs, who volunteered to help her for reasonable pay. He had overheard her conversation about paint swatches and offered his services. He approached her, "I'm free for the next few weeks until my next job starts. I can paint, do carpentry and anything else your heart desires. The owner of this paint store can vouch for me."

Lily Rose looked at the man behind the counter and got a nod. "Alright then. Does tomorrow morning work?"

"Yup, see you at nine." He held out his hand. "Liam, pleased to meet you. Where do you live?"

Lily Rose spent the afternoon spacing swipes of paint on the wall and checking and rechecking it in different light and times of the day. Before Liam showed up the next morning, she decided on an almost white, sky blue with a pale, sunny ceiling for the master bedroom. She rushed out to buy the paint before Liam's anticipated arrival time.

Liam tackled the ceiling first, promising to have the entire room finished in two days. He was a man of his word. Letting the touch-up paint dry on day three they shared a late lunch and chatted about what to tackle next. Lily Rose planned to use Liam's muscles to move furniture around and strategically position her own favorites where she envisioned them. She kept Marina's two matching whitewashed night tables in the bedroom, but added her own dresser from the city. She kept the small white café table by the window and exchanged the two matching chairs with the oversized pastel paisley armchair Marina used to sit in for their bedtime stories. Marina's old furniture was moved to the sparse guest room, thus creating a more spacious master bedroom and a pleasing second bedroom. Her belongings fit easily into Marina's closet with room to spare for Mingyu.

Lily Rose also splurged on a flat screen smart TV which Liam hung over the single dresser. Marina's old TV set was added to the donation pile in the garage. Next, she rehung the artwork around the house, hiding the pieces she didn't care for behind the love seat in the library alcove. Her mom could pick what she liked and the rest she would sell at auction.

In the linen closet she found light blue and white striped bedding which she readily used for the master bed. The room looked fresh with a shabby chic touch. The paisley armchair created the warmth she desired and kept the wonderful memories embedded in it alive and close. She envisioned herself curled up there on a grey or cold day with a good book.

Lily Rose eyed the bedside lamps and unscrewed the finials removing the shades. Getting modern white lampshades without bug splats and mystery marks was the final touch needed. She remembered when Marina and she had picked the lamps together on a home improvement shopping spree at Hildreth's in Southampton. Funny how things aged and got moldy by the water. To escape the penetrating paint smell, she slept in her old room, leaving all the upstairs windows wide open.

By Friday the house was in ship shape for her friends' arrival. Furniture had been repositioned, walls touched up, art work relocated and rehung, and rugs rolled up for cleaning or repurposing. Fine, polished oak floors shone with a fresh coat of polish and cluttered counters were cleared. Lily Rose moved into the master bedroom before Tina and Zoe arrived. The paint smell had finally subsided. Their initial reunion on the front porch was emotional and loud.

"Wow, nice upgrade. Even your violet couch is here! I was wondering if you were going to give that up," Tina exclaimed. "I contemplated buying it from you when I heard you were leaving the city."

"My couch was never for sale, girlie. It's the crowning piece of my furniture collection. I moved my best pieces prior to leaving for Asia."

"Collection? You mean all of three pieces? How does it feel to be back? When is Mingyu coming? We're dying to meet him." Zoe chimed in, plopping herself on the couch and patting the pillows.

"I'm not sure yet. He's still moving out of his apartment. Wine or Margaritas?" Lily Rose inquired as she headed to the kitchen.

"Margaritas," both girls replied in unison traipsing behind her.

"I'm still upset I never made it to Hong Kong while you were there. Starting a new job killed my vacation time," Zoe explained.

"I understand. You may have another chance though." Lily Rose winked.

"What do you mean?"

"I may be getting married there. You both have to come for that."

"Really? When?" Zoe perked up. "Wait. Let's see that ring."

"No date yet, but you'll be among the first to know. So, what's your excuse for not visiting me, Tina? "Lily Rose held out her hand to Zoe.

"The long flight? Zoe wasn't available to go with me? Ok, I don't have one." Tina shrugged.

"But I'll save up and come for the wedding for sure. Wow, girl. Your ring is spectacular!"

"Sweet. Ver-ry nice rock; is that a princess cut?" Zoe interrupted.

"Quadrillion. Just under two carats."

"Not too shabby." Zoe nodded her approval with enthusiasm.

"Thanks, guys. Now that I have your blessings and promises to come to Hong Kong, let's celebrate.

Lily Rose poured the margarita mix into the blender, adding ice chips. When it looked frothy enough, she swished the blended mix into three glasses fortified with tequila. She added a sliver of lime in each. They toasted their reunion with a loud clink. "Cheers."

Turning up popular streamed music, they moved to the front porch to watch the sun set, barbeque burgers, and swap stories. While mixing a refill batch of frozen margaritas, Lily Rose's phone rang. She picked it up, hoping it might be Mingyu. Why hadn't she heard from him?

"Hello? Lily Rose? Is that you? It's Jin."

"Jin? How are you? Is everything ok?" She could feel her pulse quicken.

"I'm fine. Mingyu, not so much."

Lily Rose felt panic take hold. Chen Du sprung to mind immediately. "Why? What happened?"

"Mingyu and Bao were arrested."

Lily Rose choked. "What? When? What did they do?"

Jin sighed. "They were protesting. The police came and rounded them up after dousing them with tear gas. He's pretty banged up. He wanted me to call you to tell you he won't make his flight. The family is pretty upset, but we'll do our best to resolve this so he can leave soon. He'll call you when he can."

"Oh my God. I was wondering why I hadn't heard from him. It's been a week! He'll be ok, right?" She sunk into the nearest chair scared to ask if Mingyu was still in jail. She had the feeling Jin didn't want to elaborate.

"A few bumps and bruises; he'll survive. Bao too. They were roughed up. I hope this unrest passes soon, but it doesn't look that way. Hong Kong is changing. I'm glad Mingyu agreed to try London. I'll miss him, but I think it's the right decision. Bao will only get him into more trouble if he stays here. Bao is writing anti-government articles that will get him black-listed and sent to the mainland if he doesn't watch it. I think the two of them were targeted."

"It's Bao's job to report the issues he's passionate about." While she voiced this idea, she secretly wondered if Chen Du had targeted them using his police connections. Was that what his message at the airport was about? That he would pay her back in another way despite having Carson's protection? The gangster mind was an enigma to her. It was starting to dawn on her that Carson Wu did have her back.

Although organized crime couldn't possibly be happy about the government changes, they would have paid enough people off not to be overly concerned, but what would happen moving forward? Either way, the changes in Hong Kong could not be a welcome development. She debated telling Jin about Chen Du's threat at the airport, but decided against it. That would mean disclosing her friendship with Alison. She needed to think with a clear head and right now she was completely foggy from the tequila.

"Did Mingyu finish moving out of his apartment yet? Last I heard, he was close to done."

"No, not entirely. The furniture he wants to keep is here with me, but he's still packing trunks for shipping and storing. Don't worry. We'll keep you posted. Are you enjoying New York?"

"Yes. It's nice to be home. My mom visited last weekend and my girlfriends are visiting from the city this weekend. We're catching up."

"Lovely. I won't keep you then. Mingyu will call in a few days... I'm sure."

"Thanks. Bye, Jin. I miss you all." Lily Rose's brain matter was saturated. There was nothing she could do to help right now, but send Mingyu encouraging thoughts and texts. She had to wait and trust Jin. She finished mixing a new batch of margaritas and refilled her friends' glasses, including her own. Now she had an added excuse to have another drink.

A pitcher later, the girls stumbled to bed, pleasantly tipsy. As Lily Rose's spinning head hit the pillow, she realized how much she missed Mingyu. She was worried about his safety. *Damn, Bao. Or was it Chen Du's work?* She fingered the dragon pendant at her bedside and fell asleep dreaming of Mingyu. They were being chased by Chen Du and his soldiers. They were running through the Mong Kok street markets with Chen Du hot on their heels when they hit a dead-end alley. Lily Rose woke up breathless, in a cold sweat, needing to pee. She spent the rest of the night obsessing over Mingyu's safety, praying he would make it out intact... soon.

Having her homies visiting from the city definitely softened the blow Jin delivered. There was value in a night with friends. *It's good to be home, but I should have stayed in Hong Kong. He wouldn't have protested with Bao if I was there.*

The day after Tina and Zoe left, Liam was back, ready to work. There was no word from Mingyu, so Lily Rose was thankful for the distraction. She noticed Liam silently eyeing the extensive barware in the sink and smiled, amused at what he was thinking. The pungent smell of tequila and limes lingered in her kitchen and spoke volumes. *Let him wonder….ha.*

"So, what's the plan for this week? The rest of the house looks pretty good with the touch up we did." Liam's sapphire gaze scanned Lily Rose's contours as she stretched to open one of the kitchen cabinets.

"I'd like to sand and paint the oak cabinets. Can you help me clear them?"

"Sure. What color did you have in mind?"

"A jade green wash." She handed him a paint chip.

"Hmmm. You sure about this? The usual trend out here is white. Better for resale." Liam looked skeptical as he fingered the polished, natural wood and eyed the paint chip. "This is a … …loud color."

"I'm positive. This place is not for sale."

"Ok then. Your wish is my command."

Chapter LXIX

Feathering the Nest

For the next week, Lily Rose and Liam worked side by side, sanding, painting, and moving anything that wasn't nailed down. Lily Rose fixed sandwich lunches and they shared the occasional glass of wine on the deck after long days of hard labor. At Liam's suggestion, they removed the kitchen double doors to the dining room and created a generous, open arch. Lily Rose was thrilled with the result.

In the garage, she found small glazed planters in different shades of green, ranging from soft, minty aquamarine to peridot to deep emerald. She hosed them down and planted them with herbs, scattering them on the kitchen's generously ledged windowsill. She cleared all counters of anything she didn't use on a daily basis and stood back to enjoy the new uncluttered look. The kitchen walls remained white while the ceiling was painted a pale blue with white cloud tufts that Liam expertly added with a sponge. They added a whitewashed coat beneath the jade green wash to soften the color so the cabinets simulated a mossy world floating on a cumulus cloud.

When they were done, Lily Rose looked at the pictures she took of Jin's tropical green kitchen. She needed something bamboo.

"How much do you think a bamboo counter for the island would cost?" Lily Rose asked as she ran her fingers over chipped tiles, each crack filled with its own memory. Looking upward toward the painted cabinetry, she continued, "Natural wood would be a nice contrast to the painted cabinets. I think bamboo would blend well with the ivory back splash and *Silestone* counter tops. We could stain it in the same golden color as the oak floors."

"Why not use butcher block? It's cheaper." Liam suggested, not getting her Asian drift.

"I think bamboo is more refined."

"I can price it for you. Shouldn't be too much. This is a relatively small island." Liam picked up his measuring tape, "38 by 68. With my industry discount, I bet it'll be very affordable. I can buy it pre-stained. I'll bring a sample for you tomorrow," he promised. The outer edges of his lips curled upward. Lily Rose watched him visualize her ideas as he did a 360 turn in the kitchen center.

"Thanks. Bring a few options. That will be the last transformation I can afford. I plan to get a return on my investment with future rentals."

"Glad to hear you'll enjoy our improvements first, this summer. Where will you be when you rent this place? Summer is the best time to be here."

Not wanting to get into the details of her life, she replied, "Don't know yet. Any ideas?"

"Always. We can rummage through my brain over beers later. I brought a six pack. It's in a cooler in my truck." Liam gathered up his tools and walked to his truck, throwing them in the back. Lily Rose checked her phone. She finally had a message from

Mingyu. He was out of jail. A sigh of relief washed over her when she read his message. He was coming, albeit delayed.

Mingyu's plane touched down in New York two weeks late. After weeks of worrying, texting and talking at odd hours, Lily Rose was thrilled to finally see him in person. A small part of her had been worried he would change his mind about leaving Hong Kong. She was counting on Jin to have her back and push Mingyu out the door. She knew how difficult it was for him to separate from his family and nest.

The night before his arrival, Lily Rose had given herself a much-needed lavender bath and manicure. She pulled her engagement ring out of a home renovation hiatus before she headed to the airport. When she finally saw Mingyu exit the luggage retrieval area at JFK airport, she jumped with joy, right into his arms.

"You're here! I can't believe it. Oh my God, I never should have left you alone with Bao. Bad decision. I missed you so much." Trying to keep her emotions in check, she dried an escaped tear against his shirt, "How's Jin? And the family?"

"Recovering. Actually, I think Jin was glad I finally left."

Mingyu spotted Lily Rose's blonde halo amongst a sea of signs and impatient people. She looked tan and fresh in white jeans and a loose, sky linen shirt, a luscious pearl in a sea of fragmented shells. He was spent from the flight, not having slept a wink since his Los Angeles stop over and he felt like a rumpled blanket. Saying goodbye to his family, not something he ever thought he would do, and dismantling and packing up his previous life, had taken an emotional toll. He hadn't anticipated how gut wrenching his goodbyes and transition would be. Of course, getting arrested hadn't helped his emotional state. Between the worrisome political events, the bruises he sustained inside and out, and leaving his family behind during uncertain times, he was shaken to his core. Bao admonishing him for leaving didn't help either.

Everything circulated in his brain at take-off, like a movie reel on replay. Not until Lily Rose sprung into his arms twenty hours later, almost knocking him over, did his mind end the vicious cycle. She was his reward, his reason for taking an uncalculated risk, making a leap. He held her close, feeling her thumping heart against his, inhaling her intoxicating scents. Having her back in his arms calmed him. "I missed you too. Jin sends his love. So does Myia. She wants to know when we're coming back," he laughed. "Hold on. I need to get one more item. Hang on to my bags." He walked back to the exit door and lifted a heavily packaged panel. He should have shipped this piece, but he wanted to see her reaction when he brought it.

Lily Rose's eyes widened. "You brought the carved panel from your apartment?"

"Yes. For your new kitchen."

"Our …. summer house kitchen. It'll look fabulous. Wait till you see what I've done. I took some before-renovation pictures, so you can appreciate how hard I've worked this past month. I figured my work gap and your delayed arrival was the perfect time to update the cottage. It has actually been fun and it kept my mind off worrying about you. You have to tell me in detail what happened."

Mingyu waved her off. "I will. When I catch my breath. Tell me about you."

"My friends came out to see me a few weekends ago. They're dying to meet you. I saved the city trips for your arrival. Haven't been in once."

"Much appreciated. How is your mom?"

"Good. We'll see her next weekend."

The car ride home was filled with happy chatter, mainly Lily Rose's. He briefly filled her in on his hectic last few weeks in Hong Kong. By the time they reached Southampton, the end of the highway, she was caught up. Tired, but content, he encouraged her to take over, listening to her chatter like a chirping bird at sunrise.

Turning left toward Noyack Road, Lily Rose rolled down the windows to let fresh air circulate. Hugging the Long Island Sound's coastline now, Mingyu marveled at the glistening afternoon water views between sheltered homes and lush trees as they navigated the narrow road's twists and turns. When they passed Upper Sag Harbor Cove, his eyes silently devoured the scenery. "It's beautiful here! Is this where you learned to swim?"

"Yup. *Foster Memorial Beach*. My first strokes were celebrated with strawberry lemonade and sugar sprinkle cookies baked by my grandmother." Lily Rose's voice held pride.

"So, we're close now?"

"Very. My grandmother's house overlooks this beach from the hill over there."

When they pulled up to the white house with the cornflower blue front door, Mingyu noticed the vegetation-- a mix of hydrangea and lavender bushes, trimmed yellow cypress trees and tufts of zebra grass contained between strategically placed boulders. Roses grew along a low white brick wall and by the flagstone walkway near the front door he saw the remnants of Marina's favorite flower, the peony. Sadly, their short blooming season had already ended.

When Lily Rose unlocked the entrance, allowing him to pass first, Mingyu took in the white beach cottage interior with its warm sand color accents. A majestic violet camelback couch rested on an earth toned Turkish *Oushak* rug facing the fireplace. There were beach scenes and macro flower paintings on the walls and colorful Italian pottery in a glass-doored maple wood cabinet in the dining room. The screened windows were open and a cross breeze made the embroidered white-on-white linen curtains sway like a gospel choir.

"Would you like a chilled drink? I made peach ice tea this morning," Lily Rose asked as she rolled his hand luggage inside and parked it by the stairs.

Mingyu followed her, adding his large suitcase next to the hand luggage. He walked to the fireplace and studied all the family photos. "Yes, to tea. Is this Marina?" He pointed to a portrait of Lily Rose and her grandmother. The resemblance was obvious, despite different hair colors.

"Yes."

"I can see the likeness. The pictures on your phone didn't do her justice." He followed her into the kitchen. "This is a beautiful beach home. So warm and inviting."

"Thanks. I've always loved it here."

The mottled shades of aqua and moss made him smile as he scanned the cabinetry and the row of herbs in the window. He noticed a small bamboo plant resting on a high gloss bamboo counter. "This feels like Jin's kitchen! The carving would look nice in here. We can *Zoom* with Jin, kitchen-to-kitchen."

Lily Rose smiled. That was exactly the reaction she was hoping for. Feeling at home in someone's kitchen went a long way. She prayed he would love the rest of the house as much as she loved Jin's home on Stanley Village Drive. She poured tea into two tall frosted glasses and walked out to the front porch. "Come sit and enjoy the view while I unpack the carving. I'll give you the upstairs tour later. I revamped our bedroom into a mermaid's oasis."

"A tropical jade-colored kitchen, a mermaid bedroom, I can't wait to see the bathroom."

"Don't get too excited. That's just basic white with beach glass accents, but I'm open to suggestions. My favorite shower is the outdoor one on the west side of the house. Big enough for two," she winked.

Tearing at the packaging, she spoke quietly, "I was thinking we would go into the city over the weekend. My friends are planning a dinner for us. We can do a little sight-seeing, shopping and stay at my mom's on Saturday night. What do you think?" Lily Rose cut through the bubble wrap.

"Sounds good. Or… maybe we could stay in a hotel, my treat. I can think of a few things I might like privacy for." He winked back at her.

"Even better. I would love a night alone with you, in the city. I'll make a reservation." Lily Rose leaned over to kiss him.

Satisfied, Mingyu took a huge gulp of his tea. His tired, drooping eyes perked up ever so slightly from the rush of sugar. He looked down at his jeans and noticed a few smudges. It had been a long, emotional trip, but he was glad to be sitting here, on Marina's porch. After a power nap, he would be ready to discover Lily Rose's world.

He feasted his eyes on the magnificent scenery around him. The house had its own aged charm, like Jin's. It didn't have the sophistication of his grandfather's home, but it had character and was comfortable and cozy. The perfect beach house.

He watched Lily Rose wrestle off the remaining packaging and enjoyed her excitement when the last covering was stripped off. She gently positioned his mother's Chinese carving against the porch railing and stood back to admire it.

"It's beautiful. Thanks for bringing it. When we finish our tea, let's see where we should hang this. Maybe over the kitchen table?"

Mingyu grabbed her hand and pulled her onto his lap. "I have to warn you … I'm fading fast."

"No problem. We can hang it when you wake up or tomorrow. Let's go put you to bed. I had crazy jet lag when I came home. Nothing like a few hours of sleep to remedy that."

Finishing his ice tea, he followed her back inside. Lily Rose rested the carving against the dining room wall. "You hungry?"

"Later. Let's do the bedroom tour." Walking over to his hand luggage, he pulled the zipper open and sat down on the stairs. "First, let me give you this. I brought you something I think you'll like." He handed her a flat, wrapped box.

Lily Rose shook it. "Hmm … Thanks." She unwrapped the colorful paper and opened the lid to reveal a neatly folded lilac linen dress from Master Kan's shop—the same style as her green one. "Oh my God, Mingyu. You remembered! I didn't even think you were listening when I talked about ordering this. These linen dresses are fabulous. Thank you so much. I have something for you upstairs. Local wear and a hoodie for at night. You'll need it here. I've been working around the clock to get the house in order so I haven't done much shopping." She twirled around holding the dress against her body, then kissed Mingyu on the lips. "I'll wear it when we go into the city."

She started up the stairs. "In the meantime, we'll stay local. Tomorrow we can relax at the beach. Maybe go for an early dinner in town."

"Beach sounds good." He stifled a yawn as he lugged his suitcase up the creaking stairs.

Lily Rose dropped his hand luggage and backpack at the top. Her abbreviated tour ended in the master bedroom. She closed the curtains. "Rest."

"Thanks, I'm toast. That bed looks mighty inviting. Wake me in two hours. I don't want to miss our first night together."

"You won't. I put a set of towels in the bathroom for you and a water bottle on the night table. It's in the cooler bag. The clothes on the bed are for you. Didn't have time to wrap anything. Do you need anything else?"

"No. Just the bed." Mingyu slurred his words.

Lily Rose kissed him again and closed the door behind her, tiptoeing downstairs. She called Zoe for a long chat as she prepped their dinner. She barbequed burgers and corn, placing them in the oven on a warm temperature. The garden salad was already chilling. She knew it would be an early night, so she decided to not fuss. She set the kitchen table, leaving the planned candlelight dinner on the porch for another night, when he was conscious. Since the breeze had died down, the mosquitos would be out dancing, looking for a feast. The weather changed quickly on an island. Besides, Marina had taught her that *the heart of every home, the crux of family life and the center of milestone celebrations and tragedies, all take place in the kitchen.*

-Buddha

Chapter LXX

Marina's Final Act

"Hello? Lily Rose, are you here?" Liam popped his head past the unlocked screen door.Freshly showered and scented, he was wearing a nicely tailored blue and white pin-striped shirt that hinted at the muscles beneath, and nicely fitted jeans that hugged his assets. His sockless blue suede loafers were a welcome sight from his usual bulky construction boots, saggy cargo shorts and smudged white tee shirts. In his left hand was a chilled bottle of a North Fork rose' and in his right, a single red rose.

Mingyu looked up from his laptop and watched Liam's tentative approach into the kitchen. Unaware, Liam placed the bottle on the bamboo counter and looked in the cabinet for a tall bud vase. Then he sat down at the kitchen table and waited. Mingyu watched in silence wondering how this would unfold. *This man sure knows his way around the kitchen.*

Lily Rose came down the stairs looking refreshed after a lazy day at the beach. Rested and freshly groomed, she was casually dressed in capri leggings and a loose, cropped, lemon floral top sloped down over her shoulders. Hearing movement in the kitchen, she sashayed in that direction. Liam's eyes lit up when he spotted her. Bouncing up out of his chair, he instantly made his intentions known. "Hi, Lily Rose. I stopped by to thank you for your business; I brought some wine since I drank a boatload of yours. I hope it's alright I came unannounced."

"Oh…hi, Liam. How sweet. Thank you." She turned and spotted Mingyu seated in the living room with an angled view into the kitchen. Motioning to him, she said, "This is Liam, who helped me with all the renovations. Liam, meet Mingyu. He just arrived from Hong Kong a few days ago."

"Oh, I'm sorry," Liam stuttered in obvious surprise. "I had no idea you had company. I should have called first. I'll catch up with you another night. I was going to ask you about renting your place in September." He backed up to the kitchen door, his ears blushing pink.

"Nice meeting you, Mingyu. Enjoy your night." Making a quick exit, he waved a half-hearted goodbye through the screen and scurried away to his truck.

"Are you sure you don't want to stay for a glass of wine?" Lily Rose asked politely through the aluminum mesh. She couldn't help but notice how good Liam looked tonight. She was flattered and surprised at his obvious efforts.

"Oh no. We'll talk another time. Enjoy the wine. Night all." Within seconds Liam was in his truck and flooring it out of the driveway.

Mingyu closed his laptop and walked into the kitchen. "He brought you a red rose. I think he was rather disappointed to see me." He raised an eyebrow.

"I wasn't expecting him at all."

"Clearly."

"We occasionally had a glass of wine on the porch after a long workday and chatted," she explained. "Tonight, was a nice gesture, but totally unexpected and unnecessary. So…. are you ready to sample the pizza at my favorite haunt?"

"Yes. Let's leave quickly before any other men show up."

"Very funny." Lily Rose smirked as she reached for the car keys.

After a stiff car ride, cocktails and pizza had them back on track. Over dinner they planned their next two weekends, the first in New York City, the second, in Sag Harbor for Marina's burial at sea.

"I reserved a boat large enough for circa twenty-five guests. Marina and Captain Manny were friends; she requested him. My mom and I invited everyone from my grandmother's guest list. She asked for twenty-two people. Tina and Zoe are coming too. We'll see how many friends RSVP. The invitations are out."

"That sounds like a fitting celebration of life."

"I'm ordering a selection of gourmet sandwiches in advance, all of my grandmother's favorites: lobster rolls, egg and tuna with celery and lettuce, prosciutto and figs, mozzarella, tomato and basil and grilled chicken with zucchini and goat cheese slathered in an herbed dressing. We'll have to bring the drinks: beer, wine, ice tea, fresh lemonade and water bottles. No hard liquor. That makes it easy. For dessert I ordered individual fruit cups and chocolate chip and honey oatmeal cookies from Marina's number one bakery. I'm respecting all of her wishes. What do you think?"

"It sounds wonderful--a memorial picnic at sea. I hope to learn a lot about her life from everyone who cared about her."

"Yes, I believe you will. Now, let me fill you in on Tina and Zoe."

The morning of Marina's celebration-of-life event was beautiful. The temperature was in the low eighties and there was a comfortable sea breeze swirling around the dock as family and friends gathered for a day at sea. Lily Rose, Ella May and Mingyu unloaded the car and carried the drinks and their overstuffed beach and supply bags to the boat. Captain Manny's mate was dispatched to assist with the catering delivery. Once the provisions were on board, he checked off each arriving guest and helped them up the plank. Captain Manny personally welcomed each friend on deck. When the boat left the dock, noisy, happy chatter filled the air, competing with the songbirds, shorebirds and seabirds swooping around them for fish and crumbs gone astray and scolding the loud interruption on their respective turfs. Drinks were served and cold veggie appetizers wrapped in phyllo dough circulated on nautically decorated plastic platters.

Somewhere past Shelter Island, close to Gardiner's Island the conversation shifted to Marina and the stories started circulating. Anne, a sporty neighbor, remembered the time Marina's kayak tipped over in frigid waters when a wake hit them. After they all scrambled in a panic to fish her out of the drink, Marina surprised everyone with a hidden wetsuit underneath her fleece, "She laughed at us and said…..What? Do you all really think I would go out in cold water without a wetsuit and a floating vest? Even surfers know better than that." Anne remembered the moment with a laugh and a shake of her head.

"Yeah, we were all worried she would freeze to death, but she just took her drenched fleece off and rowed back to shore in her wetsuit and aqua shoes. She always kept a change of clothes and a pair of Uggs in the car for emergencies," her friend Ron added, shaking his head side to side. "Remember the time she chipped a front tooth right before Halloween? She scared the crap out of the younger trick-or-treaters in a witch costume with that jagged smile and the cobwebs on her front porch. I think she traumatized half the neighborhood kids."

Alex chimed in, "Or what about the time she missed the bus back from Fox Woods Resort Casino because she was winning at Black Jack. She ended up staying another night, playing cards seated next to Steven Tyler."

Scarlet laughed. "Steven Tyler? Really? That must have been an interesting conversation! Do you guys remember when Marina went to the US Open with us and got hit by a stray tennis ball? I thought she was going to pass out. So, did the Bryant brothers. They stopped playing and offered her one of their fortified electrolyte drinks. She accepted it and asked if she drank it all, would she be able to play doubles like them?" Scarlet grinned. "Spending the day with Marina was never a dull experience."

Lily Rose listened to the stories that kept coming. While she hadn't heard all of them, she did recognize Marina's footprint in every memory. Marina had lived vivaciously, minute to minute, enjoying her many life experiences and friends to the fullest.

When Captain Manny anchored, Ella May and Lily Rose waved for silence. They were ready to say their good byes and complete Marina's send off. Ella May read a poem from *Khalil Gibran's, The Prophet,* and shared a few touching memories in a short narrative. Lily Rose read her thoughts from beautifully decorated rose printed rice paper Marina would have loved. Her grandmother was all about the details.

Marina, you were the best grandmother a girl could have. I feel fortunate to have spent my childhood summers in Sag Harbor, with you. We always had a blast; we kayaked, swam with the fishes, played tennis, watched scary movies and baked even scarier brownies and Chinese coconut sponge cake. Our time together was better than any summer camp I could have attended. I learned how to swim, ride a bike, fail at every water sport imaginable, play strip poker and I learned how to drive without totally wrecking your old car. The small dents gave it character you said and I believed you.

More importantly, I gleaned invaluable life lessons without realizing it--how to handle rejection with grace, how to bounce back from adversity and how to spread my wings and travel fearlessly. With your support, I've found my own happiness in a city across the world. Thank you for sharing your life experiences, for your belief in me and most of all, for your love. Not a day has gone by that I haven't missed you. Khalil Gibran, whose work you introduced me to at a young age, once said, 'Life without love is like a tree without blossoms or fruit.' I am lucky and thankful to have flourished in your garden and basked in the sunshine you radiated. Rest in Peace.... you are and always will be in my thoughts.

Lily Rose wiped the escaping tears and nodded toward her mother, who on cue scattered the urn's ashes into the ocean.

"Hear hear," said Captain Manny, raising his plastic wine glass into the air.

"Hear, hear," came the collective echo.

Drinks were elevated, chugged and refilled. One at a time, each person stepped forward and threw a red rose, handed to them, into the ocean bidding their personal parting words. Mingyu was last. He threw a rose for his grandfather—commemorating the special love Jin and Marina shared, without revealing anything too private. Zoe filmed the touching moments for the family and posterity, capturing the intensity of the sentiments and finally, the roses drifting away in the current. Oddly, before the ashes and roses scattered, they floated into a heart formation. *How very fitting,* Lily Rose observed.

Lunch was served, tears were wiped and the stories and laughter continued. After more than four hours on the water, it appeared Marina willed the party to end. The food and memories had run dry and a blustery wind kicked up, sending the seagulls squawking their warnings. Whitecaps angrily pelted the sides of the boat as if Ursula, the villainous sea witch, was commanding them to clear her darkening domain. The day honoring Marina had been successful, leaving all involved, emotionally spent, but nonetheless, with a toasty feeling in their hearts from the knowledge that their lives had been enriched by knowing her.

Hours later, in bed, Lily Rose sighed and expressed relief that the day had passed without incident. All elements out of her control had come together; the weather had cooperated, Marina's closest friends had appeared ready to share their cherished and humorous memories, and Mingyu had been given an opportunity to get to know her beloved grandmother by association. It meant a lot to Lily Rose. It was a day she would always cherish and remember.

The last few weeks of unencumbered freedom in Sag Harbor were idyllic, full of languorous beach days, summer sports, clamming, exploring the vineyards and barbeques with family and friends. Marina's house was once again a warm and vibrant home where love blossomed, friends met and life plans were hatched.

However, Lily Rose had yet to hear the full report on Mingyu's arrest. He had given her a brief synopsis on the sequence of events, but she still felt like something was missing. Knowing how hard his departure had been, she had wanted to give him a few days of rest and relaxation before she pushed for the details. For peace of mind she needed to know what exactly happened. Over breakfast one morning she broached the uncomfortable subject.

"I was wondering….did you feel like you were targeted when you were arrested? Were many people around you arrested as well?"

"A few. It happened so fast, I can barely remember. I always felt that the police targeted Bao because of his anti-government press, but that would mean they knew who he was. Bao thought it was because of him. I'm really not sure. My family thought so too."

"There's something I need to tell you. It's possible the authorities might have purposely targeted you and used Bao as an excuse."

"Come again? Why would you think that?"

"The day you dropped me at the airport, Chen Du was there, waiting. He appeared after you left and followed me in a threatening way until I went through security."

Mingyu stared at her. "Why? What happened?"

"I think I had Carson Wu's protection after the robbery of my pendant because of Alison. Chen Du was there to threaten me, but he couldn't touch me without Carson finding out, so he might have targeted you instead. He knew it would hurt me."

"Your joking." Mingyu sat down, looking at her with disbelief.

"Sadly, I'm not. It's only a hunch, but I may be right about this. Let me fill you in on a few events before I left. I didn't tell you at the time because I didn't want to scare you. You had enough on your plate to contend with."

"Lily Rose, you have to tell me everything. I need to tell Jin, too."

"More tea?"

As the days leading up to their London departure approached, Lily Rose could sense Mingyu's trepidation.

"What's going on? Are you sad to leave here?" She asked one night.

"Yes, I am. It's been a perfect summer…. but it's more than that. I'm still processing leaving my life in Hong Kong behind, especially during such troubled times. I can't help but worry about my family. I believe the Chinese government will change Hong Kong, ruin the Hong Kong I know and love. Bao is right. We're on a collision course as a self-governing entity. We're supposed to be autonomous until 2047. That's already in jeopardy in 2019." He sighed and took a deep breath, closing his eyes for a moment. "And now with what you told me, I'm nervous about bringing you back there. I hope Chen Du forgets about us."

"I hear you, but it's pointless to worry about things you have no control over. Look at the bright side. We have two beautiful homes to come back to: the beach house here and Stanley Village Road. You have a loving family and we both have great friends. That should give you comfort. Don't think about Chen Du." Lily Rose smiled and stroked his shoulder, but she wasn't sure what she was saying was convincing. Chen Du and Carson Wu had her nervous too.

"Marina's house is special. It reminds me of Jin's. I feel good here. There's a good vibe, like in my grandfather's home. It's been a peaceful place to relax and regroup. The days we've spent here were happy days, Lily Rose, and I look forward to returning, but now that we're on the cusp of leaving, I'm nervous about what lies ahead. There'll be a lot to navigate—finding a place to live, renting a strategic office space, building a successful business. I don't want to let JIn or you down. My grandfather is counting on me. He sold some of his prized jade to Carson Wu to finance this opportunity. I can't blow it."

"To Carson Wu? Really? Did Carson know why he was selling?" Lily Rose's mind was racing. *So, this is how Chen Du knew about us leaving? Did he tail me to the airport? Or did he have an eye on me all along? Scary either way.*

"I don't know. I wasn't with them every minute of the sale. Jin ordered everyone out of the viewing room at the end of the showing and he and Carsen talked alone for a long while. Jin didn't share a word about that conversation or any others after."

"Hmmm." Lily Rose pondered the possibilities. *So, I have Jin to thank for Carson Wu's protection? Maybe even for the return of my pendant? Wow.*

"Listen to me, you won't blow anything. It's not that overwhelming if we tackle one thing at a time, one day at a time. We have some contacts. My office will help with relocation and David will be there to guide us through finding the right neighborhood to live in. He emailed me and I know he cares. I'm not worried. It'll be an adventure, like all our trips together. We can do this." She reached for his hand and squeezed it, eliciting the smile she loved to see.

Hearing Mingyu's thoughts on Marina's house flooded her with warmth. It meant everything that he felt comfortable here. The Sag Harbor cottage was her true home, the one she always wanted to come back to. Maybe retire to one day.

Given Mingyu's unsettled nerves, she decided not to disclose her communications with Alison through David. She now believed that Jin and his love for jade had been the catalyst for her future and her safe return from Hong Kong. One day she would share all her thoughts with Mingyu. *What will happen when Jin is gone?*

The last thing Mingyu needed now was to worry about Alison Wu's hovering triad family. Lily Rose wondered if she still had Carson Wu's protection long distance. Nothing was beyond Carson's reach, it appeared. She had gathered that from Alison's coded messages. *Once a triad, always a triad. The only exit allowed out of our organization is by death Alison said. She was so brave to try.*

Mingyu cleared his throat, interrupting her thoughts. "The one thing I'm not worried about is you, Lily Rose. I know I made the right choice in a partner. You are the Yang to my Yin, the light to my darkness. You inspire me, make me happy and keep me grounded, all at the same time."

"Thanks. Ditto."

They sat wordlessly on the front porch sipping rum-spiked ice tea and watched the sun set in a fiery blaze over the inky, glistening water. An introspective, stretching silence loomed over them.

As usual, Lily Rose spoke first. She singled out some immediate plans and threw out her ideas. The mood lightened as options were discussed. Having common goals gave them direction as a team. Lily Rose stretched. *It's nice to have a partner.*

She had no doubt that together, she and Mingyu, could handle anything thrown at them. It was karma, not fate, that had brought them this far. Jin had taught her the difference. Now that Marina was laid to rest and they had Jin's blessing and continued support, she felt empowered; she was ready for battle, ready for the unknown and for the new chapter in their lives.

Lily Rose fingered her powerful jade dragon pendant that connected the most unlikely families—the Larsen family, the Ho family and most surprisingly, the Wu family. She felt at peace knowing she was loved, protected and assured that her life choices and future with Mingyu were her chosen destiny.

Would you like to see a sequel to this book?
Let the author know. :)

BleueRose.com

Acknowledgement

In 2020, about 93,000 residents left Hong Kong and in 2021 another 23,000 followed.
Many left for Singapore, the UK, Canada and the US. Some relocated to Japan, South Korea, Thailand and Dubai. Hong Kong's residents are still leaving in large numbers in 2022 as the erosion of their lifestyle under Chinese rule proceeds. Covid restrictions have added an extra layer of discontent. Some call the mass exodus a "brain drain" of professionals leaving the city, making Hong Kong only a shell of its former self.—CNBC News as reported by Monica Buchanan- Pitrelli

I would also like to thank:

Dave Potts- for kindly editing the final version. His suggestions, timely response and overall criticism and expertise were greatly appreciated. He added an impeccable British touch to the final draft.

Donna Mc Gullam and the Westhampton Writers Group- for their weekly critiques and enthusiastic advise and commentaries.

Lana Leonteva, an accomplished artist/ illustrator whose work I greatly admire- for her custom-designed front cover. Lalanaarts.com, lalanaarts IG

Lacegarden for the design and digital formatting of the back cover.

About the Author

Bleue Rose lives and works in New York where she makes precious hand-crafted gold jewelry in a collaborative studio. She has studied art, art history, design, gemology, jewelry making and creative writing. She loves the balance of both worlds, splicing the artist's and the writer's crafts. Bleue was born and raised in central Europe and loves to travel to remote destinations worldwide. Her writing is a reflection of her travels. Her stories are strictly her imagination at work.

Other Books by the Author

The Crenston Family Suspense Series including:

The Rogue Tangerine Tablet
Good Karma is the Best Revenge
And coming soon:
Island Allure and Black Magic

Island Allure and Black Magic is book three in the Crenston Family Suspense Series featuring the globe-trotting family and their extended inner circle. The Crenstons seem to have an uncanny propensity for encountering trouble, yet they always manage to bounce back with little more than minor scuffs and bruises. Their natural penchant for risk taking has them escaping dangerous situations on more than one occasion, but in a pinch, the family always rallies and comes through as a team. Oblivious to their frequent walks on the fringes of disaster, they live life to the fullest, averting misfortune by a mere stroke of fortuity. Will their good luck finally run out?

Then there are the Santos siblings, Casimir and Camila, formerly the Ortiz family from Tampico, Mexico. Hiding in plain sight, they recently found love on a Caribbean island. Life should be smooth sailing ever since they broke away from the dangerous

Flores cartel and their illicit smuggling operations, but their cartel past seems to lurk in the shadows, threatening to pop up like a geyser in Yellowstone park.

Leaving their childhood home and mindfully cutting all mental and physical ties to their past, Casi and Camila are struggling to embrace a new life, however, the future, even a rosy one, is never a straight path. When Casi gets a phone call from Maria Alfaro, his trusted Cuban private eye in Miami, the news surrounding his future brother-in-law shakes him to the core. To make matters worse, his loving, but vulnerable fiancée gets entangled with a dangerous psychic, thus inviting a new kind of danger into their midst. Good karma doesn't last indefinitely.

9 781733 819459